E. G. RYAN

hope u love my book!

♡, lis (EG Ryan)

Letter 16

A Novel of Time, Love, and War

Letter 16
A Novel of Time, Love, and War
By E.G. Ryan

ISBN-10: 148009160X
EAN-13: 9781480091603

www.EGRyan.com
EG Ryan Enterprises & EG Ryan World of Books
EGRyanEnterprises@gmail.com

For my Mother

Come out of the circle of time and into the circle of love

--Rumi

Brest, France

Winter 1946

"I was a mere child when I first met you, I was a child when I first wrote to you, but I am a woman now. I do not know when I changed, the transformation itself is a slow process, but the realization of this change forces itself upon the soul with quite suddenness," she spoke to the sea, which listened without judgment. "The Great Sea," as Papa had always called it. Looking out over this vast expanse of shimmering blue, she believed he was right. It was a great sea, and indestructible, at least on the surface.

"There has been so much destruction, so much devastation, so much suffering. But when I sit here and speak to you this reality disappears. It is only you and I and this never-ending vastness of ever-changing color. It is unseasonably cool for this time of year, the ocean looks restless. Maybe it is I who am restless. It is only here that I can rejoice. Exult in the smells and sights of anything alive. I have another letter, this makes sixteen—my lucky number. It shall be my last. It is not because I wish to forget you, but because I have mourned you for too long. It is time for me return to the world of the living. Maybe we will cross paths again somewhere, in a place only my heart knows exists." Her voice trailed off in a whisper, as though drifting off to sea.

No, she would never forget him she thought, as she caught the end of her woolen shawl that had come loose, forcing ice cold air down her chest. A lover's final farewell caress she thought. Pulling her arm out from beneath her woolen scarf she glanced down at the green glass bottle one last time, memorizing every detail, memorizing every instant of this time and place. Laughing aloud, laughter without joy, she wondered what Mama would think of her precious glass bottles, sixteen in all, being hurtled out to sea. The biting wind numbed her fingers, she could barely hold on to the bottle which felt heavier with each passing moment. Raising the bottle to her lips, she kissed the cool glass, but then, with a startling suddenness, she flung the bottle as far as she could into the dark, churning sea. "Auf Wiedersehen, my love," she spoke to the Great Sea as warm tears streaked down her frozen cheeks, "Auf Wiedersehen."

Los Angeles, California
Fall 2011

What am I doing? Jesus Christ what am I doing? Maybe Shiela was right, maybe a vacation somewhere close and warm like San Diego would have been better. A two-hour drive, tops. No, that would never work and Abe, Jesus Christ, Abe, he'd be there with me every minute of the day, every day. Maybe that'd be a good thing, I wouldn't be alone. I haven't been anywhere alone for God knows how many years. I didn't even like to drive the freeways alone. Speaking of Abe, the annoying doorbell tore me from my schizophrenic thoughts and away from the suitcase I had been trying hopelessly to squeeze shut for the last ten minutes. "Too much stuff, I know, I know I need to pack light," I said to Jack who rolled on his back and stretched his paws out and meowed. "Sorry, Jack, you're going to Uncle Abe's for a while. Make sure you tear up the sofa a bit," I whispered to him as I headed towards the front door. Before opening the door I paused to take a deep breath. Everything was going to be okay. There wouldn't be any emotional breakdowns in front of Abe today. Tugging at the door knob, which still hadn't been fixed, the door opened with a loud creak, revealing Abe's disapproving stare. He stepped inside, shaking his annoyingly perfect head of blonde curls.

"Ya know, it wouldn't take much to fix that," he said, pointing at the door's rusted hinge. Ignoring Abe's unsolicited home improvement comment I hugged him and gave him a quick kiss to the cheek.

"Yeah, nice to see you too. You know you're like twenty minutes late, Abe," I tried not to sound too annoyed, instead letting my frustration out on the door, slamming it a little harder than necessary.

"Well, I had a thought on the drive over, and from the looks of it you're not ready to go anyway," Abe snapped back with one of his usual retorts, while staring at himself in the large hall mirror.

"And that's what made you late? A thought? Must've been a slow thought," I mocked, attacking the suitcase's zipper again, with no response from the zipper. Ignoring my sarcastic comment, Abe continued to stare at himself in the mirror, opening his mouth like a chimpanzee.

"Di, have you ever wondered about the miracle of life?" Abe asked. I hoped my lack of response would discourage any further discussion in this direction. I wasn't exactly in the mood for some weighty meaning-of-life monologue. Obviously undeterred by my silence, my younger brother continued. "Think of it this way, not just any miracle of life, but my miracle, the miracle of me. I mean, if our grandparents, and I mean both sets of them, hadn't had sex, excuse me, made love, as you prefer to say, anyway, if they hadn't made love precisely at the moment they did, well, then neither Sheila or Dad would be here. And if Sheila and Dad…"

"I get the point, Abe," I interrupted, kicking my suitcase. "If Shiela and Dad hadn't had 'sex,' as you say, at precisely the moment in time they did, then the great Abraham Alistair Adams wouldn't be here!"

"Now that was rude," Abe replied, casually making faces at himself in the mirror. "I was going to say the magnificent, brilliant, radiant, fabulous Abe wouldn't be here." Somehow Abe always managed to make me laugh, despite his arrogance and fancy European fashions that made him look like a fruitcake.

"Yeah, well, maybe you could stop pondering procreation and making faces at yourself and help me with my suitcase," I huffed, stomping a foot on my suitcase which looked like it wasn't going to take much more of my abuse. "Duct tape," I said aloud. I'd better bring some duct tape, just in case, I thought. Abe ignored my plea for assistance, he obviously wasn't done pondering his own miracle of creation.

"No, Di, you're missing the point," he continued, as he found a toothpick from God-knows-where and picked at his teeth, "see, it's much more than just the grandparents and parents. It goes way back to our earliest ancestors—you know, caveman time. If there'd been just one event that kept any of them apart, then I wouldn't be here and neither would you."

"You've always had a flare for exaggeration, Abe. Would you stop for just one moment and listen to yourself? Who cares about all of this crap anyway, huh? I mean we're here. How we got here doesn't really matter. If it hadn't been us, it would have been others," I hissed at him, kicking my suitcase again. "And don't you dare say the universe couldn't survive without an Abraham Alistair or some crap like that," I added, just as Abe had made the motions as though he were going to speak again. "Ugh, this blasted suitcase," I swore to myself as I realized the only option was to remove items from it.

"Well, for your information, it couldn't," Abe replied, wiping the toothpick clean with his fingers.

"*That* is disgusting, Abraham. Go wash your hands!" I ordered.

"It's only a little plaque…," I was glad I couldn't hear the rest of what Abe said as he walked down the hall, hopefully to wash his hands.

Realizing the damn suitcase was never going to shut, I sat down on the ground and opened it to decide what I was going to leave behind. No, I definitely needed all the clothes I packed, but maybe not quite as many socks and underwear. Why did I always pack twice the underwear and socks needed? Who could wear twenty-five pairs of socks in two weeks? Reaching under the clothes in my suitcase I pulled out the shoebox full of letters Warren had written to me over the years. Lifting the lid off the shoebox and sifting through them was a ritual I had started the day Warren died, and now I was unable to leave the letters behind. The blow dryer, now that could stay behind, but the letters had to go back underneath all the clothes. There was no way I was going to leave my last lifeline to Warren behind. How pathetic, our love reduced to a bunch of shabby old letters.

"What are you doing, Di?" Abe asked as he watched me stuff the shoebox back into my suitcase. "What's in the box?" Ignoring him, I focused my efforts on closing the suitcase. I should have bought a new one. Abe had reclaimed his position in front of the hall mirror and continued removing plaque from his teeth with a paperclip. "Do you think my teeth are yellow? I just used those teeth whitening strips, you know. I was afraid they were going to damage my capped tooth, but they didn't seem to bleach the cap." Just who on God's green earth was Abe talking to I wondered, finally resorting to jumping up and down on the suitcase. Shouldn't he be concerned about me and my emotional state? It was me who lost a husband after all. And it was me jumping up and down on an over-stuffed suitcase.

"It was Donna, you know," Abe offered between scrapes, "She told me my teeth were yellow. We're not talking anymore."

"What do you mean you're not talking anymore?" I demanded, finally managing to force the zipper halfway around the suitcase only to catch my favorite bra in its teeth. "Damn it!" I yelled, tearing at my frayed bra.

"You know, you're my only sister now, at least until this afternoon. I've gotta meet Donna this afternoon to go over some wedding stuff." I was now convinced Abe and I did not crawl out of the same womb. I wasn't even sure what planet he was from. "You do remember the wedding, don't you, Di? You promised you wouldn't go AWOL on me, remember?" It was the first note of concern for my well being I had heard in Abe's voice since his arrival. Maybe he was tip-toeing around Warren's death for my sake. Why couldn't everyone just start acting normal around me? I felt like a freak. People died in accidents every day. It just happened to be Warren's day, and mine, when he was hit by a drunk driver.

"Of course I remember the wedding…uh, March, no, April, right?" Jeez, he was right, I didn't even know the date of my own brother's wedding. But what kind of a wedding was this anyway? Abe had just met the bimbo. What was her name? Akila? I didn't even know her last name. Shiela would kill me for calling her a bimbo, but Abe just met her three months ago and they were already engaged. What kind of love was that? True lust was more like it. What Warren and I had, now that was true love. We dated for six years before we got married and had been married for ten years. We would have lasted, I just know it

"Hey, Di, you okay? You hear me?" Abe asked with a look of consternation.

"Yeah, I heard you, and Donna was right, your teeth are yellow," I teased, trying to lighten my own somber mood.

"Ha, now I have no more sisters." Abe bent forward, motioning me to kiss his ass.

"You know, if I didn't know better, I would swear you were gay," I genuinely laughed. Abe was definitely going to keep his wife entertained.

With the suitcase finally jammed shut, I walked through the house one last time to make sure lights were turned off, timers turned on, and windows and doors properly secured. "You aren't going to do anything stupid are you?"

"What are you talking about, Abe? It's New Jersey, not Nepal," I answered defensively, while trying to catch my cat. "Get over here, Jack. Jack! Damn cat!"

"You did tell Sheila you were going to go climb Mt. Everest..."

I didn't let Abe finish his sentence, "Oh Lord, it was K2! K2! And I was joking. Warren had just died, remember? I wanted to get away." My voice quivered, and tears threatened to flow.

"Yeah, and you scared Sheila half to death." Abe had actually stopped picking at his teeth for a moment and looked straight at me, which I knew meant he was serious. His accusatory notions left me feeling defensive again. Thank God I was leaving for a while.

"I don't even know how to climb a mountain, let alone walk down the street without tripping, for God's sake! None of you have any idea what it was like for me, what it's still like for me," I yelled, stuffing Jack into his travel crate.

"Di, Di," Abe interrupted my tantrum, "hey, I get it. Okay, you're right."

"No, no, you don't get it, Abe, you won't get it! You meet women in bars every day and now you're marrying one of those little twats.

What do you know about true love, huh?" Abe didn't say anything, his look said it all. The moment I said it I wanted to wish it away. Pretend like I had never said anything. I had hurt my little brother, his silence said it all. The silence between us grew. I could feel the tension pressing down on my shoulders like a lead weight. Abashed by what I had just said, actually couldn't help saying, I looked down and didn't know if I actually resented or admired Abe's carefree attitude towards love, and that drove me crazy. Why couldn't I be more like him? Why couldn't I have spent the last sixteen years of my life *loving,* as he had, dozens of different people? Aren't we supposed to be a monogamous species? Or does that just apply to the females of our species? Or is it just reserved for some of us with unrealistic ideals? It wouldn't have been an ideal if Warren hadn't been run over by some drunk. We would have grown old together.

"Well…we should get going if you want to make your flight." Abe didn't look at me, but, unlike his usual self, he didn't say anything else to me about the wedding either. I knew I had hurt him, I didn't mean to, but had to admit I was jealous of his approaching wedding and all the merriment that always seemed to surround such occasions.

"Look, Abe, I'm sorry, for what it's worth. I'm just having trouble adjusting to this new life." Abe didn't respond to my apology, but picked up my suitcase and my cat's crate, and walked out the front door. Jesus Christ, I need to get a grip. This whole damn world was spinning out of control, Warren was gone, and there was nothing I could do to stop or slow it down.

Just as I was about to lock the front door, I heard the phone ring and decided to answer.

"Uh, I wouldn't answer that," Abe said, returning from his fancy Mercedes where he had just deposited my overweight suitcase. "It's probably Sheila, and you know how long-winded she can be." Not listening, I darted back inside and picked up the phone just as the answering machine did.

"Hello?" I knew it was my mother, the phone told me so; yet another wonder of modern technology. "Sheila?" It never occurred strange to me, until today, that our mother had always insisted we call her Sheila.

"How did you know it was me, dear?" Shiela asked, as though ignorant of modern technology.

"Hi, so what's up, Sheila? I've gotta get going ." I know I sounded impatient, but by talking to her I could delay the inevitable for just one more moment—that I had to travel without Warren.

"Honey, I just wanted to say good-bye before you left," she said, even though we had spoken earlier this morning *and* last night, both times saying goodbye. I didn't know what it was about my mother and trips. Something about her children and travel seemed to scare the pants off her.

"Sheila," I was about to remind her of our previous farewells, but decided not to offend another family member. Besides, I sensed the fear in her voice. Having her depressed daughter travel to the other side of the United States, all alone, couldn't warm any mother's heart.

"Thanks. I'll call you when I land at Newark. I've gotta run, Abe's here waiting in the car and you know how impatient he is." That's right, Diana, just blame it on Abe, that always works with Sheila.

"Alright, dear, have a safe trip and don't forget to call. I love you," she said.

"I love you too, Sheila, bye," I said and hung up the phone.

The drive to the airport felt like the beginning of a betrayal. With each mile I felt as though I was leaving Warren behind to resume a new life without him. The panic I had managed to suppress all morning was welling up inside me and threatened to erupt at any moment. Suppressing the fear of being alone forever was difficult enough. I already spent most of my time alone these days. Warren and I didn't have children. We didn't have many single friends. Most of what we did was as a couple, either alone or with other couples. Who wants a single widow around at dinner parties, anyway? Just give it some time, Diana, and you won't get any more invitations to parties or tennis dates at the club. Maybe a breakfast or coffee here and there when someone's feeling magnanimous, but that won't last either. Listening to myself, I realized I sounded like such a jerk. Our friends, my friends now, I reminded myself, had been nothing but supportive and gracious over the last six months; cooking dinners, calling to see if I was alright, even ignoring my bad behavior on more than a few occasions.

It was me who pushed them away, who declined dinner invitations and avoided phone calls. If there was any reason I wouldn't have any friends left, I had to admit, it was of my own doing. Maybe I deserved to be alone.

"Your new haircut looks nice. The color too." It was Abe who finally broke the silence. Grateful for this obvious attempt at peace making, I felt the heaviness in the air lift off us.

Rolling down the window, I smiled and asked, "You really like it? Red highlights and all?"

"Yeah, it looks kind of Euro, you know, auburn hair with red streaks. And it covers up the grey nicely," Abe winked and shook his blonde locks. "You know, Di, it's okay to lose it once in a while. I mean, it's only been six months, but, and don't get mad, at some point you've gotta start dealing and not treating people like total shit anymore. At some point people are going to start talking, you know." He was nervous, I could tell. He was biting his lower lip, which always made him look like a gerbil.

"Who's talking about me, Abe? What are they saying, huh? You better tell me, Abe!" My fury turned on like a light switch. One moment I was in a benevolent state, the next moment I wanted to wipe out anyone who crossed me.

"See, that's what I mean, Di. No one's talking about you! I'm just saying you have to stop acting like a rabid hyena." Now that stopped me in my tracks. I had never heard anyone referred to as a rabid hyena, especially not me. Leave it to Abe to call it like he sees it. He was right, and he had never said anything to me that wasn't spot on true, but that didn't mean I had to like what I was hearing.

"Okay, I'll try." I couldn't believe I had actually acquiesced. Was this really me? An admission of guilt from the rabid hyena? Even Abe seemed to notice my attempt to be conciliatory and smiled over at me.

"Hey, watch the road," I snapped as Abe drifted off to the right and we felt the car skid out on the right shoulder of the road. When Abe started talking about the various eyeglass frames that complemented his face, I was sure everything had been smoothed out between us again. Leaning back, I counted the palm trees we passed by, wondering what the future had in store for me.

10

"And you know, Di, I didn't meet Akila at a bar. It was at an airport." Abe glanced over at me. I closed my eyes and pretended not to hear. Abe knew I had heard him.

Despite my emotional rollercoaster, Abe managed to get me to the airport with time to spare for the cup of coffee I desperately needed. Grateful to relieve myself of my burdensome suitcase at the check-in counter, I went on a mission to find a cup of coffee. There just had to be a coffee bar, they were everywhere. Finding coffee wasn't difficult, but finding a secluded spot to enjoy it proved almost impossible. I found a section of undiscovered seats behind some temporary wall dividers. Maybe they had been discovered, but other travelers chose to seat themselves closer to their fellow man. Me, I was all alone now. I didn't know who I was anymore. Diana Dahl was no more. What does one do as a widow? Do I take back Adams, my maiden name? No, Diana Adams didn't sound right anymore. I am Diana Dahl, but without a Mr. Dahl, could there truly be a Mrs. Dahl?

A shuffling sound behind me caught my attention. Turning around I noticed I wasn't the only recluse. A middle-aged woman, she had to be in her early fifties, dressed in a neat but outdated green coat, slowly moved along to the row of seats opposite mine. She stopped and sat down across from me. Well, she can't be that much of a recluse if she chooses the seat facing me. Why, when there are all of these open seats did she have to choose the seat right across from me? Looking down, I thought if I just didn't make eye contact she would leave me alone. My book, that was it, if I found my book she couldn't possibly bother me. Who would disturb a woman engrossed in a juicy novel? Too bad I didn't have a juicy novel, just the New Jersey travel guide Sheila gave me two days ago, after I had assured her I had no need for it. I was, after all, just going to Cape May to spend some time collecting my thoughts. There weren't going to be any excursions to Atlantic City or hikes in Allaire State Park.

Finding the travel guide at the bottom of my backpack I pulled it out along with Warren's yellow "to do" notepad. Instead of opening the travel guide, I fingered the notepad and caressed the frayed edges. How often had I given Warren nice leather bound daily planners and electronic gadgets that were supposed to simply life? I usually found them tucked away in some closet or drawer, unopened. He had a point. It was easier to jot down "to do's" on paper. And his writing, so small and neat, a reflection of his organizational skills I so clearly lacked. How would I ever get anything done on my own? He paid the bills, figured out the taxes, and took care of everything else, dear Lord. Abe had been helping me out, but he couldn't be my crutch for the rest of my solitary confinement.

The woman cleared her throat, as though in agreement with my thoughts. Looking up, she smiled at me and nodded. I hadn't noticed the knitting needles and green yarn from which she was knitting. Her hands, large and bony, with skin so translucent I could see every blue vein from where I was sitting, seemed so at ease with the knitting needles. How much had she touched with those hands?

"What are you knitting?" I asked, surprised that I was the one to initiate a conversation with a random stranger. The woman looked up and smiled at me again.

"Nothing," She said in heavily accented English, still smiling as she continued knitting without pause. Nothing? She did say nothing, didn't she? Why knit something if it is nothing? What do you do with nothing?

"Why are you knitting nothing?" I asked, again surprised that another human being had peaked my curiosity enough to warrant another question from me.

"It helps me think," she answered with a nodding smile. Mesmerized by her hands and the large needles that moved up and down rhythmically, I stared at the dark green material she obviously had spent much time knitting.

"What about a scarf?" I asked, feeling the need to find a use for this stranger's work. Otherwise her time and effort would just be a waste.

"No, too heavy for a scarf," she shook her head and hummed, so quietly I could barely make it out. The woman looked so peaceful, almost serene. She reminded me of a painting I had seen of the Virgin Mary cradling a sleeping baby Jesus. The woman briefly looked up from her knitting with a smile that radiated an inner peace I could never hope to achieve.

"Well, what about a blanket? That wouldn't be too heavy." The woman's hands stopped their rhythmic movements and she looked up at me as though considering what I had just said. After a period of inactivity, she resumed her rhythmic hand movements and the needles moved up and down again.

"Not everything has utilitarian value. Sometimes the value, or joy, lies in the act, not the outcome," she said as she laid her knitting needles on her lap and rolled out a length of yarn.

"But it's a shame to make something, invest so much time in it, and then not have any benefit from it," I argued, realizing this woman held some secret to life for which my soul was still too immature. And why the heck was I arguing with her to begin with? It wasn't my knitting anyway. Why did I care?

"Time invested in something one enjoys, even if the outcome is nothing, is time well spent," she replied graciously as she resumed her rhythmic knitting.

Looking down at Warren's "to do" pad, I reflected on what the old woman had said. I had invested so much of my life in this relationship. We were just kids when we met, but we knew we wanted to spend the rest of our lives together. We knew that right from the start. And now, twenty-two years later, geez twenty-two years, that was a lot of time, there was nothing left. There was no one to grow old with, no one to laugh at silly commercials with, no one to love or be loved by, just nothing. And no one to call the insurance company about the small dent someone had left in the car that I noticed as my eyes scanned Warren's notes.

The woman was right though, it was better to have had those years with Warren, and now nothing, than not to have had them at all. Right? Some people go through life without ever finding their true love. Not me. I met mine the first time when I was sixteen years old and knew I'd be with him forever. If someone had told me forever would be cut short by a drunk driver, I would still do it. Sighing, I picked up Warren's notepad and safely tucked it back into my bag. It was only when I heard the shuffling sound that I noticed the woman leaving. Watching her slowly shuffle away, I noticed she had two knitting needles sticking in the tight bun at the back of her head.

It was after she had passed from my sight that I saw she had forgotten her knit green "nothing." Picking up my backpack, I snatched up her green creation and hurried to find her. At her pace she couldn't be far, but after searching for her in the bathroom and gift shop I was forced to give up my search or risk missing my flight. Tucking the green knit fabric into my backpack, I handed the flight attendant my boarding pass and boarded Flight 16 to Newark, New Jersey.

"Uh, excuse me, I think you're in my seat," I said, sounding as irritated as I felt. The man in my seat had already made himself comfortable with a travel pillow, eye shades, and headphones. God, what a travel geek. Either the guy was feigning deafness or he really couldn't hear me. Tapping him on the shoulder I repeated my question a little louder, ignoring all the stares.

"Can I help you?" the man asked, barely lifting a corner of his eye shade as I glared at him.

"You're in my seat, 12 C…," I said as I shoved my boarding card in his face.

"There must be some mistake," he replied and fumbled around in his pockets only to reveal a boarding pass with seat 12C printed on it.

"You've got to be kidding me," I complained and dropped my carry-on in the aisle while trying to attract the attention of a flight attendant.

"Here, you take the seat, I'll find a another one," the man with his eye shades now resting on his head said as he briefly smiled, picked up his belongings, and squeezed past me.

"Yeah, thanks a lot," I called after the generous stranger, who raised a hand without turning around. Finally in my seat I said a quick prayer, asking the universe, or whatever was out there, if this plane had to crash today, to please make mine a quick death. And, I added as an afterthought, I prayed my neighbor wouldn't be a talker.

Unfortunately, the universe was partially deaf, at least where the neighbor part was concerned.

"Jimmy, stop that, I said stop it," a woman said, as she dislodged two of her young son's fingers from his nostrils. "12 A and B, that's us, Jimmy," she said, smiling at me with a 'get up and let us pass' look. Obliging, I returned the smile and heaved my tired-rear from the seat, only to be hit by her over-sized carry-on. Again she smiled at me. Pushing aside her over-stuffed carry-on, she forced a hand in my direction. Was she serious? Who shakes hands on a flight?

"Give her a chance," I heard my conscience mutter. Alright, a chance, but it was still bizarre to me. Again required to respond to some unwritten rule of conduct between strangers, I took her hand and briefly squeezed it, ignoring the young boy who reached around his mother to present me with his hand. My antibacterial gel was in my checked luggage.

"I'm Ginny, Virginia Sanchez, and this here's my son, Jimmy," she said with a broad, white toothed smile. How can someone smile so much, is this woman for real? I nodded and returned a quick, toothless smile. There was something irritating about this pretty, chatty woman. This situation needed to be nipped in the bud now or she'd have little snot-covered Jimmy sitting in my lap in no time. All I wanted was to be left alone. Was that too much to ask? "We're going to meet his father," Ginny Sanchez began to say. I watched the smile melt off her face when I covered my ears with headphones and closed my eyes.

An air pocket forced me out of my half-conscious state. Momentarily confused, I looked around, half expecting to see Warren sitting next to me. I had to get up, I needed to stretch my legs and find a restroom. Some small part of me wondered where the gentleman who previously occupied my seat was now sitting. Casually pacing up and down both coach cabins, I wasn't able to find him. It wasn't until I stood in line for the small closet referred to as a bathroom that I noticed him. Peering up at the first class cabin, I saw his side profile, still wearing his headphones and eye shades. "Well I'll be...," I almost cursed under my breath as I continued to stare in his general direction. If only I'd let him keep the seat back in steerage, it'd be me relaxing in spacious comfort at the front of the plane. Walking back to my own seat, I wondered if this was karma. A stranger practices a random act of altruism and is instantly rewarded? It shouldn't be any surprise to me then that karma didn't view me quite as favorably. Thinking about the last few months, about Warren, and life without him, I suddenly recognized the strain I had placed on my entire family. Everyone tiptoed around me as though a land mine could go off any

15

second, and too frequently it did. Abe was right, I needed to get my life back under some type of control. Otherwise the people closest to me would become casualties of my own war.

Once back in my seat sleep overcame me again. It was the Captain's voice that woke me, notifying myself and my fellow passengers we had about twenty minutes to use the restroom and stow our rogue luggage before he would begin his descent into Newark International Airport. "Sorry to bother you, do you mind," my neighbor smiled at me, "he needs to use the potty." Lifting myself out of the seat to let young Jimmy pass, I briefly wondered what life would have been like if Warren and I had had children. Rubbing my head, I realized these thoughts were pointless. The young boy stopped and stared at me after he pushed past me.

"My father says live each day with as much joy as you can," little Jimmy said as he handed me a half-melted chocolate ball. Entranced, I picked the chocolate ball from his grubby little hand. I watched this little person walking towards the bathroom and wondered if one could pinpoint the precise moment when childhood vanishes and with it all of the secrets of the universe. Looking at the unsanitary chocolate in my hand, against my better judgment, I popped it in my mouth. A feeling of warmth spread through me as the tiny piece of chocolate melted on my tongue. Was it the boy or the chocolate?

Dresden, Germany
Spring 1937

"I do not like what is going on. I do not like it at all," Anna heard her father speak from behind closed doors. Her parents were not arguing. This is what their marriage was, a constant friction of ideas and beliefs. She never could understand why they ever married. Possibly it was a marriage of convenience. Her mother was one of two daughters of a wealthy gentleman farmer and her father had the von Marschalkt title, the blue blood without the property to back the name.

"Oh, Franz, you are always too narrow-minded. He is reclaiming our country, lifting us from financial ruin. Not an unworthy objective for a Chancellor if you ask me," she heard her mother say in an awe-struck voice, the tone she used whenever she spoke of her beloved Fuehrer.

"He is a dictator, Frieda, not a Chancellor," her father corrected her mother. "And he is searching for scapegoats, it frightens me. It is not only the Jews. Things will not end well for any of us," her father said, as usual speaking more softly than her mother.

"You are a paranoid old fool if you ask me, Franz," Anna heard her mother say as she quietly walked past their bedroom and out the back door.

It was a beautiful April evening despite the cold that still blanketed the countryside. As she headed for the barn, Anna looked up at the star-filled sky and knew that everything was right with the world. Even with the full moon it was still dark inside the barn. She couldn't risk taking her lantern. It would be her luck to be found by her mother here.

"Anna, Anna," she heard the voice she loved whisper down to her from the hayloft. With her heart fluttering like a hummingbird, she carefully felt her way towards the back of the barn and blindly climbed the familiar ladder. "I thought you were not coming," the voice in the darkness spoke to her, as she felt a warm hand clasp her hand.

"Mama and Papa w…w…were up late, I had to w…w…wait until they left the kitchen," Anna replied.

"Anna, my Anna, I would wait a lifetime for you, even two," Jakub said in heavily accented German, as he wrapped his arms around her and gently pulled her down into the soft hay.

"T…t…two lifetimes, is that all?" she giggled as she traced the contours of Jakub's face in this darkness. "I would w…w…wait an eternity for you, Jakub Gorski, an eternity."

"I too for you," Jakub whispered as he gently kissed Anna's ear. His warm breath on her neck sent goose bumps up and down her body. Who was this man who had stolen her heart? Her logical mind tried to tell her that she barely knew him, that it was unacceptable to consort with the hired help. But then, do not some go through a lifetime of marriage without ever truly knowing their spouse? And do not others walk through life without loving their spouse? Anna decided a forbidden love was a far better fate to suffer than a lifetime without love. Her parents thought it would be wise to marry someone with a similar background. Mama often spoke of the prosperous von Glann family and that "wonderful boy Heino" whom she had always had her eye on for Anna. As far as Anna was concerned, Heino not only exhibited the manners of a wild boar, he also looked the part.

Anna thought about the day she met Jakub, three years ago. He had just arrived with a group of Polish farm hands for the summer, with most of his possessions on his back. He needed to find work for to support his mother, he had said. His mother had taken ill with some type of sickness that left her incapacitated. Papa did not normally hire workers who were not yet grown men, but in Jakub's case he made an exception; he was almost eighteen and looked older than his age. Anna was not quite fifteen that first summer she laid eyes on the man with the emerald eyes she immediately wanted to marry.

"These are my daughters, Anna and Maria," her father had said as Maria pinched her in the arm, also obviously too aware of Jakub's striking features. It was not only his handsome face and dark curls that attracted Anna. The moment Jakub and Anna smiled at each other they both knew one could not live without the other. Maria, only eleven months older, yet a head shorter and frailer than her sister, had told Anna it was a temporary condition that would fade when the harvest season was over. Without previous experience to draw upon, Anna was unable to explain to her sister just how wrong she was, and always would be.

Anna traced the outline of Jakub's face in the darkness, running her fingers over his rough, unshaven cheeks. "Your German improves w...w...with each summer. Last summer we s...s...spoke mostly English. I spoke no P...P...Polish, and y...y...you no German." she said as she tickled his ear, grateful that she had studied her English lessons so well. She loved it when he spoke his native Polish, but rarely heard him use it. Usually it had been English, the language of prosperity, as Jakub had told her. Anna closed her eyes in the darkness and envisioned a lifetime as Frau Gorski. This vision with Jakub came so naturally for her. She even stuttered less around him. Mama never believed in love at first sight, yet Papa had always told Anna she would know. "It will hit you like a wagon full of bricks," he had said. Anna giggled to herself as she envisioned her own father run over by a wagon full of bricks, commandeered by her mother.

"What makes you laugh, Anna? I want to know. I want to know what you think, what you dream, what you feel when you breathe," Jakub said with such sincerity. Anna rolled towards him and held him tight.

"I am j...j...just so happy with you. The year is t...t...too long and dreary without you," she said, as the realization set in that he would soon be leaving again.

"I have spoken with your father," Jakub said as Anna felt the pulse on his neck quicken.

"Y…y…you have s…s…spoken with father," she asked, bewildered, "ab…b…bout what?" Somewhere hidden deep inside her mind she desperately wished he had asked her father for her hand in marriage. Her rational mind knew this was not possible. Jakub would not be here had he made her father such an impossible proposition. Anna felt Jakub breathe deeply as she visualized what Mama would say if Jakub were to ask for her hand.

"I have asked the Baron, your father, to stay. To work year round," he said, as she felt him exhale deeply.

"But w…w…what about your mother and…and," she sputtered. Anna did not know what else there was left back home for him, but she did know one thing, inside herself a flame of hope had ignited that she could not bear to extinguish.

"Mother passed away this last spring. There is no one left in Poland, and there is only one place my heart can bear to live," he said as she felt his body tense in anticipation of what she might say.

"Oh, Jakub, m…m…my love," Anna cried, overcome with emotion. Warm tears flowed down her cheeks and she felt the tension in him melt away like hot wax. "I am s…s…so sorry, Jakub, s…s…so sorry," she cried into his large, gently heaving chest. Anna did not know how long she had been asleep, but woke with a start. Her face, still resting on Jakub's warm chest, felt clammy. She heard Jakub's breathing, rhythmic and deep. He was still asleep. "Jakub. Jakub."

"What is it, my Anna?" Jakub sat up quickly. "Is something wrong?" he spoke with panic in his voice.

"No. No, Jakub. I m…m…must return to my room." She kissed Jakub and quickly made her way down the ladder, hoping no one had noticed her absence.

"This will not end well," Maria whispered to Anna as she tried to slip into the bedroom chamber she shared with her sister.

"Th…th…that is funny, I just heard Papa speak those same words tonight," she replied, frustrated that she could never hide anything from her sister.

20

"What? Papa knows?" her sister, illuminated by the full moon shining through her window, asked with horror.

"N…n…no, no, of course not," she answered, quickly removing her heavy overcoat and slipping beneath her warm down comforter.

"He and M…M…Mama were speaking, if you c…c…can call it th…th…that, about the Fuehrer again."

"Oh," Maria said with a tone of relief, "you know, I think the Fuehrer means more to our mother than Papa does. But enough of Mama, I worry for you, Anna," her sister said, with what Anna felt was exaggerated and unnecessary concern.

"B…b…but why?" Anna asked with equally exaggerated innocence.

"You know, Anna, you may be able to fool Mama and Papa, but you cannot fool your older and wiser sister," Maria spoke with a sharper tone now. "I see the look on your face when you see Jakub outside, and the way you behave when he speaks with Papa. Do not fool yourself, it is only a matter of time until Papa finds out…if he does not already know." Anna felt her face flush. She was not a child, she would be eighteen soon, a grown woman. How dare Maria, or anyone, speak to her as though she were a disobedient child.

"W…w…well, l…l…let him find out th…th…then, he will soon enough," Anna spoke with an anger she could not hide from her sister.

"What do you mean by that? What are you not telling me?" Maria questioned as she looked at her sister and felt fortunate that her bed was far away from the illuminating moonshine, hiding her face. Anna did not answer. "Oh, my dear Lord," her sister whispered, "tell me Anna, please tell me you are not with child."

Anna's explosive burst of laughter erased all feelings of anger she had felt in an instant. As her laughter ebbed she continued to snort as Maria stared over into Anna's dark corner of the room.

"*That* was not very lady like," Maria chided. Despite Maria's disapproval of her younger sister's behavior, Anna could hear the relief in her sister's voice, "and obviously you are not," Maria cleared her throat, "with child."

"N…n…no, I am n…n…not *with* child," Anna repeated, all traces of humor she had felt just moments ago vanished.

"Well, then what is it?" Maria asked, annoyed that she was unable to, as of yet, pry her sister's secret from her. Anna knew it was pointless to hide anything from Maria, she would find out soon enough herself anyway.

"He…He…He… is st…st…staying," Anna stuttered into her pillow, muffling her words.

"What was that?" Maria asked sharply.

Turning her head towards her sister Anna spoke more clearly. "I said, he is staying. He is not returning to Poland," Anna was proud of herself that she did not stutter. Her sister did not respond. Anna felt a cold sweat come over her. She continued to wait for her sister's response, which did not come. Anna listened to her heartbeat as she pushed her face deeper into her pillow, hoping the pillow might hide her forever. Still her sister did not respond. This silence annoyed her. She could almost feel her sister thinking, and Anna was much too tired to have some lengthy conversation that would likely end with an argument.

When Maria finally spoke it was, miraculously, without judgment. "You really love him, Anna?" It was more of a statement, an admission to herself, than a question for Anna. How could her sister know her so well? Sometimes their shared thoughts seemed uncanny to the even sisters themselves. "I thought it was a passing fancy. You know yourself that I have had them in the past," Maria continued in a tone that made Anna sit up and listen. "I never allowed myself anything more than passing fancies. What would Mama or Papa think? That is the question I have always asked myself. I have news of my own for you, Anna," Maria spoke with a darkness that sent shivers down Anna's spine.

With each passing moment that Maria did not speak, Anna felt an increasing sense of foreboding. "W…w…what news is th…th… this?" Anna stuttered, shattering the silence. She hated when she stuttered. It was worse when she was excited.

"Dieter has asked Papa for my hand," Maria said flatly.

"What? No!" Anna yelled out, instantly covering her mouth with both hands. "S…s…sorry, I mean, h…h…how, but, no not how, but, I don't know w…w…what I mean," Anna stumbled over her words. How could her sister marry a man she had said she did not love?

"Oh Anna, you are still a child," her sister spoke as though in a trance, "it is a good marriage. Dieter loves me, and I care for him. He will take care of me."

"B...b...but, Maria, y...y...you said yourself that you d...d...do not love him, and, and," Anna did not know what else there was to say. What kind of joining of the souls was it if there was no love? After watching her parents' marriage of convenience, as she believed it to be, she could not believe her sister would fall into that same trap.

"You do not understand, Anna." Maria, obviously out of her trance, snapped at her sister. "You are too selfish to care how your behavior affects Mama and Papa, the whole family actually."

"Th...th...this is not about me," Anna replied with a quivering voice.

"Yes, this is about you! You will disgrace our family, consorting with migrant farm hands like a common whore," Maria hissed at her sister from across the room.

"Maria!" Anna had never in her life been so insulted. How could it be that her sister would pass such harsh judgment? Had Maria not just moments before admitted to similar transgressions? Had she not just moments ago sympathized with her love for Jakub? Anna felt confused and hurt. Was there not tacit acceptance of their love in Maria's words?

It was not until she heard Maria's sobs that she understood. She was not truly the reason Maria was upset. Maria was upset with her own situation. She needed someone to lash out at. Anna suddenly remembered the conversations she and Maria had as children. Their idealistic views of love and marriage had been filled with so much hope despite the innocence of their age. The anger Anna felt disappeared in an instant. Her heart ached for Maria, who, she knew, suffered. Listening as her sister's sobs finally silenced she gathered up the courage to speak. "I *am* s...s...sorry Maria," she whispered. There was nothing more for her to say now. Nothing she could say would change anything for Maria. Anna knew it was pointless to tell her sister not to marry. Maria had always followed the rules. She had always done what was right, not just for herself, but for her family. Once committed, there was no going back for Maria. Anna laid back down on her soft down pillow and listened to the faint sounds of the night. She knew neither she nor her sister would sleep this solemn night.

Anna washed and dressed well before she heard the rooster crow. Quietly she made her way down the stairs to the kitchen. Maybe she would help Sigrid in the kitchen. The smell of coffee and baking bread made her mouth water. After a night like the last one, she could use the coffee, and this was going to be a long day.

"Good Morning, Fraulein von Marschalkt," the maid spoke to her as she pushed through the double kitchen doors.

"Good m…m…morning. Siggi," Anna said, resisting the urge to hug Sigrid as the maid carefully placed freshly gathered eggs into a pot of boiling water. She felt good about herself around Sigrid who did not make her feel insecure about her decisions. She even seemed to stutter less around the maid.

"Just when did you s…s…start calling me Fraulein von Marschalkt?" Anna asked teasingly. "It is Anna. J…j…just Anna." Sigrid had been in this house since before she was born. In many ways Anna felt closer to her than her own mother.

"When you became a woman, at least on the outside," Sigrid said as she handed Anna a large slice of sausage.

Anna sat down at the small, informal kitchen table and watched Sigrid's large, capable hands. "Siggi, c…c…can I ask you someth… th…thing?" Anna asked innocently.

"Just as long as it does not have to do with making children, I have no experience there," Sigrid answered as she placed a bowl of steaming, molasses-covered oatmeal in front of Anna, who had altogether forgotten that she had intended to help Sigrid.

"How c…c…come you never m…m…married?" she asked. Anna was always curious about Sigrid.

"There was never a right one," Sigrid answered without hesitation.

"S…s…so there were m…m…men in your life?" Anna asked almost disbelievingly.

"Of course." Sigrid answered, matter of fact. "There were men and this is not a proper conversation for a proper young woman."

Ignoring Sigrid's comment, Anna continued to deliberate Sigrid's love life. "B…b…but Siggi, was there not one s…s…special one? One you s…s…still think about?" Anna asked as she licked sweet molasses from her lips. Sigrid did not answer. Anna watched as Sigrid scrubbed her pot a little more furiously than she had just moments ago.

"I know why you ask," Sigrid said sharply, abruptly halting her scrubbing motions. Anna froze, a spoonful of oatmeal hovering just outside her open mouth.

"W…W…What do you m…m…mean by that?" she asked, dropping her uneaten spoonful of oatmeal back into the bowl. "S…S… Siggi, p…p…please tell me w…w…what you m…m…mean by that," Anna pleaded, yet horrified to hear what Sigrid had to say.

"I have fed you since you were a day old. I see what you like," Sigrid spoke tartly, turning to look straight at Anna.

"Y…y…you d…d…do know, d…d…don't you? Oh S…S… Siggi, p…p…please d…d…don't tell M…M…Mama or P…P… Papa, at least n…n…not yet," Anna begged.

"I wasn't completely sure, but now I am," Sigrid said, setting the pot down and walking towards Anna. "I never had children. You and your sister…I love you, especially you, like my own," Sigrid seemed faraway as she spoke. "There was one time in my life, you are right, where I thought I had found the right one, but the situation was not… correct."

'W…W…What do you m…m…mean not correct?" Anna pushed on, "how can t…t…true love not be correct? I do not understand."

"He is…was… married," Sigrid said as she placed her warm hand on Anna's cool one. "There is a natural order to things that can not be upset," the maid said as she squeezed Anna's hand, stood up, and returned to her work.

Anna watched as Sigrid poured cold water over the boiled eggs and pondered who this mysterious love had been that almost moved Sigrid to tears. And what did she mean by natural order? How could true love ever upset a natural order she wondered, as she scooped up her last spoonful of oatmeal. "Anna," Sigrid said, surprising her by once again using her first name, "sometimes the natural order is meant to be upset, but in most cases it is not."

Anna held Sigrid's gaze until the unspoken moment between the two women passed. Anna moved towards the woman with the warm hands, unsure about the message she had just sent her and embraced her tightly, whispering "I love you, Siggi."

"I know, child. Now leave so I can get some work done." Sigrid's attempt at sounding resolute failed with someone who knew her so well. Anna left the kitchen with a bucket of warm milk for the kittens in the barn.

Anna was surprised to find her father in the barn with Jakub and two other seasonal Polish farm hands, Ivan and Michal. Lowering her eyes, Anna called out for the mother cat and her kittens as she poured milk into small bowls, stealing glances at her beloved Jakub. What was her father doing in the barn at this early hour with Jakub and the others? She was not left in the dark for long. Father's mare was in labor.

"Anna, we need hot water! And bring Sigrid. Be quick girl!" her father called after her as she dropped her milk bucket and ran towards the house. Returning a little while later with Sigrid, both heavily laden with large pots of hot water, Anna hoped Jakub was still in the barn.

"How is she?" Anna breathlessly asked her father about the laboring mare. Her father's look of consternation worried Anna. She was not surprised to see Papa in the barn caring for an animal. Mama often scolded him. It was not proper behavior for a Baron to work with his hands. The Baron did not respond to his daughter, but looked at the men and asked them if the mare should be slaughtered and the foal birthed.

Anna and Sigrid listened in horror as they watched the men. The thought of slaughtering an animal, laboring to birth a new life, was almost too much for Anna to tolerate. White-faced, she watched as Jakub turned to his companions and spoke with them in hushed tones. Despite the situation Anna felt herself mesmerized by Jakub speaking his native language. Was it possible his features were even more handsome when he spoke Polish?

"I will try and turn the foal," Jakub said to the Baron as he stripped off his shirt, Carefully, Jakub reached his arm deep inside the laboring mare. Groaning as the contractions squeezed down on his arm, Jakub carefully shifted the unborn foal, pulling gently as the contractions continued to bear down on his own quivering limb. After what felt like an eternity, Anna watched in awe as Jakub pulled the foal from deep within its mother's womb. As he stood, covered in blood and sweat, with a newborn life in his arms, Anna found herself more in love with Jakub than ever before. Unsure whether it was the new life he held in his arms or the perspiration that glistened on his chest, Anna desired him more than anything else in her life.

"Oh, Jakub," she whispered before she realized she was not alone. Anna emerged from whatever spell she had been under, quickly gathered her empty milk bucket, and excused herself. Her father watched her sudden departure with curious eyes.

Travels of Letter Sixteen
Southern Coast, England
Spring 1946

The two English boys, covered in sand and mud, hid behind a large mound of seaweed, waiting for their reconnaissance troop to return with news of the enemy. Germans had been sighted in the forest minutes ago and an attack appeared imminent. The boys watched the forest for any signs of movement, enemy or friendly. Lacking any weapons they sifted through the mound of seaweed in search of drift wood. Better weaponry could be found strewn across the beach. A large piece of sword-like drift wood was no more than 10 meters away, but to leave their post now was to risk detection and even worse, likely death. A suicide mission they were not about to risk. The seaweed, which had been piled over half a meter high by the raging waves the night before, provided countless places to hide on this normally barren stretch of beach. The boys shivered as they searched through the heavy seaweed, but seemed otherwise impervious to the biting chill of a winter that had passed, but was not yet willing to release its icy hold on the world.

"I've found something," the younger of the two boys whispered to his brother, who nodded and saluted with approval. A green glass bottle would make a perfect gun. "Maybe we'll find another one," the younger brother whispered. He would offer his weapon to his older brother if he didn't find something himself. The reconnaissance troop was made up of three older boys who carried real weapons, wooden guns they had carved themselves. It was important that the reconnaissance team was armed. Theirs was a more dangerous job than hiding behind seaweed with hopes of launching a surprise attack.

A piercing scream filled the air, and then another, followed by yet another. The two brothers poked their heads out from behind their hideaway and watched as their reconnaissance troop fled empty-handed out of the woods towards the beach, flinging themselves behind the safety of the seaweed.

The momentary silence was broken by the sound of enemy gun fire. A group of eight boys, covered in mud themselves, charged out of the forest whooping like wild Indians. "Sieg, Heil! Sieg, Heil!" they shouted as they pursued the three retreating soldiers. Armed with wooden guns and twigs, the German aggressors fanned out across the stretch of beach in search of the three now-vanished English soldiers.

"Take this," the younger brother whispered as he handed the glass bottle to his brother. "I'll keep searching for more weapons." There was no time to search, as an instant later an enemy soldier was upon them. The older brother lifted the glass bottle, aimed and began to fire in rapid succession. The enemy soldier, no older than the boy himself, dropped to the ground, moaning audibly. With their hideout now revealed, the two boys became the main target of enemy fire. From all sides, the sounds of gun fire could be heard shattering the silence of this normally desolate beach.

"Cover my back," the older brother whispered to the younger, as he jumped up and began to fire his weapon recklessly in all directions. The younger brother, now armed with a small twig he had found in the mound of seaweed, followed his brother's lead and jumped up firing his weapon in all directions. This action was repeated across the beach by the six other English soldiers crouched behind similar seaweed mounds, waiting for just such an opportunity. The battle was short-lived. The reconnaissance troop had successfully lured the German soldiers out to the open beach where the English quickly destroyed the enemy. Across the beach the groans and moans of dying soldiers could be heard, followed by cheers of "Hitler is dead! Hitler is dead."

"Frankie and I've gotta run home, our Mum's gonna kill us," the older brother called out between cheers and groans to his friends strewn across the field. This sentiment was quickly echoed by the other boys, who realized they too had best return home before their mothers ambushed them down at the beach. "Not gonna need this anymore, eh Frankie," the boy said to his younger brother as he swung his arm wide and hurled the green glass bottle back into the sea from which it had come. "Saved our lives, wouldn't you say, Frankie boy," he said as he and his younger brother watched the bottle bob up and down in the waves until it slowly disappeared out of sight.

Frankie Adams would remember this day years later, even into adulthood. It would become the day that defined his childhood and his relationship with his brother.

Cape May, New Jersey

Fall 2011

"Hey, Dad," I said, after checking the number that came up on my ringing cell phone.

"How'd you know it was me, Diana?" my dad asked. He seemed to worry constantly about me, even when I wasn't on the other side of the United States.

"You know, Dad, you and Sheila ask me that same question every time you call. Caller ID, remember?" Somehow I was oddly comforted by this little game my parents played.

"I know you know who it is honey, I just, I don't know what," my father laughed. I listened to my father's laughter and wished I could go back in time, run into his arms, and be flung high in the air. Those were the days, I thought with a little too much melancholy. Frank Adams. I had to smile. In all of my memories he was always so strong, flawless, and practically omnipotent. I can't remember the day I saw him for who he really was. Not quite the big man of my childhood. Both he and Sheila were filled with flaws and insecurities, and I had physically towered over the little guy since I was fourteen years old, but wow, did I still love him. And if there was one thing I had to admire about my father, it was how much he still adored and loved

Sheila. Now that is what Warren and I had. He would have loved me, wrinkles and all.

"Thanks for calling, Dad. Sheila didn't tell you to call did she?" I asked, knowing full well the answer to that question.

"No, no, of course not," my father said, clearing his throat, just as he always did when he lied. "So, what are your plans for the evening?" he asked casually, trying hard not to sound like he was worrying too much. He knew that job was normally reserved for Sheila. Oh geez, the poor guy was nervous. His English accent always seemed to intensify when he was on edge.

"Well, I just checked into the hotel, but I thought I'd take a walk on the beach before it gets too dark, and then grab some dinner." I felt my throat constrict at the thought of a stroll along the beach alone, not to mention a dinner out alone. This was something I had to do though, needed to do. This was my life now, my future.

"Dad, I should really go, you know, it's three hours later here," I said half-heartedly, hoping he would keep me on the line a little longer. Maybe he would somehow dissuade me from going out on my own.

"Yeah, yeah, sure, you go, enjoy yourself, honey," my father said. I heard how hard he tried to sound cheerful, and I almost had to pity him.

"Bye, Dad." My heart hurt as I tossed the phone on the nightstand and lay down on the bed. I felt a panic attack creeping up on me, threatening to drown me. As I stared up at the ceiling, hyperventilating, I knew I wasn't going anywhere tonight, not without Warren, not yet. Rolling onto my stomach I reached for the one thing that could keep me grounded, my shoebox. As I pulled off the lid the familiar scent of cardboard and old love letters worked on me like a sedative.

"So this is it, Warren. This is what's left of us." I closed my eyes and ran my hand through the letters, selected one, and carefully unfolded it. "Love must be as much a light as it is a flame," by Henry David Thoreau. Warren always started and ended his letters with a quote. Oh God, I'm embarrassed to admit it to myself now, but I used to find these quotes rather corny. Later I came to appreciate them, only after I realized how much thought Warren had put into selecting each quote.

And here we have Thoreau at the end of the letter again. "There is no remedy for love but to love more." I read the quote again, and then again, and wondered what the quote actually meant. Did it even have any meaning for me anymore? A widow whose true love, whose soul mate, had been torn from her? I gently refolded the letter and placed it back in the shoebox only to pull out the next one. "You are not going to read these all night long," I ineffectively threatened myself.

I had no memory of falling asleep when I lifted my groggy head to check the clock, wiping away a letter that somehow managed stick itself to my cheek. "Oh damn it," I cursed when the fog in my mind lifted enough to realize I had fallen asleep on top of a few letters. It took another moment of deliberation to figure out whether it was nine a.m. or nine p.m. "I guess it's breakfast then," I finally said. My voice sounded hollow. I missed my cat and really wished Jack were here. Then at least I wouldn't be the crazy lady who talked only to herself. The ringing cell phone startled me, literally causing me to jump up and endure a momentary muscle spasm in my lower back. "Oh crap," I hissed through gritted teeth as the spasm eventually loosened its grip. It was only six a.m. on the west coast, who was up at this hour? Sheila and Dad were never up before eight, and Abe, geez he needed his beauty sleep. I was surprised to see Abe's name on my caller ID.

"Hey, Abe," I said, trying hard to sound perky.

"Hey, Di, how's it going? Get there alright?" he asked me as I wondered how many more family members might call in next the hour.

"Yeah, yeah, of course," I answered a little gruffly, what did he think? "So what's up?" I asked rather impatiently, hopefully sending the message that I had somewhere to be real soon.

"Well, if this is a bad time I can call back," Abe said. Obviously my message had arrived loud and clear. Did I really sound that impatient across the miles?

"No, it's okay, I just wanted to grab a bite to eat is all…and, uh, I just need to get going really soon," I heard myself saying, reminding me of the conversation I had with my father the night before.

"Oh, okay, well, I just wanted to know how your evening went. But you know what, I'll talk to you later," Abe suddenly seemed in a hurry to hang up the phone, and so much more serious than his normal carefree self. Likely his little bimbo, Akila, needed something from him, and of course good old Abe would have to jump real high. As I listened to my own thoughts, I felt my face flush. Was I really this bitter? Is this what I had turned into? Abe had done so much for me since Warren's death. Why was I acting so wicked? Grateful that I was alone with no one to witness my embarrassment, I quickly said goodbye and hung up the cell phone. "Well, that's the last phone call I'm accepting," I told my phone and pressed the *off* button. I really did need to get out of this room. The walls felt as though they were closing in on me. Carefully, I placed my box of letters underneath the bed. For a moment I contemplated locking them in the suitcase, but these letters wouldn't be worth anything to someone else, would they? Pulling my newly red streaked hair back into a tight pony-tail I reached for my raincoat and walked out of the room, turning one last time to stare into the eerily empty room.

This shabby motel was not what I remembered. The pool had already been emptied for the winter and it was only fall. But then again, who wants to swim in this weather I asked myself, looking up at the grey morning sky. Maybe there weren't enough guests to justify taking care of a pool past the summer. The place did seem somewhat deserted, but given the weather, if there were any guests they were likely cooped up in their rooms.

"Just why did I choose Cape May again?" I had to ask myself as I stood on the beach, facing the dingy motel. The question actually begged to be asked again. "The Surf and Sand Motel," I whispered to myself. This was the first motel I shared with Warren. Love truly does blind. If I hadn't seen the dilapidated place for what it was, then I sure saw it now. I had more important things to focus on back then. My husband. The whole town in general seemed to have lost its flare. "Well, what were you expecting?" I chided myself as I realized, with an accompanying wave of nausea, that no place I'd been with Warren would ever be the same again. Why should I bother going out at all anymore? Everything seemed tied to a memory of Warren. "Well you did choose a place where the two of you probably made love more passionately than anywhere else," my rational voice reminded me, making my blood flow more quickly at the memory. "Oh Warren, I miss you," I cried, as tears flowed down my face, mixing with the raindrops that had begun to fall from the sky. The pain I hid inside had found a way out. I don't know how long the tears flowed. All perception of time disappeared.

Somewhere in the blur of tears and raindrops, I found my way to the water's edge and sat down. As I sat alone on the normally busy beach, I realized the weather would of course keep most sane people inside today, but oh no, not me. Sanity did not want to keep me company these days. The few scattered souls who did venture outside moved quickly, hunched forward, to avoid the wind and the rain. As I looked out at the agitated sea, I realized how different the Atlantic Ocean looked from the Pacific that I was used to. The one I stared out at every day, but rarely saw. Today I looked out at the Atlantic and tried to see, not just stare as I did so often at the Pacific. Somehow the necessary peace for such a Zen moment eluded me and my mind drifted. I was staring again, not seeing, wondering what exactly I would do with my life now? Now that I was alone, without the partner who was supposed to be around for my whole life. Mourning the loss of my future, I picked up a cool wet rock and watched as rain drops fell onto it. Why couldn't I just turn into a rock, unfeeling and hard? The rain came down harder, almost blurring my vision. Like the last six months I thought, just a great big blur.

Looking out at the ocean I watched as some brave soul commandeered his small catamaran out towards the high sea. It was getting colder. I would have to get up and move around soon. Standing up, I shook the damp sand off my rain coat and walked slowly along the beach looking for sea shells. The sound of crashing waves soothed my soul. Stooping down, I picked up a skate egg case with its long tendrils and wondered if the small skate inside was alive. Hoping it was alive, I walked as close as I dared to the pounding waves and threw the case into the churning water. So many shells and other ocean debris littered this part of the Jersey shore, probably because of the storm. Spying a scallop shell, I picked up the fan-shaped beauty, marveling at its perfect construction. Life is so beautiful, but at the same time so horrible, I thought, allowing the shell to fill with rain drops. As though to spite me, the rain suddenly stopped and a single ray of sunshine managed to pierce through the thick blanket of clouds. It was beautiful. I soaked in this moment of beauty which I knew would be fleeting. All beautiful things were.

Feelings of guilt washed over me. How could I enjoy life, when a life had been taken, the life of my beloved? Just as I was about to let my soul succumb again to the misery of the last six months, I tripped over a bottle. I have no idea what it was about this bottle that caught my attention. Squatting down to examine it more closely I noticed that it had a worn look about it. Different from other discarded bottles I had seen in the past, often remnants from some drunken beach fest. This one seemed special. "Now you're sounding just a little bit crazier, woman," I whispered to myself as I rubbed the last of the damp sand off the bottle. No, I convinced myself, this bottle *was* different, somehow special. It reminding me of a giant piece of cloudy green sea glass, something I would have treasured as a little girl.

"Diana, Diana, Diana," I heard a whisper, or was it the wind? Turning around I felt as though someone or something watched me.

"You are crazy, woman," I said aloud to shake the creepy feeling. Inspecting the glass, I wondered if there was anything inside. The neck had been filled to the rim with some sort of substance. Was it wax? Raising my head, I felt the warmth of the sun shine down on me. "Wow," I nearly gasped as I stared up at the most magnificent rainbow I had ever seen. Rarely did I see rainbows, never before had I seen both ends of the rainbow.

"They say you find a pot of gold at the end of the rainbow. That is *if* you can find the little leprechaun. Scheming little fellers I hear," a somewhat familiar voice behind me spoke. Startled, I turned around, dropping the bottle into the soft sand. "Sorry to make you jump," the man laughed as he bent to pick up the fallen bottle. "Here you go," he said as he handed me the bottle, "nice artifact." I reached for the bottle and awkwardly held onto it, staring at the handsome stranger as recognition slowly set in.

"You. It's you, from the plane. You were in my seat, I mean, well, we both had the same seat, but you moved." I stuttered and stumbled over my words. I felt my face flush. What was it about this man that evoked such unexpected emotion in me? I had no idea what was going on. I wasn't sure I wanted to know. Thoughts of Warren pushed themselves into my mind, only to be pushed away again, colliding with the waves of guilt that passed over me.

"Are you alright?" the handsome stranger asked, as he gently guided me by the elbow to sit down in the wet sand again.

"Yeah, uh, thanks," I said somewhat abashed, as I hugged the bottle tightly to my chest.

"I'm sorry, the name is Charles. Charlie actually, Charlie Gordon from the plane," he said extending his hand out to me as he chuckled. I looked at his hand for a moment before slowly reaching out to touch it.

There was no logical explanation for what it was. At least I couldn't think of one, but I felt as though I moved through a dream. My only lifeline to reality was this stranger's hand, onto which I firmly held. A current or pulse moved through my body that I couldn't comprehend. One thing was certain though, this was no ordinary encounter between two strangers.

"Uh, I should be getting back to my hotel," I abruptly said, pulling away from this Charlie man.

"Where are you staying? I could walk you back," he said. He looked hopeful.

"No, uh, no thank you, I've got some things I've got to take care of…in town," I stammered, twisting the glass bottle in my hands.

"Well, it was a pleasure meeting you, again," Charlie said, extending his hand in my direction once again. I didn't want to reach for his hand.

"Yes, likewise," I stiffly replied, reaching for his hand, only to quickly drop it again. With that, I quickly walked away from this stranger, whose eyes I could still feel watching me as I moved away. Had he felt it too? Maybe I was crazy. Probably that was it, since I still held on to this cloudy green glass bottle. I needed to get back to the motel.

I don't know how long I'd been sitting on the corner of the bed. It could have been a few minutes, or maybe an hour. It wasn't the first time I'd lost track of time. The damp rain coat I was still wearing was glued to my body. What was the matter with me? I stared at my reflection in the large mirror and knew what was wrong, but couldn't bring myself to admit it, even though there was no stopping it. Somehow my thoughts constantly drifted towards a stranger, the man I had just met. Charles. Charlie.

Sitting on this small corner of space I occupied in this big world, I wondered if this was destiny or just random chance. Which was it? There had to be more to life than random events that brought two people together. But true love, what Warren and I had, couldn't possibly happen more than once. What I have, or had, I corrected myself, with Warren, only happens once in a lifetime. Then why can't I explain the sparks I felt with Charlie? I know it sounded ridiculous, but what had happened in those brief moments when our hands touched, was like nothing I had ever felt. There was some sort of electricity, I don't know how better to describe it. "What is wrong with you, Di?" I asked myself again, trying hard to repress feelings I hadn't felt in a long time.

Laying back on the bed, I stared up at the ceiling filled with cracks I hadn't noticed before. I had forgotten all about the glass bottle I found on the beach. Closing my eyes, my mind swung back and forth between the conscious and subconscious worlds, both of which led to bizarre thoughts and images.

It was a shattering sound from the bathroom that brought me back to the conscious world. Leaping to my feet like the rabid hyena my brother had labeled me as, I darted towards the bathroom and flung open the door. As I stared at the shards of green glass on the white tile floor, I was momentarily befuddled and confused.

"What in the name of..." I spoke aloud. The beautiful bottle had met a violent end. Broken glass meant seven years bad luck, at least according to Sheila. Mourning the loss of the bottle, I pondered how it could have possibly fallen. Maybe I *had* placed it too close to the edge of the sink while I was in my catatonic state. As I surveyed the scene of devastation, I noticed what looked like a rolled up piece of paper. Squatting down, I carefully lifted the paper from amongst the shards. It felt old, and fragile.

"Ha. So there was something inside. My instincts weren't so off." Carefully, I unrolled the paper and quickly scanned what I held in my hands. It looked like a letter written some time ago. I inhaled sharply when my eyes came to rest on the date of the letter. Either my eyes were playing tricks on me, or this letter was dated December, 1946. This had to be a hoax I thought, as a voice from somewhere seemed to whisper to me. Now I knew I was going mad as the words, "A Night of Broken Glass," popped into my mind. A shiver ran down my spine as I looked from the letter to the broken glass and back to the letter again. Was I really going insane?

Dresden, Germany

Late Spring 1938

"It is too d…d…dangerous for you n…n…now. I worry for you, f…f…for us," Anna said to Jakub as he tossed hay from the loft.

"They do not know I am Jew. It is only you who does," Jakub grunted as he heaved down another bale of hay, "and the other Jews no longer work for your father. They have all gone." He laid down the pitchfork and turned to the woman he loved. "Oh, Anna, I feel safe when we are together." Anna did not share his current sentiment. She feared for Jakub's safety, for the safety of her family. Possibly even for her own well-being.

"It is a w…w…witch hunt, I just kn…kn…know it. I have heard Papa say so often enough. I am not so sure about Mama." Anna was not sure why she was unable to meet Jakub's gaze. What would he think if he knew how her mother really felt about the Jews? Would he leave her, disappear in the middle of the night back to…back to where she wondered. Jakub gently lifted her chin, forcing her to look at him.

"Tomorrow is your sister's wedding. Let us not worry about these things tonight."

"W…W…Will you be h…h…here tonight?" she asked him as her heart raced, unable to quiet the voice inside that she was going to lose him. Trying hard to dispel her negative thoughts, she looked up at the man whose eyes held nothing but love and desire for her.

"Of course I will," he answered, placing a soft, warm kiss on her lips.

As Anna slipped out of the barn, she did not notice the man who stood in the shadows of the old wagon. Her thoughts were with Jakub and their joint future. Would it ever be possible to have a future together? Turning back to look at the barn, she could have sworn she felt as though someone watched her. "Silly girl," she chided herself, it is only Jakub, but the suspicious voice inside could not be quieted.

The rain beat down on her as Anna finally made her way to the dark hayloft that evening. It was later than usual. She had many errands to tend to for Maria, not to mention her own preparations for tomorrow. A melancholy surrounded her as she quietly climbed up the familiar ladder in darkness. Tomorrow was a day of celebration. Yet she knew it was not what Maria's heart truly wanted. Marrying for the sake of appearances was something Anna could not understand, but then Maria acted with her head and Anna with her heart. She had listened to Maria quietly weep all evening, but Anna felt helpless as she was unable to comfort her in any way. She had wanted to tell her sister that maybe a true love could grow from this union, but Anna did not believe this herself. Especially not with Dieter, whose rigid posture and eccentric mannerisms made Anna shudder. "No, that will never be me," she swore to herself as unwanted visions of her sister's wedding night forced their way into her mind. "Uuuugh," she said as she shook herself in an attempt to rid herself of these unwanted images. Reaching the top of the ladder, she squinted into the darkness, sensing his presence. "Jakub," she whispered into the darkness. "Jakub, are you here?"

"Anna," she heard him whisper as the hay beneath him rustled. "I am sorry I fell asleep," he said groggily as he blindly reached for her.

"N...N...No, it is I who am s...s...sorry. There was much to be done, but I did not expect it to take so long," she explained as she felt his warm hands reach around her waist and pull her down to the hay with him. This was the first time she had not stuttered around Jakub.

44

"I would wait a lifetime and a thousand more for you, even soaking wet as you are," Jakub spoke, with his head so close to hers she could feel his lips moving. Anna laughed quietly and inhaled, enjoying his rich scent, a warm blend of hay, perspiration, and soap.

"And I for you," she answered, trying hard not to bring up the morning's conversation again. Her physical proximity to Jakub soon allowed her to relax. Here, in this dark hayloft, there was only room for the two of them. Nothing else mattered. Nothing else would ever matter she thought, as she embraced her lover in the darkness.

"I am ready," she whispered into his ear, her voice barely audible above the rain pounding down on the barn roof. Anna heard Jakub inhale sharply, obviously surprised.

"I thought you…," he began to say as she pressed her fingers on his lips. "You are sure about this?" Jakub asked without further attempts to discourage her.

"Yes," she replied resolutely. She was more certain of this than anything else in her life. Anna had visions of this moment from the day she met Jakub. She had been raised well, she had been taught to serve a man, but all these rules only applied to a married woman. Somewhere she had always wanted to break out of the chains that society imposed upon her. She knew now was that time. Anna was unable to explain this urgency to Jakub, but somehow she believed he felt it too. Her fingers trembled as she pulled him close to her. She felt his manhood press against her. Gently Jakub removed her dress. His warm hands on her body made every part of her tingle. No other thought could enter her mind. There was only Jakub on this earth. There were no words for what she felt. The moment she had thought about for so long was here. Tenderly Jakub rolled on top of her, lovingly kissing her neck, stroking her arms, her legs, her stomach. Anna felt Jakub's weight begin to press down on her. Carefully he nudged her legs apart. As she felt Jakub's manhood slowly enter her most private of parts she knew, this act would forever change her. Anna inhaled quickly as a sharp pain cut through her, followed by Jakub's gentle rocking back and forth.

During the wedding ceremony the next day, Anna could not focus on what was going on around her. Her mind was trapped in the moments of beauty she had shared with Jakub. She had to tear her mind away from him. She felt a smile tug at her lips as she realized this was an impossibility she now had to live with.

"And who bears witness to this union?" the priest asked the congregation.

"We do," the gathered family and guests replied in unison.

"Before God, you Dieter Schiller and you Anna von Marschalkt, are now husband and wife." Anna continued to watch with an odd detachment as the priest introduced the new couple. Her mind wandered and played back *the* evening with Jakub again and again. She felt her face flush at the memory of his body on top of hers and felt a warm throbbing between her thighs.

"Are you alright, Anna?" her father asked as she fanned herself, "you look flushed." Her father placed a hand to her forehead as though she were a child.

"Yes, yes, Papa, I am fine, I just need a bit of air," she replied, as she gently removed his hand from her face, grateful the wedding ceremony had concluded and guests were filing out of the dank chapel. The heavens must not be pleased with this union she thought, as she looked up at the ominous dark grey sky that had relentlessly thundered throughout the wedding ceremony. Rain continued to fall as the guests exited the chapel. This is not right, Anna thought to herself. Jakub should be here with me. She knew this was not possible, but wished she could change the social structure she lived in. It took all of her self-control not to leave the wedding festivities and search for her beloved. What was he doing at this moment? Did he think of her? Anna could not help her obsessive thoughts. She had been counting down the minutes until she would see him again. Many hours still remained. It was her mother who interrupted her thoughts.

"Go help your sister in the wash closet, she is ill," she brusquely ordered. Anna looked at her mother, somewhat surprised by her tone of voice.

"Is everything alright, Mama?" she asked as her own suspicious mind whispered to her, rousing previously repressed fears.

Her mother had turned to leave, but stopped abruptly. Slowly turning around she stared at her daughter. "It must be now," she hissed between clenched teeth. "Go to your sister, now." The Baroness commanded Anna like one of her staff, but Anna did not move. Anna felt lightheaded. She needed to sit down. Her sister would have to wait. Pale faced, Anna ran away from her mother, away from the main house, to the garden gazebo where she sat down on a cold stone bench. Drenched to the bone, she felt her body begin to shiver, a combination of fear and cold.

"She can't know, she couldn't possibly know," Anna repeatedly told herself as she rocked back and forth. "How would she know, no one knew besides Maria and she would never…," Anna felt her heart begin to race. "Maria," she thought, as a rage she had never experienced began to well up inside of her. Storming out of the gazebo, she lifted her dress as she ran towards the main house in search of Maria. "The wash closet, that is where Mama said she was," she said aloud as she stormed up the stairs, hoping her sister was still feeling ill in the wash closet.

Anna found Maria bent over the toilet expelling the remnants of whatever she had eaten earlier that morning. Undeterred by the vision of a new bride in her wedding gown, bent over a toilet bowl, Anna began interrogating her sister. "D…id you t…t…tell her, Maria? D… id you t…t…tell Mother?"

Maria, still otherwise engaged, did momentarily look up at her wet sister whose chaotic ramblings were making no sense to her at all. Maria slowly straightened herself as Anna handed her a tissue to dab the corners of her mouth. Sitting down at a small vanity table she again looked at Anna.

"What are you talking about, Anna?" she asked, as she critically viewed her reflection in the mirror.

"I s…s…said, d…d…did you tell Mama or Papa about Jakub?" Anna demanded as she placed her hands on her hips, her posture resembling that of the Baroness.

"I have no idea what you are talking about, Anna," a fatigued Maria replied. "And stop shouting please, I have excellent hearing and would like to keep it that way," Maria said as she stood up to face her sister. "Now, Anna, would you please tell me what is going on? And start from the beginning."

Anna explained her mother's angry behavior to Maria, who pondered the situation for a moment.

"So, Mama did not say anything about Jakub, but you believe she knows?" Maria asked dubiously, straightening out her wedding gown.

"N...n...no, it was more of a...f...f...feeling...a sense...I c...c... cannot explain it," Anna tried to make her sister believe, as doubt began to settle in her own mind.

"Well, I think you should forget about it," Maria said, speaking to Anna's reflection in the mirror. "And, Anna, for what it is worth, I wish nothing but happiness for you, but is it not time to let him go?" Anna heard her sister's words but did not want to hear them. Ignoring the comment, Anna glared at her sister's reflection in the mirror. "And I have a secret for you, Anna," Maria spoke with a conspiratorial tone, ignoring her sister's hostile stare. Anna watched as her sister patted her abdomen.

Looking from her sister's face to her sister's abdomen, it took Anna a moment to understand. "Y...y...you...you are w...w...with child?" she stuttered, as the realization set in that she was not the only one who broke the rules of proper conduct. A half-hearted smile crossed Maria's face as she nodded. Anna felt a sudden weakness overcome her.

"What is the matter, Anna? You look as though you have seen a ghost," Maria said as she moved towards her sister. Taking her by the elbow, she sat Anna down, patting her forehead with a damp rag. "Is it not I who should worry?" Maria asked as she peered at her sister with concern. Anna felt her own stomach turn. She feared she would soon replace her sister at the toilet.

"Why did I not think that Jakub and I may conceive a child?" Anna mumbled to herself. Somehow her impulsive nature had once again silenced her rational mind. She had never given such concerns any thought. "Why did such thoughts not cross my mind?" she continued to mumble, wondering what she would do if the worst were true. What might Jakub say or even do? Her mind raced, as she envisioned herself a societal outcast. What would Mama say, and Papa? Mama would be furious if she knew, but her theatrical thoughts of ending up on the street penniless seemed exaggerated even to herself.

"Anna, Anna," her sister said, looking her over with genuine concern. "Did you…with Jakub?" Maria asked her sister hesitantly. Anna nodded as the silence around her threatened to crush her. Of course Maria knew.

Neither sister noticed their mother standing at the door. "You are still in here?" the Baroness chided the young women as she stepped through the doorway. How long had she been there, both sisters wondered. Surely the Baroness noticed the guilt-laden looks on both of her daughters' faces Anna thought. Anna mutely followed her sister and mother out of the wash closet.

Anna could not shake the feeling that her mother knew about Jakub, but then it was not like the Baroness to ever walk away from a problem. Quite the contrary, she was one to charge into it, head on, like a raging bull. "But a problem of such magnitude…I am not so sure she would acknowledge such a problem at all," Anna whispered to herself, as she swallowed hard. Her mother would desire such a secret never be given a voice, she thought with a strange degree of relief. As Anna looked at her sister, whose wedding gown was already stained with filth at the bottom edges from the damp ground, she wondered if her mother knew of Maria's condition. It did not really matter anymore, did it? Maria was married now. Watching as her sister's otherwise cream colored gown continued to drag along the ground, picking up more filth with each step, Anna knew that the childhood she had loved was lost forever.

Anna's heart beat quickly as she moved toward the hayloft. Her day had felt empty without Jakub. Her Jakub. "Jakub? Jakub, where are you?" Anna whispered softly into the darkness. The hayloft felt somehow different, she did not know why. Maybe Jakub had fallen asleep again. It was even later than last night. "Jakub? Jakub?" she whispered urgently, her voice quivering with fear. Slowly, she crawled around the hayloft searching for her lover. Her irrational mind would not accept the fact that he was not here, that he was not coming, and, quite possibly, would never come back to her again.

Anna did not know how long she sat in the hay, unable to move, incapable of feeling anything. It was not until she heard the rooster crow that she realized she had fallen asleep. Quickly shaking the straw from her long coat, she slipped out of the barn and ran towards the main house. "If Mama finds me out here," she worried to herself just as she reached the back entrance. Unable to understand what had happened to Jakub, her mind conjured up different scenarios as to why her beloved had remained absent from the hayloft last night. He had fallen ill she told herself, only to convince herself a moment later he lay injured somewhere, unable to help himself. Possibly he no longer respected her and now avoided her. No, he loved her too much, and she him, of that she was sure. Possibly he had been there, but had waited too long. "Yes, and then he left again," she said aloud, trying to drown the voice of reason that told her otherwise.

Anna momentarily forgot about Jakub as she passed by the kitchen and heard Sigrid's familiar humming.

"Oh, Lena," Anna looked up, startled as she nearly collided with the gardener's daughter.

"Excuse me, Fraulein von Marschalkt," the young woman said, avoiding eye contact with Anna and quickly moving past her. Anna turned to watch as the woman slithered silently away. How was it she could always appear out of nowhere? As Anna watched the pale-faced woman move down the hall Lena turned, with fish-like fluidity, and their eyes met for one brief moment. An uncomfortable feeling spread down Anna's spine as she briefly held the gaze of this woman. What was it she saw in those eyes? Quickly turning, Anna ran up the stairs and slipped into the bedroom she no longer shared with her sister. Removing her boots and coat, she slipped under her soft down covers, unsure whether she would ever emerge from this small haven again.

It was past noon when Anna awoke. The smell of chicken fricassee filled the air. Had her mother been in her room earlier or was that just part of a departed dream? Rolling on her side, she realized this was the first time since childhood she had not shared a room with her sister. Her sister...she had not even asked Maria how far along her condition had progressed. Anna laid a hand on her own midsection. "What if I too am with child?" she whispered with a deep sigh. And where was Jakub? Was it not just one night past that she had committed her soul to him? Anna inhaled deeply, trying to clear her mind of all the irrational thoughts that persisted in pushing themselves to the surface. It was time for her to find the man and find out what he had to say for himself. "I will find the truth, Jakub, whatever and wherever that truth is," Anna told herself firmly. Pulling herself from the security of her comforter, she forced herself to wash and dress.

"Good day, Mama, good day, Frau Steinmeyer," Anna greeted her mother and Sigrid as she entered the kitchen. Mama was not usually in the kitchen with Sigrid. Looking from one woman to the other, Anna realized she had interrupted a private conversation. There was an odd similarity between the two women Anna thought, as she saw the pained expression in Sigrid's eyes. They shared a similar build, with similar features and complexion, as well as their age. Oddly, years of hard work in the household had not affected Sigrid as much as years of running a household had affected her own mother. What was Mama saying to the poor woman now, she wondered as she picked up a roll and quietly excused herself. Neither woman acknowledged her coming or going, so Anna felt spared from whatever was going on. She had more important matters to tend to, such as finding the man she loved, and, God forbid, the father of a child she may be carrying.

Anna collapsed on the bench in the garden gazebo. She had looked everywhere for Jakub. Initially she was cautious in her quest to find him, but caution was soon thrown to the wind, as she approached any and all farm personnel to cross her path, asking detailed questions about Jakub's whereabouts. Not a single person had seen him since last night. How could that be, she asked herself, as she stared out towards the main house. "With this many people running around here, nothing remains private for long," she whispered. The words stuck in her throat. "Nothing c…c…could remain p…p…private," she spoke aloud as sheer terror seized her person. "Oh no, Jakub, oh no," Anna cried as she ran into the garden, unsure which way to run, not sure exactly why she was running. Had someone found out? And if so, who? If Sigrid knows, then others might have figured it out. She tried to breathe and make a list of the people she was sure knew about her relationship and those she was sure did not. Of those she was sure about, only Maria and Sigrid came to mind. Of those she was unsure about, everyone else came to mind.

As her mind raced to put pieces of a puzzle together she did not even know were missing, her mind pushed her to consider the possibility that her mother really did know about Jakub. Was that what the conversation in the kitchen with Sigrid had been about? Was that why the gardener's daughter gave her that bone chilling glare? Would Sigrid betray her confidence? Had Maria betrayed her, but was unable to face the truth when confronted in the wash closet? Anna felt her head spin. Dizzy with panic, she dropped herself into the cool, wet grass and prayed to an invisible God that He may open up the earth and swallow her whole.

"What is the matter with you, child?" Anna heard her father's voice above her. Looking up at her father, the great Baron, she wondered if he might know as well. She doubted it. He seemed somehow insulated from the world of intrigues his mother always seemed to be a part of. He was more at home in the forest or in the barn with the animals than in a house full of women.

"Oh, P...p...apa," she cried as he gently pulled her up from the damp grass.

"Come, child, inside with you before you catch your death," he spoke to her, the same way he had when she was a little girl. Anna allowed herself to be led away like one of his favorite mares when she abruptly stopped and faced her father.

"P...p...papa, th...th...there is a matter of utmost importance I m...m...must discuss with you," she said with as much authority as her youth would allow. As she looked into her father's eyes, she mourned the lost days of childhood when she could seek comfort on her father's lap as he stroked her back, the smoke of his pipe gently lulling her into an almost trance like state.

"I have been expecting this," her father said with a solemnity about his voice that shocked Anna to the core.

"Y...y....you....h...have b...b...been expecting this?" she asked, furious with herself that her stuttering problem resurfaced so intensely during anxious moments. Her father nodded and gently took her by the arm.

"Come, Anna, you are no longer a child, it is time you learn some truths," he said as he led her to his private study.

Travels of Letter 16
Barents Sea—Off the Norwegian Coast February 1949

The waves crashed against the small fishing vessel, tossing it as though it were a toy in child's bath. The fishermen, hardened to such weather, heaved one net after another, filled with large cod, out of the Barents Sea. It was February, a good month to catch cod. A month with an "R" in it, the old Captain thought as he chewed on the stub of his long since deceased cigar. September to April, the best time to catch fish, that's what his grandfather had told him. Most likely time to get yourself killed too, he thought, as a wave the size of a house crashed over the vessel, blacking out his vision momentarily. The shouts from the men on deck were barely audible. The only thing between them and death was the rope to which they were hopefully securely tethered. Barely managing to control the vessel, the old Captain chuckled, it was not he who controlled this vessel. It was she, the Great Sea, who could snap him in two in the blink of an eye. She had been his Mistress since as far back as he could remember. He spent more time with her than his own wife. If he had to choose between the two, the decision would not be a difficult one. It never had been. His wife cursed her, but he could not blame the woman, who was but weak flesh and blood. How could she compete with the infinite power of the sea? He had missed the births of all three of their children and even wondered at times how they had come to exist. Were they even his? Anika resembled neither him nor his wife, Annborg.

Another wave slammed into the vessel, almost knocking the Captain to the floor. By sheer strength of will, he held onto the helm and called to the men to come inside. Drowned out by the crashing of the waves, the men were unable to hear him, but had sense enough to stop casting the nets. This storm did not want to let up, and from the looks of it the Captain believed it would only get worse before it got any better. The season had already been profitable, they had pulled in not only cod this year, but halibut, pollack, cusk, haddock, ling, wolf fish, and red fish.

Another wave crashed into the small vessel, and the floorboards screamed at the seams as the vessel lurched sideways. The Captain caught the eye of one crewman and risked losing his balance by releasing one hand from the helm, motioning him to move himself and the others below deck.

As though responding to this withdrawal of the crew, the sea suddenly quieted as though Jesus Himself had spoken. Superstitious by nature, the old Captain chewed furiously on his cigar stub and wondered if he had angered the sea. Had he taken too much from her this season? He had adhered to all the old traditions of his forefathers, blessed the Sea and all of her bounty, and even returned a portion of each catch as a sign of gratitude. Had that not been enough? The men had argued with him, called him an old fool. Even his own son, Olaf, defied him and thought him feeble minded. What did they know about the old way? There was too much greed these days and too little respect for the laws of Mother Nature. He had always listened to nature, but these days his hearing seemed impaired. The voices of the younger generations, so sure of themselves and their self righteous ways, threatened to drown out the old ways. Had he become deaf to the laws of nature, to the laws of the Sea? Her laws, the ones on which his very survival depended.

He heard the men reemerge from below deck. Whoops and cheers now filled his ears, which just moments before, it seemed, had been filled with the screams of certain death. The old Captain did not fear death, had seen its face many times, but he worried about his son. He had tried to convince Olaf to find a job in the city, but he himself knew the inescapable lure of the sea. It is indescribable to those whose fates have kept them locked to the land. The freedom, the exhilaration, neither can be replicated on land. If his son was anything like him he would never feel at home on land, where the rules of society maintained an iron grip on individuals. The Captain scoffed at the notion of individuals. There was no individuality left. Society had dulled the soul. He saw it in his wife and two daughters, whose notions of acceptable behavior constantly clashed with those of his free spirited son, as well as his own. He feared for his son though, for the new generation of seamen. There was spirit, but little respect for the Sea. She was not a forgiving mistress. The Captain had warned his son that she could take quicker than she gave.

"Men," his son called from the bow, "cast out the nets," not waiting for the Captain's order. The Captain ordered the crew to pull in the nets, but realized for the first time this was no longer his vessel. The crew paid him no heed and proceeded with the casting. This would not bode well for them, the Captain thought as he spat his salt water drenched cigar stub onto the floor. The old Mistress had warned them. Realizing he was still tethered to the vessel, the Captain untied himself and sat down for the first time in a very long time. His legs, shaking with weariness, were grateful for the rest. Maybe it was time he passed the vessel to his son, at least make it official, he thought. He felt a jolt of pain pass through his heart at the thought of losing his vessel, but hadn't he lost it already? The crew heeded Olaf, the younger ones even worshiped him.

The storm that had so quickly disappeared, reappeared, as if summoned by black magic. The Captain heard a loud whistling sound and watched as a thirty foot wave appeared out of nowhere. In his sixty-two years at sea he had never seen anything like this before. A rogue wave. He had heard of them. He did not mourn his own imminent death. He mourned the death of his only son whose pregnant wife would not know, possibly for weeks or even months, of the fate that befell her husband.

The small fishing vessel sank within moments. A green glass bottle, trapped inside one of the fishing nets, managed to free itself and surfaced at the precise spot the vessel sank. The bottle floated on a, once again, calm sea.

Cape May, New Jersey
Fall 2011

I stood in the foyer of the *Japanese Ocean Grille* and stared at a picture of the owner with whom I assumed was her mother. The caption read, "Opening Day, April 16, 1958." I was surprised when an elderly Japanese woman appeared before me, traces of the young woman in the photograph still clearly etched in her face that seemed to have lived a thousand lives.

"Konnichiwa," the woman said as to me as she bowed gracefully. Awkwardly returning the bow, I felt a sense of déjà vu as my eyes met those of this old woman. You've been here before, silly, I reassured myself, but I was certain I had never met the old woman before.

"Why did I come here?" I mumbled to myself, smoothing out my wind blown hair. There were plenty of good restaurants in Cape May. Why do I pour salt in my wounds and go to the place Warren proposed to me? As I followed the woman who held a lonely menu in her hand, I felt as though the letter I had pulled from the shards of green glass was burning a hole in my coat pocket. Thanking the woman with a quick bow, I sat down and pulled the letter out with trembling hands. What was this I had found? A sixty-four year old love letter? Was this for real? What did the fates want with me? What were the odds that some glass bottle survived the ocean for over sixty years, not to mention traversed the entire Atlantic ocean? This has got to be a hoax, I told myself, hoping it was not. As I pondered these questions, I noticed the only other patrons were an old couple seated immediately beside me. The old woman with her nearly blue hair caught my attention, as she gently patted her husband on the hand. At least I think they were married. I could make out one wedding band, and what are the chances either of them is out on a weekend fling at their ages? The gentle way this old couple interacted with each other almost moved me to tears. She patted him, he gently touched her on the cheek, on the arm. That, sitting right next to me, was all I had ever wanted out of life. "My true love to grow old with," I whispered.

This odd fascination with the old couple grew as I observed them and wondered how long they had been married. "Oh Walter, you old fool," I overheard the old woman say with a voice like thick molasses.

"Oh Warren, you old fool," I whispered to the ghost I felt by my side.

Slowly I unrolled the letter. "What are the odds?" I asked myself again as I held onto the letter with hands that were steady now, and began to read it for the third time.

Letter 16   *Brest, France 14. December 1946*

My Beloved Jakub,

It is with a heavy heart I write this letter to you. However, it eases my sorrow to bear my soul to you in such a manner. Hopefully, somewhere across the great seas, or possibly the great heavens, this final letter shall reach you.

Much has come to pass since I last wrote to you from my home, which is no longer. At the conclusion of this horrible battle, which cost so many so much, we, along with the rest of Dresden, suffered tremendous losses. We are no longer a unified Germany, but divided on many fronts. It was the Americans and the British, Papa said, who bombed our city—devastated our city, yet the war was over. This, like so much, fails to make sense to me. Our house and all but one of the surrounding buildings were destroyed in two waves of attacks. The noise, Jakub, my beloved Jakub, the noise as the bombs dropped with a high pitched whizzing, ending in a deafening explosion, that noise alone could send one to an early grave. I shall never in my life forget the dank bunker we huddled in, waiting for death to greet us. Never before have I looked so closely into the dark face of death. The worst, however, was the actual loss of human and animal life. Sigrid, Siggi you recall, and Lena, the gardener's daughter, were both lost in the first wave of attacks. Seven others, Papa's farm hands, died in the second wave that rained down on us. The bunkers they were in collapsed from the weight of the bombs. It was chance, Jakub, chance which bunker we entered, was it not? Why them and not me? Was it their destiny, or was another destiny imposed on them? Siggi's death was a torment I did not think my fragile heart would survive. But, as you can see, I have survived. Such is human nature, I suppose. The will to continue must

59

persevere if mankind is to survive such an ordeal. Others have suffered far worse fates.

With nothing left in Dresden, we have left the city for the time being. Papa's conscience weighs heavily on him. He feels responsible for the loss of his workers. In a strange way, the loss of his animals, especially Estelle, his favorite mare, causes him more grief than the loss of our home. He does hope to return to Dresden some day, but for now we have moved our family to the summer house just outside of Brest in France. You may recall it, the one I had one day hoped to visit with you. Mama's sister Helga lives not far away and has graciously supplied us with the bare necessities for daily life, despite the fact that she has been left so little herself. Mama has not accepted this change well. She continues to live in a past that is no more, a homeland that is forever scarred with the memories of a great and horrible war. Her mental state has affected her physical state, which continues to deteriorate. She spends many hours knitting without purpose, only to unravel what she has so painstakingly created. Often I sit with her, but cannot share in her passion for knitting, another thing for which she chides me. Unfortunately, I have neither the talent nor the patience for such tasks. It is a comfort to know that Papa still supports her in these trying times where there is no household for her to run, no staff to control, and no Fuehrer to worship. The Fuehrer, I believe, was the second greatest betrayal of her life. She placed so much hope in one man, worshiped his every word, as so many did, thereby blinding herself to the real world. It took losing almost everything for her to see the treachery of it all. She does not find comfort in having survived this great war. Rather, it is a constant reminder to her of all that is gone. I have forgiven her for all that has come to pass, and still try to forgive all those whose action separated me from you. But, in the end, it may have saved your life, although I'll never know.

I speak of such weighty things, when there is again lightness in my life. Maria and Dieter accompanied us here. For this I am eternally grateful. It was an arduous journey for all of us, without any of the amenities we have been accustomed to our whole lives. It was especially hard for Maria, who has four young children and a new daughter to care for. The little one is in good health, which is a blessing, as her mother was in an awful state for nine months. Maria says this is the last child she will bear for Dieter, if she wishes to remain amongst the living. It warms my heart to know that Maria has found her own inner peace. She has, and I quote her, "Grown fond of Dieter and loves the father and husband he is." I find myself at peace without children now, but one does not know if my feelings shall depart from this sentiment in the future. Mama believes I betray my purpose in life without a proper husband and children. She neither understands true love nor free will. For me there has been enough betrayal to last a lifetime. Our love, as short as our physical time together may have been, had been my purpose, my reason, the one true constant through-out, free of the machinations that dictate this modern world. We loved outside the rules of society, outside the rules of religion. It was only our hearts that guided us, hearts that knew no boundaries. Yet, it is I who betrayed you, my beloved. It is I who committed our love to secrecy, yet how wrong I was. The greatest secret of my life was never a secret at all. And as this tale, which is my life, continues to unravel, I come to find that everyone has a secret. For this I beg your forgiveness, Jakub.

My dearest, I carry on, for I know this is my last letter. I am tempted to leave it unfinished, adding to it with each new day, but this cycle must now end. I have mourned you now for eight years, and I could do so for the rest of my life. There is one thing you have shown me, Jakub, and that is the power of love. Ours was true and pure, and a part of me believes I shall find such love again, possibly I have already. It is time I release you from the love that chains you to me. My heart would find comfort knowing that you too can love again. That your heart has not hardened. Never will I forget you, my dear Jakub, and I will continue to pray, as I do every day, for your safety, wherever in the world or heavens one finds you. I could fill a book expressing my love for you, but in the end it is all the same. With this I say to you one last time, I have always loved you, I love you now, and I will forever love you.

With Love Eternally,
Anna Alexa Elisabeth von Marschalkt

Post Script. As I sit here alone I can not help think what cruelty man is capable of, yet, in the same human animal, what beauty we can create. Please forgive the world you were born into.

Placing the letter on the table where I watched it roll itself back up into a cigar shape, which it had likely held for the last sixty four years, I felt a strange sense of calm. There was something about this letter that called out to me like an invisible force urging me to read it again. I know I barely moved or breathed as I read the letter a fourth, fifth, and, finally, a sixth time. Inhaling deeply, I caught the scent of the sea somewhere between the powerful smells of the restaurant. The old couple beside me had gone. When had they left? My enthrallment with them had obviously been overcome by my fascination with the letter. Something about this letter, no, it was not the letter, but the woman that fascinated me. What was it about this woman, Anna? How was it possible for a person I didn't know, one who might not even exist, to touch my soul in a way that nothing else ever had? Who was this woman? Part of me couldn't believe I was actually taking this seriously, but the other part was sold the moment that glass bottle shattered. Looking down at the letter, I found myself rooting for this woman, almost desperately hoping she had found her lover again. I fantasized that they had married, gone on to have children together, and had grown old together. Was Anna still alive? Was her lover alive? One question fueled another, and I began to experience this woman's anguish as though it were my own. "It is my own," I whispered, stroking the rolled letter with one finger.

"We have to stop meeting like this," I heard a familiar voice speak from behind me. Well, what do you know? I turned around and stared into Charlie Gordon's handsome, smiling face. Wow, the guy doesn't even wait for an invitation, I thought as he pulled out a chair and seated himself beside me. A pleasant smell of laundry detergent and after shave wafted over and stimulated my senses. Somehow I had the urge to get close to him and sniff each scent individually.

"What are you doing here?" I asked, confused and embarrassed, realizing a little too late how rude I sounded.

"Having dinner," he replied, as he unabashedly picked up my menu. "Sake alright with you?" he asked as a young waitress approached our table.

"Uh, well, uh, yes, that would be…that is…fine," I managed to mumble, as I felt my face flush and armpits dampen in a most uncomfortable manner.

"I did introduce myself down at the beach, right? You remember me, Charlie?" he asked with raised eyebrows and a broad smile, revealing perfect white teeth. "And I would really like to know your name."

"Oh, I'm sorry...the beach...I guess I...you've got to excuse my manners, I'm Diana." I hesitated before I told him my last name. Do I go with my maiden name or my married name? I am still married after all. "Dahl," I answered, feeling good about my decision to use my married name.

"Is that German?" he asked as he inched his way closer to me. God, I could almost *feel* the heat this guy radiated. This was doing nothing for my already agitated nerves.

"Uh, no, it's Norwegian, actually, my husband's family is Norwegian," I said quietly as a shudder of guilt passed over me. "Adams is my maiden name, it's English." Feeling flustered, I realized I had no idea what to do in a situation like this. Do I tell the guy I'm a widow? Will he try and take advantage of me then, or will it just scare him away?

"Relax, Di." It was Abe's voice I heard that pushed me in the right direction. Nervously clasping my hands, I knew I had to be straight with him. No matter what impact that had on him or ultimately me. It was only fair to Warren. "I'm sorry, I have to be honest with you," I said, and had to lower my eyes. There was something about his penetrating eyes that...they weren't unnerving, but somehow they rattled me. "My husband died recently and I just can't...," I wasn't sure *what* I wanted to say to this stranger. What? That I wasn't ready to have a relationship? But wasn't that presumptuous and premature? To assume he wanted anything from me anyway.

"Oh, I'm sorry. Wow, that's gotta be tough," Charlie said, saving me from the uncomfortable position I had placed myself in again.

There was an odd silence between the two of us as we looked out the window towards the dark sea. The odd part was that the silence did not bring with it the uncomfortable feeling usually shared by two strangers. Like the letter, I had to steal a second, and then a third, and a fourth glance at Charlie.

"No, I'm sorry, I shouldn't dump something like this on a complete stranger," I said, surprising myself that I had scanned his hands for signs of a wedding band. Charlie laughed, making me smile for reasons even I didn't understand. "What is so funny?" I asked, realizing I enjoyed this stranger's company.

"We don't know each other, yet we have already apologized to each other one too many times," he said as he looked at the menu again. "Please, let me start again," he said in a serious tone. Looking at him I couldn't figure out why he felt less like a stranger with each passing moment. "First off, I am *not* stalking you. Please note the emphasis on the word *not,*" he joked. "Secondly, I swear on my Grandmother Jezebel's soul that I craved Japanese food tonight, and finally," he hesitated as I watched his ears turn crimson. "And finally," he repeated, "I am most pleased to find you here." A jumble of emotions welled up inside of me. It wasn't only his ears that were a crimson color, of that I was sure. Was this guy for real?

"What brings you to Cape May?" I asked, attempting to direct the conversation back into safer territory.

"Work. Actually, Cape May's not my final destination, it's just a little side trip for old times sake," he said, as I waited for elaboration. "I'm an attorney. We've got a big case in both New York and London. A guy got a "get out of jail free" card and went right on doing what he does best. Bloody bastard traffics in young girls. You may've seen something in the papers?"

I had to smile to cover my embarrassment. What the heck was he talking about? I didn't know my head from my rear when it came to matters of the law, or what was going on in the world right now.

"I used to come to Cape May with my family," he said, as I noticed his eyes glance at the rolled up letter on the table. Inconspicuously, I pulled the letter from the table and tucked it into the pocket of my coat.

"So you live in New York now?" I asked, feeling disappointed by this possibility. "Oh no, I moved out to L.A. when I took a job with Simon & Baker," he answered as he looked at me with soft green eyes that forced me to look away. I felt a small rush of relief when I heard that he lived in California.

"I live in L.A. too," I said almost too quickly. The poor guy was probably confused by my mixed signals, but I couldn't change my behavior. "I'm here on, well, I don't know if it's a vacation. I guess it's just to get away for a while," I said, somewhat embarrassed. "I just needed a break is all," I admitted, feeling oddly safe with this man, Charlie.

"What do you do in L.A.?" Charlie asked. Ah, the "what do you do" question, the inevitable question everyone always asks when first introduced.

"Well, we, I, sell fish, I guess. It's really just a family business. My husband Warren, and his brother Morton, sell fish, I just help out in the office." Somehow, with this guy staring at me I wasn't in full control of my motor functions. "I don't know if I'll still help out, maybe I'll try something new, like candle making." It was supposed to be a joke, but Charlie didn't laugh and neither did I. What *would* I do now? I had to do something, something I enjoyed. And God knows I never enjoyed the fish business. No, it would definitely be something I enjoyed, not something I had to do.

Charlie continued to regard me in silence. What was he thinking? "I *do* really like candles you know," I said to break the silence and lighten the mood, as Charlie continued to study me with silent interest.

"You do your own fishing? I mean, do you have your own boats?" Charlie asked with a slight smile, breaking his silence.

"No, uh, no Warren purchased the fish and sold them to local restaurants. He never wanted to be on the open sea. Some bizarre story about an old relative whose boat disappeared a long time ago. The sea kind of just swallowed them up on a bright, sunny day." I felt silly, and also guilty, explaining Warren's superstitions to this handsome man who seemed so grounded in the realities of life. "When do you go back to New York?" I quickly asked to change the subject.

"Day after tomorrow," Charlie answered, watching closely as I picked up the letter from the table. "How 'bout you?" he asked.

"I don't know yet, I've sort of left things open for myself." That was the truth. I really didn't know what I was going to do I thought, as the waitress appeared with the sake.

"Whatcha two havin?" the young girl asked in a thick Jersey accent, as she set down the sake. Panic coursed through my body again. Why do servers have this effect on me? Feeling rushed, I nervously glanced at the menu. Warren used to tell me I did this it to myself, that it was self-imposed pressure, but pointing this out never helped solve my problem.

"Oh God, I have no idea what I want," I said apologetically, staring at the menu as my mind raced to find something, anything.

"Hey, give us a few more minutes will you," Charlie said in a relaxed manner.

"Sure, no problem," the young waitress said as she turned to leave. It wasn't until she had left that I loosened up enough to study the menu.

Charlie, Charles, Chucky, Chaz. I liked the name, no matter how I said it, I thought as I gazed at him. I just couldn't seem to take my eyes off the man. It didn't help matters that we had ordered and finished a third bottle of sake. "I've got to remain in control," I told myself, stifling a hiccup, as I wondered how old Charlie was. He had to be in his late forties, maybe even fifty by my guesstimate. A nice age for a man, like a ripe banana. Why I compared him to a banana was likely due to the sake. But it was his smell, his "man scent" as Abe called it, which fueled my desire for him. There it was again, the smell of laundry detergent, after shave and his "man scent." Maybe that was what pheromones really were. Stifling a giggle with my fist, I wondered if Charlie was as drunk as I was. For reasons I didn't even understand, I pulled the letter back out of my coat pocket and handed it to Charlie.

"Do you want to see something bizarre, but strangely wonderful?" I asked, handing him the letter. As he reached for the letter our fingers briefly touched. There it was again. That odd, yet pleasant, sensation that passed between us when our bodies touched. It was a tingling, almost as though some light vibration passed through my body. Did he feel it too? Were these the mythical sparks I had heard about when two destined lovers touched? As I wondered what our first kiss might feel like, I realized with a start that this electricity, or whatever it was, never had sparked with Warren. Reaching out to gently touch

Charlie's fingertips once more, I felt the odd sensation again, and from his reaction he did too.

"What *is* this?" Charlie asked as he looked up, gently waving the letter in front of his face.

"Remember the bottle at the beach?" He had to see the glow of excitement in my eyes. Charlie's momentary confusion was quickly replaced with curiosity.

"You mean that old green bottle you dropped," he asked, his interest now piqued.

"Precisely the one," I slurred slightly. "Read it."

Closely watching Charlie read the letter, I noted the subtle facial transformations that took place as he moved his way through this small piece of history.

"Is this for real?" he asked when he finished reading the letter and placed it on the table. The air around us felt magical, I thought as a warmth passed through my body. Expectantly, I watched as the letter rolled itself up again into its cigar shape.

"I don't know, but it sure looks real," I answered excitedly. The more sake I consumed, the more I did not want to consider the possibility that this could be a hoax. I wanted it to be real. Needed it to be real. Just like Warren's letters. The only things that still told me Warren loved me.

"This is amazing, Diana," Charlie said with glowing cheeks, compliments of the sake. "You know, it wouldn't be difficult to find the woman. Find out if it's for real. Find out if she's still alive, we've got her name." I heard the excitement in Charlie's voice as he talked on about the various possibilities associated with the letter, but wasn't sure how much the alcohol had to do with it. Surprisingly, I hadn't considered actually looking for this woman. Was it possible she could be found? That she was alive? Or possibly a relative who could shed light on her and her beloved Jakub? It was I now who searched Charlie's eyes in silence. The powerful feelings he evoked in me were indescribable. Without knowing what overcame me, I leaned forward and gently kissed him as a light tingling sensation again pulsed through my body.

"Can I walk you back to your room?" Charlie asked, leaning in for another kiss.

"Yes," I whispered as he gently stroked my hand.

The snoring woke me early in the morning. I nearly panicked when I saw a peacefully sleeping Charlie in the bed beside me. With an aching head and dry mouth, I stole out of bed and headed for the bathroom.

"Good Lord, you look like crap," I told the reflection in the mirror and gulped down a glass of water. The air in the room smelled stale. Propping open the front door with a chair, I inhaled the fresh scents of the salty sea. What do I do now, I wondered, as I turned to watch Charlie, whose chest still rose and fell with the rhythm of sleep. He was likely to sleep until noon after last night I thought. What did I do? I'm not the kind of woman who boozes all night and throws herself at the first guy she meets. I hadn't even mourned Warren long enough. Wasn't one year the societal norm? Or was that dated information? I should have felt guilty, but as I looked over at Charlie, my guilt seemed to melt away, and as far as I was concerned, society could shove it.

Society or no society, I had other things that occupied my mind. Now it was the letter I obsessed over. Was it really possible to find this woman? Charlie thought so, or was that sake-induced confidence? Once the liquor left his system he'd likely think this was some hare-brained idea. Either way, it wouldn't hurt to look her up online, would it?

I was surprised to find this shoddy little motel actually had an internet connection. I sat down in front of my laptop with the letter in my hand.

"Who are you, Anna?" I whispered as my computer welcomed me with melodic pinging noises.

Dresden, Germany

Spring 1938

Anna paced back and forth along the length of her father's study, running a finger along the spines of the heavily bound books that filled the room. She had never seen Papa, or anyone for that matter, pull a book from one of these ancient shelves, evidenced by the dust on her finger. Not to mention Lena's lack of attention to detail, Anna thought as she impatiently watched her father stuff tobacco into his pipe and light it. What truth about Jakub would he reveal she wondered, and she caught herself chewing on the nail of her thumb, just as Papa glanced up at her with a disapproving look. Quickly removing the finger from her mouth, she seated herself on the small leather ottoman and straightened her skirt.

"Your mother is ill," her father said in his direct manner as he puffed rings of smoke into the air. He did not look at her when he spoke.

Anna was confused by the words her father had just spoken. What did this have to do with Jakub?

"The doctor requires that she not excite herself in any manner," he spoke, as though discussing one of his sick horses. Anna had long suspected there was something wrong with her mother, who dismissed her increasingly frequent periods of incapacitation as overexertion. She had heard the coughing at night, especially in the winter months. Again she wondered what this had to do with the disappearance of Jakub.

"W…w…where is Jakub?" she blurted out, unable to control her emotions.

"Jakub? What of him? I speak to you regarding your mother's illness and you speak of Jakub? What insolent behavior is this?" the Baron asked with an undertone that anyone else would have missed. Casually he leaned back in his large leather armchair and puffed on his pipe.

Anna studied every movement on her father's face. Did he truly not know?

"Y…y…yes, Jakub, h…h….he is gone. Disappeared. I demand to know w….w…where he is, or do you not know wh…wh…what takes place on your own estate?" she asked in a high pitched voice, jumping up from the ottoman, furious with herself for always stuttering. "W….w…. where is he, P…P…Papa?" she pleaded, as her father observed her with raised eyebrows.

"There is not a thing, young lady, I am not aware of on my own estate," he replied, narrowing his eyes. "Now, I have told you, Anna, your mother is ill. Her lungs are weak. There has been too much excitement these last weeks. The wedding, the witch hunt, I suggest you occupy your time with more important matters." Slowly Anna realized that somehow her father not only knew of Jakub's disappearance, he was also involved in it.

"W…w…why, Papa?" she yelled at him, slamming both fists on his large oak desk. "W….w…why?"

Staring at his daughter, Baron von Marschalkt calculated the risks and benefits of telling his daughter the truth. He had made a promise, but at what cost would he honor that promise? It pained him to watch his daughter suffer, but he knew it was for the best. For herself. For the family.

"I kn…kn…know you know about Jakub," Anna accusingly shouted at him, pointing her finger close to his face, unprepared to give up. "I just kn…kn…know it. Mama is right, you are a h…h…

horrible liar," Anna sobbed between the tears that streamed down her face. "I love him," she said without a stutter, as she turned away from her father and moved to leave the room.

"Anna," her father said, a crack in his voice revealing his own emotional turmoil, "Anna, I...," Anna waited for her father to finish the sentence he never did.

Anna felt ill. She turned to the one person she felt safe with, Sigrid. No one had seen Jakub since the evening before Maria's wedding. "No one admits to seeing him," she corrected herself aloud, as she looked down at the cold roll Sigrid had placed before her.

"Eat something, Anna," Sigrid said to her, sitting down beside her at the informal kitchen table. "You look pale and your weight has dropped," Sigrid reprimanded, as Anna poked the roll with a finger, shoving it off the plate.

"I have n...n...no appetite. I do n...n...not think I sh...sh...shall ever eat again," Anna said resolutely, as Sigrid picked up the roll and spread butter and honey on it.

"Open," Sigrid commanded, as she lifted the sweet roll to Anna's lips. Like a small child, Anna opened her mouth and allowed herself one small bite.

"Oh, Siggi, y...y...you are the only one I c...c...can talk to. I h...h...have looked everywhere for h...h...him, inquired at th...th...the train station, with every shopkeeper. I even s...s...sketched his portrait," Anna said dejectedly. "It is th...th...the only memory I h...h...have of him," she said, for once grateful for some artistic ability.

"Oh, child, you will forget him soon. There is not just a handful, but a whole land full of young men," Sigrid said without conviction as she tried to comfort Anna.

"N...N...No, Siggi, no, no no. I th...th...thought you understood," Anna cried accusingly. "I thought if anyone w...w...would understand it would be you."

"I do understand, my dear Anna," the maid spoke as she embraced Anna and gently pulled her head down to her soft bosom. "I do understand," she whispered into the girl's long red hair as she stroked her back.

"What is going on here?" the Baroness demanded, as she stormed into the kitchen. "Anna, I asked what is going on?"

"M…M…Mama," Anna stammered, as she sat upright, wiping at her tear- streaked face. "I was not feeling well," she lied with greater skill than her father.

"Frau Steinmeyer, there is laundry in the hamper upstairs I need for tomorrow," she ordered the maid, who silently stood up and removed herself. Her mother appeared to take pleasure in ordering Sigrid about. Anna watched her mother approach the table. She looked more fierce than usual this morning. Maybe it was the tight bun she had pulled her hair into, which Anna noticed still had a knitting needle in it. It was rare to see her mother in the kitchen. The Baroness normally enjoyed her breakfast in the formal dining room.

"The von Glann family," her mother began without looking at her, "will be joining us for dinner tomorrow night. I ask that you mind your manners and behave like a lady," she said, fixing her eyes on Anna. Anna knew her mother. She was waiting for a response, a tacit agreement that Anna not betray the family tomorrow night. Nodding her head, Anna watched her mother turn to leave. "And, Anna," her mother spoke less severely, "Heino will be here too. He would be a good match for you," she said as she left the kitchen.

Anna felt her stomach turn. A rage she barely managed to suppress moved through her body. Running upstairs to her room, Anna threw herself on her bed and clutched her midsection.

"Oh Jakub, how could you leave me?" she cried into her pillow, as raindrops began to pound against her window.

Anna slept fitfully that night. Dreams of Jakub in peril haunted her throughout the next day. Pulling on her warm overcoat and riding boots, she headed outside into the rainy spring and headed for the stables. She needed to clear her head. Neither Mama nor Papa would forgive her if she was not on her best behavior tonight. "Good behavior I will give you," she whispered as she pushed open the heavy stable door, "but a von Glann woman I will never be," she said aloud as the smell of damp hay tickled her nose. Sneezing three times, she heard a muffled, "Gesundheit," from the shadows.

"Th…th…thank you," she replied politely, straining her eyes to see who it was.

"Good morning, Fraulein von Marschalkt," Ingo Zimmerman, the young gardener's son, cheerily spoke as he appeared at the door of an empty box stall. Unlike his sister Lena, Ingo was a friendly, honest soul whose face betrayed his inner thoughts. How could the same woman have born such disparate souls she wondered, as she forced her lips into a quick smile.

"G…g…ood morning to you, Mr. Zimmerman."

"I am sorry about your loss," he said, just as Anna was about to pull the blanket she preferred to ride on, instead of a saddle, down from the hook upon which it hung.

"W…W…What loss?" she asked sharply, spinning around to look at the young man. She observed his normally pleasant face change to one of fright, no, one of horror. Anna felt almost sorry for this young man who was not more than a year older than herself, but had somehow not yet outgrown the awkward stage every boy must traverse on his path to manhood. "I asked w…w…what loss?" she demanded, approaching him fiercely. Backing the lanky young man into the corner of the empty stall he had been cleaning out, she placed her hands on her hips and repeated her question, reminding herself of her own mother.

"I w…w…will ask you one last time M…M…Mr. Zimmermann, and you will answer me truthfully or I will tell your father I caught you sleeping in the stables. W…w…what loss?"

"The Jew you…," he stopped in mid-sentence holding on to a pitch fork so tightly his knuckles turned white.

"W…w…what do you know of th…th…this Jew?" she asked calmly, feeling her heart beat in her ears.

"He was sent away," Ingo cried as he tried to move around Anna, who felt as though she had been rooted to the ground she stood on.

"Sent away," she whispered to herself. "S…s…sent away? By w…w…whom," she demanded of her captive, finally moving to block Ingo's attempted escape. "I will not let you out of th…th…this stall, Mr. Z…Z…Zimmerman, until you s…s…speak all that you know," she yelled.

"She will have my head," he muttered, as he stared at the Baron's daughter with horror-filled eyes.

"W...w...who?" Anna stuttered, "w...w...who will have your head," she asked as she tried to swallow the lump that had formed in her throat.

"My sister. I promise you I do not know anymore, Fraulein, I promise you."

Anna allowed her prisoner to pass. As though drunk, she moved slowly towards the box stall where the mare Dagmar impatiently stomped her hooves. Stroking the old mare, Anna pulled two apples from her coat and fed them to her horse. "Did you hear that, Dagmar? It was Lena. I will find out what this Lena has to do with my Jakub. Do you hear me, Dagmar? I will find out," she whispered to the mare, as she stroked the horse again and turned to leave the stable.

That evening the Baroness, outraged and humiliated in front of her guests, waited in vain for her daughter to appear at the dinner she had so meticulously planned. The only satisfaction Frieda von Marschalkt had as she watched the von Glann family depart on this damp, bone chilling day was that the Jew was gone. Her only regret was that she had not reported him.

Letter One   *Dresden, 1 August 1938*

My Dearest Jakub,

Possibly I am mad. Does one know when one dives into insanity, or is one protected by the madness itself? As you may gather, my mental state is somewhat precarious, teetering on the brink of an inescapable abyss. Have I already fallen into this abyss? It is only my thoughts of you which tether me to a shred of sanity. I write to you in English; it is how we first expressed our love to each other, and how I feel most comfortable expressing these emotions to you now. There has quite possibly been, as you will read, one major development as to your whereabouts. What little remains of my logical mind dismissed such notions, but one must, at times, discard logic, especially where matters of the heart are concerned.

It has been over five months since your disappearance. There is no other way for me to describe your abrupt departure. Life has not been easy without you, Jakub. All my waking moments are filled with memories of you, and my nights are haunted by visions of what horrible fate has befallen you. I have decided to write you this letter in hopes of relieving some of the burden which threatens to destroy my soul. If I do not communicate with you, Jakub, I fear what is left of my mind will vanish, just as you have. There are so many unanswered questions, but to every question, somewhere an answer waits. Never believe for an instant that I shall give up the search for this answer. While this search has not brought me physically closer to you, I do know there are those on the estate who know more than they are willing to share. Some amount of pressure, I believe, can bring these guilty individuals to speak. It was Papa, however, who has, thus far, revealed the most information. I do not believe he intended to reveal such information, but given the state of my health, he believed my soul already departed. "To

77

Australia," he whispered as I lay shivering on a bed of ice, suffering from a most malevolent illness. I must admit, I would have thought it a dream given my fevered state, had Papa not asked me, once the fever broke and some strength returned to my weakened body, if I had any memory of what he had spoken to me. A look of fear, so brief as to go unnoticed by any who do not know Papa, took hold of his being when I nodded to him. He has not spoken of the incident since, but when the time is right I will use this information to my advantage.

Is it truly Australia you are bound for my dearest? What awaits you there? Was there such urgency that you were unable to meet me one last time? Is it the dangerous political climate, especially for a Jew, that forced you to leave under cover of darkness? Did someone uncover your secret or divulge it? What does Papa know? Why does he believe I should not know? I am not a child. What does a stable boy know of your disappearance? Or his reprehensible sister? Did Mama have a hand in your leaving? Was it her desire to force me into a relationship with the man of her choosing that drove you away? Since your departure she seems to watch me with alternating looks of disappointment and disapproval. However, I believe I have successfully destroyed all Mama's future attempts at finding me an appropriate suitor. Did Sigrid reveal our forbidden love, possibly unintentionally, to Mama or Papa? Or Maria? Was she driven by jealousy? Envious enough of our true love so as to destroy that which she will never know? Who confronted you, my love? If only the wind could carry your thoughts so that I may avenge what love we have already lost. I cannot believe it was me who sent you away. Am I naïve to believe that it was not I? Was it our act of passion that drove you away? My heart aches with questions for which the mind provides no answers. My heart knows it was not I who drove you away, my mind speaks otherwise. I must confess, my conscience weighs heavily on me, my beloved. I am only human, mortal and flawed, and not free from the suspicions that can destroy the bond between lovers. My rational mind tells me you did not leave of your own free will, but that your hand was forced. However, a small voice inside threatens to undermine this belief. Once the seeds of mistrust have been sown, they firmly root themselves and take on a life of their own, only to eventually grow into irreparable resentment. I must be honest, more for my sake than yours. As I write, doubt clouds my rational mind. I find myself wondering how and why the daughter of a gardener could be involved with the disappearance of my beloved. Feelings of jealousy and betrayal creep into my being late at night, when the soul is weak and demons reign. It is then that my anger and resentment take hold. Anger directed at you, at my family, at my country. It is in these darkest hours that I must remind myself, transport myself back to our last evening together, and remember the true love that binds us forever. I must remind myself that whatever reason my family has for hiding the truth, they believed they were acting in my best interest. I must remind myself that a whole people, a whole country, are victims of this same blindness.

Oh, Jakub, mein Schatz, I do not want to breathe another day without you. Why did you have to leave me? Yes, there is anger in my sentiment. Anger for what is lost and never may be again. Anger that I can not rise above this human emotion of love, that has the power to move mountains, or send one spiraling into an inescapable abyss. The hour is late, but somehow I sense your spirit, alive and well. It is not death that separates us. I am certain my soul would detect such a horrible loss. Please send me a sign that our love can survive geographical separation. I do not know if I can continue to traverse this earth without a sign.

Love Eternally,
Anna Alexa Elisabeth v. Marschalkt

Post Script: There is one more matter I must share with you. The child I carried, your child, was lost during the fever. You are surprised? Yes, Jakub, you and I created a child. Every night I pray for his soul, the ultimate gift of our love. Guilt pursues me during the day and hunts me at night. I did not mourn the death of this innocent being. I welcomed it for self-ish reasons. My conscience is not quieted by telling myself the world into which it would be born was an unjust one. Hiding his existence from my family betrays not only him, but my love for you. But I am weak. I know someday I must find the cour-age to reveal my own secrets, atone for my own sins.

Anna's shaking hand dropped the fountain pen on the desk. She stared at the letter she had just written. A cold sweat covered her body. The exertion of merely getting out of bed and sitting up to write had been too much. Her body shook and her hand ached. Stretching her cramped fingers, she picked up her letter and slowly moved back to bed. An overwhelming sense of melancholy swept over her as she touched her midsection and suddenly mourned the loss of her son, born over four months premature. She had managed to keep her condition and its termination a secret. That she had survived the ordeal of bringing a lifeless child into this world alone was nothing short of a miracle. There had been so much blood. Was it the loss of the child that had made her so sick? Was it her wicked ways that had poisoned her baby? Infested her body with fevers and chills? Would the baby have lived if *he* had been there? Anna did not feel the tears that flowed down her cheeks and dropped on the letter. Anna only vaguely remembered returning to her bed.

When Anna awoke the next morning she was startled to find Sigrid holding her hand, asleep in the chair beside her bed.

"Siggi," Anna croaked hoarsely, her throat dry from the heat that could already be felt so early in the morning. "Siggi," Anna whispered again, just as she realized she had fallen asleep with her letter. Panicked, Anna carefully removed her hand from Sigrid's grasp and rolled the letter up, sliding it into an empty apple juice bottle that stood on her nightstand. She shoved the bottle under her pillow just as Sigrid lifted her head.

"Anna, you are awake," Sigrid smiled down at her, gently pushing a tangle of red hair from her damp face. "How do you feel this morning? I will fetch you something to eat. You need your strength," Sigrid said, showing no signs that she had read Anna's letter.

"I am not hungry," Anna said as she reached for the glass of water on her nightstand.

"Fraulein, I have heard enough of that over these last few days," Sigrid reprimanded her, "you must eat, you have lost a lot of blood." Anna stared at her with her mouth agape.

"Y…y…you read my letter? H…h…how could you?" Anna demanded, not hiding her outrage at such an obvious violation of privacy.

"What? That paper you sleep with? Ach," Sigrid said, waving a dismissive hand at her. "I would be a blind mule not to see that you were with child," Sigrid spoke firmly, yet with an underlying tone of genuine concern. "I have seen," Sigrid paused and turned away from Anna. Lifting herself from the chair, the maid walked to Anna's window and looked out at the lightening sky. "I have," she began again, "seen many children born, and too many lost."

"Siggi, you told me you know nothing of childbirth, did you not?" Anna's words hung in the air like a dark cloud. She could not see the maid's face, but knew it was best to let the matter rest. Sigrid was not one who could be pressured to reveal a secret she did not want to reveal. Not even Mama was able to penetrate the steel-plated armor Sigrid could wrap herself in. Anna stared down at her empty hands, feeling a loss she never thought possible.

"These hands will never hold a child," Anna cried as the maid moved from the window and embraced her. Why was it always Sigrid who comforted her? Why did she not share this bond with her own mother? Her own mother did not even know that she had lost her son. The maid held Anna until her sobs ebbed.

"Now," Sigrid spoke gently, "I will come up with a tray. You and I shall have breakfast together." Anna did not answer, but silently watched as Sigrid straightened her comforter and headed towards the door.

Dozing off, Anna was awakened by the creak of her bedroom door. "Maria," she said, feeling a slight burst of energy at the sight of her sister. Now that Maria was a married woman she did not see her as frequently, even though Maria lived only a short bicycle ride away. Somehow, the bond of sisterhood had never been the same. But in this moment, she felt as though she and Maria were still children, sharing a room, discussing the advantages of riding a horse with or without a saddle.

"What are you doing here? And in your condition," Anna reprimanded, looking at her sister's swollen midsection, afraid she would bring a child into this world right here in the bedroom.

"Sigrid came to visit. She said you, ah, you may need me. Which was enough for me to know that you do. How are you feeling?" Maria asked, slowly seating herself at the foot of Anna's bed, one hand resting on her large belly.

"I think it is you who needs support. You are too thin...in most parts, and you look almost a shade of...green," Anna said, concerned for her sister's well-being. Did Maria know of her own predicament?

"Yes, and you do not look much better yourself," Maria replied squeezing her sister's big toe which poked out from beneath the comforter, causing her to squeal. The sounds of running footsteps and a swinging door silenced both young women, as Sigrid burst in.

"Anna, what is the matter? I heard a scream," Sigrid said, gasping heavily from the exertion of sudden, quick movement. Looking from one young woman to the other, both of whom burst out laughing at the same instant, Sigrid shook her head. "Yes, you two amuse yourselves at the expense of an old woman," she said gruffly, dropping a full tray of food on Anna's small desk. "You and you," she commanded, pointing at the sisters, "will both now breakfast with me. One would think neither of you have enough to eat...and you," she pointed at Maria, "who brings a child into this world any day now...I will lose my mind yet."

Stifling another giggle, which was quickly followed by one from Maria, Anna sat up straight in bed and watched as Sigrid began handing out various plates with rolls and cheese. Why was food so important to Siggi, Anna wondered, as she held out her hand to receive a soft boiled egg. Maybe it was having lived through a war that made people that way, she guessed as she nibbled on a roll.

"Now take care not to spill on the comforter," Sigrid told both women as though addressing two five year olds.

"Will you ever see us as grown women, Siggi?" Maria asked with a mouth full of egg.

"I do not know any grown women of good birth who speak with a mouth full of food," the well-endowed maid said, as she seated herself on the bed across from Maria and smiled at the two young women.

"Well, that answers your question, Maria," Anna teased, enjoying her breakfast for the first time in a long time. It was the first moment since Jakub's disappearance where she had not spent every waking and resting moment obsessed with the unfair fate that had befallen her. She knew the moment would not last, but she wished it could.

Two weeks later Anna had regained enough strength to go outside. It was not until this point in time that she realized how close she had been to death. She was eager to visit her sister, who had given birth and cared for a new daughter. The world outside seemed almost foreign and strange in some way. The sky seemed too bright, the birds too loud, and the walk to the stream at the edge of the woods too far. Slowly she made her way across the stubbles of wheat, all that remained of the recent harvest, that reminded her of a shorn sheep. Anna carefully carried the empty glass juice bottle that held her letter safely inside.

"Now how did I think of this?" she asked herself, questioning her sanity as she reached the edge of the wood. She peered through the glass. The dark green made it virtually impossible to see what was inside. Tapping her finger on the top of the glass bottle, she made sure the thick wax seal which filled the neck was solidly in place, something she had watched Sigrid do with much greater skill. Reaching the stream, she sat down to rest her quivering limbs, resting the bottle on her legs. Anna inhaled deeply, enjoying the smell of the woods so close by. She watched as the water rippled along and wondered how far her bottle might travel.

"My d...d...dear, Jakub," she spoke, feeling self-conscious even though there was no one to witness her foolish act. "I h...h...have written a l...l...letter to you, and I, uh, uh," Anna did not know what to say. She did not want to admit that he was really gone and never coming back. "But do I know that for sure?" she whispered, staring down at the bottle. "No, I do not." Standing up she stood in silence for a moment, enjoying the warmth of the summer sun on her face. "Jakub, p...p...please be safe wh...wh...wherever you are," she finally spoke as tears threatened to flow. Somehow, Anna managed to control her emotions. Squatting down, she gently shoved the bottle into the stream. Anna still stood by the stream long after the bottle disappeared around the bend in the stream. "Be safe, my love," she whispered to the trees.

Anna did not see the bottle, with its heartfelt letter, become entangled by the roots of a large tree at the water's edge. She would never know that same tree, struck by lightning the following fall, would crush her bottle and bury her letter forever.

Travels of Letter 16
Japan
Summer 1956

Kiyomi sat in a secluded corner of the beach, waiting for her husband to arrive. It was a Sunday, he had a lot of work to do today and did not have much time he had said. He usually worked on Sundays, but only for a half day. Lately, he seemed to be working a lot more, and often he worked straight through to Monday. Kiyomi wiggled her toes in the sand and felt the warmth of the sun through her long skirt. She felt guilty. Was it asking too much to have her husband meet her here? It had been so long since they spent any time together, and now with her mother living with them there was even less time. Kiyomi knew Takashi resented her mother, but what could she or her mother do? After Kiyomi's father passed away, it was only natural for her mother to come and live with them. It was a great burden on Takashi though, three women to care for besides himself, especially given her mother's frail health. His mother, Nobuko, had always lived with them. Nobuko never accepted Kiyomi and let her know this whenever any opportunity presented itself, especially when Takashi was not present, which was almost always. Kiyomi had accepted her fate, and even responded with lowered eyes to the abusive names Nobuko called her. But Kiyomi could not tolerate the ill treatment of her mother, by both her husband and her mother-in-law. Kiyomi had endured the physical abuse for so long, she did not feel the slaps and kicks the two inflicted on her for the slightest infraction. However, watching her mother slapped and kicked, in her frail condition, was unbearable.

Kiyomi cherished this moment of peace away from Nobuko, and even from her own husband, whose imminent arrival almost frightened her. Most of all she wondered what she would say to Takashi when he arrived. He did not speak much to her anymore, aside from ordering specific tasks be completed by the day's end. He hadn't come to her bed in over two months, and when he had, it was abrupt and increasingly violent. The broken nose she suffered a month and a half ago was almost healed, the bruising was gone, but the resentment she felt towards him was very alive. It took everything out of her to quell the hatred for him. Kiyomi had to remind herself every day, every hour, how lucky she was to be married, how lucky she was to be taken care of. She could have been one of the unlucky ones, and ended up an old maid. What would she do then? Yes, she was beautiful, even now, but beauty fades, and without her beauty, no one would ever take care of her.

Tossing her head back, Kiyomi felt her long black hair graze the sand. She hadn't worn her hair unbound for years. Her long hair was what had attracted Takashi to her in the first place. These days he demanded she wear it tied back in a tight bun, calling her a whore if he caught her with it down, even within the confines of their own home. Her mother-in-law had threatened to cut it off on more than one occasion, even chasing her with a pair of scissors once. Kiyomi was sure she would awaken one morning and all of her beautiful hair would be gone.

Kiyomi wondered what was taking her husband so long. He probably had more work than anticipated today. Or was he with her again, she wondered. She did not know who this "her" was, or how many of them there were, but she knew they existed. It was not something she spoke of, not even to her own mother. It was her own fault, after all, there must be something she was doing wrong to push her husband to other women. She couldn't help the feelings of anger that welled up inside of her when Takashi came home, smelling of cheap perfume with lipstick smudges on the collar of his white shirt. Was this acceptable behavior everywhere, she wondered, even in America? Was this what being a woman was all about, being submissive in every way to her husband and her mother-in-law? Kiyomi felt the color rise in her cheeks when she wondered what her life would have been like if she had packed her things and moved to America, the land of opportunity. Would she have met an American and fallen in love? She had seen American movies and love seemed different in America.

Staring at the waves, she noticed a bottle bobbing up and down in the shallow surf. It seemed odd to her that a bottle should float. Shouldn't it sink, she wondered, as she lifted herself and walked towards the water. The cool saltwater on her feet felt good, a contrast to the warm sand she had just walked through. Picking up the bottle floating straight towards her, she held it up and peered inside. She was sure there was something in it, a paper of some kind, which had been sealed inside with what looked like wax. Carrying the bottle back up the beach to her blanket, she wondered about the contents of the bottle and felt a surge of excitement. She couldn't wait to pry out whatever sealant plugged the bottle and investigate its contents. Kiyomi felt as though she were starring in an American movie. Daydreaming, she failed to notice Takashi until he stood right in front of her, blocking out the sun.

"I told you not to wear your hair down, you filthy whore," Takashi yelled, kicking sand into her face. Coughing, Kiyomi felt the tears well up in her eyes, as she tried to rub the sand out of them. Takashi again kicked, this time it was the back of her head he struck. Kiyomi was thrown forward and landed in the sand, face first. Quickly gathering herself, she jumped up and hurried to pull her hair back into a knot. "What's this?" Takashi demanded, staring at the cloudy green glass bottle.

"It just washed up on the shore," Kiyomi meekly replied with averted eyes, as the pain in her head throbbed.

"It's filthy and you touched it. You are filthy," Takashi snapped, as he slapped her across the forehead. Kiyomi knew better than to cry again. Any signs of weakness fueled his rage. Instead, she kneeled beside her husband and began to unpack the picnic she had packed. Kiyomi did not need to get too close to smell the foreign perfume that it seemed her husband had bathed in. Stealing quick glances at him, she noticed Takashi's general disheveled look.

A rage rose in her like a tidal wave, a rage that was as unstoppable as a charging bull. Without thought, she lifted the green bottle and slammed it into her husband's temple with a loud smack. Takashi looked at his wife as though seeing her for the first time, while knowing it would be for the last time. His eyes rolled back in his head, and he landed in the sand face first. Strangely, Kiyomi felt no remorse. She quietly picked up the bottle and walked down the length of the beach to the cave where the water churned wildly and dangerously. Without ceremony, she tossed the bottle into the water and returned to her husband, still face down in the sand.

Kiyomi couldn't help wondering about the green bottle as she sat next to her mother on a plane bound for New Jersey. Was it a sign from the gods? The authorities had accepted her story that her husband had complained about a headache after bumping his head and then suddenly keeled over. Surprisingly, the bottle left no evidence on his temple of the violent impact. A ruptured vessel was the official cause of death. With Nobuko placed with Takashi's youngest brother, Kiyomi felt a sense of freedom she had never before experienced. She and her mother could start over in America with all of the money she never knew her husband had. She looked over at her mother, who smiled at her and patted her hand. "You did well my daughter," she said, and closed her eyes to sleep.

Cape May, New Jersey
Fall 2011

Not a thing. I couldn't find a thing on Anna in the internet. So it was a hoax I tried to tell myself, but didn't really want to believe it. Charlie was still asleep so I slipped into the shower and tried to wash away the night's memories. What now? When the shower door slid open I didn't have to wonder about the "now" for a moment.

"Good morning," Charlie said as he poked his head into the shower. "Care if I join you?" he asked, stepping inside. The last thing I wanted right now was a naked man in my cramped shower.

"I'm just about finished here, actually," I quickly replied, turning off the water, and feeling suddenly very self-conscious.

"Oh, uh, ok, uh…well…here," Charlie said dejectedly as he backed out of the shower and handed me a towel. I couldn't make eye contact with him right now so I quickly snatched the towel and wrapped it around my body.

"Uh, do you mind giving me a moment, I've gotta, you know…," I tilted my head in the general direction of the toilet.

"Oh yeah, right, of course, I'm sorry," Charlie apologized, clumsily removing himself and his rejected manhood from the bathroom.

Sitting down on top of the toilet with my towel still tightly wrapped around me, the "what now" question shot back into my mind. What to do? What to do? "Alright think, woman," I whispered to myself, staring at the tile covered floor. Just an hour ago I had awoken, renewed, with a new lease on life. Somehow, in that moment, all of the sadness and guilt of the last six months had not been forgotten, but had definitely been locked up in some corner of my mind. So, what key had suddenly unlocked this hidden door and caused all these feelings of grief and guilt to flood out again?

Still seated on the toilet, I dropped my head into my hands and knew I couldn't do this with Charlie. Not yet. I just met the guy and he was leaving tomorrow, back to New York and then to London. I'd likely never see him again. "I will never, ever see him again. I am doomed to never, ever love again," I said aloud, as I caught a, likely imaginary, glance of Warren in the steam of the bathroom. Was he laughing?

"Didn't I tell you? You don't have to say 'ever' after never. It's redundant," the steamy apparition spoke without moving his mouth. Was the laughter I heard in my mind? God knows it wouldn't be the first time I had some type of hallucinatory experience. The steam in the bathroom slowly disappeared as I, still sitting on the porcelain throne, searched for the ghost of my deceased husband.

"Great," I said aloud, "I see my deceased husband and he gives me a lesson in grammar." Shouldn't a ghost say something profound? I realize English was never my strength, but I expected something like, I love you forever, Diana. The bathroom walls suddenly felt as though they were closing in on me, forcing me out of the bathroom. I needed air.

"I was going to grab some breakfast, then I've gotta head out to meet some old friends," Charlie casually said after I finished blow drying my hair. Did he just say that a little too casually? I had managed to avoid talking to him, but there was no way around that anymore. Was this jealousy I was feeling? Who was I jealous of? The supposed old friends he was meeting? I didn't quite understand the emotion I experienced. Looking away from Charlie, who expected an answer, I resisted the urge to ask him if his friends were women.

"Sure, uh, breakfast sounds great," I mumbled distractedly, searching for my shoes. Glancing up, I saw a brief look of disappoint skitter across his face. Is he the one trying to find a way out? Does he feel some sort of obligation to the poor widow he hooked up with last night? Was this his M.O.? Preying on vulnerable women he meets while on travel? Was it just widows? Or any woman for that matter, when he was traveling for *business*? Does he then go back to a family somewhere?

"Great, I know the perfect place," Charlie glumly said, buttoning his pants. Watching this man I hardly knew, I couldn't bring myself to believe someone like him was for real. The man he showed me, the caring, funny, confident, successful man, just had to be hiding something. What did he want with someone like me? The overwhelming self-doubt I felt seeped through, making me resentful and hostile on the outside. Could Charlie sense my hostility?

"There has to be some angle he's playing," I whispered to myself as we left the motel room together. Somehow the motel seemed even grimier than when I had first arrived. As we walked past the empty motel pool, it dawned on me it was Charlie Gordon I should have looked up on the internet. Not some woman who, given the lack of any information about her, likely did not exist at all.

"These pancakes are great. And the coffee...not bad," I lied, searching for anything to say to this man who was more a stranger now than when we first met on the plane. Why did sex change everything?

"Diana," Charlie said as he placed his fork down and wiped syrup from his chin. He definitely is a handsome man with that strong square jaw and dark curly brown hair with a sprinkling of grey just above the ears. "The pancakes are lousy and the coffee is cold," he said as he leaned back against the booth the two of us shared, forcing us to sit much too close. "It used to be a great little place, I swear." Charlie said, obviously upset.

"Well, I didn't want to be a bad sport, you know, I thought this was your favorite breakfast spot I mean," I said, fumbling with my napkin, nearly knocking over the largest glass of water I'd ever seen.

"Look, Diana, I'm sorry," Charlie said with seemingly genuine remorse.

"The pancakes aren't *that* bad," I quickly said, hiding my face in the gargantuan glass of water. Charlie briefly smiled.

"No, I mean about last night…I shouldn't have... I mean, I didn't want too…." Now it was Charlie who stumbled over his words. "What I'm trying to say is, I don't want you to think last night meant nothing to me. I don't want you to feel like I was taking advantage of you." Setting my glass down I studied Charlie as though he was a fifth grade science experiment. What was the guy going to say next?

"Did you hear me, Diana? I don't want you to think I took advantage of you," he finished with his ears the same crimson color I remembered from the night before.

"I'm a grown woman, I know what I'm doing," I replied almost caustically. Where did this anger come from? What was it about Charlie, or what he had said that brought these strong emotions to the surface? "Or do you think I'm easy prey because I'm a lonely widow," I hissed, staring him in the eyes.

"No, Diana, for God's sake, no. What you went through is horrible, but…, but…," Charlie stammered as I looked down to my cup of cold coffee for answers. "I didn't know about your husband when I first met you," he said defensively as a large blue vein emerged on his forehead. Still staring at my cup of coffee, half searching for Warren's ghost, I wondered what he would think of my previous evening's activities. What was it I saw in the bathroom this morning? Maybe he did know. Whatever I saw, whatever I searched for, I doubt I was going to find it in this cup of coffee, but then again, people have seen Jesus in a stick of butter.

"Hey, you know what, Charlie?" it was the first time I called him by name. It felt strange to call this man by his first name, but after last night that really didn't make sense. It also made me suddenly regret my misdirected or unjustified anger toward him. "You know, I had a great time last night… let's, uh, let's just leave it at that." Now it was Charlie who seemed to study me for a moment, making me feel uncomfortable.

"What if I don't want to leave it at just that, Diana?" he asked leaning up on his elbows. It wasn't the first time I heard Charlie speak my name, but the first time I realized with what ease he spoke it. Why had I waited so long to acknowledge him? Was it because of Sheila? My own mother rarely called anyone by their first name, part of the reason

I called her Sheila and not Mom. As far back as I could recall, Sheila introduced herself as Mrs. Adams. "Calling someone by their first name is an invitation for further conversation," she had said. Well, she was right there, I thought. Calling someone by their first name does breed a familiarity, and that is not always desirable. In this case, I wasn't so sure. There was a lot more to this Charlie than I was giving him credit for. I think I seriously underestimated the guy. Charlie waited in silence, waited for an answer to his question, but I remained silent as my internal tug of war raged on.

"Well, I've got to get going, Diana," Charlie finally said, looking at me, searching my face as though looking for a sign. A sign I clearly was not ready to give. Looking away I rummaged through my backpack, wishing myself out of this awkward situation. There in my backpack I noticed the odd knit "nothing" the strange woman had left at the airport. Stroking the soft wool, I glanced up as Charlie deposited a twenty dollar bill on the table and then pushed a business card in my direction.

"Look, if you ever want to meet, you know, just for a cup of coffee, when you're back in L.A., gimme a call o.k.?" Watching Charlie stand up and pull on his coat, part of me wanted to scream and yell for him to stay, but the more powerful part of my being remained stoic. As he leaned down towards me, I could feel my chances with this man slipping away. When his warm, soft lips brushed my cheeks, I again felt that spark I had tried to deny all morning. Did he feel it too? I had never bothered to ask. If he did, wouldn't he have said something? I could barely look up at Charlie to say goodbye. Forcing my lips into a smile, I lifted my hand in a slight wave as Charlie headed towards the door.

"Well, bye," I meekly called after him. Briefly turning to wave, he walked out the door of the diner and didn't turn back again. Now I suddenly felt more alone than ever before. Part of me wanted to run out, grab Charlie, and drag him back. The other part still clung to a life with a man who was definitely never coming back.

"Well, this one's not coming back either," I whispered to myself, pulling the green knit something onto my lap to twist between my fingers.

Is that what I was afraid of? Again I stared into my cold coffee. "Afraid that anyone I meet might just up and disappear some day, as though they never existed?" I didn't realize I had spoken aloud until I noticed the old woman in the adjacent booth turn and stare. It took an effort on my part not to glare at her. Instead, I found something else when I looked at this woman in the booth. Her eyes held no hostility or contempt for me. No, her eyes, as dark as bottomless pits, were filled with a grief, with despair that not even I knew. Geez, how old was this woman?

I watched the old woman slowly pry herself out from behind her booth; it was as though watching a movie in slow motion. The small woman, dressed in a Sari, began a slow shuffle towards the door. She abruptly straightened, turned and shuffled intently back toward my table. The, I assumed, Indian woman who stood before me, clutching her Sari with one hand, placed a small, black stone on the table.

"You do not ask my opinion, but I speak it now," the old woman spoke with a heavy Indian accent. "If you love him and he loves you, you must follow him. Let nothing stand in your way."

The old Indian woman turned and left before the speech centers in my brain began functioning once again. I still felt tongue tied and confused, upset that I lacked any innate ability to think on my feet. Why on earth did this woman, whom I had never met, give me a rock and relationship advice? Picking up the small black rock, I was surprised by its warmth. What does she know about my love life that I seem to be missing? Standing up to leave, I placed the rock in my pocket and thought of the odd assortment of items I had collected so far on this trip.

Letter Two   *Dresden, 30 November, 1938*

My Beloved Jakub,

Why does my worry for you persist? One would think there is a time when the worry might ease, but it has not. Over nine months, Jakub, it has been over nine months since your disappearance. And if anything, my fears are greater now than before. This world I live in, my family lives in, it is not the world of my childhood. The world where we are judged, based on what we accomplish and how we behave, not what we believe, is gone. What is happening here, the persecution, the awfulness of it all, is more than I can bear. When is it all going to end? Sometimes I wake up still trapped in a nightmare, envisioning you locked up in a prison somewhere, cold and alone, or left to die on that Night of Broken Glass. *But then, for the sake of my own sanity, I envision you far from Dresden, far from Germany, safely in Australia somewhere, possibly living on a warm beach surrounded by sunlight and life. I sound foolish, I know, but it helps me survive the day, every day. I still search for signs, miracles, anything that may strengthen my belief that you are not only alive, but safe. Despite the grave situation, I still climb the ladder to the hayloft, hoping to find you tucked safely in the hay, waiting for me with an explanation of why you went, and a promise that you shall never again leave.*

These last four months, my dear Jakub, have been difficult for the family. Papa is in a constant state of anxiety. I hear him at night, behind closed doors, arguing with Mama. He fears the annexation of Austria is only the beginning, with violence inevitable. Sigrid tells me he has directed her to begin hoarding supplies for what he calls "the great horror to come." Sometimes I help Sigrid in the kitchen, late into the night, boiling fruits and vegetables to be stored in jars. The food we prepare is hidden well in underground cellars. The work, and Sigrid's moral support, helps ease my mind, but it is when I am alone with my thoughts that I cannot escape the reality of what is. Sigrid has confided in me that she prepares more food than even what Papa has requested. Mama does not share Papa's sentiment. She believes it is a wasteful use of precious time, even shattering seven prepared jars of red beets on one occasion. The Fuehrer, she claims, has only noble intentions. He has strengthened the infrastructure and brought prosperity to the German people who suffer so greatly. Papa does not condone the persecution of innocent people, he says. It seems this topic divides even close families. Papa has told Mama she chooses not to see the truth. This "movement," he believes, has taken on a life of its own. Usually he does not argue with her, I believe he fears for her health. She has not had coughing fits since my last letter, but Papa forces her to sit an hour each day to rest her body, if not her soul. I know this drives her mad, as she is normally so restless.

Just yesterday two men arrived, dressed in the official party uniform. I was unable to hear what they spoke to Papa about, but they did interview him alone. It would have been less difficult to listen had it been at a later hour. It is always difficult to be inconspicuous before the noon hour with the maids moving back and forth through the house, cleaning and laundering. Later I heard Mama speak of a list, an accounting of all estate workers in the last two years, and their current whereabouts. I fear your name is on this list. And Jakub, your secret, that which I would have died to protect, is not a secret. The gardener's son knows. It is not only I who knows. Never before or since has what you believe been of consequence to me, to our love. Yet my whole world is now divided on this subject. Maybe it is meant to be that your whereabouts remain unknown to me. Oh Jakub, what I would give for this knowledge, but at what risk to you? What I would give for just one more moment with you.

You may remember Lena, the gardener's daughter. It took much time before I had a chance to confront her regarding your situation. She swears she knows nothing of your current whereabouts, but does admit to knowledge of our relations. It was her brother Ingo who passed this information on to her, which confused me given my past conversation with him. How he came by this knowledge, she does not know. Who is he protecting? Or was he lurking in the shadows the night we expressed our love most intimately? It is a horror to believe such a thing, but, as you can understand, I cannot report any of this to Papa, despite the fact that he knows more than he is willing to admit. But believe me, my love, I shall get to the bottom of this.

I have shared my burden with Sigrid, and Maria. Without Sigrid and Maria, God protect their souls, I do not believe I could survive this world. As for Maria, I am convinced I falsely accused her the night of her wedding. She did not betray me, us. On the contrary, she lends great moral support and has given of herself, despite the condition she was in for nine months. There is further great news to share about Maria. She has a new daughter, Alexandra Anna Frieda. It is a great relief to us all especially given how weak Maria's body was before the arrival of the child. Both Sigrid and I cannot spend enough time with this sweet child. Oh, Jakub, it is hard to imagine how tiny and innocent we are when we enter this world. When is this pure innocence lost? How is it that something so pure can grow into something so horrible? As I watch Alexandra, though, I do feel hope for all of us.

After much thought, I named our child. Possibly this pleases you, but quite possibly it does not. In either case, I hope you do not mind the names I have chosen. He is named after his father and grandfather, Jakub Franz Gorski. It was Sigrid who convinced me to name your child, to help ease the sorrow. Sigrid, Maria, and I found a special spot where I can retreat and

97

honor his brief existence. It has helped me mourn his loss, and in an odd way, it helps me mourn you. If that is what you are, lost? Sometimes, in my darkest hours, my dearest Jakub, my mind wanders. Would this child have been born healthy had you not disappeared? Anger at you, uncontrollable anger I do not want to experience, surfaces during these hours of stillness. Oh Jakub, I do not want resentment to cloud my memory of you. I do not want to blame you when I do not know the reasons you had for leaving. Maybe it was me you protected. The hour is late, I no longer make sense to myself. With this, my love, I take my leave.

Love Eternally,
Anna Alexa Elisabeth v. Marschalkt

Post Script: Wherever you are Jakub, is it not strange that we look up at the same moon, the same sun, and the same stars? How small we really are. What do we and all of our trivialities mean? Maybe someday we will know.

Anna gently set her fountain pen down and blew upon the letter to help the ink dry. Carefully she picked up the letter, rolled it tightly, and shoved it into the empty green apple juice bottle that stood waiting on her desk. She cautiously prepared her wax plug, shoving it deep into the throat of the bottle, then filling the sides with hot liquid wax. Anna was exhausted. Setting the bottle down she stared up at the moon and the beautiful light it cast over the earth. Was he looking at the moon right now? "Of course not, he's in Australia," she whispered as she reminded herself that he was likely looking at the sun. Part of her soul wished him to the safety of this unknown land, but the selfish part of her soul desired him at any cost.

Anna shivered as a small gust of wind crept beneath her closed window. Pulling her robe tightly around her body, she blew out her two candles, picked up her bottle, and quickly walked to her bed. She crawled under the down comforter and hid the bottle safely beneath her pillow. As she lay in her bed, with her head resting on the pillow hiding the glass bottle, she stared up at the dark ceiling, enjoying the smell of smoldering candle wicks. Would this be like every other night? Would sleep elude her once again, only to find her in the morning hours? Mama had asked her if she was sick as she often slept late into the day. Did she suspect anything? How could she *not* have noticed that her daughter had been with child? "You'll never know your grandson, Mama," she whispered to the moon, as she shifted her position again.

Unlike most other nights, Anna quickly dropped into a deep sleep. Dreams of Jakub floated in and out of her subconscious. It was her Papa and his stern face, so unlike his usual demeanor, which she remembered when she first awoke to the crowing rooster. There was something she knew she should remember about Papa, to use as a negotiating tool, but could not recall what it was. Confounded by the fact that dreams tend to disappear before the individual is fully awake to remember them, she lifted herself out of bed and made her way towards the wash closet. She stepped out into the chilly hallway pulling the robe she had slept in tightly around her body. The sound of singing downstairs lifted her gloomy outlook a bit, as the smell of frying sausages reached her nostrils.

Anna descended towards the kitchen, tying her hair back in a bun and fastening it quickly with hairpins, hoping she would not run into anyone. She felt a wave of disappointment pass over her as she saw Lena burst through the side door and disappear into the kitchen. Obviously, Lena, holding a large slice of bread in her hand, had no intention of remaining in the kitchen, as she rushed out and, once again, nearly into Anna.

"Excuse me, Fraulein," Lena spoke with lowered voice.

"Lena," Anna spoke before her mind had time to decide what she wanted to ask this woman. "I w…w…wish to…," Anna's mouth continued to move, but emitted no sound as she looked down at this woman's midsection. Was everyone here with child, she wondered, blatantly staring at Lena's prominent bump. How had she missed this before? Well, she reminded herself, she did not spend her days closely observing the staff. Lena noticed Anna's stare and protectively placed her hand over her midsection.

"Please, Fraulein, please," Lena spoke with a cracking voice, as tears filled her eyes. "Please, I did not judge you," she sobbed, as she wiped her dripping nose with a small handkerchief. "I did not judge you," she repeated, as Anna tried to figure out what this woman was talking about.

"W…w…what do you speak of? N…n…not judge me, f…f…for what?" Anna asked, as suspicions arose in her.

"I told my brother never to let on…never let on to anyone that we knew of you and the Jew," she cried as tears streamed down her cheeks. An odd feeling of déjà vu passed over Anna as she watched the gardener's daughter sob and beg her for discretion. Did she not recently stand before this young woman and have a similar conversation?

"Is it gone?" Lena asked, with a look Anna could not contrive to be anything but sympathy. Lena knew about the child. Her child. Anna felt as though she were far away in a dark cloud. One she could never escape from. Feeling drops of perspiration form on her forehead, Anna grabbed the young woman and pulled her into the small sitting room.

Anna had never been fond of Lena, whom she had grown up with, but had never conversed with. Anna had always thought of Lena simply as the gardener's daughter. She had tried to convince both her mother and her father not to bring her into the house as a maid. What was it her mother had said to her? "You know nothing of loyalty, Anna," her mother had said. To whom was her mother loyal? To the gardener and his family? Was it because they had always been part of the estate? Was it a sense of allegiance to the gardener's deceased wife who used to assist Sigrid in the kitchen? To her own family her mother surely did not demonstrate the proper degree of loyalty, Anna thought as she looked at the sobbing woman from head to toe.

"S...s...stop it," Anna hissed and handed Lena a handkerchief. "You are c...c...causing a scene," she said with as much authority as she could muster given the circumstances. "W...w...who is the father?" Anna demanded, hearing her own voice quiver, furious once again at her stuttering.

"I cannot, please, I cannot," Lena begged.

"Is it U...U...Ulrich? I saw y...y...you in the vegetable g...g... garden with him. Or...or...or is it Otto? I've seen you with h...h... him too. Oh, n...n...no, it must be Gerold, he makes eyes at all the w...w...women..." Anna spoke in an accusing tone. How could this woman with no morals compare herself with me, she wondered as her mind raced. Which of her father's farm hands had she allowed to violate her? Was it more than one? "W...w...well, if you will not tell me, I w...w...will tell the Baron and th...th...then...,"

"No, oh no, you can not do that he will...," Lena's voice trailed off as she covered her face with both hands and sobbed uncontrollably.

Anna waited until the young woman calmed down. "S...s...sit, Fraulein Zimmerman," Anna ordered as she retrieved chocolates from her mother's special chest. Somehow this woman, whom she had resented her whole life, did not seem as threatening anymore. Quite the opposite, she seemed rather vulnerable. Anna could not even remember for what reasons she so disliked the gardener's daughter. There must be a reason why Lena had behaved indecently, could it have been love? And the truth of the matter was, Anna thought, she herself had behaved as unacceptably as this maid she judged so harshly. "N...n... now, you and I will g...g...get to the bottom of...all of th...th...this," she gestured with a box of Swiss chocolates in her hand, which she then placed before Lena. "First, h...h...how did you know...a...a... about me?" she asked, watching Lena intently.

"It shames me to speak," Lena cried, seemingly on the verge of hysteria. "I have watched you, Fraulein von Marschalkt, since we were young girls," Lena sniffled, dabbing her nose with her handkerchief. "You wore fancy dresses, played with beautiful toys, and I...," the young woman stared out the window as though reliving a past she wished she could forget. "And I, I lived with nothing but a father who sought out the belt when he drank too much." Lena spoke with an undercurrent of hatred. "But you, I have never meant you harm. I watched you, pretended to be you, always secretly wanted to be a friend to you." Lena sobbed uncontrollably.

Anna felt as though she could not breathe. How could she have been so selfish all these years, not to notice a lonely, motherless girl? She knew that her own mother's loyalties would allow this gardener's daughter into her house as a maid, but never as a friend to her daughter.

"I am s...s...sorry...," Anna whispered as she felt a sense of guilt spread throughout her being, guilt she would only later truly begin to understand. "I w...w...will not tell my father of your c...c...condition, Fraulein Zimmerman, on the one c...c...condition that you tell me everything you kn...kn...know of Jakub G...G...Gorski," Anna said more gently, as it occurred to her that what this woman knew about Jakub was more important to her than what Lena knew about her past condition.

"I will...," Lena spoke quietly as she cleared her voice, "I will tell you everything I know."

The two young women sat in silence as they regarded each other. One born into a world of prestige and limitless opportunity, the other into a life of seeming inescapable servitude; yet they shared a similar spirit, a common thread. They followed their hearts instead of the rules that a strict, unforgiving society placed on young women.

Three days later, Anna would walk to her stream by the woods, never knowing the fate of the second bottle she tossed into slow moving water. As the bottle traveled around the bend and continued on towards the Elbe River, it slowly filled with water, washing away all evidence of Anna's written love. Anna would never know she had not properly sealed her second bottle. Sinking to the bottom of the river, the bottle was eventually covered with silt, never again to see the light of day.

Travels of Letter 16
Eastern Australian Coast
Summer 1958

"I don't want to go, not tonight," Sheila said, as she rolled over in bed and pretended to sleep.

"I know you're not sleeping, Sheila. Come on, it'll be fun, everyone's gonna be there," Hunter prodded, knowing he would eventually persuade his American girlfriend to come along, like he always did. "Come on, babe, I'll drive. You can sleep in the truck."

Sheila rolled back over to stare at her boyfriend. Yes, she could call him that now, couldn't she? She'd been with him for almost four months, almost the entire time she had been in Australia. He'd even invited her into his inner circle, his 'sanctum of righteousness' as he called it. She would do anything for him she thought as she stared into his intense green eyes. Almost anything, she corrected herself.

"Here ya go, babe, something to help get you in the mood," Hunter whispered into her ear, stroking her back with one hand and handing her an odd looking cigarette with the other. How did he do that, she wondered. How was he able to get her to do things she really didn't want to? Was it her lack of will power, or his amazing power of persuasion? Somewhere deep inside she knew it was futile to try and resist him. Kissing him on the mouth she reached for the cigarette and inhaled deeply, coughing violently as the smoke filled her lungs. She giggled, only to lapse back into another coughing fit. Giggling helped cover her embarrassment. After four months of this she should be used to the smoke. Maybe it was her guilty conscience that wanted to remind her how wrong this all was. Inhaling once more, too deeply, she felt the smoke travel down her throat and into her lungs. The smoke burned her lungs and throat, forcing her to jerk forward as a coughing spasm wracked her body again.

"Hey babe, you okay there? Sounds like you're just about ready to eject a lung or something," Hunter said with what appeared to be genuine concern as he pounded her on the back.

"You know, my Mom would kill me if she found out I was still seeing you. And for this," she said, pointing at what he called his homemade cigarette he now held firmly between his teeth, "she would rip your eyeballs out and feed 'em to the sharks," Sheila giggled as she covered her mouth with both hands to stifle her laughter. Somehow everything seemed hilarious now as she giggled uncontrollably. Irritated, Hunter reached for her arm and dragged her out of the bed.

"Well, I guess we're lucky Mommy's screwing Daddy an ocean away, aren't we," he said sarcastically, throwing her boots at her. "Put these on, move, we've got to get going, everyone's waiting." Giggling, Sheila picked up her boots and followed Hunter out to his truck.

Sheila didn't know how long they had been driving, or where they were driving to. Time had somehow slipped away from her again. She wondered if she had dozed off for a moment, maybe longer. Nothing seemed funny anymore. Looking over at Hunter she decided not to risk asking him what time it was. There was something about his eyes that scared her tonight. His eyes revealed an untamed, almost predatory side she had never seen before.

"I am such an idiot," she whispered to herself when she realized how little she really knew about Hunter. Maybe her Mom was right, maybe there was something sinister about this guy. And her mother had only met him once for a couple of hours. It didn't help that she had no idea where she was and that Hunter drove like a madman down an unpaved road to God only knew where. Maybe the sea? She became more certain it was the sea he was headed towards as an unmistakable salty smell intensified with each passing moment. Were they really going to meet *the others*?

Hunter, who had turned off the truck's headlamps a few kilometers back, suddenly braked. Luckily it was a full moon, Sheila thought, as Hunter jumped out of the car. "Come on, don't lag behind," he ordered as he moved towards the sandy beach at a rapid pace. Sheila followed him, but, unable to move through the sand as swiftly, paused for a moment in an attempt to identify any landmarks, anything familiar. She had not grown up in this country, how could she know where she was? Down the beach she heard voices, Hunter's, but who else? She had been in an altered mental state when she first met the other members of the "sanctum of righteousness." Actually, she had been "altered" every time she met any of the members, she thought, disgusted with herself.

"You stupid fool, you wouldn't recognize a single one of them," she whispered, wanting to kick herself. Reaching the small group, she counted five others including Hunter. Had she met these people before? She must have, she thought, unless this righteous group, or whatever they were, had more members. Somehow she doubted it.

"Hey, Sheila," an oddly familiar voice called out to her. From somewhere in her mind the name Brian jumped up.

"Uh, Brian," she replied cautiously, as every hair on her neck stood straight up. Something about this group wasn't right, every part of her being sensed it, but what was it? Two of the others were women. That much she could make out. Had she gotten herself involved with some strange cult? Sheila spun around, there were voices behind her. She peered into the moonlit darkness and waited as the voices closed in on her.

The white bag covering the man's head reflected the moonlight, making him appear like a headless apparition. The two men flanking him held him tightly as he struggled to be free. Sheila gasped at the scene unfolding before her. The man, shackled at both the wrists and ankles, continued to struggle until he was kicked in the back and forced to his knees.

"Is everyone here?" It was Hunter who spoke, his face eerily lit by the moonlight.

"Everyone accounted for mate," answered Brian. "Are you sure about her?" Sheila assumed Brian was talking about her.

"Yeah, she's fine, she'll do whatever I tell her to," Hunter answered into the ghostly night. Sheila wanted to turn and run, but where would she run to and how far would she get? Would they chase her? What would they do to her if they caught her? With her survival instinct running in high gear, Sheila realized the best course of action was to comply with whatever they required. Make them believe she would do whatever Hunter, that creep, wanted.

Sheila watched in horror, as the male members of the group turned on flashlights and shined them on their prisoner. Hunter approached the prisoner and removed the white bag, revealing a gagged man beaten beyond recognition. Sheila knew she would be sick, and turned away from the group to empty the contents of her stomach. It took her a moment to recognize that the man was an Aborigine.

"Where did you find this one, mate?" Hunter asked one of the captors, as though speaking of an animal.

"Found this half-breed hitchin' a ride into town. Can't hide behind these white man clothes, now can ya, mate," the larger of the two captors said as he kicked the man in the back again.

"Everyone assembled here knows what it is we need to rid ourselves of," Hunter spoke solemnly with raised hands. "Bring the boat. The women stay here," he ordered.

Sheila watched in horror as two men secured a rock to the man's back and placed him in a wooden row boat. Sheila continued to watch, frozen with terror, as the men pushed the boat into the waves and one by one jumped inside, the boat and its occupants a dark silhouette against the bright sea.

"Do we have the sheep blood?" Sheila heard Hunter ask. The waves carried his voice to the shore as though he were standing next to her. Minutes, possibly only a moment later, a splash and the ensuing laughter made her blood run cold.

She didn't know how long she had been standing in frozen terror when she heard Hunter's distinct voice float over the calm sea again. "Let us pray now, brothers."

"There's one, and there's another," she heard a strange voice cry out, obviously interrupting Hunter's religious moment. "Bloody hell, there's a whole shiver of 'em out there, mates."

Shiela knew it had to be sharks. Why else the blood? To attract the sharks of course, even a child knew sharks smelled blood from far away. Who were these people and what was wrong with them? And these women, how could they stand by and watch this happen? Too late, Sheila realized that she too had stood by and let *this* happen. Just as she was seriously contemplating making a run for it, she heard what she thought was Brian's voice for the last time, "Hey mates, there's a bottle floating out there," he shouted. Sheila watched as flashlights illuminated a small patch of ocean.

How the small boat capsized would forever remain a mystery. Maybe Hunter tried to reach the bottle and the boat flipped. It was a small boat after all. Maybe it was something else, maybe a higher justice had been served. Not one of the boat's occupants survived the fall into the shiver of frenzied bull sharks. Sheila never spoke about what happened that summer evening, she assumed the other women hadn't either. Maybe the cosmos had heard her comment about feeding Hunter's eyes to the sharks. One thing she knew for certain, she would never find peace again.

Cape May, New Jersey

Fall 2011

The sign over the door read *Jenna's Curiosities*. Since my breakfast with Charlie I'd been walking around the town aimlessly for who knows how long. Absentmindedly, I rolled the smooth black stone in my pocket. I couldn't shake the old Indian woman and what she had said from my mind. The weather had partially cleared, with large rays of sunshine beaming down from the sky between large white clouds. It was beautiful. Deciding to take a walk along the beach, I headed in its general direction. It would definitely be more enjoyable now without the rain. Was it the sign that caught my eye? I wasn't quite sure. Examining the weathered sign more closely, I noted that nothing out here was immune from the salty air and severe weather. The door jingled and creaked, reminding me of my own broken door that still needed to be repaired, and I pushed my way into the small store that smelled of incense and lavender.

"Anything I can help you with?" A voice from nowhere asked. Looking around I was surprised to see a woman directly in front of me. She looked almost like a mannequin, dressed in some type of Tibetan or Asian garb, so I hadn't noticed her sitting right in front of me.

"No, thanks, I'm just looking," I replied, feeling oddly soothed by the scents that permeated the air.

"It's the jasmine," the woman spoke, looking up from behind her glasses. The woman smiled at me as I looked at her with an obviously confused expression. "The smell in here, it's the jasmine," the woman said, pointing to a tray of incense sticks she sold for twenty five cents a piece.

"Hmmm, it does smell nice," I had to admit, picking up one of the fragile sticks to examine it more closely. Abe used to burn these things in his room and drive Sheila crazy.

"I've got over a hundred different scents, in case you're interested," the woman offered as she continued to read whatever magazine captured her attention.

"Thanks, I think I'll take a few of the jasmine," I answered, surprising myself by picking up six of the jasmine incense sticks. I had never purchased an incense stick. Somehow I always thought of them as hokey and associated them with all those new age fakers. "Well, people change," spoke the incense neophyte as I sniffed my sticks and admired the embroidered clothing the woman had for sale.

"Where do you buy your merchandise?" I casually asked, still inhaling whiffs of jasmine and picking up a small elephant ornately decorated with tiny red beads.

"Oh, from all over. Asia and Africa primarily though," the woman said, still engrossed in her article. "Sometimes my husband brings back things for me from his diving vacations, but that stuff really doesn't sell well. I've just never had the heart to tell him, you know what I mean?" The woman looked up from her paper and pointed to shelves in the back of the store. "Anything you find back there, seventy-five percent off...no, make that eighty percent off."

I moved to the back of the store and studied the odd assortment of swords, gaudy plastic bracelets, faux hula necklaces and other various junk that littered the shelves. I was sure I heard the woman chuckle to herself. Picking up a pen with a bobbing turtle on it, I wondered what smart ass comment Warren would have made about the store and its odd assortment of knick-knacks.

"That you can have, and fifty more if you like. Got a box of five hundred in the back. Don't know what the guy was thinking. Ah, Men. Gotta love 'em, they sure try," said the woman as she shook her head. She looked about forty, but had an aura about her as though she should be eighty. Was it her hair with the premature grey streaks that made her seem older? No, it was her personality. She was so self-assured, I thought, as I gave in to the urge to stroke a roughly knit light green scarf that reminded me of the green knit "nothing" I still carried in my backpack. "Why did I keep that thing?" I quietly asked myself, placing a multi-colored Rasta type hat on my head. It seemed I was collecting my own rather odd assortment of things on this trip. The knit "nothing," the glass bottle with the letter, and then the odd stone.

"No, that's not you," the woman said as she raised herself from her chair and moved towards me to pull this obvious fashion violation from my head. "Now this," she said as she reached for a knit, beige beret, with a matching knit flower, "this is you." Stepping back to admire me, making me feel more uncomfortable than anything else, she smiled, motioning for me to look at myself in the mirror. "Beautiful," the woman said to my reflection in the mirror, "just beautiful."

I didn't exactly see what the woman saw as I stared at my reflection in the mirror. A round face with a beige, flowered beret on dark hair with red highlights is what stared back at me. Hmmm. The hat was growing on me though. My mind managed to travel down Warren's memory lane once again. No one had called me beautiful, not since Warren. Never before, nor since, had I felt beautiful. That was one of the things that made him so wonderfully special. He managed to find a beauty in me I did not know existed, and in those moments always made me believe it myself. Would Warren tell me I looked beautiful today? Ok, now I'm really hitting a new pathetic low. Come on Di, how lame are you? I had to ask myself the question. Had to snap myself out of whatever self-pitying moment I was about to wallow in again for God knows how long. It was such an easy out to always play the victim. For once I didn't want to play the victim. I wanted to be the heroine. To hell with all of the beauty talk and two thumbs up for making up my own damn mind.

"I'm not really a hat kind of person, but surprisingly I do like this one on me…so I'll take it," I said resolutely, rummaging through my backpack to find my wallet.

As I paid for my beret and smelling sticks, I pondered how much of what I thought about myself and did was because of Warren, because of the words he spoke to me and how much I always wanted to please him. A vision of Charlie briefly wiggled its way into my mind like a worm eating through an apple. Would I ever find anyone as…what exactly are the words I'm looking for here? Would I ever find someone, so full of love for me, that I could become what it was they saw in me? Is that what all of it came down to? Was there anyone out there who could ever see me the way Warren did? Was there anyone out there *I* could ever feel that strongly about? My face flushed as I recalled the previous evening with Charlie. I was so engrossed with my own thoughts I didn't hear the woman speaking to me again.

"What is it you search for?" the woman asked for the second time, placing a diving magazine on the glass counter. "What is it you search for?" she asked, stepping close enough to me that I could smell her minty breath. Taking a step back, I turned away from the woman whose closeness made me a bit uncomfortable.

"Oh, I'm just looking around a bit," I answered, not sure where she was going with her question.

"No, no, no, not in here, out there," the woman said pointing towards the window and the world beyond it. I have to admit, I was a bit confused by the question and must have looked at her like a dog with its head tilted while his master barks strange sounds at him.

"I'm sorry, I don't understand the question….searching for what?" I finally had to ask.

"Honey, people come in here every day. Everybody's got a look about them," she spoke as though she was talking about the weather. "Some look lost, some confused, some angry or sad, some even look genuinely happy, but you, you're searching, honey." Well, how the heck do you respond to a question like that? Not to mention that it's a blatant intrusion into the sanctity of the mind. "Definitely searching," she repeated.

Goose bumps covered my body. "Does everyone in this town think they have some strange cosmic connection?" I finally asked, pulling the beret down over my ears, a sign that I didn't want to hear anymore crazy talk. This strange woman reached over the counter and pulled the beret up, exposing one of my ears.

"I don't know about everyone, I just know about me," the woman said as she continued to fuss with my beret. "There ya go, honey, gotta wear it right, you know," she said, winking at me and then motioning me to leave. "Go on, get outta here. Get out and enjoy that weather while it lasts." Pulling my arms through my backpack I left the store, stealing one last glance at the strange woman.

"Is everyone in this town just a little bizarre?" I whispered to myself as the jingling, creaking door fell shut behind me.

Letter Three   *Dresden, 15 March 1939*

My Beloved Jakub,

With every passing day the innocence of youth and all that is familiar moves further from my grasp. Even as I reach, Jakub, reach back to a past that is no longer, I am unable to find anything solid on which to grab hold. Oh, it is horrible, life is horrible. It is not fair of me to burden your soul with such sentiment, but it is my passion for you, my obsession with you, the one true thing in my past which I still dream to hold in my future. It is this hope for the future, a future together, which does not allow me to free myself from this past that never can be again.

The days pass, the seasons change and it has been well over a year since you disappeared. I know Maria and Sigrid worry for me. I still have night terrors, and occasional day terrors, but regularly convince myself that you are living in Australia. The horror that you have departed this world, or worse, that you suffer somewhere is too much for my soul to bear. For my own sanity I can no longer think of you anywhere but in the safety of a distant land, waiting to return to me. Someday. Please Jakub, do not let the memory of our love diminish. Do you remember what you said to me the night we bound each other with our love? "It is only you I love, Anna, it always has been, it always will be, forever." I repeat those words to myself every evening, praying for the night you again whisper them into my ear. The night when your warm breath on my neck makes my heart soar again. Is it not strange, Jakub, how fragile the human heart is in matters of love, yet it is strong enough not to miss a beat until it rests forever? Just yesterday I climbed the ladder to the hayloft. I have not been there for over a month. What used to seem so familiar about the loft, now seems foreign and strange, even the smells that permeate

114

*the air. I looked at where we laid together as lovers and won-
der if, in a different time and place, we would still be together.*

*You must believe that I continue to search for the truth. I have
met much resistance in my efforts. All know of my search,
futile as it may seem to them. Even Mama knows and has reprimanded me on more than one occasion. She does not want
staff on the estate burdened with foolish questions. "Foolish
questions raise suspicions," she warned. I believe her worries are exacerbated by the military officers who frequently
appear unexpectedly at the door to meet with Papa. What they
speak of with Papa I do not know. Whatever it is has changed
the color of his hair to a shimmering gray. Often I find him in
his study smoking his pipe, staring out the window as though
in a different world. Oddly, Mama does not discourage these
official military visits, but receives the officers with her finest
china and cream tortes. I was never aware what charms my
mother was capable of casting onto unwitting men. Somehow
I know that, while she believes in the movement that is afoot
here in Dresden, in all of Germany, she does have the best
interest of the family at heart.*

*Now I must write to you of what I have learned. Do you
recall Lena from my previous letters? She has given birth to
a healthy baby boy she named Thomas Walter Zimmermann.
I only found out of her condition some months ago when I
looked upon her midsection. She continues to hide the iden-
tity of the father, but suspicions point to Ulrich, or possibly
even Otto, or Gerold. Mama has provided her a room in the
main house. The house she shares with her father and brother
was not suitable for a woman carrying a child. But it is fear
for the child's life which prompted Papa to move Lena to our
home. Strangely, I care as much for little Thomas Walter as I
do for Maria's young daughter, who grows stronger with each
passing day. The bruises on Lena's body told us that the old
Mr. Zimmermann did not receive the news of Lena's condition*

well. As far as I am concerned, the old man could just disappear. Who would beat a woman with child?

I am sorry, I digress. What I did uncover is the role the gardener played in your disappearance. With some degree of persuasion, Lena confided that it was her father who knew of our relationship. Her father's normally tight lips had been sufficiently loosened after an evening of drink. Oh, Jakub, even the act of writing these words sends shivers of horror down my spine. The gardener, in his drunken stupor, confided that he had witnessed our expression of love. Lena assured me that he did not witness anything, but was in the barn that evening, listening, as he had many evenings before to the "Jew and the whore." Oh, God forgive us, forgive me Jakub. Please, send me a sign, a signal, something that confirms that our love had to be. That it was not I who selfishly took what was not mine to take? I do not care what names I am called behind my back, I plan to defend my honor, our honor, without words. Lena swore on her then-unborn child that she had no further information regarding her father. With whom would she have shared this information? Is this who betrayed you? Old Mr. Zimmermann? And to whom? I try to hold on to the belief of you on a warm beach somewhere, but find difficulty with this notion given the current political climate and how many on the estate seem to have been privy to what I believed was our sacred secret.

Last night I dreamt of you, Jakub. I cherish the dreams with you that cradle me with warmth and lull me to sleep like an innocent child, not tear me from my sleep with screams that wake Sigrid. You find me silly, I am sure, to speak of my dream, but the oddity of it requires repeating. It was you and I, tightly embraced, on a warm bed of straw. No, it was not the hayloft as you may assume, but the middle of a large field. We were, my dear, without clothing and surrounded by everyone I know, possibly everyone I have ever known. In this dream, in front of these people, neither you nor I demonstrated any remorse for our actions. We loved, Jakub, without restraints, without rules. Oh, but for a world where rules do not exist for lovers. My dearest, the morning calls, and with it hope of a new day. The aroma of Sigrid's breakfast travels up to my room, and makes my stomach emit noises most unbecoming a lady. With thoughts of love and food I leave you for another day.

Love Eternally,
Anna Alexa Elisabeth v. Marschalkt

Post Script: As I sit at my desk a few moments more, and watch the rising sun, I have faith that today must be a better day than yesterday, and pray that tomorrow shall bring stability to this world we live in. There is, my dearest Jakub, a small hummingbird outside my window. Could it still be one of the two my Papa's cousin returned with from his travels last year? Is it true the speed at which its heart beats? Up to six hundred beats per minute? Is this a sign?

Anna quickly placed her fountain pen in her desk and hastily rolled up her letter. The audible growling noises from her stomach and her watering mouth hastened her movements. As she reached for the empty green glass bottle in which to place her letter, she accidentally knocked it over, sending it to the ground with a crash. Anna stared at the broken shards of glass as she slowly stood up, pale faced, to find a broom. "Is this your sign, Jakub?" she whispered to herself as she left her room, angry that she would now have to sneak back down into the dark cellar to retrieve and prepare another of Mama's green glass apple juice bottles. In her distracted state Anna did not remember the letter she had left on her desk.

"F...F...Frau Ahrens?" Anna asked, surprised to find the old maid in the kitchen. She had not seen Henriette Ahrens in the kitchen since the last year when Sigrid was ill and unable to leave her bed for two weeks. Anna barely knew this woman who had fed her own mother as a child.

"Good morning, Fraulein," the old maid said, looking up at Anna with a nod of the head.

"Wh...wh...where is Sigrid?" Anna asked, disappointed that Sigrid was not in the kitchen. She had looked forward to speaking with her this morning. Something about this day had seemed positive, and full of possibility, at least until she dropped her bottle and then found Henriette in the kitchen.

"She has left for the sea," the old maid said as she added a pinch of salt to the boiling eggs."

"W...w...when did she leave?" Anna stuttered, frustrated by her stuttering and that the day was turning against her.

"The Baroness sent for me early this morning," the old woman said glancing at Anna with a peculiar expression. "Frau Steinmeyer was not...feeling well," the maid said, as Anna glanced at her sideways and turned to leave.

"W...w...what was wrong with her?" Anna burst out, momentarily forgetting her own troubles. Henriette considered Anna for a moment before answering, as though weighing the impact of her answer.

"It is none of my concern, nor yours, Fraulein, but I believe it is a delicate matter...of the heart."

"W…w…what?" Anna half shouted in disbelief. "W…w…what sort of matter of the heart? P…p…please, Frau Ahrens," she begged as she looked at this old woman who likely knew more family secrets than anyone on the estate. Henriette looked at Anna with quick, bright eyes that belied the years spent observing the world. Anna knew, without pushing it any further, that Frau Ahrens had already spoken all she was going to. Any further questioning would be met with stoic silence. She did not begrudge the old maid her silence. She herself knew all too well that the old woman would not have been around as long as she had, especially with her mother in charge, if she betrayed every secret she witnessed or heard.

"Why did she tell me of Sigrid's matter of the heart?" Anna whispered to herself, as she left the kitchen with neither the answer to her question on the whereabouts of Sigrid, nor something tasty to quiet her angry stomach. Sigrid's love life sparked Anna's interest even more than the broken glass on the floor of her bedroom. "Why do they all disappear without a word?" she wondered aloud as she closed the kitchen door.

"Maria! Maria," Anna called out breathlessly as she stormed into her sister's home. She welcomed the smell of fresh baked bread, thankful she had decided to leave the main house and question Maria about Sigrid's mysterious and abrupt departure.

"Quiet! In here," her sister called from the sitting room, sounding agitated. Anna quickly ran through the kitchen, stealing a freshly baked roll, as Adelgunde, Maria's recently hired maid, gave her an irritated look. Apologizing, Anna carefully opened the door to the sitting room, where she found her sister seated before the small stove with her sleeping daughter cradled in her arms. Anna quietly walked over to her sister and gently touched the light red fuzz on the top of her niece's head, so similar in color to her own hair and Maria's.

"Have you heard?" Maria asked her sister as she gently rocked little Alexandra back and forth.

"I j…j…just found out," Anna answered with a mouth full of bread. Anna watched as her sister shook her head in disapproval.

"Anna, please, wait to speak until you have swallowed," Maria whispered. "Did Mama tell you?" she asked Anna, who was busy shoving another large piece of bread into her mouth.

119

"Mmm, Mmm," she answered with closed mouth, shaking her head. "F…F…Frau Ahrens told me," she continued, covering her full mouth with her hand as she spoke.

"Anna!" Maria chided, disturbing the sleeping baby. Both women waited and held their breath, sighing with relief when the infant continued to sleep. "I could not understand a word you said," Maria whispered, still shaking her head.

"I said, F…F…Frau Ahrens told me," Anna repeated more clearly, "just now."

"Old Henriette? How on earth does she already know that I am with child again," Maria asked with a perplexed expression, "I only just told Mama yesterday."

"W…w…what? You are with child…again?" Anna blurted out, quickly covering her mouth with her free hand. The confused expression on Maria's face quickly changed.

"You did not know I was with child, did you?"

"Nnn, Nnn," Anna replied shaking her head, trying hard to chew and swallow the last of her roll quickly.

"So, if you came with news, and it is not about me, then it must be something important to you," Maria spoke slowly, as she studied her sister's face which was so similar to her own. They shared the same green eyes and red hair, only Maria was petite, and Anna was large boned.

Anna recounted what she had learned from the old maid. Maria listened intently as Anna listed off her theories as to why Sigrid had really left.

"Do you really believe she has a secret lover?" Maria asked, intrigued by the whole situation.

"F…F…Frau Ahrens specifically said it was a m…m…matter of the heart," Anna said, as she tried to guess what else would possess Sigrid to leave abruptly in the middle of the night.

"But how do you know she went to Ruegen? There are many places she could have gone." Maria said, annoying Anna with her rational question.

"Oh Maria, I do not know, I just assumed she was going to the summer cottage at the shore. That is the only sea I have ever known her to frequent, and always with us." As the two sisters sat next to each other and attempted to figure out this new mystery, Sigrid sat in a lonely passenger train, headed towards Ruegen, the one place she could be alone with her thoughts for a while.

Anna did not return back to the main house until after dinner. As she walked under the dark, moonless sky, with all traces of stars hidden behind thick clouds, she thought of the unexpected day she had spent with her sister. Anna and Maria were intrigued by the thought that Sigrid had a secret lover somewhere out there, one she had kept hidden from the sisters. But now her own life's questions again came to the forefront of her mind. Maria, always the wiser older sister, had suggested Anna, with her exceptional English skills, work as a translator of foreign papers. Anna knew Maria wanted her to direct her thoughts in other directions.

"Many of my friends, women of good social standing, have volunteered their time," Maria had suggested to her. Anna knew her sister meant well, but Maria did not understand the hope to which she still clung. The hope that Jakub would return to her, with arms spread wide, eager to spend the rest of his days with her. "You know, Anna," her sister had said with averted eyes, "he will not return." Anna did not want this, how could Maria be so sure? "Anna, look at what is happening in our world. He is a Jew. You told me so yourself," Maria stated, knowing what emotional turmoil Anna had been through, a condition exacerbated by the loss of a child. Reaching for Anna's hand, she asked, "What kind of life is left for him here? What kind of life is there for you anywhere but here?" Anna could not find any words with which to respond to her sister. Her mind felt suddenly numb. The pleasant day she had spent with her sister seemed to disappear, as memories of Jakub and her lost child took over her thoughts. She suddenly felt stifled by the warm room. Picking up her coat she had squeezed Maria's hand and walked outside into the cool night.

Anna returned to her own room. It took her a moment to realize that something in her room was amiss. The pillows on her bed had been lined up straight across the headboard. Also, the room looked tidier than she had remembered leaving it. Suddenly, the thought struck her that she had never returned to sweep up the shards of glass, all that remained of her mother's apple juice bottle. A sudden heat swept over her as she felt her heart race. "M...m...my letter," she cried, almost in a squeal. "M...m...my letter!" Initial panic quickly gave way to a rage which suddenly surged through her veins. The letter she had left on her desk was gone. "W...W...Who?" she demanded of the dimly lit room, "Who...w...w...would violate m...m...my private quarters?"

Storming down the stairs she first entered the dark, empty kitchen, and then continued her march towards her father's study. Swinging the door open, she stomped in, her face a shade of crimson, which complemented her hair, giving her the overall appearance of a tomato about to burst.

"Wh... Wh...Who was in my room?" Anna yelled at her father, unaware that her father was in the middle of a discussion with a young official. Slowly leaning back in his large chair, the Baron puffed his pipe and removed his spectacles.

"Officer Geist, may I introduce my daughter, Anna," he spoke with a cold calm that startled Anna enough to knock some sense into her raging brain.

"Sir," Anna managed to utter without stuttering, avoiding the young man's eyes. "Papa." Anna quickly turned to leave, but was surprised when her father invited her to stay.

"Please, Anna, be so kind as to grace us with your company for a little while," the Baron spoke to his daughter, daring her to reject his invitation.

"Papa," Anna nodded in acknowledgment and demurely sat down on the small ottoman that she had sat on so many times.

It did not take long for Anna to figure out what her father was doing. Was this one of her mother's ideas, or had he come up with this one on his own? Somehow she could not believe that her mother did not have a hand in this. "Always scheming," Anna spoke silently to herself, as she wondered why her mother was not here to witness this theatrical performance.

"Anna, Officer Geist was...," the Baron addressed his daughter. He had known Anna his whole life, and knew his wife's plans to introduce his daughter to a young officer of good breeding would fail miserably, but he was forced to keep up the charade to appease the Baroness. It was fortunate Anna had walked in when she did, the young man was just getting ready to leave.

"Please, call me Dieter," the young man nervously interrupted.

"Yes, Dieter, he must leave now, but maybe there is an opportunity for the two of you to visit together in the near future," said the Baron. The level of discomfort the Baron felt was not visible, and even his daughter was unable to see through him this time. Anna watched her father, marveling at his sudden ability to hide emotions. Young Officer Geist, not as practiced in the ways of facial deception, looked as red as fire. The uniform he wore appeared like a costume to Anna, and she watched beads of perspiration form on his brow and travel first slowly and then more quickly down his flushed face.

"It was nice to meet you, Dieter," Anna said, as she curtsied and handed the young officer her handkerchief with which to dry his perspiration. Officer Geist, incorrectly interpreting this small act, promptly managed to drop the handkerchief. As he scrambled to pick it up, Anna used the opportunity to steal away from her father and suitor, but not before she gave her father her own cold stare.

Anna would later find out it was Henriette who had swept away the shards of glass in her room. Anna never would believe that the old maid had no knowledge of the letter left on a desk. The fate of the letter, number three to her beloved Jakub, would never be known to her; it had somehow slipped into the small space between her desk and the wall.

Travels of Letter 16
South Island, New Zealand
December 1964

"E tangi ana koe, Hine e hine, E egenge ana koe, Hine e hine," the young boy sang as he built his sand castle. Sensing a presence behind him, the boy turned and peered up at a girl who stood silently watching him. How long had she been standing there? He didn't want to know. Had the girl heard him singing, he wondered, feeling a heat rise in his face. Building his sand castle was a private matter. Singing was a private matter for him too. It wasn't meant for the ears of another, especially not a Pakeha. Grandfather had told him the Pakeha did not understand the traditions of the Maori and needed to be educated. Unlike his grandfather, he had no interest in educating them, he did not trust them. Grandmother did not trust them either, she said they did not respect their traditions. Looking back down at his sandcastle, he decided to ignore the Pakeha, maybe she would go away.

"What are you building?" the pale faced girl asked with a strange accent. Ignoring her question he dug a little faster, hoping she would get the message and leave him alone. He was a man after all, doing man's work. He shouldn't be bothered while he was working. That's what Grandfather told Grandmother when he was out in the shed, but Grandfather was usually smoking and playing cards with his friends. "Is it a mountain?" the girl asked, sitting down on her knees next to him and interrupting his work again.

"No, it's a sand castle," he answered, annoyed with her stupidity.

"Why does your castle have a bottle on top of it?" she asked as she carefully touched the cool green glass with her finger. "Did you find it on the beach?"

"It's not a bottle, it's a tower," he snapped, repressing the urge to throw sand at the girl.

"Are you a Maori?" the girl asked, patting sand on his castle. He didn't answer, but watched as the girl gathered wet sand and dripped it on his castle, making tall pointed towers. Wondering where the girl was from, he picked up some wet sand and tried it himself. Pleased with the tower he had built, he made another one.

"Make some more around here," he said to the girl, pointing at the base of sandcastle. It was his sandcastle and he needed to take charge again. Ignoring his orders, the girl dripped wet sand on his glass tower. Watching the sand slide slowly down the glass, he thought he should probably ask the girl something, maybe where she was from.

As though reading his thoughts, she said, "I'm from Philadelphia, the city of brotherly love. We all love each other."

"That's stupid," he said, deepening the moat around the castle and pondering just how all the people in a city could all love each other.

"Well, not everyone loves each other. My mom says you can't love everyone, but you can try," the girl added as an afterthought, placing tiny shells around the base of the glass bottle. "Have you ever been to Philadelphia?" the girl asked as she sat back on her heels to look at him. He had no idea where Philadelphia was, but he didn't want her to know that.

"No," he answered casually.

"Well, if you ever come to Philadelphia, you can stay with me. I have a bunk bed, but you would have to sleep on the bottom. I sleep on the top." The boy stopped working to examine the pale girl more closely. Had she just invited him to her home, just like that? She didn't even know him.

"You are, aren't you?" she asked, looking at him patiently with clear blue eyes that reminded him of water.

"Are what?" he asked gruffly.

"Maori," she replied as she examined the neat row of shells she had placed on the sandcastle. "Do you have any tattoos? Dad says they're part of your culture or something like that. Mom says only bikers and criminals have tattoos, but he says she doesn't know what she's talking about, and he's going to get one on his," she pointed at her backside, making both of them laugh. The boy realized that he actually liked this girl with all of her stories. "My dad's a, I don't know what you call it, but he studies different people and how they live and stuff, you know the kinds of things they do." The boy listened in silence as the girl talked on about her dad and her friend Tommy from a place called Jamaica, and the cat with fleas her mom wanted to get rid of. The boy had never had many friends, especially not a friend from someplace faraway. He was happy he had not walked to the market with his grandmother and two younger brothers today.

Wishing the day would never end, he looked at the girl and said, "I am."

"Am what?" she asked a little confused.

"Maori," he answered with obvious pride.

"I know," she said and smiled at him with straight, white teeth. Should he invite her to the Meeting House tonight? There was a party tonight for his dad's cousin, but what would his grandmother say? As long as he could remember, his family had not invited a foreigner to the Meeting House, maybe it was time someone did. The boy and girl continued to work on their sandcastle, toiling side-by-side in silence. It was not an uncomfortable silence, but a silence that comes from knowing that all is right with the world. When he finally spoke he hoped the girl did not hear the tremor in his voice,

"So, we're having a party, over at the Meeting House, tonight. It's, uh, for my dad's cousin." The girl watched him with a curious expression that reminded him of his dog when the dog wanted something from him, but didn't know what. "You wanna come?" he asked, nervously rubbing his sandy hands on his legs.

The girl's eyes grew wide at the offer, "Really?" she asked, unable to hide her excitement.

"Yeah, sure," the boy answered, trying to sound casual.

"My dad says you need a special invitation from a Maori to enter the Meeting House." The boy was pleased the girl was familiar with this tradition. "It's no big deal," he answered, his rapid heartbeat belying his outwardly casual demeanor.

"Hahona! Hahona!" he heard his grandmother's calls, but ignored her for the moment. "Hahona! Come now, boy," his grandmother persisted, as she turned to leave.

"I've gotta go help, you know, for tonight," the boy said, as a strange sad feeling washed over him like a wave. "So I'll see you tonight?" he asked.

The pale girl with the clear blue eyes looked at him with a big smile. "Yeah," she answered as Hahona backed away from her. "I'm Sally," the girl said, just as Hahona turned around to walk away. Glancing back at her, he raised a hand to wave goodbye.

The tide came in and washed away the sand castle, and along with it, the glass bottle. A sand castle two strangers had built together, only to part later as friends. This friendship, created in a moment, would endure across the seas and over a lifetime.

Cape May, New Jersey
Fall 2011

The strange woman was right, it was a beautiful day. The weather this time of year was really hit or miss, usually it missed. But on the days it didn't rain, the turning leaves and the warm noon-day sun lent an almost heavenly feel to the world around me. Inhaling deeply, I dragged my bare feet in the sand, wishing Warren was here to give me some advice. The thought made me almost laugh out loud. Was I serious? Ask my deceased husband advice about another man? What kind of lunatic was I? The light breeze was just enough to force me to keep my coat on, and brought unfamiliar ocean smells inland from the east. The Pacific smells different than the Atlantic I thought, looking out at the mildly choppy sea. Reaching my hand into my pocket, I gently fingered the rolled up letter I had carefully wrapped in plastic along with my odd little black stone. What was wrong with me? It was as though the letter reminded me of its presence; ensured I did not forget its existence. Resisting the urge to sit down and read the letter yet again, I stood and looked out over the wide sea. No matter what I did, I couldn't get the letter out of my mind. Everything about it seemed to be legitimate, even the paper. Then again, I wasn't an expert on old letters, so it could very likely be a hoax. Any moment some hidden television crew could jump out of the bushes, airing my idiocy on national television. I needed medication.

For me, temptation always won out over self-control. No longer resisting my urges to read the letter again, I sat down on the dry sand and wiggled my toes deep into the underlying damp sand. Sensing a presence, I turned around abruptly. Half-expecting Charlie, I was surprised to find no one there. I couldn't shake the feeling that someone or something was watching me, but as far as I could see, there was no one around. Off in the distance there was a young mother with her three children, dressed in warm coats and bare feet. I had heard the mother say they were digging holes to China when I passed by earlier. I had to smile at the thought. Did every young child think they would reach China? I know I did. At what point does the human mind mature enough to realize you weren't going to get remotely close to China? Or figure out the Santa Claus lie? As for me, I still wished Santa was real.

Gently stroking Anna's letter, I wished I could transport myself back to such an innocent time. Where death and work and bills were not a part of reality, where they didn't even exist. A movement out on the ocean caught my eye. Shading my eyes with the letter, I tried to see past the glare of the reflecting sun. Where were my sunglasses? No one from Los Angeles goes anywhere without their sunglasses. Squinting, I stared at the blur on the sea, chiding myself that I had not yet visited an optometrist. Warren had repeatedly urged me to visit the eye doctor. It was clear I needed glasses.

As the small object came into focus, I realized it was a boat, still too far out for me to distinguish further details. Watching as the boat drew closer, the people aboard also came into focus, barely. Something about the boat and the people on it struck me as odd, but I couldn't figure out what. And speaking of odd, I had to steal another glance at my letter. "Who are you, Jakub?" I whispered. What has this woman Anna endured for you? And for so many years? This letter had to be legitimate. How could so much emotion otherwise be trapped in one glass bottle? What was it about these mysterious lovers, whose unfinished love story so captivated my own imagination? I thought of my own love letters from Warren which accompanied me on this trip. They had been such a source of consolation for me over the last six months, when nothing and no one else was. It was only these last two days since…since "I met Charlie," I said aloud, that I had not obsessed over Warren's letters. "Well, you've got someone else's love letter to obsess over," my rational mind spoke, as I briefly looked up at the boat that had come into full view on an ocean that was now completely calm. I had never seen the ocean this still before.

Now that I had a clear view of the boat, I could see there was definitely something odd about it. Its wooden frame with oars lacked any sails, giving it an almost primitive appearance. And the people aboard…it was the young, dark-skinned woman, amongst all the men, who caught my eye. I sat frozen in time, watching the young woman, dressed in a loose-fitted summer dress, raise her hand slightly, as though in greeting. Turning around, now convinced there was someone behind me, I was again surprised to find no-one. A chill ran down my spine as I watched the young woman hold out her hand, as though reaching out to me. Was it me she wanted, I wondered, as Anna's letter that I was still holding rolled itself up. Reaching in my pocket for my plastic bag, I briefly looked down to slip the precious letter into the protective plastic.

"The boat," I half-shouted when I looked up again. The boat was gone. It was just there, and the woman. I know I saw the waving woman. Looking up and down the shore, I felt my heart beating in my ears. I quickly jumped up and walked to the water's edge. Where was the woman? Where was the damn boat? Looking out at the sea I really began questioning my sanity. "My eyes aren't that bad," I whispered as I felt an imminent panic attack.

"Calm down, Di." I tried to reassure myself. "Yeah, I'm going to calm down," I spoke to the sea. There is a logical explanation, right? Hadn't I heard that one too many times in my life? "Yeah, sure, a reason for everything," I said, still speaking aloud, still trying hard to convince myself, as I walked back to retrieve my shoes and backpack, that I had not gone insane.

The sun had disappeared, its warmth replaced by dark, ripe clouds, and the temperature instantly dropped at least ten degrees. Shivering, I fell to the sand and stared out at where I was sure I had just seen this strange vessel. "I have gone mad," I said aloud as another shiver passed through my body. The sand beneath my bottom felt cold. Pulling the green knit "nothing" out of my backpack, I folded it and shoved it under my bottom, hoping the woman from the airport wouldn't mind too much. "Well, at least it is good for something," I spoke absently, thinking of the woman who likely mourned the loss of her green knit "nothing."

Sitting in the quickly cooling sand, I looked down the shore. The mother with her children was still lugging one bucket of water after another to a large sand castle they had built. "They would have seen something, they would have seen the boat," I reasoned aloud, hearing the doubt in my voice. Oh God, Warren, am I going mad? I see your face in the shower steam, I see a boat that disappears before my eyes, what's next? A padded cell? "The next thing I know I'll be wearing a straight jacket, and looking at white padded walls…the crazy lady who talks to herself," I said sarcastically, realizing with horror that I had been spending a lot of time talking to myself these days. And then there was Charlie. How does he figure into all of this? Into my crazy world? Making an effort to keep my inner conversations silent, I wondered what Warren would think about Charlie. Would he feel betrayed? I couldn't help myself, but somehow my mind steered itself toward Charlie. Was I beginning to forget Warren?

The tears that streaked down my face felt warm. Rubbing my eyes with my sleeve, I pulled my beret further down over both ears, and watched as the three children on the beach continued to carry buckets of water up the beach. Their shrieks and shouts resounded down the shore. It was time for me to leave. Bending down, I picked up the knit "nothing" I had been sitting on and shook out the sand. The soft thud on the sand barely registered in my brain. I don't know what made me look, but I bent down to pick up whatever it was that had fallen out of the green knit thing. "A brooch," I said aloud as I turned the delicate red-gold rose brooch, no bigger than a quarter, in my hand. How the heck did I miss this? I have to say I felt a bit more guilty about the woman's lost knit "nothing" knowing it had a possibly valuable brooch attached to it. But what was I to do? Nothing, I thought, gently turning the small treasure over in my hands, unable to make out what looked like letters, rubbed away, likely from years of wear? I wrapped the brooch in a clean tissue and packed it safely in the front of my backpack. Slipping on my shoes, I glanced towards the woman on the beach playing with her children one last time, and wondered what it was I had seen on the ocean.

Letter Four   *Dresden, 31. August 1939*

My Beloved Jakub,

I cannot breathe, Jakub, I cannot breathe. I awoke in the middle of another endless night and felt a weight crushing down on my chest. Have I gone mad? I was unable to breathe, unable to scream. I called out for you, my beloved, called out for you without a voice. You could not hear me. How much time has passed since you have gone? Are your thoughts ever with me? With us? Do you note the passing of time as I do? A measurement of time that begins with the day you left? It has been almost two years since you left, but my memory of you could belong to yesterday. What use is a measurement of time, when time is truly measured in moments shared, moving along much too quickly during those precious, wonderful moments, and nearly grinding to a halt during life's most unpleasant times? For myself, a day could be a week, a month, even a whole year. Sleep still eludes me many nights, but I believe that writing to you, in these darkest hours, is the only chance I have of lifting my soul from the depths into which it has fallen. I am sorry, Jakub, I know I sound mad. It is when I move between the world of dreams and waking that I am most confused and most vulnerable. The act of writing to you is a cure for my broken soul.

Much has transpired these last months, the most awful of which pertains to Maria. She bore a daughter, Marlene Elsa Alke, whose life ended the moment she saw the light of this world. There is nothing more horrible, to this I can attest, than the loss of a child. The love a mother feels for her unborn child is indescribable, Jakub. The strength with which Maria saw herself through this situation was a consolation for me, but sometimes I fear she has closed off many of her emotions. She is with child again and I fear for her health. The doctor told Maria she should have waited until she was fully healed, both physically and spiritually, before carrying another child. I heard Mama tell Papa this matter was not the concern of the doctor, but a matter that must be resolved between Maria and her husband. I have not spoken to Maria about Dieter, there are certain boundaries I feel a sister cannot cross. And besides, I must admit, he is not solely responsible; Maria will do anything to please this man and uphold her marriage.

Both Maria and Lena's small children continue to provide a ray of light where often there appears to be none. Even Papa is not immune to the infectious laughter and affections of these young ones. It is only Mama who reserves her affections, only rarely allowing any glimpse of the woman she could be to shine through. Somehow a friction has developed between Mama and I, one which has festered for some time, but has now, on occasion, ended with a regrettable exchange of words. Maria does not interpret Mama's behavior as any different, but then she does not live under the same roof as her any longer. Somehow I cannot help believing that Mama's emotional state has something to do with Sigrid, but what? I questioned her about Sigrid, who spent over two months at the Baltic Sea. Her caustic reaction to my questions and the resentment she seems to feel for Sigrid surprised me. I have never known Mama to become this emotionally involved with anyone. What surprises me even more is that Mama has not insisted that Sigrid leave. On some level, Sigrid has left though. After her two month sojourn to the sea, she spent a mere three weeks here before she departed for Munich, where she spent another month. She has returned, but seems distant, as though Mama has forbidden her to speak with me. Even Maria has noticed a change in Sigrid's behavior. And the long discussions and emotional support she provided since your disappearance have also all but vanished. Oh, Jakub, I am no longer sure who betrays whom.

Oddly, I have found almost a friend in Lena. If I am honest with myself though, I wonder if this friendship is not truly a plot to find out more information about your disappearance, as well as any evidence identifying the father of her child. As of this point in time, she has not uttered a word regarding the father of Thomas. Lena did confide in me, and I apologize that I did not mention this earlier in the letter, that her father went to meet someone the night before your disappearance to "talk about the Jew." Our night. Could that be? Is it you of whom he spoke? Could he be the catalyst which set this string of events in motion, leading to your disappearance? I have not properly thought out the details of my plan, but somehow, somewhere, I will find a way to pry this information out of old Mr. Zimmerman.

This may come as a surprise to you, Jakub, but I have found employment within the city at the "Dresden Tagesblatt." Two, and sometimes three, times a week I cycle into the city and translate foreign newspaper articles along with a number of other young women hired for the same purpose, some of whom Maria knows. I feared it would be tedious work, but actually find it quite stimulating and, at times, challenging. It is interesting to read articles about one's own country, written by someone from another country. Strange, how different their perspectives are from our own. There is only one woman at the Gazette whose political views I find not only disturbing, but offensive. For most of us, voicing our political opinions does not seem proper. Mama does not support my decision to work. She has told me, on not just one occasion, it was time for me to find a suitable husband. She has tried on three separate occasions to introduce suitors whom I find dull and boring. Even Maria, whose idea it was that I should work as an interpreter, no longer finds such employment fitting for a young woman who should be married. It is you, Jakub, and you alone I shall marry when our paths again cross one day. Am I a fool to believe in a shared future with both of us in it? I climbed up

136

the hayloft yesterday. Somehow I sensed the love we shared, as though it again lingers there. When I closed my eyes I smelled the hay and could almost hear your laughter, feel your warm kisses. Oh, Jakub, I so yearn for your embrace. With thoughts of you in my mind, and love for only you in my heart, I say goodnight.

Love Eternally,
Anna v. Marschalkt

Post Script: There is an underlying tension in this home that parallels the rising tensions in my country. This tension which surrounds me, surrounds all I know, threatens to consume me, but when I hold you close through my letters all I sense is an eternal calm. How I wish this sensation were not of such a fleeting nature.

Anna, with her comforter wrapped around her, held onto her fountain pen as she looked out her window. The cool fall wind howled outside as branches from the oak tree tapped against her window. "Why?" she asked the darkness, "why?"

When Anna awoke the next morning with her head resting on her desk it took her a moment to gather her thoughts, and move her stiff neck. Had she written a letter last night or had that been a dream? Looking down at the smeared letter, she felt rather disconcerted at having little memory of writing it. Picking up the smudged paper, she read the words that seemed almost foreign to her. These were definitely her words, but why did the late hours, or maybe the darkness itself, bring out such dark and helpless emotions? Why did the new morning often bring with it the hope for a new beginning, the anticipation or expectation that anything was possible?

As Anna stared out the window, which now painted a very different picture than the darkness she last viewed through it, she realized it was all about hope. In the solitude of darkness, crystal clear logic defeated idealistic hope. No, logic did not defeat hope, it did not even allow hope to exist. There was no opportunity to keep hope alive. "No," Anna argued with herself, "it is not the opportunity that is lacking, it is the reason to keep it alive that is lacking." And now, on a beautiful day, she basked once again in the hope that love, her love for Jakub, and his love for her, would endure not just another day, but all eternity. "It is because you are not alone with your thoughts during the day," her rational mind spoke as though chiding her for her ignorance. No, Anna thought, that was not correct either. She was, after all, still alone with her thoughts at the present moment.

Anna felt her head begin to spin. This was all too much to think about this early in the morning. Stretching her neck, she lifted herself and the comforter and walked to her bed. Somehow, she did not get the rest she so desperately needed while sleeping in a seated position. Drifting into a state of unconscious bliss, Anna dreamt of Jakub on a beach. "Jakub," she called out to the man she loved, who seemed always a few centimeters beyond her grasp.

Waking with a start, Anna pushed her comforter from her body and slipped out of bed, gasping as the cold air in the room wrapped itself around her body. She picked up the letter, tightly rolled it up and shoved it into an empty green apple juice jar. As she melted her wax to form an airtight seal, she thought about the day ahead and what it would have in store for her. There was no work for her today at the newspaper, maybe it was time to talk to Sigrid.

This morning she had a plan, she thought, as she walked down the stairs towards the kitchen. She was going to confront Sigrid about her mystery lover. Why did she keep him so secret? She hoped Sigrid would be in the kitchen as usual, but one never did know these days, given Sigrid's odd behavior and frequent disappearances. Anna opened the kitchen door and was relieved to find Sigrid there, and not old Frau Ahrens. She approached the maid with the same emotions she had since she was a small child.

"Good m....m...morning, Siggi," Anna spoke cheerfully, almost swallowing her words when she saw the look on Sigrid's face. It was then that Anna smelled chamomile and realized Sigrid was not alone in the kitchen. Someone sat at the kitchen table with a towel covering her head, presumably to inhale the steam from a pot of hot chamomile tea. The sounds of protest escaping from beneath the towel, as well as an occasional small arm, made it apparent that it was Lena with her young son, Thomas. But why did Sigrid look upon them with such disapproval? Anna watched as Sigrid prepared the breakfast, all the while mumbling to herself and intermittently shaking her head.

"Oh, Fraulein von Marschalkt," Lena said, as she appeared from under her towel with a bright red, damp face, very similar to the small, plump red-faced child who emerged with her. "I am sorry that you must find me in such a state," Lena said, pointing to her tousled hair with one hand, while keeping her young son's hands away from the hot liquid in front of them with the other hand. "It is Thomas, he has been up all night with a horrible cough...the chamomile steam soothes him."

"Good m...m...morning, little T...T...Thomas," Anna said, stroking his damp, cheek. "I think you g...g...grew a few centimeters s...s...since yesterday." It always made Anna's heart skip to see the little boy and the smile that spread across his face when he saw her. "Will y..y..you call th...th...the doctor?" Anna asked, as she watched Lena dry her young son's face.

"No, he seems a bit better now," Lena answered and picked up the pot and carried it to the wash basin, staying clear of Sigrid. It was apparent to Anna that Lena knew of Sigrid's sentiments, or was smart enough to avoid her altogether.

"Leave it," Sigrid hissed at Lena, motioning for her to leave the kitchen. Distressed by Sigrid's behavior, Lena nodded at Anna and quickly departed the kitchen.

"I am n...n...not leaving th....th...this kitchen until you t...t... tell me what is g...g...going on, Siggi," Anna demanded, realizing full well she had no power whatsoever over this woman. If Sigrid was going to tell her something, she would, and then only on her terms. If Sigrid chose not to, well, then she would never know, but there was no reason she could not try to extract at least some information from her.

"How can he allow that...that...common whore into this house?" Sigrid spoke, with an anger Anna had never heard before.

"Sigrid," Anna cried, "How c...c...can you speak of h...h...her in such a manner? We know n...n...nothing of her situation. And Thomas, he is such a sw...sw...sweet boy." Anna watched as Sigrid furiously dropped an egg into a pot of boiling water, causing it to rupture, only to be joined a moment later by two more ruptured eggs. Well, there won't be any boiled eggs for breakfast, Anna thought, somewhat disappointed by the idea.

"And w...w...who is th...th...this 'he' you s...s...speak of, Siggi?" Anna asked as she watched Sigrid's chest rise and fall too quickly.

"The Baron, your father," Sigrid shouted, dropping an egg to the ground. Quickly running to fetch a rag, Anna wondered if Sigrid felt threatened by Lena's presence. Did she fear she was going to be replaced? Sigrid herself replaced Frau Ahrens at one point in time.

"You are m...m...mistaken, Siggi," Anna said softly, "it was not Papa, but Mama who demanded Lena join us in the big house." Sigrid turned with her mouth agape to stare at Anna. Sigrid moved her lips, but no sound came out. Anna watched the maid's face change from pale to ashen and helped her sit down at the kitchen table when it became evident that her knees were shaking.

"The Baroness?" Sigrid muttered to herself.

"I h...h...heard Mama and Papa arguing in th...th...their bed ch...ch...chamber, as they always do," Anna said, feeling her face flush with embarrassment. She was angry, she did not normally stutter this much with Sigrid. "I...i....it was M...M...Mama."

"Eavesdropping again!" Sigrid snapped, with an anger that wasn't truly directed at Anna.

"W...w...well," Anna stuttered, embarrassed over her eavesdropping. How could she not, she tried to convince herself. They did nothing to lower their voices. No, this was not true either, Anna remembered. There were times when she knew her parents spoke in angry, hushed tones to one another. She had been tempted, but had never actually pressed her ear to the door, to listen like Maria had when they were children.

Anna had been sure Sigrid would be relieved by the news that it was the Baroness who had insisted Lena live in the house, but it hadn't improved Sigrid's state of mind. Mama would never let Sigrid go, of this Anna was sure. Sigrid had been with them too long. Anna watched Sigrid's facial expression slowly change from shock to a nod of understanding. "Now I understand," the maid spoke, but not to Anna.

"What am *I* missing? Where is *my* understanding?" Anna whispered to herself, as she watched Sigrid gain control of her emotions and remove the boiling mass of smashed eggs from the water. Anna wondered why she never stuttered when she whispered or sang. "Maybe I should just whisper all the time," she again whispered to herself.

Unexpectedly, Sigrid turned to Anna and stroked her cheek, the way Anna herself had done just minutes ago with little Thomas. With a brief smile passing over her lips, Sigrid stepped back and considered Anna for a moment with eyes that seared into Anna's soul.

"Siggi, w...w...what is it really?" Anna asked, wishing Sigrid would confide in her so she could help. Why would Sigrid not confide in her? Why wouldn't anyone confide in her, Anna wondered.

Removing her apron, Sigrid handed it to Anna. "I believe, young Fraulein, you will be making the breakfast this morning," Sigrid said, leaving a stunned Anna standing in the kitchen.

The Baroness did not appear surprised when she saw her daughter enter the dining room with the breakfast cart, one hour later than the regular breakfast schedule.

"G…g…good morning, M…M…Mama," Anna stuttered, expecting her mother to fall over from shock at the sight of her daughter serving the morning meal. Anna was surprised her mother sat in silence as she served the cold coffee and burnt rolls. What was even more surprising was the fact that her mother did not once question why exactly she was serving the meal and not Sigrid. Nor did she comment on the lack of her morning egg. In the all years she had dined with her mother, Anna could not remember a day where the Baroness did not consume a soft boiled egg for the morning meal.

Anna sat down to join her mother and wondered where her father was. In the past her mother and father always shared their morning meal together. It had been the noon meal that brought the whole family together. But in recent months there was always some reason why at least one family member did not appear at the noon meal. There was an awkward silence between the two women as both joylessly partook of their meal.

It was Anna who broke the silence. "I a…a…am s…s…sorry, M…M…Mama. I d…d…do n…n…not wish to shame you." The Baroness looked at her daughter with expressionless eyes. Anna had often envied her mother's ability to look at another individual without revealing even the slightest emotion, often making her subjects squirm. Anna felt herself squirming in her seat as her mother continued to stare at her. If there was one person on this earth who really made her stutter, it was her mother. "W…w…why do you treat m…m…me as a stranger?" Anna blurted out before she had the chance to think about what she had said. She knew that she had grabbed her mother's attention by the sound of her mother's coffee cup dropping onto the saucer.

"It is you who makes herself the stranger," her mother replied without emotion, as she patted the corner of her mouth with a napkin and pushed her chair back, as though to leave.

"Oh, M…m…mama," Anna said softly as tears threatened to overflow, "why d…d…do you not l…l…love me?"

The Baroness stood and moved towards the door. Haltingly, this proud woman turned to meet Anna's eyes. "I have always loved you. It is what you do that I can not love," her mother spoke, with such conviction that Anna wanted to run and embrace her, begging her forgiveness. Unable to move from her chair, Anna watched as her mother left the dining room, and with her departure, the moment of reconciliation was gone as well. Anna felt alone as the sound of her mother's rhythmic footsteps faded as she walked down the long hallway. This was a loneliness that transcended the large dining room, a loneliness devoid of anything living. It was a void that even a mother, a sister, or a dear maid could not fill. It was a void that comes with the knowledge that we are born alone and we die alone.

"Oh, Jakub," Anna cried as the tears finally broke, streaming down her face. "Oh, my love," she sobbed, dabbing at her nose with her handkerchief, "That you m…m…may never die alone."

That evening Anna did not appear for the evening meal, which was not unusual, as she often shared the evening meal with her sister's family. On this cool summer evening she cycled the three kilometers to where her stream met the Elbe River. Grateful for the clear sky, Anna spoke a brief prayer for her beloved and tossed her fourth bottle into the fast moving river. Anna would never know that two days later a fisherman would find the bottle. The bottle would remain with the fisherman for over five years, at which point it, along with the fisherman, would be destroyed by an enemy bomb.

Travels of Letter 16
Research Station 6, Antarctica
January, 1969

Dave, the Research Team Leader, had warned them, in no uncertain terms, to follow three cardinal rules when leaving the station. Rule one: no one, and he meant no one, went anywhere alone. Rule number two: tell the others at the station where you're headed. And rule number three: always take the walkie talkies. He had followed the rules, that much he could remember. Or had he? He could feel the walkie talkie pressed beneath him, likely smashed to bits. Oh God, he was starting to feel delirious with the cold, at least those parts of his body he could still feel. He was sure he had broken his back, but at least it wasn't his neck. Or maybe it was his neck. No, he'd be dead if it were his neck, and this sure wasn't Heaven, more likely Hell. And Sherri, God, where was Sherri? He couldn't hear her, couldn't move to help her. Goddamn it, if something happened to Sherri, he may as well die right now. Floating in and out of consciousness, Edmund wondered how long it would be before Death stood before him, maybe he was here already. With his face pressed almost into the wall of a crevasse though, he couldn't see anything around him.

145

How had he come to be in this desolate place, he wondered with increasing apathy. Captain Cook had been right, the world didn't need Antarctica. No, he knew that wasn't true, he wasn't thinking clearly anymore. The world desperately needed Antarctica and its ice shelf to regulate world climate. So, how was it that he came to be here? He tried to think and make sense of things. As long as he could think clearly, hold one rational thought, he was still alive, not necessarily alright, but alive. Unfortunately, his thoughts were no longer clear and rational. He knew his name was Edmund Steiner; yes, that's right, he was named after Sir Edmund Hillary, his father used to joke, because of his love for the mountains. The joke was pretty accurate though, it was his love of the mountains and the extreme places on earth that drew him to this place.

The morning had started so well, hadn't it? There had been reason to celebrate something, only he didn't recall what the reason was. Was it Sherri, he was sure it had been about Sherri. An anniversary, that's what it was, an anniversary. He and Sherri had been at Station 16 for one year. But there was more, much more. He closed his eyes to rest just a little while. He was so tired, but strangely at peace.

From somewhere deep inside he heard his mother's voice calling out to him, "Edmund, wake up dear, you'll be late for school." No, he wasn't late for school, his subconscious mind reminded him as he drifted back to consciousness. Jesus, if he fell asleep he would be done for.

"You are done for, you old fool," he tried to whisper between violently chattering teeth. He had no idea how long he had been lying in the crevasse or where Sherri was. Had she fallen in too? Sherri, his fiancé. That is what he had tried so hard to recall. He had proposed to her this morning, at the Station, in front of everyone. Everyone. That was the problem with this place. So desolate, yet one could never be alone. Then again, none of the others had made a love connection now, had they?

"Hey, Frosty, that you," he asked without moving his lips, as he stared at the large snowman walking around before his eyes.

"Sure is, Edmund, and if you're really talking to me then you're more crazy than even you thought," the large snowman with coal

146

black eyes replied without moving his mouth. "You know, Edmund, why don't you come with me to some place warm, someplace dry? How about Hawaii?" the snowman asked, again without moving the smile plastered to his face.

"I knew you'd show up sooner or later. Just didn't think you'd look like a snowman," Edmund replied, with blue lips tightly pressed together, "but then again, snowmen always scared the daylights outta me as a kid."

Sherri. Her name, or was it her voice, rocketed into his sub-conscious, pulling at him, pleading with him to wake up. Sherri, he thought groggily as he struggled to regain consciousness, she was why he was out here today. It wasn't to gather data, it was to find a moment alone, for just the two of them to enjoy a small part of their engagement in private. Somehow the snowman had managed to creep out of his subconscious, and now confronted him head on.

"Come on, Eddie! You don't mind if I call you Eddie, do you? They're never gonna find you, you didn't even tell em where you were headed," the snowman smiled. "You broke rule number two, Ed. You don't mind if I call you Ed, do you?"

They hadn't told the others where they were headed. The snow-man was right, they hadn't. The Goddamn rules. "We followed two outta three of them. That should count for something!" Edmund yelled without a voice, as he was suddenly hit by the harsh realization that no one would ever find them alive.

Edmund heard a moan somewhere close by. Was it close by? Was it the snowman? Sound had a way of playing tricks on you in a cre-vasse. Something beneath you could sound like it was above you. That had to be Sherri. He tried to call out to her, but his chattering teeth and frozen vocal chords only let out a quiet croak. Frozen, something about the word triggered his memory. Damn fool, he thought, every-thing around here was frozen. No, it was something else. That's right, the green bottle, the green bottle Sherri found frozen in the ice. Why was she so fascinated with the damn thing, it was only a bottle. She said it could be of historical importance, something from Shackleton's crew, maybe. The damn thing probably slid down the crevasse and straight into hell, he thought, as the snowman stared at him with an open mouth, revealing sharp, pointy teeth.

"Edmund, Edmund," he heard her calling for him, but she sounded weak, so weak. His own pulse felt weak and his breathing labored. Feeling the darkness begin to surround him once again like a warm blanket, he knew the snowman was standing close by. He didn't hear Sherri again, likely she too had already slipped into unconsciousness, blessed unconsciousness, maybe the snowman had engulfed her already. Edmund was certain, as he closed his eyes, that he would never again open them to this world.

Edmund felt the snowman surround him. Death felt warm and comfortable he thought, and its voice was so soft and soothing now. He heard Death calling out to him by name again, "Edmund, Edmund? Can you hear me Edmund?" He tried to make sense of it all. Why would the snowman ask if he could hear him? Of course he could hear him.

"I think he'll be okay, his pulse is stable and his breathing is normal," the same voice stated, with what sounded like great relief. Edmund recognized this voice. Confused, he wondered how the voice of the snowman could sound so familiar, so comforting. It didn't make sense, he felt as though he were swimming through a giant bowl of jell-o, with the surface just out of reach. It was when he heard Sherri's voice and felt her small hand on his arm that he opened his eyes again.

"Sherri," he croaked in a barely recognizable voice, "Sherri, you're alive."

"Honey, you are too, and you're gonna be alright, do you hear me? You're going to be okay."

"Am I...," Edmund started, too scared to finish the question. He stared at Sherri who was bundled up on a cot right next to him.

"Paralyzed?" she asked, finishing his question for him. "No, but you've got to hold real still. You did break your back, but I swear, you're gonna be fine," she reassured him with a light stroke of the hand.

"And you, everything ok?" he asked, tapping her hand with his stiff fingers, three of which were blackened with frostbite. Sherri nodded with a smile.

"How, how'd you find us?" he croaked at the man beside his cot.

"The bottle," Dave answered flatly, "We never woulda found ya'all without it." Answering Edmund's confused look, he added, "we spotted the bottle ya'all left in the snow. Damn thing fell in after ya, just after we reached the crevasse. Damn lucky we saw it, I say. We would never have found you otherwise."

Cape May, New Jersey
Fall 2011

Lost in thought, I moved through the town in a daze. The events of the day were like a jumbled dream now. The woman in the boat, the woman in the store, the woman in the diner, and now the beautiful brooch. Was this all some strange coincidence or was there something bizarre about the women in Cape May? A shiver ran down my spine as a strong gust of wind almost blew my beret from my head. Grabbing for it at the last moment, I heard someone calling my name. It was him. How could I forget about him? Turning around I looked for the now familiar face that belonged to the voice.

"Diana, over here," Charlie called, waving from across the street. Wow, I barely recognized the guy with the Irish cap and long overcoat, even though Charlie was wearing those same clothes at the beach just a day ago. There was something different about him. But what? Ah, now I knew. Once you see a man undressed, putting clothes back on him never really dresses him again. My mind only saw an undressed Charlie, peacefully sleeping on a dingy motel bed.

"He wasn't kidding when he said 'old friends,' was he?" I whispered to myself, looking from Charlie to the elderly couple who accompanied him. I hesitated before acknowledging him with a brief wave, half irritated that my body seemed to gravitate towards him against my will, or at least my conscious will. Why couldn't I just keep walking and ignore this guy? What did I want from him anyway? Why lead him on when I knew this wasn't going anywhere? He was leaving tomorrow and me...geez, I had no idea what I wanted anymore. I was about as stable as a mound of pudding. Folding my arms tightly across my chest, I stepped into the street towards Charlie as butterflies fluttered in my stomach and my heart pounded in my ears.

"Charlie...I didn't expect to run into you again," I said, confused by the struggle between what my mind thought I should feel for him and the physiological attraction he evoked in me.

"Diana," Charlie cleared his throat, "these are the friends I told you about. Sheridan and Edmund are, ah, old friends of the family." Charlie ran a hand through his hair, knocking his cap from his head. Obviously I wasn't the only one feeling uncomfortable, but his self-conscious behavior surprised me.

"Nice to meet you," I said, extending my hand to the elderly woman and then the old man.

"The pleasure is all ours," the woman said, as she considered me with a knowing, broad smile, "Sherri, please call me Sherri."

"Chuckie, we are going to go on ahead, we'll meet up with you two in a bit." Now that was rather presumptuous I thought, watching the elderly woman with the blue hair take her husband by the arm and turn him towards their unknown destination. How did she just presume to think I would be joining them anywhere?

As soon as they were out of earshot, Charlie turned to me with his crimson colored ears, a color I was getting used to seeing on him. He gave me a shy, lopsided smile.

"I'm sorry, they're, uh, kind of like family, you know," he said, holding his elbow out towards me. Well, he was as presumptuous as his old lady friend, but there was something about his take-charge attitude that appealed to me. Definitely a man who knows what he wants. Still, I hesitated, wondering what I was doing with this man and exactly where all of this was going. My rational voice, which was quickly being drowned out, tried to remind me that this man, this almost stranger, was leaving tomorrow and I'd likely never see him again.

"What the heck," I said more in response to my own thoughts than to Charlie's waiting elbow, silencing that nagging rational mind that could be so annoying.

"Chuckie, huh," I said, grasping his waiting arm.

"Yeah, yeah, yeah," Charlie snorted with a half-smile, "don't you go calling me that now, you hear," he teased, as we headed in the direction the elderly couple had gone. I guess the old woman was right about me. How did she know?

"I'm just getting used to saying Charlie," I answered, half amused with the whole situation. "Where are we going anyway?"

"Lunch," Charlie answered, as though that was sufficient explanation. Under most other circumstances I would have protested. I would have needed to know exactly where I was headed and for how long, and would have never accepted such an invitation to begin with. But this was not "normal circumstances" I reminded myself, briefly glancing over at this man I had been so intimate with, yet hardly knew. What was it that continued to force him into my life? Was it fate to stumble into him repeatedly? Oh come on, Diana, I told myself. Stop this hokus pokus monkey business. There is random chance after all. Either way, walking beside this handsome man with his dark curls, I felt an odd, almost natural calm. It was only when I was physically with him that the emotional roller coaster I had ridden for the past forty-eight hours slowed down and I actually found a comfort zone. How long is it going to last this time, though? It's only a matter of time before I fall into my dark abyss of loneliness again.

"He's just smitten with you," this blue-haired Sherri told me, when we were both in the Crab Shack restroom. Studying this woman as she applied lipstick to her wrinkled lips, I wondered how much Charlie had told her about us. How could she know about me otherwise, I wondered, trying to straighten my disheveled hair.

"I've known him for a long time, and seen him with a lot of women," Sherri said matter of fact as she lowered her lipstick and glanced at me in the mirror, "I shouldn't have said that, honey, it'll give you the wrong idea." I stood frozen, listening to this woman, who obviously knew much more about Charlie than I ever would.

"You know, I've known Charlie since he was a little boy," she turned to look directly at me. "I don't know why he never did get married, he's quite a catch you know. Sometimes you've got to wait for the right one to come along, I guess." And then she winked at me.

A surge of emotion coursed through my veins, forcing me to lower my eyes. I had the right one, but *he* was taken away from me. And now, here, in some strange bathroom, I have to listen to some blue-haired woman talk to me about a man I just met. Warning bells sounded so loudly in my mind, I was surprised I could hear myself think. Bells warning me to run while I still had the chance, even though my heart told me otherwise. Maybe everything about this situation was wrong, but then why couldn't I walk away? Something had to be right.

"He told me," Sherri spoke calmly and gently squeezed my hand. Looking up, confused, I wondered what *exactly* Charlie had told her. Oh God, it couldn't be about last night, could it? I felt a wave of heat move up my neck and face. Oh come on, he wouldn't talk to her about *that*. He's a grown man, for God's sake.

"I almost lost mine once too," the elderly woman said, as she stared off into some distant secret place to which only she held the key. "Only God brought him back to me." Sherri looked almost startled to see me, as though suddenly realizing she was not alone. "I'm sorry about your husband. Fate can play cruel tricks on us," she said, as she straightened her blue hair. "But don't forget for a minute that, call it what you like, fate, fortune, it doesn't really matter…don't forget it has some pretty amazing, unexpected tricks up its sleeve." The eccentric blue-haired woman with her oversized beaded necklace winked at me again.

Something prevented me from asking Sherri what happened to her husband. It wasn't that I didn't want to know, but we had spent too much time in the restroom as it was. And besides, whatever it was, it likely happened a long time ago, I thought, placing my brush into my backpack.

"We should get back, the two of them'll think we've left 'em for some younger men," Sherri said with a lightness of being that was at odds with the heavy air that still hung in the bathroom.

"Right," I replied, obediently following this woman back to the table.

"Ah, there they are," Edmund said, attempting to wink at me as he briefly squeezed both eyes shut. "Charlie here tells me you're in the fish business."

"I, uh, well, my husband is, or was I should say." I resisted the urge to bite my nails. Could we please just not talk about Warren? Why does everything always come back to that? I looked around at the three sets of eyes staring at me. "I, uh, did a lot of the paperwork," I replied, embarrassed by my inability to carry on any type of normal, intelligible conversation about my deceased husband. Charlie sensed my discomfort and picked up the conversation, saving me any further humiliation.

"I was telling Ed about the letter you found, we've been arguing about whether it's a hoax or not," Charlie said.

How could Charlie tell them? I glared at him, feeling as though a bond of trust had been broken. This letter, the one I found, the one I had shown to Charlie only to later find myself in bed with him, was something very personal. Not to mention, pretty ludicrous. I had contemplated not showing the letter to him, but whatever emotion, or sake, had overcome me last night, it seemed like something I had to do. Now I wasn't so sure it had been the right move.

"Oh, come on, Diana." It was Warren's voice I heard, as clear and crisp as though he sat beside me. "You have no personal claim to this letter. It is as much his as anyone else's."

So lost in angry thought, I barely heard Charlie ask me for the letter, and Sherri ask whether I was alright. The world, my world, closed in on me and my vision darkened from all sides, until only a pin-sized hole of light was left. It was in this moment between conscious and unconscious worlds that I recognized the letter for what it was. "The letter," I spoke without sound and without words, "it is a catalyst." Someone, in some great beyond, or possibly in my own mind, agreed with me.

The three individuals seated at the table never heard my revelation. The three people seated at the table merely saw a woman pass from a state of consciousness into a state of unconsciousness.

Eyes stared down at me. A lot of them. I could sense as much even before I opened my eyes. Blinking a number of times, the faces slowly came into focus.

"Are you alright?" Again there was that familiar voice I should have known. It took a moment to gather my wits and make sense of what happened. Aha, I must have passed out.

"Charlie," I hoarsely said, as I pulled myself up from a humiliating horizontal position. This was just great. And here I thought I couldn't humiliate myself any more.

"Hey, I'm here. You okay?" he asked, helping me up and into a chair.

"How long...how long was I out?" I asked, rubbing my throbbing head. "Did I hit my head?"

"No, no, you just slumped forward," Charlie spoke with a quivering voice, "and I laid you down...and you came right to." With Charlie's assistance, I stood up. "Do you want to go to the hospital?" he asked with obvious concern.

"No, I'm fine, just a little tired, and I had a late night uh...last night." I hadn't meant to say it, but glancing over at Charlie, whose ears once again changed color, made me smile. It may have been my imagination, but the old couple passed a knowing glance between them. And you know what, who cares? So I slept with the guy. It wasn't the first time in the history of the world a woman slept with a man.

"You know, I think I'll head back to the motel and take a nap." The three people at the table smiled at me with sympathetic eyes. God, how I hated the "poor little widow we feel sorry for" look. Okay, I needed to calm down, and, as my brother would agree, stop being such a bitch.

"You do that, honey, everyone here understands," Sherri said, as Charlie draped my coat over my shoulders. Lifting my backpack, I noticed the unspoken conversation going on between Charlie and Sherri. The elderly woman motioned, quite clearly, for Charlie to leave with me. "I'll walk you back," Charlie offered, which I hoped he would have done even if the old woman hadn't encouraged him.

"You really don't have to...," I started to lie, but quickly realized Charlie had made up his mind on the matter. Apologizing for the scene

I could have done without, I wished Sheridan and Ed a good day, only then noticing that three of Ed's fingers on his left hand were missing.

"So that was, ah, how can I say it mildly…uh, completely and totally embarrassing." I didn't look at Charlie as I walked slowly beside him. A chuckle from my companion eased my tension somewhat. Maybe he didn't think I was a complete moron after all.

"Oh, that was nothing," Charlie said, grinning at me with his straight white teeth and strong jaw. "You should have seen what happened to me in the elevator at work last month. I'll leave it at that for now." I stole a glance at this man who was beginning to feel dangerously familiar.

"Why does that scare you, Di?" the voice I knew and had loved for so long asked, as though Warren were standing beside me. Turning, I caught a glimpse of a reflection between Charlie and myself in a store window. Stopping, I gasped for air as I again felt my head spin. Now that could not have been real. I just passed out and now I'm hallucinating again? Come on rational mind, say something encouraging. Well, what a great moment for my common sense to remain silent. And what about the voice? Was that my conscience? But then why didn't it make me feel guilty?

"You ok? Diana?" Charlie interrupted my recurring mad thoughts. "Maybe we should get you to a hospital," he suggested with the annoying concerned tone I was getting much too used to. My face tingled as he gently pushed a loose strand of hair from my face. Goose bumps moved up and down my back at just the slightest of his touches. Straightening myself, I lifted my chin, looked him in the eyes, and spoke that which directly contradicted my heart.

"Go back to your friends, Charlie, go back to your life." Freeing myself from Charlie's grasp, without another glance in his direction, I headed back towards my lonely motel. Yes, I'm psychotic. I know.

Why was I staring at the motel ceiling again? What is it about this ceiling? Would I find answers to my crazy life in the cracks? As I lay on the bed I fingered the brooch I had found in the knit "nothing" in one hand, and in the other hand I held the black stone the old Indian woman had given me.

"This is *really* a bizarre little place, isn't it?" I asked the black stone, which seemed to reflect a star-shaped light. And what about the brooch? Who was this woman? Closing my eyes, I tried to turn off my mind. Somehow the events of the day wouldn't allow that. One crazy thought collided smack into the next one, making me once again question my own sanity.

Here I was, exhausted and alone, in a decrepit motel room where I really didn't have to be. Why was I being such a goddamned martyr? The sound of my cell phone tore me from my dark thoughts and made my heart skip. Maybe it was him. Maybe he was at the other end of this small piece of vital technology so casually placed on my night stand. Who was I kidding? I had been waiting for his phone call; schizophrenic me. Push him away, yet wait for his phone call. Hey, wait a minute. He can only call me on the hotel phone. He doesn't have my cell phone, at least I don't remember giving it to him. But why would he call, after the way I treated him? Cursing myself, I realized it was probably Sheila or my father, neither of whom I cared to converse with at this moment in time. Abe, maybe, but actually I wasn't in the mood for his concerned line of questioning either. Why hadn't I given Charlie my cell phone number? He could still call the hotel, I guess.

"How pathetic are you, Di?" I asked myself as the phone silenced itself and the unknown caller was routed to voicemail.

Sighing, I returned my attention to the brooch, only to be immediately interrupted by the screaming cell phone once again. I don't know whether it was my imagination, but even my phone seemed to emit a sense of urgency. Was I supposed to take this phone call? Rolling over onto my side, I glanced at my phone, which told me an "unknown caller" awaited me on the other line. Well at least it's not Sheila or Dad, or Abe, for that matter, rousing my curiosity as to who *was* calling me.

"Hello," my voice echoed, as I spoke into this lifeless piece of technology on which so much of life depended. The sound of crackling static at the other end of the line was all that reached my auditory senses. Somewhere, as though faraway, there was a voice, barely audible so that at first I thought I had imagined it. It was a woman's voice, of that I was certain. A voice with a tone of, what was it, desperation?

"Diana," or was it "Anna" I heard over the crackling air waves? My heart raced. What name she called out I would never be sure of, but it wasn't the first time goose bumps covered my body today, but this time from fear. The connection was suddenly broken, followed by the eerie dial tone that had always disconcerted me for some reason.

Still holding the phone long after the connection had been severed, I stared at it, frightened that it might ring again, but also frightened that it might not. The sudden piercing tone emitted by the phone caused me to drop it. "Geez, get a grip woman," I chided myself, picking up the phone, which showed me that one new voicemail had been received. Quickly looking at my missed calls list, as though expecting to find out something, I dialed into my voicemail. There it was again, a woman's voice nearly drowned out by static. After listening to the voicemail six times, I still wasn't able to make out what name this woman called out, sending chills down my spine each time I listened. Why would she call out Anna? That just didn't make sense. Not only did it not make sense, it was just plain crazy, I told myself, most unconvincingly.

"It's your name, idiot. The "Di" was just drowned out," I said, hoping that speaking it aloud would strengthen my conviction that it was indeed me this person called out for. But the next question that would logically follow would be to ask 'who is this woman' and 'why did she call out for me?' Wouldn't one leave a message instead of calling out someone's name? I realized my hands were shaking as I nervously twisted the brooch and the black stone in one hand. Gently placing the cell phone back down on the night stand, I rolled onto my back and stared up at the familiar ceiling that was as cracked as I was. "Diana, Anna…Anna, Diana," I said to the ceiling, which seemed to smile at me with an evil, crooked grin. Could this be a coincidence I wondered, repressing the urge to read Anna's letter once again.

Dresden, Germany

November 1939

Anna sat at her desk and waited, listening to the other women gossip about rumors they had heard. Anna was not interested in rumors, just facts. At least not the kind of rumors she heard these days. She had always enjoyed English, it had come easy to her, and politics, while not really a field of study for women, did marginally interest her as well. Her job at the *Dresden Tagesblatt* was normally something she found stimulating, but today there had not been much to do. The normal shipment of foreign newspapers to be translated had been lost in transit. At least that is what they are telling us, she thought as she fingered the tightly rolled letter in the pocket of her skirt, wondering which direction the current political environment would go. Her father believed foreign newspaper shipments were delayed or destroyed because they contained anti-German propaganda that was not allowed to reach the German population.

"We are at war," she whispered to herself as she looked around at the smiling faces of the young women around her. Nothing here even remotely indicated as much.

"What about you, Anna?" Ingrid, a stocky young woman with brunette curls, asked her with a broad smile, revealing a set of crooked, stained teeth.

"About wh...wh...what?" Anna asked, somewhat abashed that she had no idea what these women were once again giggling about.

"Is there someone? You know, a special someone for you, Anna?" Ingrid asked, as all eyes turned to stare at Anna.

"Err, uh," Anna stammered as she felt the heat rise in her face and tried to find a way out of this most unpleasant situation. These matters of the heart, as Frau Ahrens had said, were not things she chose to share with random strangers. She had to admit, some of the women were not random strangers, they were even friends of Maria, and the others had become acquaintances, but that made it almost worse. "N...n...no," was the only word she managed to stutter. Anna felt a sudden sense of betrayal for her beloved. Again she had denied Jakub, but what was she to say to this group of gossiping hens? That yes, she did have a lover? One who disappeared to Australia without mentioning a word to her? Anna felt a mixed sense of betrayal and anger suddenly surface. Picking up her coat, she walked through the sea of crammed desks and headed outside, noticing along the way that the women had long since forgotten about her and had moved on to other banal chit-chat.

Anna walked across the cobblestone courtyard and made her way to the small church at the end of the road. She had ridden past it on her bicycle so many times on her way into and out of the city, but had never taken the time to really see it. Pushing open the old rusted gate, she slowly walked between ancient graves until she reached the church doors. Half expecting the door to be locked, she pushed down the door handle just as someone else pushed open the door from the inside. The door knocked her in the forehead, and she felt her world spin and darken.

When Anna opened her eyes, she stared into a pair of worried yellow-green eyes that reminded her of her favorite cat she had not seen in the last few weeks.

"Oh, dear God, I am so sorry...here, no, maybe you should stay put, ah," a young man stammered as he nervously rubbed his hands together.

"W…w…what happened?" Anna asked as she rubbed her forehead and tried to remember what *had* just happened.

"I was in a hurry…oh, I am so sorry…I, am always in such a hurry these days, much too much of a hurry…hurry, hurry, hurry…I am sorry. Please let me take a look at that," he said, peering closely at Anna's forehead. "Cold, yes, that is right, cold…something cold, you, ah, need something cold…for the forehead," he seemed to say to himself, turning around frantically, wondering where he could find something cold.

"I am fine," Anna said as she picked herself up off the cold ground. "I have no intention of joining them any time soon," she spoke, motioning at the graves that surrounded the old church just as her stomach threatened to empty its contents. The young man nervously looked from Anna to his watch.

"I again apologize for my behavior…here, I must…oh, the baby is on the way," the man mumbled, as though to himself. "I must go, but please, ah, allow me to write down your name to inquire about your welfare…I am a doctor." The young man handed Anna a small book and his fountain pen. Without responding, Anna accepted the pen and complied. The young man looked startled, almost pale when he read the name in his book.

"Werner Wenke," he introduced himself with a slight bow as he shoved his small book into his coat pocket. "Fraulein, again, my apologies," he said, as he peered at Anna's forehead on more time and turned to leave. Anna reached up and felt the now egg-sized lump on her forehead as she watched this odd, disheveled young man quickly depart down the small church path. Shaking her head in disbelief, she turned and entered the cool church.

Anna breathed deeply when she entered the church. There was something about places of worship, it did not matter how large or small they were; they all had a similar scent. Was it the cool walls, the silence, the dead entombed in the walls and beneath? She did not find the odd smell offensive, rather it was quite comforting, especially when combined with the smell of burning candles. Anna briefly wondered what the strange young man, who had said he was a doctor, was doing in an empty church. A deep coughing from behind a small closed door answered her constantly wandering mind.

Walking down the center church aisle she realized what the scent was. It was the scent of stale air. How many souls had breathed this air she wondered, as she paused at one of the pews and decided to sit down to ease her throbbing head which threatened to explode. Anna contemplated whether she should go and find a real doctor, not some strange simpleton she had just met. Shifting position on the hard wood bench beneath her, she was reminded that, no matter how often she shifted her weight, she would never find comfort on this bench. "It is so we do not fall asleep," she whispered up at the God or spirits she felt surrounding her. The sound of deep coughing, accompanied by the sound of someone blowing their nose, interrupted her thoughts. Anna hoped whoever found themselves behind the small closed door remained where they were. She enjoyed her moment of solitude after spending her morning listening to idle gossip and unsubstantiated rumors.

Placing her hand into her skirt pocket, she pulled out the letter she had written to her beloved Jakub the night before. "Why is it always in the late hours that I cannot bear your disappearance?" she whispered, raising the letter to her lips. She had not been able to locate an empty apple juice bottle, and did not dare to leave the letter in her room. "You could use a different type of bottle," her rational mind had told her at two o'clock in the morning. "It must be the same type of bottle," her irrational mind had argued, making no sense to even her, but somehow the irrational mind carried more weight. Reminding herself that she must ask Sigrid for a bottle when she returned home, she slowly unrolled the letter as her heart began beating more rapidly.

Letter Five   *Dresden, 20. November 1939*

My beloved Jakub,

We are at war! At war! Now we are to be enemies based on the country of our birth as well? Oh, Jakub, where will this all end? I rarely sense your spirit, even in the hayloft. Rather, I hope to remember that one night where our shared love was to begin an eternity together. I now visit what I call "our place" where "we" can quietly mourn the loss of our son.

I must tell you, Jakub, if you are indeed far away, you would not believe what goes on in this country, in this home. Mama proudly flies the party flag over the main house entrance. She argues that the flag is flown by most of Dresden's prominent citizens. She would not want to be singled out for such a trivial matter. I know Papa secretly opposes this overt act of support, but Mama has convinced him of the necessity to show our support for the cause. Especially him. Papa, as all in this house, knows better than to argue with Mama when she has made up her mind about the way things should be. Mama and Papa continue to argue about other aspects of this war. Often I hear them arguing about the Fuhrer, but more often it is my situation they argue about. Mama does not find my work suitable employment for a young woman who should be married, but fails to see that I am not made for the world that she and Maria seem to so willingly or easily accept. I do not know what I plan to do with the rest of my life, but for now I know that I survive with your memory, one day at a time.

I prayed for you tonight, as I do every night, but tonight I prayed that you are far from here and even further from your homeland. It has been many months since I pushed Papa to tell me what he knows of your disappearance. He stands by what he has told me in the past, but there are some things I have uncovered. It was two days ago when I rode my bicycle home from the city. I saw a man laying in a ditch beside one of Papa's fields—the field with the two large oak trees you may remember. It was the gardener, old Mr. Zimmerman. You can imagine the scare he gave me. I believed he was dead. His face was pressed into the ground, but it was clear to me who this man was. I pulled at him and managed to roll him onto his side. Papa, and everyone else on the estate know Mr. Zimmerman frequents the bottle, but I had never seen him in such a state. It startled me when he coughed and emptied his stomach near my shoes. Jakub, it was horrid. I should not speak of such vulgar things, but it was the state I found him in which allowed me to obtain this information. Yes, I realize I took advantage of his weakness, but I shall stop at nothing to uncover what has happened to you. It was in the ditch, where this man laid in soiled clothing, smelling as though he had been drowned in Sigrid's wine sauce, where I demanded he tell me anything he knows of your disappearance or current whereabouts. He swore to me, on the life of his children, but that is not worth much given how he has treated them in the past, that he knew nothing of your whereabouts, but he did say he saw you leave, Jakub. The hour he did not recall, only that he had fallen asleep after a long day and had awoken hours later in the darkness of night. Normally he would not have seen or heard anything, but, possibly as fate should have it, he walked outside the front door with the intent of smoking his pipe and heard hushed voices and footsteps approaching along the gravel path. As you know, anyone entering or departing the estate passes by the house Papa allows him to occupy. Hidden in the shadows, he watched as three men passed by his home and headed into the woods. It was a short while later he heard the sound of a car engine starting. I asked the gardener how he could be sure it was you, upon which he answered that one of men called you by name.

Oh, Jakub, Mr. Zimmerman swears that it appeared you were in no manner forced by these men to leave, but that there seemed to be an urgency to the voices he heard, yet no hostility. My love, maybe it is true, Jakub, maybe you did leave for Australia. My belief that you are not dead has been strengthened, but I find myself experiencing an odd jumble of emotions. While I pray continuously for your safety, and my heart beats easier believing you alive and hopefully safe, I cannot help wonder why you did not find a way to take proper leave from me. At a minimum, a short note that I could hold on to, as I have no comforting words to cling to. Maybe someday, when this letter finds you, or we are reunited, you will explain all of this to me. Please forgive these negative thoughts. As I have written before, I do not want anything to taint my memories of "us." For now though, I hope I will rest easier with the knowledge I have gained.

I must tell you of Maria. She, as I wrote to you just recently, is with child again. Her condition seems much improved. She has a healthy appetite and has not felt any of the illness she experienced previously. We all hope she maintains this appetite and level of energy. It must be difficult to carry a child and have another to care for at home. Sigrid continues to behave most erratically. At times she wears a most strange expression. As though she is about to tell me something, but then decides not to. It seems to bother her deeply that the gardener's daughter and her young son share a home with us. It would be most horrible for a child to grow up with a grandfather such as his. As far as I know, Mr. Zimmerman no longer speaks with his daughter and has never spoken to his grandson. It is a tragedy that such things occur in life. I no longer ask Sigrid about her "matters of the heart," just as I have given up speculating who the father of Lena's young child might be. I do have my suspicions, but does it truly matter?

My beloved Jakub, the hour is late and I must find some rest. Tomorrow I shall continue where I left off today, hopefully one step closer to you.

Love Eternally,
Anna v. Marschalkt

Post Script: Again my mind wanders, Jakub. What is it about the nature of mankind that we cannot live peacefully with one another? Am I naïve to believe that we cannot survive if we do not dominate our neighbors? If we do not take what is not ours to take? How is it that we teach our children not to strike out, yet we adults show no such restraint in our affairs? As I grow, I find the world does not have room for idealistic minds.

Anna sighed as she stared down at the unfamiliar words she knew she had written sometime in the late hours of the previous night. What spirit possessed her at night she wondered as she rolled her letter up tightly and carefully placed it back into her skirt pocket. Anna slouched down slightly on the hard bench and looked up at the magnificent ceiling. Even for such a small church, there was such attention paid to detail. The sound of coughing and a door opening pulled her from her thoughts as a short, heavy-set pastor waddled into the main church toward the altar, thumbing through a thick Bible. Fairly certain he had not seen her, Anna sat motionless, hoping she could remain unnoticed. It was as though the pastor read her thoughts and looked up, directly at her. Mortified by what she must look like, Anna pulled at her loose scarf and attempted to tie it around her head as the pastor waddled towards her.

"Are you alright, Fraulein?" he asked, glowering at Anna, who tried unsuccessfully to hide the lump beneath her scarf.

"Y...y...yes, ah, I am fine. Th...Th...Thank you," Anna looked away from him as she spoke. She did not know why an odd-smelling church could make her feel so comfortable, yet the man who represented God within the church evoked the opposite sentiment. "I, sh... sh...should be going," Anna said, as she gave up trying to hide her swollen forehead.

"God sees all," the pastor said to her as she stood up, grateful to leave the hard bench behind.

"It w...w...was a door, uh I ran into it," Anna felt the need to explain, embarrassed by her stuttering.

"Fraulein, the house of God is always open to you, if ever you find yourself in such need," the pastor offered, as Anna nodded and quickly walked away. "The devil reveals himself in her hair," Anna was sure she heard the pastor whisper as she walked away.

What was it about her red hair that often elicited such negative responses in her fellow man? With a shiver Anna recalled the day she and Maria had ridden their bicycles into the city to visit the weekend market. It was the old woman selling flowers who started the unrest.

"Daughters of the Devil," the old woman had chanted, as Anna and Maria pushed their bicycles closer towards her corner flower stall.

It was not until Maria pointed it out that Anna realized of whom the old woman spoke. A group of unruly youths, eager to join the witch hunt, added their own lines to the chant as they surrounded Maria and Anna.

"Devil's daughters! Devils daughters!" the agitated youths chanted as they tightened their circle around the horrified girls.

What may have started as a joke for these young men turned serious, as an angry mob formed, pushing and shoving, voices calling out in unison. It was when the fruits and vegetables, followed by stones, began to fly that Maria had grabbed her and forced their way through the mob. To this day, Anna could not figure out how they managed to flee from the ensuing scuffle without injury. Never before that moment in time had Anna been so aware of her hair and how it made her and Maria somehow different from most of the rest of their city. Never before that incident had she been so aware of how one's exterior could have such a powerful emotional impact on others. Never again would Anna feel comfortable in large crowds. Anna shook herself, as though to rid herself of this past memory, and the more recent one of the disingenuous pastor.

As Anna walked down the street towards the newspaper office, she briefly considered going home. There was likely little, if anything, to do there, and she, with her large bulging forehead, would surely be the immediate focus of attention for the next hour. She heard her father's words resounding through her mind, "If you make a commitment, you must follow through with it." These words, combined with her own sense of duty forced her back in the direction of the newspaper office. Dragging her feet, she slowly trudged up the stairs towards the back office.

Anna sensed something was wrong the moment she set foot in the room. An eerie silence, penetrated only by occasional hushed whispers, gripped the office. What had happened? She hadn't been gone that long. Anna tried to figure out just when she had left. Lightly fingering her swollen forehead, she thought that whatever it was couldn't have happened more than an hour ago, likely less. What could have happened here she wondered, scanning the group of silent, pale-faced women. Even Ingrid, who always displayed a large smile looked as though she had seen a devil.

"Maybe it is me," Anna whispered sarcastically to herself as she quietly walked to her small desk and sat down. It worried here that not one of the gossip hens had filled her in on what had happened. "No one's even noticed the horn on my forehead," she whispered to herself, quietly sitting down. Anna leaned over towards Helga, a small boned young woman who reminded her of a plucked hen.

"W…w…what has h…h…happened, Helga? W…W…Why do all of y…y…you look as th…th…though you h…h…have seen a ghost?" Anna was surprised by the urgency she heard in her own voice. Helga turned and stared at Anna, briefly looking up at Anna's forehead as though the large lump were just another freckle that speckled her face.

"You don't know?" Helga asked with disbelief. "Where have you been, Anna? They escorted her out," the young woman said, as she moved her mouth like a pecking chicken. "She is gone. Who would have known?" Helga said as she stared at Anna.

Anna felt the irritation rising in her. She wanted a clear answer.

"Wh…Wh…Who is gone?" Anna asked trying to hide the growing annoyance she felt. "And wh…wh…who would have kn…kn…known w…w…what?" she added, resisting the urge to slap this hen-like woman across the face.

"Giesela," Helga responded with a whisper. "It was Giesela. They took her away."

"G…G…Giesela Steinherz? Who?" Anna snapped, feeling immediately guilty about her misdirected anger. Patience was not one of her virtues. "Who took her away…and why?" She asked less caustically as she watched the scared face before her twitch nervously

"I am not sure, Mr. Zeller called Giesela to his office…two men, uniformed, were already waiting," Helga recounted as she nervously wrung her hands together.

"Wh…wh…what did th…th…they w…w…want with Giesela?" Anna asked, confused by what this frail, frightened woman told her. Helga leaned in close enough for Anna to feel her warm breath on her face.

"She is a Jew. And a spy." Helga said as though one was as bad as the other. Helga sat back and Anna watched as an almost satisfied look momentarily transformed Helga's face from the scared chicken

171

to something, what was it, sinister? The hairs on the back of Anna's neck stood straight up as she looked around the room which seemed to have taken on a new dimension.

"Ladies," Mr. Zeller's voice sounded through the room like a trumpet, "papers have arrived. We have papers to translate now," he stated, as he dropped a stack of foreign newspapers on a desk in the middle in the room. Anna watched as one by one the women retrieved a paper and quietly returned to their desks. Slowly the room transformed itself back to what it had been like before she left. Anna decided it was time for her to return home. As she packed her things together, she glanced over at the empty desk. She had never exchanged many words with Giesela, aside from the normal pleasantries required to survive in cultured society. Anna would never see Giesela again. She would never know what fate had befallen this young woman, but forever her conscience would haunt her.

Anna climbed up to her room and, without removing her coat, threw herself onto her soft comforter. "Oh, Jakub," she cried into her pillow. "Was it these same men who took you?" Anna sobbed as the events of the day replayed in her overwhelmed mind. "No, no the gardener said you walked freely…that there was a familiarity about the way the two dark shadows spoke to you." She tried to persuade herself as she sat up, remembering the rolled up letter in her skirt pocket. Pulling the letter from her pocket she smoothed the wrinkled paper as she walked to her desk and sat down. Picking up her fountain pen she stared down at the words, the only connection to her lover, and began to write.

Post Script 2: I am guilty, Jakub, guilty of ignorance. An ignorance which insulates my being from the realities of the world. There is a movement, Jakub, cunningly creeping along, that threatens to shake the world I live in. What world will this be when the shaking ceases?

It was a week before Anna found her way back into the cellar and found a box of empty green apple juice bottles. It would be another three days before she melted the wax and entombed her letter in the glass bottle. The morning Anna walked to her stream at the edge of the wood was cold. Thoughts of the war occupied her mind as she stood at the water's edge.

"May you be safe wherever you are," she spoke to her beloved, as she kissed the bottle and tossed it into the fast moving stream. Anna would never know that heavy rains would cause her stream to spill over onto the surrounding pastures. She would never know her bottle survived the winter intact beneath a layer of snow on one of her father's cow pastures, only to be destroyed the following spring by the wheels of a military vehicle.

Travels of Letter 16
Bengal Coast, India
March 1972

Devi remembered the evening she paused outside her home and listened to the raised voices inside. She had never heard her mother raise her voice, let alone yell at anyone. Devi had not even been sure at first if it was her mother inside the house. She knew her father would not tolerate such behavior from a woman, ever. The sounds of her father beating her mother after that were too much to bear, she couldn't bring herself to enter the house so she had walked down to the ocean and sat on the warm sand, clutching the small black stone she had possessed since she was a child. There was a crescent moon that night that reminded her of a painting she had seen as a child; that moment seared itself into her memory, she wasn't sure why.

Her mother's unsuccessful pleas echoed in her head now, "They are not a good match, things will not go well for them. For Devi." She had always suspected her mother was not in favor of the match, but had little voice in the matter. Devi herself had no choice. Were there really places on earth where women did have a choice? Would her soul come back in one of these women, or would she now rejoin the ultimate soul, she pondered as she coughed, a weak, dry cough. Her lungs seemed to have lost all ability to expand and contract. The urge to cough overcame her again as it had so often these last two days.

Devi closed her eyes, wishing she did not have to breathe, and recalled how she had come back from the fields exhausted just two days ago. Her back ached and her hands had been covered with blisters after twelve hours outside. She almost found some type of sadistic humor in the situation. She had been worried about the blisters on her hands, but today she was nothing but one big blister. The days spent in the field were made more difficult by the heat. All she had wanted to do was lie down on her mat and go to sleep, just for a little while. She hadn't heard her mother-in-law enter her husband's home until it was too late. Devi had sat up, filled with horror as she realized she had not prepared the evening meal. She had watched, still frozen with panic, as her mother-in-law dragged in some old glass bottles that she had found on the beach, bottles that would soon join many others already neatly stacked next to the stove. Tomorrow her mother-in-law would surely blow more glass trinkets for the tourists. Devi barely had time to cover her head as her mother-in-law started beating her with the old broom, once again. Oddly, as she cowered in the corner, covering her head, she barely felt the broom handle adding more colorful bruises to her body. She was covered with an array or colors, as bruises of varying ages progressed through the healing process.

A spasm of coughs rattled Devi's body, she wanted her mother. Her mother wouldn't know she was here, how could she? Or was there some mother-daughter bond that could defy time and space? She hadn't seen her mother since she left her father's home for her husband's home. Not until she herself was married did she understand the courage it took for her mother to speak her own mind.

"She is too young, I beg you Rajeev, she is just fourteen years old, it isn't even legal," her mother had pleaded with her father.

"Legal, I will you show you legal," her father had shouted. How did it come to be this way Devi wondered. How can a world be just, when women are treated worse than animals? When Devi had finally left the calming peace of the ocean and returned home, she heard muffled whimpering noises from a small bundle of rags in a corner of her father's home. The small bundle of rags turned out to be her mother, whose arm was grotesquely bent out of shape. The next morning her mother prepared the morning meal with her arm wrapped in a make-shift sling as though nothing had transpired the night before. The only indication that something *had* happened the night before was the unprovoked slap her father had placed squarely on Devi's cheek, leaving her with the metallic taste of blood inside her mouth. "Worthless, stupid girl," he had said as he left the home without turning around.

Devi opened her eyes. Her mouth was so dry, she needed water, but she couldn't swallow, could she? Trying to swallow, she realized, almost indifferently, that even those muscles were frozen. Two days ago she hadn't prayed. Was she being punished? Did Brahma feel betrayed? She had prayed to one of her gods every day, usually Brahma, but not two days ago. Working too much was no excuse to forget her spiritual obligations. Maybe the gods worked their revenge through the hands of her mother-in-law and her husband.

"Worthless girl," her mother-in-law had said to her with cold black eyes. When they poured the cooking oil over her body that night, Devi asked the gods for forgiveness; forgiveness for her own soul, but also for the souls of her mother-in-law and her husband.

"Worthless girl, your parents won't even pay for your life," she had heard her husband say between her own screams, begging for mercy, pleading for her life. When they lit the cooking oil with the blow torch she had asked forgiveness for the souls of her father and mother. She had never felt so much physical pain, yet strangely, she experienced a sense of spiritual peace. Devi knew she would be free soon.

"It is a miracle she is still alive. She should be dead, poor thing," Devi heard a nurse say to another nurse who briefly appeared in her line of vision. Aside from her weak cough and shallow breathing, she had no means of communicating with anyone. In a detached way she wondered what she must look like. Visions of a mutilated cow she had seen filled her mind. Devi wondered why, if her body was so broken, so burned, could she still see, hear, and think so clearly. How much longer would she be trapped in this earthly cage? When would her spirit be freed? Could the gods not find mercy for her? She did not know if she still had arms and legs or if they had been burned off entirely.

Closing her eyes again, Devi remembered running outside her husband's home, engulfed in flames as neighbors passively watched. She had managed to strip off some of her burning clothing which, she had heard the nurses say, was why she still lived. Again, she heard an unfamiliar, sarcastic voice inside her ask what kind of life this was. Would her husband marry again, she wondered. He had visited her yesterday. "It was a cooking accident," Devi heard him tell a nurse. Devi heard the sarcasm in the nurse's voice when the nurse told her husband, "We seem to have a lot of *cooking* accidents. Look around, Sir, there are six *cooking* accidents in here. I hope *you* do not have a *cooking* accident."

Devi felt another silent cough shake her rigid body, but this time there was no air left in her lungs. She had been conscious of her last breath, and grateful for it. As she looked ahead she saw something indescribably wonderful, and imagined to breathe out a deep, full sigh of relief. Devi dropped her black stone talisman, unaware of her hand that had tightly held on to it for two days.

Two days later there was another *cooking* accident. It was presumed a bottle from a neat stack next to a stove had rolled off and knocked over cooking oil, which had somehow alighted and burned down a home. The occupants of the home, a man and his elderly mother, were burned to death, but the stack of bottles remained unburned. Neighbors later cleared out the home, throwing out all of its charred remains, even the bottles. No one wanted the cursed bottles. Two weeks later the surviving bottles, and one green glass bottle in particular, were loaded on a truck, and, along with all the neighborhood trash, deposited into the ocean.

Cape May, New Jersey
Fall 2011

"What on earth...?" The frantic knocking startled me out of my half sleep. Dropping the television remote that I had fallen asleep holding, I jumped up and rushed towards the door. "Who is it? I'm coming," I heard myself answer, still groggy and not thinking straight.

"Diana! Open up, it's me!" The urgency in his voice was unmistakable. "Come on, Diana, open up, it's important."

"Charlie, what's going on?" I asked, as I tore open the door and self-consciously stood before this man, nervously running my fingers through my disheveled hair.

"I found her," he half shouted, as he pushed his way into my motel room. I was confused. Who in the heck was Charlie talking about?

"Found who?" I asked, still confused, wondering if it was the late hour or just my mind that had decided to move like molasses. There was something arousing about Charlie's current state. I hadn't seen him like this before; this excited. His eyes gleamed as he smiled at me with near perfect white teeth. I hadn't noticed his crooked bottom tooth before. Charlie motioned me to sit down beside him. Oh, I see, he's trying to get me back in the sack. A notion, I had to admit, I wasn't entirely opposed to.

179

"It's not what you think," he said, as though reading my mind. "It's about Anna...your Anna."

"My Anna?" I asked, perplexed, "You mean Anna from the letter...that Anna?"

"Precisely, that Anna. You and I don't both know any other Anna do we?" he teased, gently covering my warm hand with his chilly one.

"I don't understand...where, I mean, how did you find her? I checked online, at least as much as my limited research abilities go...is that how you found her? Are you even being serious with me? Come on, you're pulling my leg, aren't you?" I asked, pinching him in the chest. Charlie squealed like a pig and shook his head, holding both hands up.

"I swear, this is for real," he said, defending himself from my renewed pinching assault. He was serious wasn't he? That means she could possibly be alive. And if she's alive, then I could find her, couldn't I? God, I am insane, aren't I?

"Is...is...she alive?" I could barely breathe.

"Let me start at the beginning," Charlie answered calmly, which did nothing to lessen the suspense. Actually it made it quite a bit worse. Sensing my impatience, Charlie patted my hand, as though appeasing a fidgety child, which oddly did not bother me. Quite the opposite, this whole Anna affair seemed to act as some bizarre aphrodisiac. I had to restrain myself from pushing Charlie back on the bed. Fanning my flushed face, I listened intently, expectantly.

"First off, I don't know if she's alive or not. At least not yet," he said as he tapped his feet, revealing his own excitement.

"What do you mean not yet?" I asked impatiently, becoming more confused by the minute.

"Okay, wait, wait...I'm getting ahead of myself," Charlie answered tapping his feet more quickly. "I mentioned the name, von Marschalkt, to my friend in London."

"Why would you do that," I interrupted, feeling suddenly protective of the letter, and possibly Anna as well.

"Okay, let me back up further," Charlie said, looking down as he nervously tapped his feet. "I tried to look up Anna online. You know, it was just out of, you know, curiosity. I can't even explain why your letter…why, this sounds crazy, but I just had to check, to see if she exists…existed. I didn't get anywhere, but did find one hit for a Baron von Marschalkt." My mouth hung open as I watched Charlie with pure amazement. How could this letter, this woman have affected him this way? He seemed almost more crazed than me. "There wasn't much about the man, only some reference to a race horse he had before World War II," Charlie said.

"Is he Anna's husband? Father? Maybe a brother?" I interrupted as Charlie's excitement fueled my own.

"I'm getting there, just…hold yer horses," Charlie gripped my hand more tightly with his hand, which was now sweating. "So, I thought to myself, who could help me and 'pop,' I just knew." Charlie looked at me as I started to giggle. "What's so funny?" he asked, poking me in the ribs.

"Oh, just your 'pop' is all, but please…please do go on, Charlie," I laughed, watching this man, who was beginning to grow on me. Actually, if I'm being honest with myself, he grew roots on me the moment I met him.

"Anyway, I called my friend Stephen…uh, Stephen White. He works for Interpol in the U.K., and I asked him for a small favor. He owes me a few, actually." Charlie looked up at me with his broad smile. The temptation was too great, I had to lean into him and plant a kiss on his beautiful, soft, warm lips. His body immediately responded to my advances, but I had to push him away. I had to hear the rest of the story before, well, before whatever was going to obviously happen next. It wasn't that I pushed him away, but the need to know about Anna was far greater than the need to satisfy my animal desires right then.

"Keep talking, Mister, *that* can wait," I coyly said, nibbling at his ear.

"Yes, Ma'am, you drive a hard bargain. Like I said, I called Stephen and he said he'd look into it for me. I wasn't sure about the spelling, but I thought I was pretty close." Listening as Charlie spelled out "von Marschalkt," I wondered how he could have remembered the spelling after just one reading, not to mention his alcohol-induced state at the time.

"Geez, Abe would have a field day with this," I mumbled, envisioning my brother shaking his head in disbelief.

"What was that?" Charlie asked.

"Nothing, go on…please."

"Well, it didn't take long for him to get back to me with an answer," Charlie paused, looking at me.

"Well, go on, go on," I insisted, picking nervously at my nail.

The anticipation of what he was about to say was so great, I was sure I was going to burst. It didn't help that Charlie seemed to have a flare for the dramatic. He obviously knew how to captivate an audience, likely his experience arguing cases before a jury.

"Well, it didn't take long for good old Stephen to get back to me, and Diana, there is a record of an Anna von Marschalkt." Charlie seemed as moved as I felt. Reaching for Charlie, I had to hold on to him as the tears streaked down my cheeks and onto his shirt.

"You said you didn't know if she was alive. 'Not yet' is what you said. When will you know?" I asked between sobs, wondering if I needed to apologize for my childish behavior. After all, what grown woman cried about another woman she didn't even know? But somehow, here, in this small motel room, in the middle of Cape May, New Jersey, with this man I had only recently met, yet had shared so much with, my emotional breakdown felt justified, almost right. I wasn't even surprised to see that even Charlie's eyes weren't dry. Charlie cleared his throat.

"He's going to get in touch with his Interpol contact in Germany. Then he'll call me back."

"So what do we do now?" I asked, trying to manage my emotions.

"We wait," he answered calmly.

"We wait," I repeated in almost a whisper. Charlie lay back on the bed and reached both hands out to me. Dropping into his warm embrace I felt safe, and content, as I pushed Warren into the back of my mind. For right now, for this moment, I wanted to be free of guilt, free of painful memories, and free of whatever consequences my actions may have in the future. Right now there was just Diana and Charlie, and somewhere there is or was Anna, who somehow had brought us together.

"And so we shall wait," I said, unbuttoning Charlie's pants.

Baltic Sea Coast, Germany
March 1940

Anna unpacked her suitcase and neatly hung her dresses in the musty closet. She had not been to the island of Ruegen for years. Coughing as she looked out the window at the Baltic Sea, she did not understand why it had been so long. She loved the island, especially the town of Sassnitz, where she had spent many childhood summers with her family at their summer cottage. Would it be different now that she and Maria were no longer children, she pondered, watching through her window as a flock of seagulls stood motionlessly facing the gusting winds? In the distance she could barely make out Maria with two small children in tow.

"Should you be out there in your condition?" Anna spoke to herself without stuttering, as she thought of the child her sister carried so soon after the birth of her most recent child. Speaking a short prayer for her sister and her born and unborn offspring, she wondered if she herself would ever be with child again. Anna coughed and shivered momentarily, reminding her she needed to finish unpacking, Sigrid had asked to speak with her privately before the evening meal. Anna was grateful her mother was not here yet. It was refreshing to be free of her constant scrutiny. She and Papa had stayed behind in order to take care of unfinished business.

"Whatever that might be," she spoke aloud, momentarily suppressing the worries this war caused her family. Her mother did not seem as concerned about the war as her father, who had foreseen much of what had come to pass. It was the human injustices that most profoundly disturbed him. Only once did she hear her mother complain when she was unable to obtain her favorite French cologne.

"Does she not see how more and more goods and services are no longer available?" Anna asked herself, as she thought of the extra supplies they had brought along in case of a shortage.

Coughing again, Anna bent forward to ease the pain in her chest. It had been Papa's idea to send her up here. Maria too, he had said, could benefit from the healing powers of the sea. He had great belief in the "magic" of the sea as he called it. Mama had called him an "old fool" as usual, but did not argue that the salty air had various health benefits. There was another reason, Anna believed, why her father had sent his daughters up to the sea. It was the war. He feared it could spread onto German soil, and Dresden might not be safe.

"But is one safe anywhere, once war is upon us?" Anna asked herself as she thought about what her father had said. "War will be upon us, it is only a matter of time." Was he right?

Anna coughed again as she thought of her beloved Jakub. What life would his be now if he had remained? Surely he would have been taken from her. It was folly to think of a life together, in the world she lived in today. "Our world, Jakub...ours was a different time," she whispered between coughs, as she thought of the world she had once known and how much it had transformed in a short span of time. "How much more of our own humanity will we lose before this is all over?"

A dark depression settled over Anna's being as she looked out at a sky that mirrored her emotions. "I h...h...have lost everything," she cried, as she opened up the diary she had neglected for so long. Inside she found, safely tucked between the pages, what was left of the small daisy Jakub had given her. It had been an innocent gesture when he bent down and picked the small white daisy from amongst

184

the wildflowers. She barely knew him then, he had been nothing more than a fancy that should have passed. But even then, so long ago, when he had first arrived from Poland to work on the estate, somewhere deep inside, she knew he would never be just a passing fancy.

Pulling a wool scarf from her suitcase, she tightly wrapped it around her throat and went downstairs to look for Sigrid in the kitchen.

"W…w…where is Sigrid?" Anna asked, when she saw that only Lena was in the kitchen, preparing the evening meal. Anna was not sure, but thought she saw a dark cloud pass over Lena's face at the mention of Sigrid's name.

"I believe she is in the sitting room, Fraulein von Marschalkt, with the baby." Lena said, surprising Anna with her formal tone. Why had Lena assumed this formality again, Anna wondered. Anna had enjoyed the more informal relationship between the two of them

"I am sorry, she asked that I address you properly," Lena added as though sensing Anna's thoughts. Anna was about to ask Lena who the "she" was when she heard Maria returning with Alexandra and Thomas. Anna watched as little Thomas toddled to his mother, who picked him up in a loving embrace. Turning, Anna left the kitchen with more than a pain in her lungs.

Anna found Sigrid sitting in the rocking chair beside Maria's infant daughter, Hannelore Maria Liesel, knitting what looked like a green scarf.

"I did n…n…not know you kn…kn…knit so well, Siggi," Anna teased, as a cough wracked her body. Somehow her mood always improved when Sigrid was near. Sigrid stopped knitting as she watched Anna bend forward in evident discomfort.

"Come, child, we will make you some tea," Sigrid said, wrinkling her brow with obvious concern.

"N…n…no, Siggi. I am fine," Anna protested as she touched the soft green yarn. "You must w…w…watch the child, and…wh…wh…what are you knitting?" Anna asked as she looked up at Sigrid, who studied her with a peculiar expression.

"I'm not sure yet," Sigrid answered as she laid the needles in her lap. "It soothes my soul, it helps me to think," she added, as she turned to look out the window which revealed a quickly darkening sky. Anna studied Sigrid's familiar features and wondered about the woman she had known her whole life, but knew so little about.

"Siggi, d...d...do you believe t...t...true love comes only once in a l...l...lifetime?" Anna asked before she could think about what she had said. Sigrid considered the question as she looked straight at Anna.

"For some of us this may be the case, but for most, I believe love is in the mind as much as it is in the heart," Sigrid answered, as she bent down to pick up the ball of yarn that had fallen to the ground und unraveled. "What the mind decides, the heart will follow...," Sigrid's voice trailed off as she looked down at her creation. "There is something you must know. And it is time that you know."

The lump Anna felt in her throat, along with the cough that wracked her body every few moments, did nothing to help ease her fears. There was something about the way Sigrid had spoken that scared her. Was she now, finally, going to find out what happened to her beloved Jakub? She had been sure Sigrid knew nothing of his disappearance, yet what did she really know of this woman's secret life?

"Anna, you ask me of true love, and it is time I tell you of mine. You are old enough. There is a war. No one knows what the future will bring. I must follow my path with a clear conscience. I can no longer carry this burden." Anna did not know whether it was relief or disappointment that washed over her when she heard Sigrid was going to reveal something about her own lover, and not about Jakub.

"So, th...th...this is n...n...not about Jakub?" she stuttered, just as another cough overcame her. Sigrid did not answer, but briefly looked at her with a mix of concern and, what she interpreted as, disapproval.

"Listen, child," Sigrid said impatiently, "I must speak now, for in the morning I shall depart." The confusion written all over Anna's face was apparent.

"B...b...but we h...h...have only just arrived. Mama d...d... doesn't need you in D...D...Dresden. Maria n...n...needs you here. I n...n...need you," Anna protested, believing Sigrid was to return to Dresden.

"It is not to Dresden that I depart for, it is to France, but that is of no consequence," Sigrid said with a dismissive gesture. "I did love a man once, many years ago…and he loved me, but this love…was not right," Sigrid's tone had softened as she spoke.

"I know, you t…t…told me," Anna blurted out, excited to find out more of Siggi's enigmatic past.

"That man…," Sigrid hesitated as tears welled up in her eyes, "is the father of my two children." Anna stared at Sigrid with her mouth agape. She did have children, and all these years Sigrid had led Anna to believe she knew nothing of childbirth. "Oh, Anna, I have wanted to tell you and Maria…oh, how many times have I tried, only to remember my promise." Anna could barely make out what Sigrid said between sobs.

"Oh, Siggi, y…y…your private life is y…y…yours alone," Anna said, as she knelt before Sigrid and tried to comfort the woman who had spent her life comforting herself and Maria. Sigrid's sobs ebbed as she looked up and gently held Anna's face in her hands.

"Anna, that man is your father."

Anna heard the thump, but felt nothing as she sat down hard on the wood floor. Staring up at Sigrid, she mouthed the words she had just heard spoken. Her mind raced as she tried to make sense of it all. What would Mama say if she found out? Oh, Mama could not find out, she thought.

"Does she know? Does Mama know?" Anna whispered, unaware that she had spoken loud enough for Sigrid to hear. "Of course not, she would never allow Siggi near the house, or even in the city for that matter," Anna mumbled, as her mind tried to understand what she had just heard.

"H…h…how could he? H…h…how could you?" she finally asked. "H…h…how could you do th…th…that to Mama? She trusted you, S…S…Siggi." Anna said with a cracking voice as tears threatened to flow. "And w…w…where are the children? W…w…where are your two children, Siggi?" she asked, realizing with a start that she possibly had half-siblings somewhere. Anna rejected the hands Sigrid held out to her. Standing up, she backed away from Sigrid and asked again with a strangled voice, "Wh…wh…where are your children, Siggi?"

It was more than a dark feeling that crawled up Anna's spine like a spider, as she stared at this woman; it was a horrible certainty of what

Sigrid was about to say that made Anna's stomach turn. "N...n...no," she whispered, "n...n...no, you can't be m...m...my m...m...mother. A...a...and Maria too?" she asked with a whisper. Sigrid nodded her head in affirmation.

"I was never supposed to tell you or Maria...,"

"N...n...no! No! Lies. All lies! Lies! H....h...how can you d...d... do this to me? And M...M...Maria?" Anna shouted as she backed towards the door.

"Anna, please listen child, I must explain to you," Sigrid called after her as Anna ran out the door. She needed air. She could not breathe. A cough wracked her body as Anna pulled on her thick wool coat.

"Where are you going?" she barely heard Maria's voice as she ran out the back door.

It was late when Anna, half frozen with cold, slipped back into the house. Someone had left the back porch light on for her. Quietly she slipped up the stairs and walked into her room. She was not surprised when she heard a soft knock on her door.

"Can I come in?" Maria asked with a hushed voice. Shivering, Anna nodded, overcome by a body rattling cough, as she wrapped herself in a woolen blanket and lay down on her bed. Maria joined her coughing sister on the bed.

"H...h...how long h...h...have you known, Maria?" Anna asked, searching her sister's face.

"I only found out today. But....but I have had a suspicion for some time now," her sister replied without betraying any emotion. Anna looked at her sister and contemplated just how her barely older, yet seemingly much wiser sister, always seemed to have a sense for such things.

"Do I walk through life with my head buried beneath the ground?" Anna mumbled to herself, suddenly realizing that she too should have noticed something odd about the relationship between Sigrid, Maria, and herself. A strangled laugh, combined with a cough escaped from Anna's tired body.

"A m...m...maid. We t...t...treated her as a m...m...maid all these years, M...M...Maria," she said as she felt a sudden overwhelming sense of guilt. "W…W…Why, Maria?" Anna asked, "W…W…Why would M…M…Mama raise us as her own?" Anna heard her sister inhale sharply. Moments passed before Maria answered.

"I do not know. Possibly she and Papa protected us. We are Papa's children," Maria finally answered with a quivering voice.

"W…W…What do we do now?" Anna asked as she turned her head to look up at the ceiling.

"Nothing," Maria resolutely replied, "*We* do nothing."

Anna sighed audibly, as she wondered what strange twist life now had in store for her, for all of them.

Letter 6   *Sassnitz, 15. March 1940*

My Beloved Jakub,

I pray, as always, this letter finds you well. Two weeks ago I should have begun this letter, however illness prevented me from writing you. It is only now that I have the strength, and a moment between coughs to catch my breath, that I can begin to pour my soul out to you once again. My beloved Jakub, I write to you not from my beloved Dresden, but from the Baltic Sea where I have spent many a day and night dreaming of you. How I wish you here with me, more than the salty sea air I breathe, more than the sunlight that rarely breaks through the clouds. Again I find myself in emotional turmoil,I Jakub, but this time it is not I alone who suffers. If only you were here to wrap your arms around me, I know I would survive. Now, I feel as though I drown with each breath I take. How I will extract myself from this whirlwind of emotions I do not know. Somehow I must remind myself there are others out there, especially at this time of war, who suffer fates far more horrible than my own.

Please forgive my scattered thoughts, I have much on mind. It is not every day that one discovers the life one has led, the life one has known, has all been a lie. I write to you now because tomorrow Mama arrives and I do not know how to face her. Mama, the woman I have known all my life as such, is not the woman who bore myself or Maria. It was Sigrid, a woman I have treated as a maid all these years, who carried two daughters for Papa. Was this the true love she hid from me, from all of us, for all these years? How can she live under the same roof with Mama? How much betrayal Mama has suffered all these years, with the living proof of this treachery under her same roof? Oh, my heart bleeds for Mama. And Papa, what burden must now rest on his shoulders? A burden he can never relieve himself of. He is responsible for the misery of so many. But, when it comes to a question of the heart, can one truly assign blame anywhere? I have taken a step back from the whole matter and have considered heeding Maria's advice to do nothing, at least for now. Yes, this knowledge changes everything, but now is not the time to dig deeper into wounds that shall never heal. And yes, I have many unanswered questions, Jakub, with each new question leading to further questions, but I must wait to have these answered, if ever they shall be. Sigrid departed the morning after her confession, but did not disclose when, or if, she should return.

Do you see it, Jakub? Do you see the irony of it all? I have wasted so many days of my life, or our lives together, worrying that someone may uncover our secret love. And to what end? To hide our love from people whose own lives are shrouded in betrayal? Whose infidelity is a far greater sin than the pure, true love we share. I worry for Mama now. If any good should come of all this, it is that for the first time in my life I feel I understand her. It is no wonder she has worn a shield of armor around herself for so long, never allowing anyone close enough to penetrate her hard shell. Is this why she places so much faith in the Fuehrer? A belief that he shall not betray her or the Fatherland? How can she stand by Papa when his betrayal is visible every day in flesh and blood? She is a stronger woman than I. And Sigrid, how can she deny her own children for so long? Is it the war and its unpredictable outcome that forced her to reveal her secret? A fear of death? I have come to a crossroad in my own life, Jakub. I shall no longer hide my love for you. I know Papa and Mama know of my feelings for you. It is time they all learn the truth. The truth about you, about me, and about the son they will never become acquainted with. Maybe this path shall lead me to understand why and where you have gone.

Now, my dear Jakub, you understand why it is with great anxiety I face Mama tomorrow. Does she know Sigrid has disclosed

191

their secret? Does Papa know? I cannot be sure, but somehow I do not believe so. Strangely, with each day that passes, another piece of my youth, of my fond childhood memories, is peeled away, like an onion, to eventually leave what? A hardened soul which no longer has room for dreams and magic? As a child, this place, the Baltic Sea, was a magical place, filled with wonder and great expectations. It is different now, almost dull and faded, as though someone has painted it a shade of grey. I do not know how much the current revelations have to do with my state of mind, but the Baltic Sea shall never again be the same.

It is odd, Jakub, how wrapped up in my own world I can still be, when the world around me is at war. When so many I do not know or see suffer. A war which threatens my own existence, as well as that of my family and all I know to be real. The war too has taken so much more than the eye can see. The increasing lack of goods we are able to purchase is the overt effect of the war, but the wounded and destroyed spirits of man are the true victims of this war. I too have become disillusioned with reality, Jakub. But then what is reality? It is not the static constant I once naively believed it to be, but a dynamic, unpredictable state with infinite variables which enter at will into this equation of life. Oh, my love, how I long for the days of predictability and consistency. How I yearn for long nights spent in the hayloft with you, where I rest my head on your chest and hear the constant beat of your heart. Will we ever again be together? Or will this war forever sever our earthly ties? I dreamt of you again, Jakub, not in Australia, but in some other distant land, I was not sure of where. You were not alone, but surrounded by people, friends, who cared for you, Jakub. Of this I was glad. Yet somewhere I envy the life you lead without me in it...resent those who are close enough to touch you. Do you remember the flower you gave me so long ago? I carry it with me in my diary wherever I go. I shall never forget you, my beloved Jakub, and someday I will uncover all truths.

Love Eternally,
Anna v. Marschalkt

Post Script: As I sit here and look out to the sea I wonder how well I truly know the people whose lives I share every day. Secrets, secrets, secrets. They are all around us, are they not? Is there a man, woman or child alive who does not hide a secret somewhere in the depths of their soul? But what is it about a secret that allows it to wield so much power? The secret itself or the nature of any secret?

Post Script 2: I believe the fates have decided my sister shall only bring daughters to this world. The latest member of the Dieter Irmer Gottfried family is healthy Hannelore Maria Liesel, who, I am told, resembles me. Maria, whose sanity I question, is again with child.

Anna felt her hands shake as she placed her fountain pen carefully back into her small purse. Tomorrow Mama would be here. The thought of facing her mother made her stomach turn. What would she say to this woman, who had acted in the role of a mother, her mother, for so long? "Possibly Maria is right," Anna whispered to herself as she stared down at the letter she had just written. She carefully rolled her sixth letter to Jakub into a tight roll and inserted it into a green glass apple juice bottle she had confiscated for her journey to the sea.

Anna's mother would not arrive the next morning. Instead, a telegram arrived, urging them to leave the sea and return home at once. Hastily packing her things, Anna looked at the green bottle that stood on her desk. "You. I must send you on your way first," she spoke to her bottle, picking it up as though it were a sleeping child. Anna slipped out of the house unnoticed. Both mothers were too preoccupied with their children and packing to notice her leave. As she walked towards the churning waters of the Baltic Sea, which looked almost grey green beneath the dark grey sky, she briefly pondered her own mental state.

"What is wrong with you, Anna?" she whispered to herself, as she looked down at the cool bottle in her hands. "It soothes my soul," she replied, defensively, as she thought of Sigrid knitting to free her own soul. One needs an outlet, she told herself, as she approached the crashing waves. Standing before this unfathomable body of water, she picked up her bottle and briefly kissed the cold glass. From somewhere an image of kissing a cold, dead fish pushed itself into her mind. Anna shook her head to rid herself of the disturbing imagery.

"Jakub, my dearest, I apologize for my brevity, but we depart for Dresden shortly," Anna spoke, as a wave crashed close to her, drenching her shoes. "May you always be safe…and loved," she spoke without conviction, as unwelcome feelings of jealousy rose in her. "May you always be safe," she repeated, as she threw the bottle into the agitated sea and quickly turned to leave. There was still much packing to be done.

Anna did not turn around again. She would never know her green glass bottle was immediately washed back to the shore, where it would repeat this cycle, coming and going as the tides ebbed and flowed. Anna would never know a storm tossed her bottle onto the rocky Reugen shoreline, where the bottle shattered, forever destroying her words of love.

Travels of Letter 16
Indian Ocean, 13 miles off the
Indonesian Coast
April 1979

Standing on the deck of the *Oliana* he watched the horizon. It would be any moment now. Yuri rubbed his large abdomen, oily with suntan lotion. He was oblivious that years of vodka, beef stroganoff, and fried pirozhki had not improved his physique or general state of health. No one would ever dare tell him so. Uninhibited, he scratched his rear and dropped his shorts just far enough to urinate into the Indian Ocean. Watching as the long yellow stream of urine reached the ocean, he felt a surge of self importance swell up inside him. He had shown them all, he thought, his father, his mother, his brother, even his so-called friends who now called on him regularly. Yes, he had made more money than any of them, than all of them put together actually, and that in such a short amount of time. More money than he knew what to do with now, he thought, and chuckled as he spat his chewing tobacco into the green sea below. His mother had called him a drunk and his father a failure, he recalled with emotions he did

197

not even know how to describe, possibly feelings of inadequacy, he wondered.

"Sir, your drink," the young Malay boy said, interrupting Yuri's thoughts. Without looking at the boy Yuri reached for his martini.

"Two olives, I said," Yuri spoke softly, "two olives," he repeated, as he poured the contents of his glass over the frightened boy. "Now be a good boy and clean up this mess you made," Yuri spoke sweetly to the boy, but with an undertone the young boy was most familiar with. The half-naked boy quickly scampered away and returned a moment later with a towel in hand. The boy frantically wiped away the liquid on the deck as Yuri patiently scrutinized his work. "You missed a spot over there," Yuri pointed out as he casually kicked the boy in the ribs and turned towards the ocean once again.

"It's here, Sir," the Captain called down to him from the bridge. Well of course *it's* here, you dimwit, I can see the vessel with my own eyes, Yuri thought as he watched the wreck of a vessel slowly approach the *Oliana*. It amazed him that this rotten carcass of a boat could float, let alone navigate any body of water. But, then again, what did he care, as long as he received his cargo. Yuri felt a surge of excitement as the vessel drew near. He could see the red and white flag, could almost hear the fluttering of it, he thought. His excitement had not lessened one bit from his morning meditation. He was torn between the excitement of what was to come and disappointment in himself that an external variable could take control of his physiology. He liked to be in charge, in complete control at all times. It was only behind closed doors that he should let his guard down. His composed exterior hid an internal rollercoaster of emotions. He glanced around the *Oliana* to assure himself his guards were all present with their weapons drawn.

The small vessel pulled up alongside his pristine 100-foot yacht. Yuri raised his hand as a small, wiry man dressed in black made motions as though to board his vessel.

"That won't be necessary, Dong," Yuri said to the man, as he wiped away beads of sweat that poured from his forehead, as much from anticipation as from the sun beating down on his uncovered head. He wondered how these Indonesians could run around fully clothed so close to the equator, without even a drop of perspiration oozing out of their oily skin.

"Still no trust the Dong, eh?" the small, heavily accented man spoke without antagonism.

"It's your breath I could do without," Yuri replied nonchalantly, as he wondered where on this tiny vessel his cargo was hidden.

"You dirtier than slime round my hole, man," the small man said as he pointed at his behind. "We say twelve miles out. You boat 13 miles out. Cost you more. You no trust man, no trust," the small man snapped, revealing rotted and missing teeth.

"Maksim," Yuri called to his personal body guard. The body guard handed him a small locked case, which Yuri slowly opened with the key that had hung around his neck. He then held out the diamonds for Dong to see, payment for his cargo, just as the Captain called down to him from the bridge.

"Sir, we have confirmation, cargo has been delivered to the United States."

"What was the final count?" Yuri asked the Captain without taking his eyes off the small man.

"79 Sir," the Captain answered, and disappeared from sight again. The small man held his hand out for the case, as Yuri shook his head.

"Dong, Dong, Dong, you're getting sloppy my friend. I ordered 100, not 79," he said, as he waved a short meaty finger at the small man.

"You always lose some, man. Rot along the way, part of the contract," the small man said, as he impatiently held his hand out for the case again.

"You always lose some, you always do," Yuri laughed making his large abdomen quake. "First things first. Where is *my* order?" he asked, unable to adequately mask all of his excitement.

"No trust, asshole," the small man said, as he smiled and nodded at one of his own heavily armed guards. Moments later three young Malay girls were brusquely dragged on deck by the hair and shoved towards the Oliana.

"Not so rough with the cargo," Yuri warned lightheartedly.

Yuri watched as a guard helped the three girls across a narrow plank between the two vessels. He felt the adrenalin pulse through him, just as he always did when he watched his new girls cross the plank. Feeling his manhood ache and throb with desire, he was suddenly overcome by the sensation that he could do anything. He felt like a czar, no, he thought, he was a czar. He could have these girls right here, right now, in front of all these men. It became clear to him these weren't men, these were slaves, all of them, here at his beck and call. Sure he paid them, but what was money if not a means to enslave others? Yuri smiled at the thought and reminded himself that he was a benevolent, gentle man with manners, despite the family he was raised in.

Yuri followed the girls below deck, escorted by an armed guard. Pinching the girl immediately in front of him until she screamed, he contemplated how many times he had followed three young girls into his private room. How much cargo had he delivered to the United States? Business was definitely good in the U.S, he thought, as he watched the guard shackle each of the girls to a ring on the floorboards. Opening the tiny window, he motioned the guard to leave. Yuri locked the door behind him and turned to look at his most recent acquisitions. It was a shame to have to dispose of such beautiful creatures after he was done with them, but what else could he do? He couldn't exactly travel around with young girls crawling all over the *Oliana*. The fear he saw in their faces, smelled on their beings, increased his excitement and desire, fueled by his knowledge that he was in complete control of their lives. Rubbing his oily abdomen in anticipation, he pulled back his slick black hair and dropped his shorts, only to be interrupted by a furious banging on the door.

"Boats, Yuri, lots of em, come quick," Maksim called from behind the locked door. Pulling his shorts up, Yuri quickly unlocked the door and exited the soundproof room without closing the tiny window he had opened. Pulling a shade down over the door and surrounding wall, he stepped back momentarily to make sure the door was completely hidden, before he casually climbed the stairs and strolled on deck.

Four armed military boats had surrounded the *Oliana* after it had drifted out of international waters and into Indonesian waters. A team of heavily armed military officers boarded the yacht. The men conducted a thorough inspection and head count of all those on board.

Unable to find anything amiss, the military officer in charge ordered the *Oliana* to return to international waters. As the military detachment prepared to leave, a young Lieutenant leaned over the deck railing and spotted a green glass bottle being waved from an almost invisible window, followed by muffled voices; slight sounds he would have ignored had he not seen the glass bottle. The young Lieutenant, sensing something amiss, requested another search of the vessel.

Another more thorough search of the *Oliana* revealed a hidden room with three captive young girls. The owner of the vessel, along with the crew, was placed in an Indonesian prison, and later in a United States prison, where they were charged with human trafficking.

Cape May, New Jersey
Fall 2011

"Geez, this has gotta stop," I said with a hoarse voice as a loud ring tone wrenched me from a particularly good dream, one that I now was already in the process of forgetting. The conscious world began to creep into my awareness once again and I recognized the ring tone.

"Anna," I half-shouted, pounding on Charlie's back. The fact that he remained comatose despite the phone's annoying ring didn't surprise me after what I had done to him. I felt my face flush. "Charlie, your phone. Wake up!" I yelled, crawling over him to grab his cell phone. "Damn it," I cried, as the incessant ringing abated. "How can you not hear that annoying thing?" I accusingly asked the half-asleep man beside me. "Jesus Christ, you would sleep through an earthquake!"

"Huh…sorry, I uh, you know, I don't know," Charlie answered in a nonsensical way.

"Anna, maybe it was about Anna," I protested, as Charlie began to drift off into dreamland again.

"Anna?" Charlie sounded confused.

"Yes, Anna…your friend from Interpol's got a friend, or something like that, and he was going to call, blah, blah, blah. Remember?" I impatiently explained. "What is it about you men? How is it you can sleep through anything, but you're never too tired for sex?" Charlie suddenly sat up, catching me off guard, as he grabbed his cell phone and dialed his voicemail.

Despite closely watching Charlie's blank facial expression, I couldn't begin to guess who had called and what information they may have left. What a poker face this guy had. His face revealed absolutely nothing.

"Well? Who was it…what did they say?" I asked the moment Charlie pulled the phone from his ear. I know I sounded frantic, I even gave in to the urge to chew one of my fingernails. Not a habit I needed Charlie to find out about just yet, but I couldn't help myself.

"There is a record of Anna von Marschalkt's birth, but there is no record of her death," said Charlie, repeating the message he had just heard.

"Which means she could still be alive," I shouted, jumping into Charlie's lap to kiss him, but toppling him over instead.

"Hey, hey, easy there woman, I'd like children some day," Charlie teased, as I stretched out on top of him.

"So what do we do now?" I asked, feeling a burst of energy pulse through my veins, something I hadn't experienced in a long time.

"Well, we could make some more calls and try to locate her or…," Charlie looked at me with an odd expression.

"Or what?" I asked rather impatiently. Now was not the time to withhold information.

"Or you…we…you could fly to Germany and find her." My heartbeat pulsed in my ears, as I lay motionless on top of Charlie, digesting what he had just said. It had never crossed my mind to actually go out and search for this woman.

"Me? Go to Germany and find her?" Saying it aloud made my jumbled thoughts even more confused. "What if I can't find her? What if I do? What do I say if I find her?" Taking a deep breath, I had to stop myself. This was all just plain crazy talk, as Abe would say, but somewhere in the depths of my mind, the idea had already taken hold of me.

"Are you serious?" I asked, watching Charlie. I had to know if he was serious or if he just threw the comment out there to test my response; to determine how far my insanity would really go. But then again, it was Charlie who had kept all of this insanity alive. Charlie nodded in affirmation.

"I'm going," I said quite suddenly, surprising even myself. Charlie didn't flinch when he heard my words, but he had to wonder what his role would be in all of this. He had offered to go with me, hadn't he? "So, what's my next step?" I found myself asking, feeling like this was all an out-of-body experience.

"You really are serious, aren't you?" Charlie commented, seemingly impressed with my spontaneity.

"I've got nothing else to do, and the weather here hasn't exactly been the best beach weather," I said, smiling at Charlie as I felt his manhood come alive beneath me.

"Well," he moaned, "you likely won't find beach weather in northern Europe this time of year either," he said, suddenly distractedly.

"Hey, what's the matter?" I asked, sensing a shift in Charlie's enthusiasm.

"Nothing, it's uh, just, I don't want you to fly all the way out there and, you know, be disappointed." Charlie's tone sounded doubtful to me.

"Aww, that is sweet. Worried I can't handle it if I don't find her? Or worried what I'll do if I do find her?" I asked, actually touched by his protective feelings for me. "Don't worry, I'm a big girl, I can take care of myself," I said with more confidence than I felt. Why did I do that? Why couldn't I admit to him I didn't want to always have to take care of myself? Ever since Warren's death I was always proving to myself and everyone around me that I didn't need anyone. That I could do it alone. But the truth was I wouldn't mind having a shoulder to lean on once in a while.

"Alright, but you know, if you need me, you can always call me. I'll be in London soon you know," Charlie offered, as he gently pushed my tousled hair aside to kiss my neck, sending goose bumps up and down my body. I am a moron, why can't I just ask him to come along with me? And besides, it'd make things a heck of a lot easier with his connections.

"I'll be alright," I whispered in Charlie's ear. "And besides, I'm sure you've got better things to do in London than fly to Germany and follow some crazy woman around," I casually said, hoping Charlie would take the bait and insist he was coming along.

"Look, this whole Anna things got me pretty interested too. Make sure you call and give me an update on what you find," he breathed into my hair, squeezing my rear as his naked, throbbing manhood took what I no longer could resist. I could remain entwined with this man forever. But, all good things must end, right?

Propped up on my elbows, I watched with a heavy heart as Charlie wrote down his personal contact information. "And I'll call you if I find out anything else," he added, bending down for one last kiss before he left the motel room. Never in a million years would I have believed that separation from this man would be so painful. Why did I have to say goodbye? Why were there always goodbyes? Today he was headed back to New York and in a few days he would be in London. There was a really good chance that I'd never see him again. These types of holiday romances had a way of fizzing out as soon as the respective individuals returned home. At least that is what I've heard, but didn't want to believe. Was I crazy?

"Oh, Warren, I am so sorry," I said to the ghost that suddenly seemed to have materialized in this empty, lonely room. Just as I began to wallow in pity again, my singing cell phone interrupted my thoughts. My caller ID identified Abe.

"Hi, Abe," I answered, strangling my phone's annoying ring.

"Hey, Di," the voice on the other end of the continent rang in my ear.

"It's so good to hear your voice, Abe," I said honestly, feeling somewhat comforted by the sound of my brother's voice.

"So, everything A-okay on your end?"

"Yeah, ah, yeah, sure…of course," I lied.

"You sure? I just had this odd feeling…this sounds crazy, but I had a feeling you could use a call from your brother right about now." The concern in his voice transmitted clearly across the miles.

"Hey, I'm fine, little brother. So, look, I am glad you called. Could you do me a favor?" I felt my heart beat in my ears as I spoke.

"Yeah, sure. Hey, wait a minute. I forgot this was Diana I'm talking to. Maybe I should ask what the favor is before I find myself in some compromising position, *again,*" Abe teased, with just a hint of an undertone, likely remembering past favors I'd requested.

"Ha ha, funny guy. Look, it's really no big deal, but since I've got you on the line I won't have to call Sheila and Dad to tell them I'm going to Germany…"

"You're what? Why are you going to Germany? When'd all of this come about? And why can't you call them yourself?" Abe asked.

"I've, uh, I've got some things to take care of over there. Look, I'll explain everything when I get back. I promise," I said, questioning the sanity of my decision. Abe had always told me there were different levels of bad decisions. His always happened to center around women, bars, and booze. Well, this might rank up there with his bad decisions I thought, envisioning the look on Abe's face if I told him about Charlie and the search for the enigmatic Anna.

"You sound different, Di. Is this about a guy?"

"Look, Abe, I told you I'll explain everything when I'm back. Now tell me, are you going call Sheila and Dad for me or not?" I asked with my usual impatience.

"Fine. Fine. Just take it easy will you," Abe said. I was relieved to have Abe talk to Sheila for me, but I did feel a little sorry for him. Boy, was he going to get an earful from her.

After promising Abe that I'd be safe and take care of myself in Germany, I finally managed to wrangle him off the phone. His concern, I had to admit, while touching, could border on the annoying. Laying back on the springy motel bed, I again stared up at my familiar ceiling.

"So, what do I do now?" I asked the spider slowly making its way along a web it had spun in the corner of the ceiling. "Do I really go for it?" Why I was engaging in this conversation with myself I didn't understand. My mind was made up a second after Charlie suggested going to Germany to find Anna. It wasn't much later that I had a travel agent on the line, assisting me with my flight arrangements. The earliest flight out, at a reasonably outrageous price, was three days from now, flying into Berlin. That would have to do. Oddly enough, I didn't hear any protests from my normally ever-present, annoying, rational mind. Only when my thoughts wandered to Warren did I second guess my decision. What was my true motivation for going? To find this woman who had no ties to me whatsoever? Or was it the hope of meeting up with Charlie? The desire to keep this fairytale alive a little longer? Fear of going back to Los Angeles and my solitary confinement? Breathing deeply, I knew whatever life had in store for me, life did progress one day at a time. That is how I was going to walk through life now. One day at a time.

Before I knew it, only one day remained before I was to fly over the Atlantic. Charlie had assured me there'd be plenty of people, probably most people, who spoke English. "It shouldn't be a problem," the travel agent had told me. No, it shouldn't be a problem, but this cold I had picked up was turning into a problem. The evening had been miserable, and the day didn't seem like it would be much better. Bronchitis knocked me out flat for a month last year. I was in no mood for a repeat experience. "There's nothing like a walk in the salty air," I said aloud, reminded of a salt cave spa I visited with Warren. "What a waste of money," I had insisted, but when my allergy symptoms diminished significantly I had to admit there must be some hidden health benefits in the salt.

Searching the room for my coat, I wondered how I could manage to be such a slob. There was a reason the motel provided drawers, but somehow my things always ended up on the floor. As my eyes darted past the mirror, I saw something my mind immediately registered as wrong. Something that shouldn't be reflected in it. It was Warren. I immediately looked back in the mirror, but the vision had disappeared. I wanted to tell myself that it was just my mind playing tricks again, but somehow I couldn't.

"Warren, Warren, are you here?" I whispered, as the temperature in the room dropped. Shivering, I stared at my own reflection in the mirror. "What do you want me to do, Warren?" I pleaded with my reflection, as the room started to feel particularly suffocating. Out. I had to get out.

Walking along the Jersey shore, I was overcome by an odd feeling of tranquility. These moments had been few and far between since Warren's death, but strangely I experienced most of them since arriving in this bizarre little corner of the world. Maybe this is what's necessary to heal the soul. At least my soul. Maybe I should stay here and continue to heal. Maybe this is what Warren wants. Am I losing my mind? Or is it already lost? Looking down the length of the shore, I recognized the spot where I'd run into Charlie just a few days earlier. This trip really had done me a world of good, even if my guilty conscience wouldn't lessen its grip on my soul. Deep in thought, I startled when my cell phone started ringing yet again. Answering, I was surprised to hear Charlie's voice on the other end.

"Diana?" The voice on the other end sounded nervous.

"Charlie. Hi." My voice sounded hoarse, compliments of the cold I contracted God knows where. Why was he calling?

"I'm sorry, did, uh, did I get you at a bad time? You sound, uh, sick," Charlie said as a cough wracked his body and nearly shattered my ear drum.

"No and yes…no it's not a bad time, and yeah, I caught some bug, sounds like you did too. I'm okay though, just staring out at the ocean wondering what to do with myself," I said, hearing a sneeze transmit through the phone. "Gesundheit. We sound like a hospital ward," I said, not surprised in the least that we shared the same cold. We had, after all, spent quite a bit of intimate time together.

"Thanks, Diana," Charlie spoke hastily. "Look, I've gotta run here in a second, but I wanted to tell you we found an address for Anna's place in Dresden," he said in a rushed, but excited manner. "No guarantees though, keep that in mind." Time slowed down for me in that instant. It was one thing to know Anna was a flesh and blood person, but it was another thing to know her last known address. If I had wavered for even an instant as to whether I would search for this woman, my sign had come. There was no more doubt in my mind. I knew what I wanted to do. What I had to do. Was that it?

"One more day," I whispered to myself. Just one more day and I would be off.

Packing my bags the next day, I wondered if I should leave my worn undergarments behind. No one likes to travel with less than fresh undies. With my luck they'd choose my bags to rifle through. And besides, it'd give me some extra room. I tossed my worn underwear in the trashcan, and hoped the cleaning staff wouldn't find them. My disorganized packing was interrupted by the sound of a lock turning. Spinning around, I watched as my motel room door opened.

"Oh, I am sorry, Ma'am," a young cleaning woman said as she noticed me standing in the room, staring at her. "They told me you checked out, Ma'am," she said, holding a piece of paper towards me.

"Oh, I'm sorry, I didn't realize it was past ten. I've got an afternoon flight, and I forgot about the early check out time," I said, feeling somewhat abashed. Flustered by the maid's presence, I hurriedly packed the rest of my suitcase, stuffing clothing into any available space.

"I can come back later, if you need a little more time? Our little secret," the maid said, smiling broadly.

"Uh, no...no it's alright, I'm just about done. You could probably start on the bed, right?" I asked, looking around the room, realizing I still had personal items in the bathroom.

"I'm in no rush," the young woman said, handing me the bracelet I had left on the nightstand the evening before.

"Oh, thank you." I said, grateful for her honesty. "I would have been sad if I had lost this."

"Things are never lost, just misplaced," the maid said in her odd dialect. "Hmm," I replied, somewhat absent mindedly as I pushed down on my suitcase, which didn't appear to be bursting at the seams anymore.

"I guess speed makes for a better packer," I said to myself, but I'll just keep the discarded underwear to myself.

"You need help carrying that out?" the woman asked, pointing at my suitcase.

"No, thanks, it's got wheels," I answered, looking up. I just now noticed her beautiful, almond shaped eyes and dark espresso colored skin.

"Are you from Jamaica or someplace like that?" I asked as I sneezed in the maid's direction with such suddenness of force that I had no time to cover my nose and mouth. Horrified, I stared at the young woman who had just received millions of microscopic viruses hurtling through the air, and directly into her face.

"Oh God, I am so sorry...not to mention so completely embarrassed." Rushing into the bathroom, I continued to apologize profusely as I retrieved tissues for the maid, who wiped at her face with the back of her hand.

"No problem, I have had worse come my way, and besides I have never been sick. Not a single day in my life," the young black woman spoke with an undertone of pride.

"Not even a tiny little cold?" I asked, still horrified by what had just happened.

"Not one day, Ma'am. And it is not Jamaica, it is Somalia. My country is Somalia." Again I heard that unmistakable tone of pride in her voice. Handing her the tissues, I quickly packed up my toiletries and jammed them into my suitcase. Now I was not only embarrassed, but felt like an ignorant fool as well. With a brief glance around the room, I threw on my backpack, thanked the young woman, and handed her a ten dollar bill. With my suitcase in tow, I headed towards the door.

"Thank you, Ma'am, every bit helps pay for night school," the young maid smiled with a glowing face. I sneezed as I slowly walked down the hall, and then immediately coughed, wondering how someone could walk through life without so much as a cold. As the taxi cab approached, an odd feeling passed over me, as though I had left something behind. The feeling intensified as the cab sped towards the airport. God I hated this feeling. Did I leave something behind? Possibly something important? I had no idea.

Dresden, Germany

November 1940

Anna ran her fingers along the spines of the books in her father's study, the way she had so many times since she was a little girl. Only this time it was different. This time she was actually looking for something. She was searching for a world map. The map she had, the one Dieter had given her at Maria's urging, depicted the continent Australia with its geography, but provided no further details. Anna needed to find a more detailed map.

Anna had spent many hours huddled over her map, at times with her sister, contemplating and discussing which route Jakub would have likely taken to get there. Would he have traveled overland, and then by sea possibly? What type of vessel would he have found that would ship him all the way to Australia?

"I never realized how far away Australia truly is," Anna had told her sister, as the physical separation between herself and her lover felt even greater now that she saw it right in front of her on a map.

"Maybe he is not there. Maybe he is not far, maybe he is in London," Maria had said as she stroked her sister's hand. Anna had felt a lump in her throat when her sister mentioned London. Maybe she was right. What if he had not made it to Australia? What if he still awaited passage and was stuck in London, or even worse some-where here, confined along with other Jews? What if the Fuehrer took England too? Anna knew she had to stop, but she had no control over the dark paths her thoughts chose to wander.

"I pray to God every night that he is far from Europe," Anna whis-pered as she thought of all the unfortunate souls whose lives were torn from them, those who had no chance to flee, those who disappeared, from one day to the next, never to be heard from again. Her sister was right, it was not a good time to be a Jew in Europe

Anna moved her finger along the top of a large book, watching the trail her finger left as it moved through thick dust. How could her sister remain so calm she wondered, recalling how peacefully Maria had nursed her young daughter.

"What kind of future will they have?" Anna had asked Maria as she gently touched Anneliese Eva Maria's tiny hand and looked down at the older siblings playing with a wooden horse on the ground.

"It is not a good time to have young ones," Maria had said as she gently rocked her sleeping daughter.

"He has to have an atlas, a modern one," Anna said aloud, annoyed with her father's lack of organization. "At least one from this cen-tury," she added acerbically as she scanned the books that were out of reach. She was sure she had seen him looking at an atlas in the past, but she could not remember when that was, nor what it was he had been looking for. Asking him was out of the question, he would likely ask about her sudden interest in geography. Maria's suggestion she tell him it was an interest in seeing which countries the Fuehrer and Russia had already conquered was not convincing enough. Her father knew her thoughts on the war all to well, he would more likely find her reading Karl von Clausewitz's *On War* than following the Fuehrer's latest conquests. If Sigrid were here she would have asked her about an atlas. Sigrid knew every corner of this house, includ-ing Papa's study. Anna felt her face flush as she envisioned Sigrid and Papa in a tight embrace, engaged in inappropriate behavior. "My mother...," she whispered to herself as she looked around the room and wondered where it was she and Maria had been conceived. Trying to dispel the images of her father and Sigrid she wondered whether

Mama was aware that Sigrid had told her. "She must have been sworn to secrecy...why else would she have been able to live here," Anna pondered aloud as she absentmindedly chewed on a piece of her long red hair. "Mama would never stand for it," she spoke aloud again as she realized that her mother had stood for it for all these years.

There must be more to it then. There just had to be, she thought as she spied an oversized world Atlas she had seen her father examining some time ago. Absentmindedly climbing the wooden wall ladder she reached the Atlas. She had not yet addressed the issue of Sigrid with either her mother or her father, just as Maria had suggested, but there was a smoldering ember inside of her that insisted on knowing more, that demanded seeking out the truth. It was only a matter of time, she knew, before this ember alighted into a giant flame.

Oddly, despite the war and increasingly frequent bomb raid sirens, life for her family was almost normal, aside from the fact that Sigrid had not been seen since their short sojourn to the Baltic Sea. While goods had become more difficult to acquire, somehow her father had enough connections to ensure the family always had more than enough to live as they always had, evidenced by the box of Swiss chocolates on her father's desk. On occasion she would take a box of these chocolates and share them with the other women at the newspaper, some of whom did not share her privileged circumstances.

Pulling the Atlas out from amongst the other books proved a chore in itself. Almost losing her footing on the ladder, Anna lost her grip on the large book and watched as the Atlas crashed to the ground with a loud bang.

"Well, that solves that problem of trying to carry it down the ladder," she said to herself, hoping her father would not walk in at this moment. He seemed more distant lately, but that was no surprise, given the war and his constant worry. Her mother continued to search for appropriate suitors, but this was not an opportune time for such endeavors, as most young men were actively engaged to the war effort, as were many young women. "I believe I do my share," Anna again spoke to herself and thought of her job translating foreign newspaper articles. Both her mother and father believed her time would be better spent closer to home. Her father had told her she was safer close to home. He had told her their bunkers were smaller and safer than the public ones, but Anna would not listen. She now enjoyed the three, sometimes four, days a week she rode her bicycle the few kilometers into the city.

"I know where all the public bunkers are," she had said, hoping to ease her father's fears. It was her mother, oddly, who was most opposed to her leaving, "and she isn't even my real mother," Anna whispered to herself as she climbed down the ladder, immediately ashamed at herself for having such thoughts. "She may not be my mother by blood, but she has always acted in the role of mother," Anna said, thinking she must at least be grateful to her for that.

The book was heavy, and larger than any book she had ever seen. Instead of carrying it to her father's desk she sat down on the floor beside it. Carefully turning the pages of this oversized volume, Anna wondered how many of the books in her father's study had ever actually seen the light of day. Some of them had to be hundreds of years old. Slowly turning one large page after another she finally reached the Australian continent, depicted on two pages. Her eyes drifted across the continent from Western Australia to New South Wales. The continent was large, much larger than she imagined. "How will I ever find you, Jakub?" she asked as she looked at the various details seemingly drawn by hand. Her heart sank as she stared at the vastness of this continent a world away.

"This is outrageous...a despoliation of private property," Anna heard her father's voice resounding through the house. The Baron was rarely upset, and when he was, it usually took an accustomed eye to notice any difference in his behavior. For her father to be yelling, something appalling must have happened. Scrambling to her feet Anna rushed out of the study, forgetting about Australia and Jakub for the moment. And where was her mother, Anna wondered. Normally it was her mother's voice that boomed through the house from behind closed doors, not her father's more gentle voice. Anna raced down the hall with her skirts lifted. He was at the front door. She was not the only who had been attracted by her father's yelling, the house staff too had come, like moths drawn to the light. Even Lena, who had assumed Sigrid's role in the kitchen, came out with her son clinging to her leg.

Anna slowed her approach as she came to the large entrance hall and peered around the corner.

"It is your duty as a German citizen, a German solider, to assist with the war effort," she heard a man's voice speak with caustic precision as she peered around the corner to see the front entrance. Her father's back was turned to her, but she could just make out two, no three, officials, neatly dressed in the party uniform adorned with the black spider, the most senior of whom addressed her father.

"It is by direct order of the Fuehrer," the official, obviously attempting to emulate his Fuehrer in appearance, stated as he twitched his small moustache. "Every German citizen shall provide for the war effort…willingly." Anna did not like the emphasis this man placed on the word willingly.

"Willingly or what?" she mouthed to Lena and her mother who had come to witness this latest confrontation. Her mother, firmly pressing a finger to her lips, did not take her eyes away from her husband. Anna resisted the urge to ask her mother what these men wanted and turned to watch just as her father stepped outside and closed the door behind him. The small group of onlookers turned to step towards the windows.

Anna lifted her skirts and ran towards the back of the house. "No, I don't like gossip, but it isn't gossip when it's happening to your own family," she whispered to herself and barged out the back door. Someone was going to have to warn Maria about this. As Anna ran down the small back road to her sister's house, one she normally did not use, she turned and briefly paused to watch her father. He stood motionlessly as one of the three men stepped into his Mercedes automobile and, followed closely by another car, drove down their long driveway, only to disappear moments later into the woods that would take them to the main road.

Anna felt her heart sink as she continued to stare at the shape of her father and the dark woods. It was not the loss of her father's prized automobile that caused her grief, it was the way he too stood and watched the woods, utterly powerless. Here was not the infallible man she had grown up knowing. Here stood a man, bent forward, as though the weight of the world pressed down on him. A man who normally controlled his future and that of his family, but could no longer do so. Here stood a man whose spirit had been broken. Anna watched a moment longer, but the urgency to reach her sister pressed her onward. Had these men been to see Dieter and Maria yet?

That evening, under cover of a cloudy sky, Anna found herself beside her mother, father, and Dieter, digging a hole not 300 meters from the three holes previously dug to hide food preserved in glass jars for a war she had hoped would never come. Besides the preserves, her family placed what jewelry, silverware and gold her they possessed into thick wooden crates and carefully lowered them into the cold, dark earth.

As Anna watched one crate after another disappear, she was reminded of a coffin being lowered into the darkness, soon to be consumed by the unforgiving creatures of the earth. "When will all of this end?" she whispered to her mother who stood silently by her side. She could not see her mother, but she was sure she felt her shudder. It was the sniffle that startled her the most. Was the Baroness crying? Anna had never seen this woman shed tears, but under this darkened sky she realized, with an acute ache in her heart, that the Baroness was not without feeling.

Letter Seven   *Dresden, 15. November 1940*

My Beloved Jakub,

*I pray this letter finds you safe, well, and far from this dis-
ease that continues to spread its scourge throughout Europe
and beyond. How can one ever speak of humanity again?
How can one ever equate the human experience with anything
resembling compassion? Is civilization destined to repeat its
mistakes for eternity? The hour is late, Jakub, the night once
again seeps into my soul. Oh, Jakub, it is at night, in this darkness that I feel so alone. It is in this obscurity that the line
between reality and whatever lies beyond it blur. It is here I see
shadows. Shadows with voices that whisper to me, call to me.
Prayer is not enough to silence these voices. I hear the voice
of our son, of our children who yearn to be born. It has been
too long, Jakub, so long that I do not know if I can continue to
live without you, but know that possibly I must.*

*The war is taking its toll on Papa. He is not the man I have known
all these years. He worries constantly about the future, about
the family, about all the rumors of war, and especially about
Mama. Mama appears impervious to the incessant rumors. It
is rare that I hear Mama and Papa argue about the Fuehrer
and the war anymore. I believe Papa realizes this is a battle
he cannot win. Mama's health may have much to do with his
capitulation. Mama proudly flies the party flag and denies any
reference to her poor health, but it is with greater frequency, and
for longer periods of time, that she is forced to remain inactive.
Extraordinarily, my relation with Mama has improved since
Sigrid confessed her secret. I have even taken up knitting, and
to my own surprise, have knit the most hideous hats for the children. Maria, I must say, was not pleased with these gifts.*

Without Maria in my life I fear I would be lost. Sigrid has not yet returned, I do not know that she ever will. There are so many questions I would like to ask, need to ask. There are too many unanswered questions. Questions I could never ask Mama or Papa. There was a time I felt bitter towards Sigrid, and Papa too, but it is not my place to try and understand what it was that passed between the two of them. Now I feel almost indifferent, as though what happened does not really matter. Maria has been my pillar of strength through all of this. I have leaned on her too much. Sometimes I forget that she too has many unanswered questions of her own, and is quite busy with the children. Often I sit with the children, who, despite the war, grow stronger and more beautiful with each passing day, even Lena's young Thomas. It is in the innocence of youth that I search for hope in the future. Maria continues to amaze me. She has embraced her role in life and proves to be a wonderful mother and a seemingly attentive wife. What occurs when she and Dieter are in private I do not wish to know, but it is clear that Dieter is very much in love with Maria. Maybe that is what makes her marriage bearable–the knowledge that there is a person who loves her so deeply, even if she is unable to reciprocate that same love.

It has been almost three years since you last held me in your arms. So much time has passed, yet it seems as though just yesterday you disappeared. I feel I have reached a impasse in my search for you. Daily I study the map of Australia, dreaming of the places you may walk, wondering if I am a part of your dreams. But sometimes, Jakub, sometimes the realities of the war and the human suffering slither into my thoughts. It is then that I convince myself you are locked away somewhere, tortured, possibly awaiting death. Jakub, may the power of my love reach you wherever you are. I fervently await the day our paths shall again cross.

Love Eternally,
Anna v. Marschalkt

Post Script: I have again seen the hummingbird outside my window. Can it really still be one of two released by Papa's cousin? How can the poor creature possibly survive here?

Anna felt tired. She did not want to wake up at her desk again, but she also could not find the energy to move herself to the bed. Staring out the window she felt sleep tugging at her being. A movement in the garden beneath the lamppost caught her eyes. If there was someone out there they would surely pass by the next lamppost in either direction she thought. As she waited, she could hear her own heart racing in her chest. She did not have to wait long to see someone pass quickly beneath the light cast by the lamppost. Rarely erring on the side of caution, she grabbed her coat and headed down the stairs as fast and quietly as possible.

The air outside was too cold for slippers, but they would have to do for now, she thought, as she heard someone breathing not far from her, but rapidly moving away. Whoever it was had disappeared behind the side of the main house and was headed for the back lawn. Silently, Anna followed the heavy breathing that she thought she recognized. It was a dark night and almost impossible to see anything. Without the sounds of heavy breathing and footsteps she would never know in which direction this mysterious person was headed.

The footsteps stopped abruptly and were followed by the sound of digging. Anna realized she should have known better than to confront a thief likely attempting to dig up the jewelry and silverware her family had buried. It could not be her mother or father, and it certainly would not be Dieter. As she stepped closer, she recognized the wheezing cough.

"M...M...Mr. Zimmerman!" Anna nearly shouted, as she stepped towards the dark outlines of a man with a shovel. Her eyes had adjusted enough that she could make out his silhouette under this dark sky. Anna heard a gasp and the shovel drop with a dull thud. "W...w...what are you doing?" she stammered with fear as she realized the precarious position she had placed herself in. The gardener did not answer, which only heightened her agitated state. "I w...w... will scream," she quickly threatened, taking two large steps backward when she sensed her life might actually be in danger. "I can outrun him," she whispered to herself when she felt she was far enough out of the shovel's range. "I have a proposition for you," Anna said, grateful that she had not stuttered. "I say n...n...nothing of this if you t...t... tell me whom you told about Jakub." Anna was surprised by her own

222

authoritative tone. Something she must have learned from her mother she thought. The gardener's silence did not ease her tension. Anna heard his quick, labored breathing.

"The Jew?" Mr. Zimmerman asked, finally speaking. "You want to know of the Jew?" Anna could smell his breath from where she stood. Obviously he had been at the bottle again. "I will tell you about the Jew."

Travels of Letter 16
Somalia Coast, Africa
March 1988

The old woman felt her knees buckle and dropped to the warm ground, grateful for the soft sand her old bones landed on. Unwilling to move, she felt anger, a boiling rage, for her God. Was he her God, or was he only the God of the men, deaf to the laments of women? She watched as a small boat with two young men drifted by, waving to her as they passed. Disregarding the young men, she wondered where the justice was in all of this. It was not hers to question but, undeterred by social and religious limitations, she poured her soul out to this unjust God.

"Why do you take from me my children? What evil spell is this? What curse has been placed on my children? On me? Why do you not take me? I am old, of no use," she cried. "What horrible crimes have I committed that you leave me no child, and only one grandchild?" Dizzy with anger and sadness the old woman alternated between mourning wails and depressing silence.

"Nadifa. Nadifa," she heard her husband's third wife, Aziza, and also the youngest, call out. The old woman chose not to answer and stared silently into the wide blue hazy nothingness. "Nadifa, there you are. Come, you have been without drink for too long, and there is fresh camel meat, it would do you good," Aziza said as she gently tried to lift the old woman from the sand. Unable to move the old woman, Aziza squatted beside her. "He was my son too. I too mourn him," she spoke, gently laying a hand on the old woman.

"He was not your son, none of them were your sons," the old woman spoke with a fierceness that startled Aziza. "I alone bore them into this world," she hissed. Slowly raising herself, Aziza backed away from the old woman, realizing she needed this time alone. "I alone cared for these children," Nadifa spoke, more softly now.

"I am sorry," Aziza said as she left the old woman alone on the beach.

Nadifa had never been fond of her husband's choice for a third wife, but had been powerless to change his mind, even with her elevated status as first wife who bore her husband three sons. Wiping sand from her long dress, she sobbed as she recalled the loss of each of her sons. The youngest had been killed by a stray bullet, the oldest by an intentional bullet, and now there was Labaan, in whom she had placed all her hopes. What was this cruel scourge that was laying waste to so many so quickly? She had nursed him throughout, prayed throughout, and watched him wither away before her eyes, just as his first and only wife and two of their children had before him. Lightheaded with grief, she closed her eyes and searched for a hidden corner within herself that she could crawl into and hide. "Why not me?" she again begged the God who had forgotten her, "Why not me?" she thought as she heard her name called from somewhere faraway.

"Nadifa, come back with me," the old woman heard her sister say. The old woman felt as though she was unable to move, and stared blankly at the woman who mirrored her own image, the one she had shared a womb with, and now had grown old with.

"Why?" she whispered as her sister sat down beside her.

"I do not know why, Nadifa, but I do know that you must drink," her sister answered with a fierceness she recognized as her own. Momentarily shaken from the stupor she had been trapped in, Nadifa looked at her sister who held out a wooden cup filled with camel's milk. Reaching for the cup with a shaking hand, her sister helped her guide the cup to her lips. "And when you have finished this you will eat," her sister commanded, as she raised herself from the hot sand. "I must go and help with the food."

The old woman nodded in silent acquiescence as she lifted the cup to her lips again. She felt the fluid pass through her and revitalize her life's blood. Watching her sister disappear in the distance, she envied this woman who never bore any children, who never knew the anguish that the loss of a child, young or old, caused. The old woman continued to sit on the warm sand. Her rage at this peculiar God had subsided, but left in its place was a dull, throbbing pain she could feel in her heart. On this day she would not pray again.

She did not know how long she had been sitting under the hot African sun when she saw a child approach, leading a goat with one hand, and holding a bottle in the other.

"Grandmother, she says you are going to be okay, we both are. We have to take care of each other now," the small girl spoke, as the goat tugged at the rope she held onto tightly with her little hand.

"Who is she?" the old woman asked Ayan, closely watching her young granddaughter. She had Labaan's eyes. She had seen that the day Ayan was born and she first looked into those beautiful innocent eyes. Eyes that did not yet know this world and all the cruelty it had to offer. As she looked deeper into those eyes, she saw innocence lost, but eyes still filled with hope, despite the cruelty and despair that surrounded them.

"Who is she?" she asked her young granddaughter again, more gently than she spoke with anyone else.

"The woman from the sea," Ayan answered, as she dropped a shadowy green bottle in the sand beside her grandmother and sat down in Nadifa's lap, tugging the goat down beside her. "She was with me when I found this. She came out of the sea," Ayan said as she pointed at the bottle. "It's for you she said," Ayan spoke as she looked down the beach as though searching for someone. "She's gone now. She went back into the sea. Father's with her."

Superstitious by nature, the old woman stared at the bottle, half expecting it to move on its own. "Why did you pick this up child?

227

Speak the truth," the old woman demanded, pointing briefly at the old bottle. The young girl turned to look at her grandmother.

"I told you, Grandmother. It is for you. She said so." The girl sighed as she turned back to face the ocean again. The old woman studied the bottle, afraid to touch it. What evil curse was at work here? Was her granddaughter next? Had some evil curse been placed on her whole family? Was this a sign? This one, she thought, as she hugged her granddaughter against her body, was all she had left. No one was going to take her. Cautiously picking up the bottle the old woman suddenly dropped it again, as though she had picked up a venomous snake. She did not know whether the odd vibrations she sensed had come from her own body, her imagination, or from the bottle that now lay motionless beside her. Upset with her own ridiculous behavior, the old woman gently lifted the young girl from her lap.

"Come, child," Nadifa said as she carefully lifted the bottle with two fingers. These were childish fantasies, she told herself unconvincingly. The girl had just lost her father. "We will return this to the sea, to your woman," she said. The young girl followed her grandmother to the edge of the water, the goat at her side, and watched as her grandmother tossed the bottle back into the sea.

The old woman and the young child stood silently, side by side, and watched the bottle drift away. It was time to take care of things Nadifa thought as she watched the bottle drift out of sight.

Ayan forgot about the day she found a shadowy green glass bottle on the beach. She was devastated when her grandmother passed away at a very old age, but found peace in the knowledge that her grandmother had seen her marry and had received the news from America that each of Ayan's three children were born healthy. Like Ayan, none of her children would ever fall ill. Ayan often wondered about her grandmother's last words to her, "The woman from the sea."

Newark International Airport, New Jersey
Fall 2011

"Well, now you really think I'm stalking you," the voice behind me teased. Turning around abruptly, I found myself staring up at Charlie's gorgeous smiling face.

"You have to say, it is just a little weird," I replied, smiling as I stood up to embrace him. "What are you doing here?" I had to admit, he was about the last person I expected to see right about now.

"My case, remember the one I told you about?" Charlie asked as he sat down and patted the seat next to him, inviting me to sit.

"Uh huh," I answered dumbly, fighting the urge to nervously chew my fingernails. Could it be? Could it really be that his case was canceled and he was going with me? On the same flight?

"Remember when I said part of the case was in New York, part of it in London?" Nodding I watched Charlie, not really wanting to give in to hope, yet feeling as though I already had. "Well, it turns out the London part of the trip is no longer necessary." Charlie seemed excited, almost nervous himself, as he spoke. But why would he be excited? That would mean he didn't have to go anymore. Unless that

meant he *was* coming with me now. He looked at me as though waiting for me to say something.

"What? I mean, what does that mean, you're not going to London?"
I asked, wondering just what this perfect man could possibly find so
attractive about me. It definitely wasn't my brains—I lost all mental
abilities around him. Did he feel the same?

"Well, let's just say the witness that was to be deposed, has been...
disposed of," Charlie said with a satisfied look on his face.

"You mean the guy is dead?" I asked incredulously. "And you...
you are okay with this? So it is, uh, good news...that this guy's dead?"

Charlie nodded his head. "This guy's the other half of a major
venture in trafficking sex slaves. Young girls. Somehow he's managed
to slip through one loophole after another. We weren't even close to
building a case against this creep. He wouldn't have helped my case...
and that's putting it mildly."

As I listened to Charlie talk about sex slaves and dead witnesses, I
couldn't help thinking of his naked body pressed firmly against mine.

"He's managed to find ways around the law, what I mean by loop-
holes, for years. He didn't even need to run from the law, but used it to
his advantage. He, how should I say it mildly, had it coming." Charlie
said, as he twitched his nose and then released a thunderous sneeze.

"And Gesundheit to you too," I offered, handing him a tissue, trying to distract myself from the throbbing sensation between my legs.

"Looks like the two of us make a dandy pair, huh?" Charlie eyed
me, just as I blew my own red nose. I suddenly felt self-conscious and
wondered what he saw when he looked at me with those beautiful
eyes that could even seduce a grieving widow. I watched his eyebrow
twitch as he looked at me and winked. Was he thinking what I had just
been thinking? They say men think of sex every few seconds. But then
who was I kidding, he walked past plenty of beautiful women every
day. I'm sure he had plenty of sexual fantasies that didn't include me.
And I had been up all night with this dang cold, so I wasn't exactly
looking my best with a red bulbous nose.

Charlie squeezed my thigh, a little higher than normally acceptable in public places, but hell, did I care right now? No, not after that
little jolt of lighting shot straight up my body and into my heart. He

could press me down on these uncomfortable airport lounge seats and I'd be willing. How did he do that? Jeez, easy girl. I had to remind myself where I was.

"Sheridan was right about you," Charlie said, whose hand still rested precariously close to the currently forbidden zone. He was still looking me up and down. "Diana, you are special, and I have to say I have fallen for you, in a really big way." Watching Charlie's ears and then his face turn the same shade of crimson mine must be, I thought the two of us must look like two guilty teenagers caught in the act. "So, if you would like to have me that is, I'd like to help you find that Anna of yours." That wasn't what I expected Charlie to say. It was what I had hoped to God he might say, but never dreamed he would. Was he for real?

"Are you serious? You want to come with me... right now?" I asked, the doubt resounding in my voice.

"Well yes, uh, I mean no, I've got this ticket to London...I'd, uh, have to meet you in...where are you flying into again?" Charlie seemed less enthusiastic now. Maybe he was second guessing his own decision. Was I not enthusiastic enough about his offer?

Taking a deep breath I looked at Charlie. "I would love you to come," I said and felt a huge weight lifted off my shoulders. Honesty was the best policy after all, right? I watched Charlie's expression transform from anxious anticipation to pure joy, and I couldn't help thinking of a child in a candy store. However much I must sound and feel like an idiot at times, it was wonderful to know that my idiocy was well received by Charlie.

"Thank God, Diana," Charlie pressed a quick kiss on my lips. "Look, I've gotta get to my own flight...I wasn't really sure I'd be on it...but if you wait for me in Berlin, I'll meet you," Charlie stammered as he nervously twisted the strap of his carry-on bag.

There wasn't any time to waste. I pulled out my hotel information and quickly copied it down for Charlie, lest he come to his senses and change his mind.

"I can help you," Charlie said, as I handed him a shred of paper with my scribbled writing on it.

I looked at him. "I know," I smiled. With one final indecent squeeze, he gently pushed me away and started for his own gate. Thoroughly content, I watched Charlie dash away.

He didn't turn around again. I watched until he was out of sight. Watching Charlie, I wondered if all of this was real. And if it was, it all seemed just a little bit insane. Didn't it? Feeling the onset of dizziness I had experienced earlier, I quickly sat down and placed my head between my legs, likely looking like an escaped lunatic. After a few minutes in this rather odd position I felt a lot better.

"Is this man really going on a European adventure with me?" I whispered aloud, unzipping my backpack to pull out the letter, still wrapped in a protective plastic bag. This letter, this was the reason Charlie had returned to the motel that night. Was this letter the reason Charlie had called me so often? It was this letter that was taking me, and a man I had recently met, on an oversea odyssey to find a woman neither of us knew anything about. A woman who may not even be alive anymore. Carefully removing it from the plastic bag, I unrolled the letter and read it for nearly the hundredth time. Each time I read it felt like the first time, as new secrets, or clues, into this woman's life were revealed, or at least I imagined them to be revealed. "You are as crazy as a loon," I whispered to myself, as I repackaged my holy letter and zipped up my backpack.

There it was again, that nagging feeling that I had forgotten something. I was leaving a motel, not my own home, so it wouldn't matter if I left the coffee pot on, the cleaning people would surely turn it off. And there was nothing left in the closet. And my toiletries, I packed all of those, but none of those items were vital anyway, all of them easily replaced. No, I don't think I left anything behind, but I still couldn't rid myself of this irritating feeling, which intensified as I walked toward the gate to board my flight. I stopped, set my backpack down and unzipped it one more time to reassure myself that I still had my passport. I had been lucky enough to bring it from Los Angeles; call it intuition. And there was the wrapped letter and the knit-work with the brooch. My wallet, tucked beneath the knit "nothing." Everything seemed to be there. Zipping up my backpack, I firmly told myself to stop worrying like an old woman. But the feeling, almost like an itch on my back that I couldn't reach, didn't want to go away.

It wasn't until the plane accelerated and was en route for the Berlin Tegel International airport that I finally realized what I had left behind in the motel. "I didn't look under the bed," I whispered hoarsely. "I didn't look under the damn bed!" Caught in an emotional tailspin, I blindly reached for the air sickness bag, and not a moment too late. I was over-come with a profound sense of loss, as I emptied the contents of my stom-ach. "Oh no, Warren, your letters. No, please not your letters," I cried helplessly into the paper-bag still pressed firmly to my face, unaware of anything or anyone around me.

Dresden, Germany

March 1941

Anna listened as the Fuehrer's voice resonated from the sitting room. Even through closed doors his voice boomed like an angry machine.

"Bulgaria too," she almost spat the words. "And this man does not even sound human. And now Bulgaria too," she repeated in a whisper. This war was not going to end until every country in the world was gobbled up, of this she was convinced. Did they not see the monster they cheered for she wondered with disgust, as the cheers and roars of thousands poured out of her mother's radio, which was rarely silent these days. Passing by the doors, she wondered if her mother was alone in the room. Unlike her mother, her father did not hang on every word the Fuehrer ranted, but Anna did find him listening to the radio almost as much as Mama these days, at least when he was home. He had been ordered to report to Berlin, and spent much of his time traveling between Dresden and Berlin. He wore a constant furrow of worry on his brow, unlike her mother's almost expressionless visage.

Anna picked up her boots and slipped them on as she headed towards the door.

"Why did she return?" she asked herself, storming out of the house like a tempest. She had just gotten used to the fact that Sigrid would not return. No one had heard from her in months, "And now she returns without an explanation of where she has been. Damn her!" she silently cursed, welcoming the evil spirit that roused in her. "*And without an apology!*" Anna felt unbounded rage toward Sigrid, but also toward her mother. She had not spoken to her mother since the evening she discovered Mr. Zimmermann attempting to steal her family's buried fortune. She had not yet recovered from the shock of what he had said, that it was her mother who was responsible for Jakub's abrupt departure. And when directly confronted, her mother did not have the strength of character to discuss Jakub. Her mother had refused to talk about Jakub with her, "but she denied nothing, just as Mr. Zimmerman predicted she would," Anna hissed, resisting the urge to stomp the ground like an angry child.

It had been a difficult time for Anna these last months. There was no one she could talk to who understood. Her bond with Sigrid had been damaged, if not severed altogether. "M...M...Maybe it was I who drove h...h...her away?" she pondered aloud, wishing she could turn back time and disappear with Jakub. "And Maria, again she is with child. She is always with child, and in need of much rest," Anna sighed, crushing the small worm of jealousy that threatened to burrow to the surface of her consciousness. She wanted Maria to be happy, of course, but somehow her own dissatisfaction with life and the world was magnified in comparison with her sister. "At least Mama leaves me be," she sighed again, kicking a rock that lay in her path. Her mother had not sought out suitors for her since the evening she had confronted the gardener about Jakub, recalling the distaste with which Mr. Zimmerman had said "Jew."

Anna grabbed her head with both hands and screamed with all her being, "Why? Why?" She bent forward to catch her breath and considered returning to the main house to interrogate the whole lot of them. Her father had warned her to leave Sigrid be, but why wouldn't he? After all, he was *her* lover at one point in time. "Or does he remain her lover," she hissed at the cool afternoon sky. Anna felt a wave of nausea wash over her. The picture of her father and Sigrid embracing in a moment of passion was one she did not care to conjure up again. Unfortunately this image managed to intrude on her thoughts too frequently. Unsure where her afternoon walk would lead, Anna headed towards the stables.

"P...P...Papa's new horse," she said aloud, deciding to view the animal she had heard so much about. "One thing Papa is right about, creatures like these are of superior character when compared to mankind," she spoke without stuttering as she entered the stables.

"Whoa, whoa, that's a good boy," Anna whispered to the black stallion that had recently been acquired. He father had warned her to stay away from him. "Who is he to speak to me about things I shall and shall not do?" she whispered with an underlying hostility the horse sensed. Undeterred, Anna opened the gate and entered the box stall.

"Whoa," she breathed, holding out her hand towards this black beauty. She slowly moved toward the agitated horse whose ears were pressed flat against his head. Suddenly rearing, the gigantic creature lashed out and nearly missed Anna's head.

"Wh...wh...whoa boy," she stammered and quickly moved back, blindly reaching for the box stall door behind her. The magnificent beast, emboldened by Anna's fear, reared again, hitting Anna in the arm with such force she was knocked to the ground. The pain in her arm shot through her like a bolt of lightning. Instinctively rolling away, she barely managed a scream as the wild creature crashed down over her, miraculously failing to damage any further body parts. Expecting to have her skull crushed at any moment, she rolled again as the beast raised itself and pounded down with such force she felt the ground quake beneath her. It was the high pitched screams the horse emitted, blind fury, that made Anna realize her life may soon end. "It is true what I have heard," she breathed with clarity as time slowed, "a lifetime does pass before one's eyes in the moment of death." She had not seen Jakub this clearly since before his disappearance. Anna did not feel the hoof of the horse hit her head.

In one instant she relived her time with Jakub with extreme intensity. She felt a peace that transcended her being, and brought with it closure and acceptance of whatever was to come. Somewhere in the back of her mind, in this same instant, she perceived the sound of sirens followed by a familiar voice shouting. And somewhere faraway the voice of her lover spoke to her. With all the power that binds the human will to life, she rolled away from this great demon of a horse, towards the door of the box stall, as the last remnants of her conscious being drifted away.

Anna's was unaware of arms pulling at her, dragging her out of the box stall. There was no pain now, only darkness. Somewhere in that darkness she heard her name called, but that no longer mattered. She knew there was someplace else she was destined to go.

"Anna! Anna!" She heard her father's voice fade as even words no longer penetrated her darkness.

Where was the horse carrying her? Anna felt a rhythmic pacing beneath her. No, it was not a horse, she slowly realized, someone was carrying her. The air raid sirens were blaring out their ominous song. The sirens, she thought to herself in her now semi-conscious state, why do we worry so about them? The sirens sound the coming of the war to the Fatherland, but the war is not here. It is far away. Time and again they sound. Time and again we flee to our living tombs. And there we wait. We wait in darkness, surrounded by a palpable fear. Where the only sound is the beating of hearts and death's approaching footsteps. We wait for the end, listening as the footsteps approach, at times slowly, at times with a quickened pace. Yet the end has not come. "Are the sirens to remind us of those dead and dying on the battlefield?" she muttered

"What do you say, child?" Anna recognized her father's voice but was unable to answer. "Quiet, child, quiet," he urged as she briefly opened her eyes. A pain in her head, as well as her arm, became more pronounced as she rose into consciousness.

"Papa," her voice sounded foreign to her, as though a much older woman had spoken. "My head," she groaned, attempting to lift her uninjured arm to her head.

"I know, child, I know. Remain still, Anna, please," her father urged, as the sirens continued to resonate.

"How is she?" It was Otto, the farm hand, peering at her as her father carried her down several steps into the dank, dark bunker.

"She needs a doctor," her father snapped, "She needs a doctor, now!"

"We need to get her out of here," a voice that she didn't recognize insisted, "She is losing much blood."

"Blood," Anna whispered hoarsely, as she stared into the darkness trying to make sense of it all. What had happened? Who was here beside Papa and Otto? Where was Mama? And Maria, and the girls? She felt tired, more tired than she had ever felt before in her life. And this place, what was this place which confused her with its odd smell. This did not smell like the hayloft, and it was so cold, much colder than it had ever been before. Anna drifted back down to the unconscious world.

"Jakub, I am here," she whispered into the darkness, as she reached out to caress his familiar face, longing for his warm embrace.

"I have missed you, Anna," he whispered, as he handed her a small wooden box.

"And I you, Jakub. But it is cold, Jakub. It is so cold," she said, opening the small box. The box emitted rays of brilliant light, warm light. A light of such beauty, Anna could not tear her eyes away from such sparkling brilliance.

"Oh, Jakub, it is beautiful," she whispered, marveling at the shimmering tiny green hummingbird she now noticed inside the box, inside the brilliant light. Gently she lifted the delicate creature from the box and held it close to her heart.

"You must set it free, Anna. It is not meant for you to keep," Jakub gently spoke as he reached for her hands and tenderly opened them. Together they watched as the hummingbird disappeared, leaving only darkness behind.

"I will go and find a doctor," Otto offered, moving through the musty darkness and up the steps to the light. The Baron did not stop him. He was willing to take any risk to save his daughter's life. He held the oil lamp close to his daughter's beautiful red hair and stared at the shirt he kept firmly pressed to her head, watching as it slowly changed from white to red.

"I have done wrong by you, Anna," he whispered, struggling with his conscience. There was so much he should have told her, but could not. "I only wanted what was best for you," he murmured, as he watched his daughter mumble unintelligibly. "Why dear God, why?"

he cried as he saw the irony of it all. They were surrounded by war, yet death was coming to his family by the hoof of a horse. His horse. "Oh, Anna, my Anna," he sobbed, as he picked up his daughter and left the bunker. "You shall not die in this dark tomb," he spoke to his unconscious child, resolved to risk anything for her. The Baron did not heed the sirens as he carefully carried his daughter towards the main house.

"Jakub," he heard his daughter speak softly.

"No, child, it is Papa," he said, attempting to maintain composure as Goethe's *Erlking* poem possessed his mind. How long would it be before Otto returned, the Baron wondered, as the eerie sirens continued their ghostly death wail.

The house became alive again the moment the incessant, bone-chilling wails ceased. The sirens had long since discontinued their alien howling when Otto returned with a young doctor in tow.

"Where is the young lady?" the doctor asked Lena, who had greeted him at the main house. Lena showed the doctor to the sitting room where Anna had been laid upon the sofa. The Baron, still holding the blood soaked shirt to his daughter's head, looked up at the doctor and then to the women who surrounded his life. They were all here: Anna, Maria, Frieda, and Sigrid, who had returned just yesterday. And now Lena, who delivered the young doctor.

"Baron," the doctor muttered with a slight nod, as he headed straight for Anna with an almost surprised look in his eyes. His new patient, who seemed to hover between two worlds, drifting in and out of consciousness, moaned as he carefully examined her head.

"I require boiled water, vinegar, and clean linens," he resolutely ordered, a contrast to his usual nervous manner, while never removing his eyes from the patient.

"The bleeding has stopped," the doctor observed a short time later. He pressed the stained shirt back on the head wound he could barely see under Anna's matted hair. Unsure as to the extent of internal brain damage, the doctor examined Anna's pupils, jumping back in surprise as his patient unexpectedly opened her eyes and reached out and to touch his face.

"It is you," Anna whispered as she gently touched the doctor's face. The Baron, dismissing his daughter's comments as hallucinations, nervously awaited the doctor's opinion. After a few moments, moments of such silence the Baron heard the beat of his own heart, the young doctor looked up as though evaluating the family.

"No, she shall not pass from this earth today. However, she has suffered a bruise to the brain and must remain very still."

"She will live?" Sigrid gasped, as though releasing a breath she had been holding for too long.

"Oh yes, I am quite certain of that," the doctor replied, as he again checked the pulse of his patient.

"She shall be quite alright now," he spoke almost casually, as he cleaned and dressed Anna's wounds, under the mumbled protests of his semi-conscious patient.

"You must change the bandage daily," the doctor instructed Lena, as he checked on his sleeping patient one last time. "I do not normally believe in miracles," he spoke, hesitating before continuing, "but in the case of your daughter...." The doctor had turned to look at the Baron, but abruptly stopped speaking, as though realizing some things need not be spoken aloud. "Well, I should be off then," he said nervously, as he finished washing his hands, "but I shall check on the patient tomorrow."

"And what of the arm?" the Baroness asked, handing him a towel just as Sigrid walked in.

"As I told the, ah, Baron, that the dislocated shoulder I reset shall cause some, ah, discomfort and should be rested for two weeks. As for the bruised arm, alternating warm and cool compresses," the doctor said, handing the damp towel back to the Baroness with a slight nod. "And the head injury, of course," he said, tapping his lips with his pointer finger as though deep in thought. "Yes, yes. As to the head injury... she must be roused from sleep every hour until my return."

"Thank you, doctor. May I inquire as to your name?" the Baroness asked with her usual arrogance.

"Oh, I beg your pardon, Madame, the name is Dr. Wenke, Werner Wenke, if you please," he said, somewhat flustered as his face changed to a shade of red more pleasant that his normal pallor. "The, uh, patient, I am sorry, my manners. I was...excuse me, it was the call to duty...I focused on the patient...," the doctor spoke haltingly, reflecting an inner turmoil that was hidden while he had been attending his patient.

Two weeks later, Anna found herself sitting at her desk in front of a blank sheet of paper and an empty apple juice bottle. Gently fingering the small bandage that now replaced the bigger ones she had been forced to wear on her head for the last two weeks, she contemplated how her mother and Sigrid could live under one roof. Both her mother and Sigrid had fretted over her these last weeks, each in her own way. Her mother with her normal aloofness and Sigrid with her never ending quest to feed Anna. Both women, however, nearly drove her mad, as it was solitude she most craved.

"It is bad enough h…h…having one worried m…m…mother. Who could t…t…tolerate two?" she said aloud, almost laughing at the irony of it all. Unfortunately, it was not really a humorous situation. Anna remembered nothing of the accident, nor why she had gone to the stables that day. "Surely not to ride th…th…that wicked creature," she spoke without anger, staring at the sheet of paper she would soon fill with words for her lover. Fingering a rose brooch someone had left on her nightstand, she picked up her fountain pen and began to write, as outside her window the bone-chilling cold refused to release its hold on the land.

Letter 8   *Dresden, 2. April 1941*

My beloved Jakub,

I sit here at my desk, and search for words to describe how I feel. Loneliness is not a strong enough word for the emotions that have taken hold of my soul. I should have written to you months ago, but was unable to find a voice for what I must tell you. Now, I have again found that voice. Oh my beloved, the whole world has gone mad. I must take care with letters I write. The suspicious nature of the world frightens me. Any minor offense and one's neighbors are only too eager to report to the officials. Papa tells me to trust no one. He need not worry. Maria aside, there is no one left here in whom I would ever confide. This world has become such a hateful place. Do not think me horrid, Jakub, but for one thing we can both be grateful—that our child must not suffer through this awful progression of humanity. Have I gone mad, Jakub? Is this a horrible dream from which you shall wake me with a kiss? Oh how often I have prayed it is.

It was the gardener, Mr. Zimmerman, whom I found in a most compromising situation one evening, preparing to steal from our family, the family that has fed him all of his years. Putting my own fears aside, I confronted him regarding your where-abouts, upon which he swore he knew nothing of your current residency, but did know why you had abruptly left. He confessed to knowing of our relationship, Jakub. And with a long-standing grudge against all Poles, he admitted, he believed he had found a way to rid himself of one Pole whom he claimed had stolen a job from hardworking Germans. Was it truly this one horrible man who forced you to leave without a word? He planned on dealing with your companions later, those who had arrived with you from Poland. Oh, Jakub, why you? Why, I asked him. Given our relations, it was least difficult to dispose of you.

Oh how it burns in me, Jakub, that this wicked creature approached Mama and falsely accused you, Jakub, of thievery. Portraying you to Mama as a dirty, thieving Jew, even worse than the Gypsies who pass through at times. Jakub, I could not breathe. Oh the injustice, Jakub! What a despicable crime! It was he who slaughtered chickens and showed them to Mama as evidence of your thievery. You would no more take what is not yours than I. I have attempted to speak with Mama. I have tried to explain to her that it was not you who stole chickens. Mama will not speak to me of you. Jakub, it was about chickens? How could she believe something so insignificant? Who was it who took you away, Jakub? Or can any of the gardener's story be believed? Did he truly see you leave with two others? Who were they, Jakub? Who was it that accompanied you the night you disappeared? Mr. Zimmerman has not been seen since that evening, nor do I think he shall again show his face on the estate.

What is it of this war that transforms men into monsters? Papa believes this war shall get much worse before it is over. The von Glann Family, friends of Mama's, were forcibly removed from their home just last week. Mr. von Glann was taken when he attempted to prevent soldiers from taking his wife and children. Oh, Jakub, I had no idea that his wife was a Jew. Some part of my being knows I shall never see any of them again. But do you know what destroys the soul, Jakub? It is when you become numb to these atrocities due to the frequency of these incidents. Even I am guilty. But how can one survive otherwise? My love, there is a part of my spirit which actually believes that you read these letters. I know I have gone mad.

My beloved, my head aches and my mind wanders. It is thoughts of you which keep me alive. At times I sense your spirit, as though you stand beside me. Tonight is not such a time. I pray, as always, for your safety and that we may walk this world together again someday.

Love Eternally,
Anna v. Marschalkt

Post Script: A shooting star passed through the night. Again I wonder how beauty and wonder can co-exist with horror and torment. But then again, I wonder if one can appreciate, or even understand, one without the other?

Anna ran her fingers over the area where her hair was beginning to grow back, grateful that it was not her face that had been kicked by the horse. The memories of what immediately preceded and followed her accident had not returned, nor memories of the accident itself. She had so much more to say to Jakub. It was when she wrote to him that she felt his spirit, but not on this night.

"Am I losing h...h...hope, Jakub?" she asked the ominous night, as she picked up the letter and pressed it to her bosom. "Am I?" she whispered again, lifting herself from the chair and walking slowly to bed. Crawling under her heavy comforter, she lay there with the letter still firmly pressed to her chest, hoping she might, in someway, rouse Jakub's spirit, wherever he may be. With tears of hopelessness streaking down her face, she saw only a bleak future ahead. "Please," she sobbed into her comforter, "please do n...n...not let me lay f...f... forever alone in this barren room."

The letter was still on her chest when she awoke. Straightening the letter, she carefully rolled it up and walked to her desk where the empty glass bottle stood. Anna stared at the bottle for a moment, contemplating her own actions. "Am I a f...f...fool?" she asked the cool green bottle, as she dropped the letter through its long neck. "I am a fool," she whispered.

That afternoon Anna walked to her stream and followed it into the woods to the small moss covered bridge she had crossed so many times as a child. It was cold and dark in the forest, but oddly she felt less alone here than in her room. She felt safe. "Be safe, Jakub, wherever you are," she quietly spoke, raising the bottle to her lips to kiss it before she tossed it into the stream. Anna watched in horror as her bottle, which she, in all of her distractions, had neglected to plug, filled with water and slowly sank.

Anna returned to her room. Disappointed with herself, she contemplated writing another letter when she heard a soft knock on her door. Startled, she turned in the direction of the knock, repressing the urge to hide behind her bed. Somehow she sensed who it was, even before Sigrid opened the door.

"Anna, may I come in?" Sigrid asked as she stepped into the room.

"You h…h…have already c…c…come in," Anna pointed out with asperity. Ignoring the young woman, Sigrid entered and sat down on Anna's bed.

"It is time we speak truthfully," Sigrid said, as she patted the bed for Anna to join her. Anna gazed at this woman whom she should have called mother all these years, and was not sure she wanted to know any more truths.

Travels of Letter 16:
Atlantic Ocean, off the Coast of Cape Town, South Africa
January 1990

Jenna was frightened. No, frightened wasn't the right word, she thought; petrified with horror was more like it. Tomorrow, just one more day, Jesus Christ, how could it be just a day away?

"Can't sleep?" David asked her, without opening his eyes. "I told you not to worry, you'll be fine.

"Yeah, fine," she repeated, still thinking about the billions of liters of water she would be under tomorrow. It wasn't natural. Humans just didn't belong *under* the water. Dry land, that is where we belong, at least where I belong, she thought. As far back as she could remember, she had been afraid of water. She couldn't remember how she had nearly drowned at the beach so long ago, despite the many times family members tried to remind her of the incident. That had to be the cause of her phobia, she thought, staring at the fluorescent green stars on the ceiling. At least that was what the therapist had convinced her of. Aqua-phobia is what he had called it. Hers was a bad case of it she assumed, since nothing she had worked through with him did anything to alleviate her fear. Her father called it crazy. Whatever it was, she hadn't set foot in the ocean for as long as she could remember. She didn't even like baths for that matter. She looked over at her boyfriend, unable to make out any of his bold, handsome features in the darkness. She knew his face so well, she could see it through the blackness. A therapist couldn't cure her, she thought, but maybe love could.

"I'm actually not fine, David, I'm scared out of my mind," Jenna whispered into the darkness, eliciting a sleepy grunt from David. She actually felt a bit better now that she had spoken the words aloud, that she had addressed her fear instead of suppressed it. "Yeah, I am scared to death that I am going to die tomorrow," she told her own demon, which grinned at her through the darkness. David, obviously awakened by her assertions, rolled over and took her in his arms.

"Look, if it makes you feel any better, I've done this over a hundred times," he spoke drowsily into her shoulder.

"I know, one hundred and sixteen to be exact," she finished his sentence for him. "You're right, it won't be so bad," she agreed, firmly pressing her eyes closed. She still couldn't comprehend that she had actually completed a diving class, but somewhere from the depths of her mind a voice tried hard to be heard, "you know that was in a mere three meters of pool water." Jenna hoped the morning would never come.

To Jenna's dismay, the morning did come. "Look at this! Will you look at this, Jenna?" David yelled with outstretched hands, reminding her of the pastor at her church. It was true, they couldn't have asked for a better diving day. The sun shone warm on her skin and the ocean looked as calm as a pond to her.

"All right, listen up fish food," the excursion leader addressed the group, "we've gone over the rules. Remember to stay close to yer buddy, and be back at one o'clock or we leave you." Jenna tightened her grip on David's arm, who reassuringly patted her hand.

"He's kidding, Jen. Relax, you're gonna be fine, I promise." David spoke with such conviction, such confidence, that Jenna felt her pulse begin to normalize again. It was his self-confidence that had first attracted her to him. Self-confidence she so obviously lacked.

Jenna looked back at the boat one last time before she submerged. She had come this far, she was actually in the water. She could sense fear trying to grip her. The fear tugged at her, wanted to drown her. Focusing on David, she submerged and followed him down and down into the liquid bowels of the earth. To her surprise, the fear she expected disappeared with each meter she descended. Locating her underwater camera, she began snapping pictures of David interacting with the local sea life. This underwater paradise took her breath away. Seeing her beloved in a place he seemed to love more than life was incredible. Her heart jumped at a close encounter with a small tiger shark, but its quick departure calmed her mind, which was ever ready to launch into worst case scenarios. He is so carefree, she thought, watching David and wishing she could be less worried about the water and everything else.

"But look at you," a voice in her mind said, "you're diving, whad-daya say to that, Dr. Dinkard?" This underwater world was so beauti-ful and new, she was unaware how much time had passed until David swam towards her. Briefly embracing her, he pointed at his watch, the sign that it was time to surface. She now realized she had done it, really done it, and felt as though a great weight had dropped off her shoulders. David would be so proud. His months of urging her, pres-suring her, had paid off. Never before had she felt such a profound sense of accomplishment.

Jenna didn't know where they came from, but unexpectedly she found herself in the middle of what seemed like millions of jelly fish. So many she was unable to see David or figure out what direction was up. There were so many of them they blocked out the little sunlight that filtered down to these depths. She felt her pulse quicken along with her breath. "Calm down, idiot," some part of her mind in charge of survival reprimanded her, "you can't hyperventilate, not down here, so just calm the hell down." Listening to herself she closed her eyes and took slow controlled breaths. "That's better, much better," the voice said.

Jenna didn't know how long she was caught in the underwater jellyfish jungle, but when the smack passed, she realized she was all alone. The voice would not allow her to panic, not until she reached the surface. "Slow," is what the voice told her, "slow and steady ascent." Slowly she ascended, up and up, pausing occasionally to look around for David. "He's close by," the voice reassured her, "you were just separated by the jellyfish."

After what seemed like an eternity, she reached the surface and tore off her face gear, unaware that her camera and watch had been dislodged and were sinking to the depths of the ocean. The panic that was barely kept in check now released itself with a vengeance. Tearing off her weight belt, she screamed and looked around wildly for any signs of David, for any signs of the boat. Nothing. There was nothing and no one. "God, I'm gonna die," she yelled. "I'm gonna die! David! David!"

Somehow the voice that had brought her to the surface safely made itself heard through her mania. "Use one of the flares," it said. Reaching for a flare, she pulled off the cap and watched with frenzied hope as 45 seconds of heavy orange smoke filled the sky. Jenna had no idea how long she waited, hoping someone would see her. With no watch, she had no idea how long she had been treading water. Her body was beginning to grow tired, but her internal mania had not slowed. She knew she wouldn't be able to keep this up indefinitely.

Looking up at the sky, she wondered how much time she had before dark. Somewhere a glimmer of sanity was beginning to shine its way back into her soul. She began to float to preserve energy. She still had one flare left, but wouldn't use that unless there was some type of boat or plane in sight. Overcome with fatigue and thirst, she was about to close her eyes for a moment when she caught sight of something floating just ahead of her. Was it a bottle? She struggled towards it, filled with hope that there was something to drink inside. "If it were empty it would have filled up and sank," she told herself as she slowly swam towards the bottle that seemed just beyond reach.

As she followed the bottle, her mind shifted into autopilot. "Just follow the bottle," it directed her muscles, which begrudgingly followed orders. As long as she had a goal, something to swim towards, she knew she was still alive. A small part of Jenna's rational mind knew that following a bottle was crazy, and noted that the sky was beginning to change color and evening was coming. As the effects of dehydration began to set in, Jenna began to wonder whether the bottle was real, or if any of this was real for that matter. What was she, with her phobia of water, doing in the middle of an ocean? "Can you tell me that, bottle, huh? What's the matter, cat git yer tongue?" she slurred, as she continued to follow the bottle. Jenna heard a noise off in the distance, a noise that restored every last ounce of hope and reserve she had left and granted her a moment of rational clarity. It was now or never. Unable to see clearly, she pulled out her last flare, detached the cap and held it as high as her fatigued arm would allow.

When the search boat found the semi-conscious diver they could not make sense of her mumblings about a bottle. When she regained consciousness and was reunited with her grateful lover, Jenna's story about a bottle was attributed to hallucinations from dehydration. Jenna was never sure about the bottle either, but one thing was certain, she loved David, enough to spend the rest of her life with him, but not enough to ever follow him into the ocean again.

Somewhere Over the Atlantic Ocean
Fall 2011

"You alright there?" I heard a man's voice ask. I had not sat up, and neither did I want to, since I realized that I had left Warren's letters underneath the motel bed in New Jersey.

"They'll keep them for me," I unsuccessfully tried to convince myself as the plane hit an air pocket, causing everyone to lurch forward. Sitting up, I looked at my neighbor, barely registering he was there.

"No, I, uh, I'm fine," I stuttered, seemingly having lost all motor control of my tongue.

"Here," the stranger said, handing me a tissue as he motioned towards my face. "For your tears."

"Oh thanks," I replied, surprised I had remembered any manners at all, but fearing this guy next to me would want to engage in some banal small talk. They always did. I knew this type of guy. Well talking is a bit better than puking your brains out again I thought, inhaling deeply. "They are only letters," I mourned quietly to myself, "only letters." This realization didn't ease the pain, but caused my tears to flow anew.

Again, my neighbor waved a tissue in front of my nose. Grabbing the tissue, I blew heartily, glancing briefly at my neighbor who resumed his reading of a newspaper. Grateful for small favors, I leaned back in the seat to continue wallowing in my own grief. "How could I do something like that? ...Oh Warren, how could I be so stupid?" I blamed myself, oblivious to the fact that I had spoken aloud.

"I don't know who your Warren is, or what happened, but tomorrow the sun will shine again, and the earth will still spin," he spoke with what sounded like a Spanish accent, although I was usually wrong about accents. My natural inclination was to glare at this man, but somehow his genuine tone comforted me, at least for the moment.

"Silly, no?" this oddball man asked with a wry smile, "it is something my mother used to say to me. I always found it rather ridiculous, so I apologize for, you know, repeating it to you." Scratching his forehead, obviously somewhat abashed by his Zen-like words, he returned his full attention to his newspaper. And me, I felt like I had to say something. I hated it when people felt embarrassed, especially on account of me. He had tried to help, hadn't he?

"No..., it was, uh, actually rather sweet," I finally said, for lack of anything better to say, confounded by my own idiocy. How could I have failed to notice a shoebox-sized container missing from my suitcase? Wasn't the first clue quite possibly that the dang suitcase managed to zip shut in a jiffy? Hell, what is the matter with me?

"I always check beneath the bed," I quietly hissed, realizing with irritation that the one time I hadn't checked, I had left my lifeline to Warren in some decrepit motel. How many countless beds had I looked under in the past to find nothing but the signs of poor housekeeping? Pulling out my compact, I wasn't surprised to find the reflection of a mad woman whose tears had turned her mascara into what looked like war paint. "Great," I sighed, passing another sidelong glance at my neighbor, who thankfully kept his nose buried in the paper, allowing me this moment of privacy with my pitiful reflection.

The hours in the plane passed painfully slow, as though Father Time had decided to take a nap, or forgotten about his job altogether. Staring past my neighbor's greasy dandruff-flaked head to the small oval window, I saw only a small piece of a radiantly sunny blue sky that did not mirror my mood in the least. I thumbed through all of the in-flight magazines, most of which tried to persuade me to purchase some useless item I'd never use, and slapped the last of them shut. "Does anyone really buy this stuff," I asked aloud, just as a flight attendant moved down the aisle, selling duty free goods.

"I usually do, for my girlfriend," my neighbor spoke, as though I had addressed him. I've got to stop talking out loud. Of course he'd think I was talking to him. Nodding at my neighbor, I shifted my body a little farther to the left to keep his stray dandruff from making contact with me. My neighbor, who suddenly shifted and sent his dandruff flying my way, folded his paper. I was able to catch a glimpse of the headlines as he shoved the paper into the storage area in front of his knees.

"Hey, do you mind if I take a look at your newspaper? I've run out of ads to read here," I said, pointing at the in-flight magazines. I didn't feel quite as depressed about the forgotten shoe box with its trove of love letters anymore. Maybe it was the bit of sunshine I spied through the window, or maybe it was bigger than that. Maybe it was the realization that Warren's letters did not define what Warren and I had. That what we had is something I will always carry with me, in my heart and soul, and not in a ratty shoebox.

"Yeah, sure. I'm done with it anyway," the man said as he pulled the paper out. "And besides," he continued with a smirk on his face, "now I've got a whole two inches of extra legroom." He did not look particularly tall sitting down, but even a dwarf's legs would feel constricted in these seats, I thought, reaching for his well read copy of today's New York Times. There was something that had caught my eye. I was sure it was on the front page. Sifting quickly through the paper, I located the front section and quickly scanned the headlines.

It only took a moment to find what I had been looking for. The headline read: *Key Witness in Ivanov Case Dead,* by Santiago Vega. *Viktor Popov, the key witness in the Yuri Ivanov case has been found dead in his home. Popov...,*" I read, wondering if this was the case Charlie was working on. He hadn't mentioned any names. Or had he? I wasn't really good with names. Charlie had said he wasn't in a position to divulge that information, but if I paid attention to the news I'd hear about it. That was what he had said, wasn't it? This had to be the case. Now convinced, I read on, overcome with a sudden desire to find myself in a romantic European hotel with Charlie.

"That's mine," my flaky neighbor said unexpectedly, reaching over to point at the article I was in the process of reading.

"Excuse me?" I asked, momentarily confused. Of course the paper was his. Or did he mean the article? I had no idea what the mildly irritating man was talking about.

"That's mine, uh, the article," he repeated, removing an unappetizing tuna sandwich from its triangular plastic box and stuffing it into his mouth. He reminded me of a frog with inflated vocal sacs.

"Hmm," I answered, still unsure what the man was talking about.

"Sorry," the man apologized with a full mouth. "I wrote that article," he explained, as small particles of food sprayed from his mouth and landed on the newspaper I still held. Quickly looking away from the paper and its unexpected additions, I eventually figured out that the man sitting next to me was Santiago Vega.

"Oh, you're Mr. Vega," I said finally, giving the man time to swallow, and hoping he would save the next bite for later.

"Yup, that's me. Who woulda thought a Cuban like me could make it in the Big Apple?" The man spoke with an undertone I couldn't figure out. He definitely wasn't boasting as he explained how he came to live in New York. No, he seemed to speak of it more with a sense of awe, or respect.

"They say one must have talent and luck in equal parts to survive this world. I say nope, they're wrong. All one needs is luck," Santiago Vega said, as he leaned back into his seat, kissed the cross he wore around his neck, and released an audible sigh. "I apologize for the rude interruption," he said, "please do read on."

Doing as Santiago suggested, I leaned back into my seat to read the rest of the article. My emotions had come full circle since boarding this flight. I had to admit, I wasn't surprised when my thoughts drifted to Charlie again. My yearning for him displaced all thoughts of my shoebox. What was it the young cleaning lady had said after all, "things aren't lost, just misplaced." Well, she'll surely find my letters and save them for me, wouldn't she? Folding up the newspaper, I handed it back to its owner and realized how deceiving looks can be. I would have never thought such an odd duck was a successful journalist. I gave him another sidelong glance. His eyes were pressed firmly shut, but somehow I knew he wasn't really asleep. *Maybe he doesn't want to talk to* me. Reclining my seat, I shut my eyes from the world and recalled the serendipitous events of the past hour.

"This really is a small world," I whispered. What were the chances that I would meet the guy who wrote a newspaper article about my lover's case? Is that what Charlie was, my lover? Could it be more than coincidence I wondered? I was grateful for the sleep that finally overcame me.

Dresden, Germany

April 1941

Anna could not bring herself to sit down on the bed next to Sigrid. Instead she walked quietly to her desk where she sat with her back facing this woman, who now seemed like a stranger. It did not surprise her that Sigrid did not ask her again to join her on the bed. That would have unsettled her more than whatever Sigrid needed to discuss. "Why can I not face her?" Anna whispered to herself, as she stared out the window and searched for something she knew was not there.

"I will tell you a love story, Anna," Sigrid spoke with a somberness in her voice that made Anna shudder. "A love story that began a very long time ago." Anna did not want to listen to Sigrid, but she could not help herself. She craved the truth, any truth. This desire to know burned in her almost as brightly as her love for Jakub, but at what cost to herself, she wondered. There had been so many secrets, so much deception. She sensed Sigrid's eyes on her back.

"One thing you must know, Anna," she heard the hesitation in Sigrid's voice, "I will tell you my side of this love story, but there is not only one other side to this story…and, it is for those others to reveal their side, in their own time."

"W…What if they do not?" Anna asked, spinning around in her chair to look at Sigrid. "W…W…What if they do not?" she asked again, revealing how important these revelations really were to her.

"Anna, I will tell you all I am able to," Sigrid said, as Anna hung on her every word, forgetting that she had wanted Sigrid to think that she did not care.

"There was a summer, very long ago…and I was such a young girl. My mother worked as a laundress on a large estate that bred horses. It was grueling work, as you can imagine," Sigrid sighed, looking down at her hands. "Often Mother needed help. I can still recall how raw my hands were after a day of scrubbing and wringing sheets and linens. I swore I would never follow in her footsteps." Sigrid smiled into space, obviously seeing a different time and place. "It was here I first met your father, Anna. He came to learn to ride. His family did not have the means to acquire and maintain horses. The feeling…what passed between your father and I the first time we met, I shall never forget." Anna watched with a heavy silence as Sigrid's eyes filled with tears.

"Mother explained my position in life would never allow me a young man such as your father. She *was* right, but that did not stop me…" Sigrid's voice trailed off as her eyes glazed over. Anna was not sure Sigrid would continue. "He came back every summer, Anna, and with each summer our love grew. Together we made plans for our future, a future I wanted so desperately to believe in. A future he too wanted, but one that was doomed from the beginning." Sigrid covered her face with both hands, as her shoulders shook uncontrollably. Anna waited impatiently for Sigrid to collect herself. Breathing deeply, as though what she was about to say pained her greatly, she continued. "I was with child."

"Seven summers after we had first met, I carried the child that love had created. I will never forget the expression of sheer horror on your father's face. He, more desperate even than I, moved me to his home where I was hidden, Anna. Hidden in a room beneath the main house. Oh, it was horrible, Anna," Sigrid cried. Anna had never witnessed such emotion from Sigrid, but then a soul cannot hide such painful memories forever. Suddenly, as though a switch had been turned off, Sigrid abruptly stopped crying and looked at Anna with haunted eyes.

"It is here that Maria… and… you were born," Sigrid spoke slowly, as though every word carried a lifetime of burdens.

"W…w…we both were b…b…born in a…a cellar?" Anna stuttered, horrified by the thought of anyone spending any amount of time in a dark, dank cellar, let alone bringing a child to this world in such a horrid place.

"It was not a cellar as you know…it was a spartanly furnished room…with one window high up at ground level. I remember…I remember cherishing the few rays of sunlight that filtered through into this dark underworld…" Anna watched Sigrid swallow hard, "it was…not easy with… two newborn babies," she spoke to the invisible ghosts of the past.

"T…T…Two b…b…babies?" Anna blurted out, confused. "T…T…Two b…b…babies…then, did one n…n…not survive?" Sigrid looked at Anna with desperation in her eyes.

"Oh, my dear child…please forgive me…forgive me…," Sigrid sobbed, "you and Maria are twins."

"W…W…What?" Anna shouted. She felt as though she had been punched in the abdomen. "B…b…but, th…th…that does not make sense…sh…sh…she is older than I. Sh…sh…she is my older sister."

Sigrid lifted herself from the bed with a heavy heart. Slowly she moved towards Anna with her arms extended.

"N…n…no, no, g…g…get away from me you…you…deceitful witch," Anna cried in a high pitched voice. "W…W…Why? Why w…w…would you deceive me? And Maria? W…w…was it not enough to lie to us all th…th…those years? Y…Y…You are my b…b…birth mother. H…H…How could you?"

"You must understand child, your father and I…,"

"Do n…n…not call me child," interrupted Anna, red-faced, and with the temper to match. As though she had not noticed Anna's outburst, Sigrid calmly continued. "Your father and I needed to do what was best, for both of you. This is when your mother…took you," Sigrid said, as an icy chill passed over Anna's soul.

"But why the lie?" Anna cried as her world began to spin.

"There were those who knew I had borne two girls. When your mother…took you…it was better… people believed the children were of different ages, they were told Maria was older, but you...you grew so much bigger than Maria," Sigrid spoke, her face a flaming red that Anna had never before seen.

"S...s...so no one could ever c...c...connect Maria and I to you," Anna spoke in a monotone voice. It was not a question, but a statement of fact.

"You must understand, Anna, there was no future for you and your sister. Your father could not marry me....and even if he had, he had no inheritance, merely a name. What little he had would have been taken from him if he married me." Warm streams of tears now freely flowed down Sigrid's face.

"If ever you are a mother, and I pray someday you are, you will know....a mother will do anything to protect her children."

"N...n...never!" Anna shouted fiercely. "N...n...never will I have another child and n...n...never would I do something, anything s...s...so...devious! So d...d...despicable. So evil!" The rage that flooded Anna's being now exploded from her. "H...h...how can you d...d...dare to make assumptions of wh...wh...what I w...w... would or w...w...would not do?" Anna yelled, further infuriated by her stuttering.

"Anna," Sigrid attempted to soothe her as she placed a warm hand on Anna's icy one.

"N...n...no, do n...n...not touch me!" Anna cried, pushing Sigrid's hand away and jumping out of her chair. Turning on Sigrid like a rabid animal, she felt a hatred she had never known. "And what about mother, how did she come to be with father?" Anna asked with a cold, calm fury that sent shivers down Sigrid's spine. It did not escape Anna that she had not stuttered.

The two women stared at each other with calculated silence. "As I told you, Anna, there are more sides to this love story that I am not in a position to discuss," Sigrid seemed to look through Anna now. Anna felt tired. More tired than she had ever felt before. She could almost see as the last shreds of her childhood and innocence died. There was nothing left now of the timid child who viewed the world through innocent eyes. No, the woman's spirit that now possessed her was capable of anything.

"Do not speak to me of love," Anna spoke in a hardened voice, without her usual stutter. "You know nothing of love or loyalty."

Anna slammed the door as she left her room, leaving Sigrid standing by her desk. She did not know what to make of what Sigrid had told her. "It does not change my life in any physical manner," Anna whispered to herself, realizing that it was her own emotional well-being Sigrid as worried about. She headed towards Maria's house on foot, instead of riding her bicycle, to give herself extra time to think. "How will Maria take this news?" she wondered, hoping it would not further affect her fragile health or the health of her unborn child.

"M…M…Maria," Anna called, shivering uncontrollably. She had forgotten her coat in her abrupt agitated departure. The cold air had not done much to clear her head though. "M…M…Maria," she called again, as she walked through her sister's kitchen.

"In here," she heard her sister call from the playroom. Anna entered the playroom and quickly seated herself in front of the warm oven.

"Aunt Anna, Aunt Anna," her young nieces cried, eagerly throwing little arms about their chilled aunt.

"Well, l…l…look at you," Anna spoke without any of her earlier hostility, kissing the girls on the head. "How are you f…f…feeling, Maria?" Anna asked, unable to suppress the concern in her voice.

Maria smiled. "I do not know why women continue to have children after going through the birthing experience just once." Anna gently placed her hand on her sister's swollen abdomen, which looked too large for how far along her sister thought she was.

"H…h…have you had anything t…t…to eat today?" Anna asked, frightened by the dark circles under Maria's eyes. Aside from her bulge, Maria's bones jutted out sharply, as though they might pierce through her pale skin at any moment. Even her normally lustrous red hair appeared dull and stringy.

"I eat, but am unable to keep anything down. Lena has been a great help with the children," Maria said, her chest heaving with the effort of speaking.

"I w…w…worry for you, Maria," Anna said, as she placed her warmed hand on Maria's arm.

"Don't fret about me, I have enough people doing that. Tell me, Anna, what is the latest gossip at the newspaper?"

Anna considered her sister's delicate situation and wondered whether she should tell Maria about Sigrid's revelations. As she looked at her frail sister, she wondered how the two of them could possibly be twins. Aside from the red color of their hair and similar facial features any sisters would share, it didn't make sense. Maria was thin and fine boned and stood a good ten centimeters shorter than she. Anna, on the other hand, was tall, with large bones. She was far more robust than her sister. "Like Sigrid," she whispered, inhaling sharply.

"What is it? Anna, your face is pale...are you not well?" Now it was Maria who had a look of concern on her face.

"Sigrid c...c...came to my room...just n...n...now, before I came here," Anna said and cleared her throat. There was no easy way to tell Maria this, but Maria too had survived the earlier shock of finding out that Sigrid was their mother.

"She told you, didn't she?" Maria said, reaching for Anna. Anna looked at her sister with a perplexed expression.

"Told m...m...me what? D...d...do you already know?" she asked Maria with incredulity.

"That we are twins? Yes...she....told me when we were at the sea." Maria could read the anger written all over her sister's face and in the rigid posture Anna's body had assumed.

"H...h...how come y...y...you did n...n...not tell me?" Anna asked with clenched fists. She felt faint.

"Now listen, Anna. I could not. And Sigrid, she tried, at the sea, Anna, but you ran out before she could explain. She made me promise not to tell, it was her burden to share," Maria explained, as a pale-faced Anna sat with her mouth agape.

"Am I surrounded by lies and deceit?" Anna whispered, as she quietly stood up to leave the playroom.

"Anna! Anna!" Maria called after her. Anna turned around to face her sister.

"You have n...n...never stood for anything, Maria" she said without emotion and turned to leave.

Letter 9   *Dresden, 29. August 1941*

My Beloved Jakub,

It has been almost four months since I last wrote you, yet it feels as though years have passed. Due to my own neglect you shall unfortunately never read my previous letter to you, Letter Eight. So much has happened these last months, so much which makes one question and condemn the nature of the human spirit. With each passing day I lose more faith in humanity, my family, and myself. As a younger woman I believed good should always triumph over evil. I no longer believe this, as the demons of my long nights have infected my days as well. Oh, Jakub, I do not know if you could still love the Anna you would find today. She is no longer the young girl you met years ago, full of enthusiasm and hope. I wonder, is this the natural progression of life? That with each passing year our eyes are further opened to the realities of life, which are securely hidden from youth? Often I study my reflection in the mirror and wonder how so much bitterness has crept into my soul.

My beloved, happiness seems such a distant memory. I fear my memories of us may disappear too. Already they feel as a dream does upon waking. Even the young children in my life, and those waiting to be born, do not fill me with the joy they used to. Every day it seems, news arrives of the death or disappearance of yet another neighbor or friend. Just yesterday a telegram arrived for Papa. His cousin Wilhelm, with whom he shared much as a child, was killed near the Russian border. Fortunately for him, Papa says, he leaves no wife or children. But it is obvious how much Papa suffers. He has not left his study since yesterday. The smell of his burning pipe has not ceased since he received the telegram. Jakub, I am a horrible person. This news of death and dying no longer surprises me. Is the human soul truly so adaptable, that even the daily atrocities of war become common place? Just another part of life? My love, I no longer know what defines normal.

Soldiers come regularly to interview Papa, to determine how much of the harvest he must "donate to the cause." I hear him complain to Mama that the soldiers do not leave us much. Many cows, goats, and pigs have been taken. Even Papa's prized stallion was taken. It is likely these animals shall serve as meat for the soldiers. Papa remained in his study for three days after this last incident, only coming out because orders required his return to Berlin. We are still lucky, compared to the many who have so little. Somehow Papa still manages to find chocolate for Mama, without which she says she cannot live, as it seems to provide some physical comfort. But how can I speak of chocolate when so much suffering surrounds me? People, especially in the city, live in such dire circumstances. They have nothing, Jakub. There is such a scarcity of goods that the people have taken to thievery, which we have witnessed firsthand. Our chickens, ducks, and geese are stolen in the dead of night, and on occasion a cow or pig disappears. There are but a handful of chickens left. Mama has ordered the staff to bring the chickens, ducks, and geese into the house at dusk every evening. What used to be our "winter garden" room is now a small menagerie. You recall the glass covered room attached to the house where Papa had many strange plants? The smell in this room is almost unbearable, but I fear soon the remaining cows, pigs, and goats may wander the halls of the house as well.

Sigrid's return to the estate has brought with it further revelations where Maria and I are concerned. It turns out we are more than sisters. We shared the womb together. The story Sigrid tells is riddled with holes, I do not know what to believe anymore. She now spends most of her time assisting Maria. Lena seems to have permanently taken over Sigrid's work in the main house. Even without Lena, Sigrid would likely assist

Maria, who recently, and quite unexpectedly, bore two young daughters, Edith Annemarie Ilse and Renate Ulrike Sigrid. It is a miracle that both girls thrive, given the difficulties of their birth and the fact that they were six weeks early, according to Maria's calculations. Without Sigrid, Maria has told me, the girls would not have survived. I still miss the relationship I once shared with Sigrid, but it is difficult for me to be in the same room with her these days, even when all the children are afoot. Mama spends most days knitting, following the war over the radio. I cannot understand what so fascinates her with this war. She is no longer the forceful person you once knew. Yet still I sense a general unease about her being. It has only been a few weeks since she and I again began to speak. It was I who broke the silence. She would rather go to her grave than capitulate on any matter. Sometimes I wonder if it is the atrocities of the Fuehrer she so vocally supported that now haunt her days. She would never admit this. No longer does she argue with Papa behind closed doors the way she used to. I have not asked her about you again, Jakub, but when the time is right I believe I may yet uncover the truth.

I still hold my job at the newspaper translating foreign papers, but the work does not provide the satisfaction it once did. Papers only trickle in these days, and much of what is translated is never used. Papa regularly urges me to reconsider work and stay at home. I would suffocate at home. Often I ride into the city just to escape the confines of the house, for a moment of personal peace in this world of war. It is here that I forget about the deception in my life. But I must admit, I have not found the strength to forgive those around me. Maybe it is I who should beg forgiveness, but I find that I am not a strong person. Possibly someday I will have the strength to rise in the face of adversity. Possibly have the courage to protest this barbaric war. But for now, I must be honest with myself and realize that I am no better than my fellow man.

Jakub, I search for meaning in my life. I still search for signs. Either the meaning and signs have disappeared, or my spirit is no longer able to see these ephemeral moments that give purpose. The only constant in my life is the small humming-bird that visits my window. I am beginning to believe he is but a fancy of my imagination, but I welcome his presence. Do you believe in signs, Jakub? Sometimes I wonder about life and its purpose. Are the religious interpretations, as varied as they may be, actually accurate? Is there some afterlife where judgment shall be handed out and justice served? Is there someplace where all those who are dear to one shall converge again, without the restrictions imposed on them by a close-minded society? Jakub, when I close my eyes I often feel your spirit. Not as frequently as in the past, but I know there is some part of you nearby. Yet, my rational mind does not believe that you have yet departed this world. Surely, some part of my own spirit would die as well. Still, I love you with all my heart and continue to pray each night for your safety.

Love Eternally,
Anna v. Marschalkt

Post Script: Last night I dreamt I could fly. I have not dreamt such things since I was a young child. Earth is such a beautiful place when seen from heaven.

Anna stared at the letter she had written. The dream she had last night floated back into her conscious memory. "What a wonderful dream," she whispered, wishing every one of her dreams could lift her the way this one had. She had awoken feeling free of mind and spirit, until the realities of the world abruptly crashed in on her, erasing all traces of this truly spiritual moment. She looked out her window at the grey sky. It had been raining without pause for three weeks. Her little stream had flooded the surrounding pastures, as it had so often in the past. The rain was uncommon for this time of year. Maybe the Gods of humanity were angry.

Listening as the rain tapped against the window like a thousand tiny feet, Anna was grateful the wheat harvest had been completed before these torrential downpours. Papa had constantly worried that rain would ruin the harvest, but three weeks of stifling heat had been a Godsend.

As Anna rolled up her letter and shoved it into the empty green bottle, she wondered when she might find an opportunity to "mail" it. Smiling at the thought of her "mail" to Jakub, she felt a sudden enthusiasm for life she had not experienced in a long time. Leaning back in her chair, she indulged in thoughts of a sun-baked Jakub reading her letters as they washed up on the shore of a tropical paradise.

It was another two weeks before Anna ventured out with her glass bottle safely stowed in the basket of her bicycle. The flood waters had receded, but the soil was damp and heavy, as was the air. She rode her bicycle towards the river, stopping at a bridge that crossed the Elbe. Wiping the perspiration from her brow, she unpacked her bottle and looked down at the unusually brown river water. "I have no idea who I am anymore," she whispered, lifting the bottle to her lips. As Anna lightly kissed the sun-warmed bottle, she imagined her lover's breath on her neck.

The creaking sounds of a bicycle interrupted her moment as an elderly man passed by, observing her with a peculiar expression. Anna thought to ask him to mind his own business, but then reconsidered. She was likely an odd sight to behold, holding her bottle in a lover's embrace. Somewhat abashed, Anna quickly tossed the bottle into the swiftly moving water below and watched as the bottle momentarily submerged, only to reemerge a moment later.

"Where will your travels take you?" she asked, as the bottle passed from her view. Anna would never know that just one day later, the old man on the bicycle, sifting through garbage washed onto the river's bank, would find her bottle and take it to his home, along with other river treasures, hoping to find some use for it. Anna would never know that the old man would eventually realize this particular bottle was not empty and remove the wax plug. Anna would never know that this illiterate old man, recognizing the contents of the bottle as worthless to him, would toss the letter into his fire.

Travels of Letter 16
South Atlantic Ocean
November 1991

The young girl screwed on the back of the radio she had just finished putting together. Briefly glancing at her uncle, she wondered why he was always nice to her. He was the one who had given her the radio kit she assembled in less than fifteen minutes. The directions said it would take an hour. She didn't need the directions. This wasn't the first radio she had put together. Akila couldn't explain why it was she loved radios so much. It wasn't just radios though, it was anything electronic. Yesterday she fixed her mother's coffee pot. It was a simple fix, merely requiring the replacement of a single wire. And two days ago there was a short in the engine room which she helped the mechanic fix. Her parents did not approve of her mechanical abilities, especially not after she reappeared back on the deck, covered in grease and stains. Gently she touched the cheek where she could almost still feel the sharp sting of her father's hand. "This is not appropriate for an eleven year old girl," he had shouted.

Fixated on her radio, she turned the dial to determine what type of reception, if any, she might receive out here in the middle of the

Atlantic Ocean. The crackling static that floated over the airwaves was still music to her ears, more so than the actual waves that crashed against the sides of her father's yacht.

"You finished it already, Akila? Why am not surprised?" Uncle Bes asked her, squatting down beside her on the hot deck. She could smell his sweat. She could even see it as it dropped on to the deck, only to evaporate moments later. Usually odors agitated her, especially human ones, but in the case of her uncle, she did not mind. She did not look at him as he spoke to her, but continued to turn the knob on her radio, more quickly now. There was probably something she was supposed to say to him, something any one of her sisters would know, but not her. She felt awkward and shy around people. But Uncle Bes was different, he didn't seem to mind her strangeness. He told her she was "unique." Her mother did not like Uncle Bes, she wasn't sure her father really liked his own brother much either. Was it because Uncle Bes liked other men, she wondered. This was information she should not know, but did.

Often her parents argued, almost uninhibited, in her presence, while around her three sisters they remained silent. It was as though she did not exist, as though they did not think she had ears. But they could never hear her silent screams.

"She does not hear anything anyway," her father would yell at her mother if ever she reprimanded him, "she only has eyes and ears for electronics...and this filth she collects." Her father was only half right though, she thought. Yes, she did love electronics, but she also desperately wanted to be like her three sisters and four cousins. And she did hear everything they said. She saw so much more than the others. Sometimes she watched the children play together and wondered how it was they knew what to say to each other. It was as though each held an invisible script from which they read at precisely the right moment. On the few occasions when they invited her to join their games she felt almost panicked, usually responding with detailed descriptions of one of her latest electronic gadgets or explaining where she found her latest glass treasure that was stored in any available space in her room. The other children never missed an opportunity to remind her that she was strange or, worse, crazy. Maybe she was, she thought, listening to the soothing sounds of static.

Uncle Bes still squatted silently beside her. Without looking up, Akila inhaled deeply, enjoying the smell of the ocean and her Uncle Bes. Despite the pleasant olfactory stimulation, the sea made her nervous. There was nothing here for her to collect, and now that the radio was done she had nothing left to build or fix. Her father had forbidden her to bring any of her projects along, and she wouldn't be spending any more time in the engine room. It was time she had "hobbies more appropriate for a normal young girl," her father had fumed. "No man will ever have an aberration such as this one," he had said after threatening to send her away to a school for girls.

When her father asked if he had made himself clear, it was obvious to her that he had. There was no reason to agree. She did not understand what offended her father so that she received the mighty slap that knocked her glasses to the deck, shattering the left lens and cracking the right. She would have to view the world through her broken glasses for the next two weeks, until they returned home to Egypt.

With more vigor she turned the knob on the radio. The thought of being sent away to a school of strangers frightened her even more than the fact that no man would ever have her. She wondered what sort of a thing an "aberration" was.

Akila felt her uncle's hand on her own, gently pulling her hand away from the radio knob. "I have found something, Akila, but you mustn't show your father," he whispered conspiringly, pulling an old green bottle out from the hand he had hidden behind his back. "It was floating near the yacht when I took a swim. I thought you might like it." She grabbed the gift and examined it closely.

"This. This is a great green glass bottle. From the looks of it, it has been in the water for quite some time. And look at this Uncle, there is a seal, it looks as though it may have something inside," she spoke breathlessly, with an odd, almost robotic cadence to her voice. Akila smiled for the first time since boarding the yacht almost two weeks earlier, even briefly looking her uncle in the eyes. The smile her uncle beamed back at her went unnoticed as she dove into her own secluded world, visually recalling and categorizing every glass object she had collected over the last eight years, even the ones her parents had disposed of and thought she would not remember. This glass bottle was different though. She recognized it the moment she held the long cool neck in her hands. It didn't make sense. On a hot day such as this, the bottle should be warm, if not hot, but it remained cool no matter how long she held onto it. For one brief moment, she understood that she was no different than the other children, than anyone for that matter. That they too had their fears and sadness, but unlike most others, she had a special gift. Not one that made her strange and weird, but, like Uncle Bes always said, made her unique and special.

"You have a gift, child. Do not worry about matters of the heart. Love shall find you and you shall find love when the time is right." Akila sat upright, jolted from her safe internal world. Looking around to find the source of the voice, she knew she would not find a face. Yet she knew the voice had been real, as were the words the faceless stranger had spoken. The bottle? Was it the bottle?

"I told you, no more trash," her father yelled, coming up to her from behind and tearing the glass bottle from her.

"Ahhh, the thing is hot," he cried out in pain, hurtling it back into the ocean from which it had come. Akila did not hear her father ask her what she had done to the bottle. Running to the guard rail, she caught one more glimpse of the bottle before it disappeared in the yacht's wake.

Seven years later Akila would travel to the United States to attend college at the California Institute of Technology, where, in less than two years, she completed more than the required coursework. Two years after that she would start and successfully run her own computer business. It wasn't until her company was listed as one of Fortune 500's most promising businesses that she was officially diagnosed with Asperger's, an autism spectrum condition. For the first time she understood her difficulties with social relationships, and the ease with which she understood technological processes.

As Akila stood in the living room of her Pasadena home, staring at her collection of treasured glass objects, she recalled the faceless voice she had heard so long ago. It had been right.

"Hurry up, child," her mother called to her in her native Arabic, interrupting her thoughts. "The groom is not going to wait all day." With her sisters picking up the train of her wedding gown, she cast one last glance at her reflection in the mirror before heading to the waiting limousine. Twenty-one years after a faceless voice had told her love would find her, it had. Akila would marry the man who would always love her, the man she would always love.

Berlin, Germany
Tegel International Airport, Fall 2011

The baggage claim signs pointed in all directions, or was it my sluggish mind? I was exhausted. Never having visited Germany, I had no idea what to expect, but I didn't see anyone running around wearing Lederhosen. Actually somewhat disappointing, but then I shouldn't be so naïve, right? But, it's not like I had a lot of time to plan and read up on travel hot spots and local customs. My trip wasn't all pleasure anyway. I was here on a, well, what was it exactly I was here on? I guess it's kind of an assignment. My own special assignment. What was I thinking? How on earth did I get myself into this crazy trip? That is what this trip was, just plain crazy. Why was I having doubts now that I was actually here, especially with Charlie here too? At least I hoped he would be here.

Couldn't I for once make a decision and stick to it without having this nagging doubt eat away at me, eventually convincing me I had made the wrong choice? Maybe it was Warren's letters I had left behind. Maybe it was because I was alone and had never traveled overseas before. It was one thing to fly to Cape May alone, but traveling over an ocean to a country where I didn't speak the language and had no idea what peculiar customs might get me in trouble, now that was a whole different story.

"Come on, Di, pull it together," I tried to encourage myself, "it's not like you've flown to the middle of the Amazon jungle." With just a fragment of my initial confidence restored, I swung my backpack over my shoulder and figured out the direction to the baggage claim area.

When I finally reached my room at the Sternblick hotel, just two kilometers from the airport, I tossed both my backpack and coat on the bed and dropped myself into one of the ultra modern oversized chairs. Wow, what a difference from my dingy Cape May hotel room. It wasn't what I expected from a German hotel. Somehow I envisioned something more along the lines of a *Heidi* movie, but then again, no one seemed to be yodeling either.

"I'll go downstairs and find something to eat...soon," I said aloud, but my body had other ideas, finding the oversized alien chairs quite tolerable. My backside wasn't about to lift its tired self anywhere.

"Warren? What are you doing here? I thought you were...you know..." Looking around the room I tried to figure out what hallucination-inducing substance I had accidentally ingested.

"You can say it, Diana, go ahead," Warren seemed to encourage me with a nod and his warm smile. I wanted to run to him, to throw myself into his arms, but somehow I felt paralyzed, as though I was rooted to this uber-modern chair.

"You are, uh, gone, right? Not alive?" I asked, as my eyes remained glued to the apparition before me. Warren nodded and without words flashed another smile that seemed as real as the chair I felt beneath my well-endowed rear.

"You...you don't exactly...ah, look like a ghost," I pointed out, staring at the two small moles on his neck that he had often talked about having removed because his shirt collars irritated them. All the details were there. Everything fit. What ghost has moles? And why exactly wasn't I just a little bit frightened if this really was a ghost? But then why would I fear Warren's ghost?

"Warren," I cried, trying in vain to lift myself from the chair, "Warren, please, just please let me touch you, just one last time." Warren's smile disappeared. "Someday, Diana, but for now, you have to look out for yourself, for your own happiness." As Warren spoke the temperature in the room dropped, sending an involuntary shiver through my body.

"What if I don't want to? What if I can't let go? Everything reminds me of you," I wept, again remembering Warren's box of letters I had forgotten at the motel. "Your letters, even your letters are gone…and I haven't even called the motel….oh please, Warren, please, don't go… Warren." Warren's smile returned to his face.

"Diana, you don't need those old letters to remember our love. Yes, our love was special, it always will be special. But you are capable of so much more love. There is still so much life ahead of you, so much love in you. So much love can still be yours." I looked at this ghost that so resembled the man I thought I would grow old with. And yet, here before me now stood the spirit of my soul mate, encouraging me to forget about him and find new love. Did he know about Charlie? A realization slowly crept into my consciousness. One I hadn't wanted to admit, for fear of losing my memories of Warren. I had already found new love. I didn't know if it would ever blossom into the love I shared with Warren, but if I didn't give it a chance, with my whole heart, I would never know.

"Give it time," Warren spoke, now more an apparition than anything human. "Good bye, Diana," he smiled, disappearing before my eyes.

"Warren! Warren!" I called out to him. "No, don't go, not yet," I cried without a voice. A dead silence overcame the room. Even the ticking clock was muted.

Mumbling, I awoke, seated in a large chair. It took a moment for me to figure out that I really was sitting in a hotel room in Germany. Shivering, I noticed the goose bumps covering my skin, but then I hadn't expected to fall asleep. The dream I had just moments ago vanished the instant I rejoined the waking world. "Warren," I whispered, realizing that somehow he had figured into this dream. I had to get up and move my stiff joints. Slowly I lifted myself from the chair and stretched my cold, stiff limbs. Unfortunately, the thermostat I found could not be adjusted. Pulling my coat from the bed, I hastily threw it over my shoulders. Time had lost all meaning. I had no idea how long I had been asleep and for a moment tried hard to figure out if the clock next to the bed was telling me it was six in the morning or six in the evening. Looking at my own watch didn't help any. It still ticked to New Jersey time. "Oh, for God's sake," I snapped, walking to the window where a gray sky didn't reveal much either. "What the heck," I muttered, remembering I had had a similar issue when I first arrived in Cape May. Well, I wasn't exactly the seasoned international travel. "Whatever time it is, I'll see Charlie soon," I told the gray German sky. Just the thought of Charlie warmed my belly, spreading quickly to the rest of my body. "Charlie," I spoke his name slowly. "Charlie, what is this going to turn into?" I asked.

My growling stomach needed to be appeased, so I decided to go downstairs and have breakfast or dinner, wondering where Charlie was right now. For the first time since I met Charlie I didn't feel guilty about the way our relationship had progressed, and was still progressing, I had to remind myself. What Einstein quote had he recited for me that first night together in the Cape May motel? "Gravitation is not responsible for people falling in love," I remembered, eagerly dialing his cell phone number. Something he shared with Warren, a love of poetic quotations. A bit on the corny side, but heck, he was a romantic too. Just the thought of Charlie warmed my belly. This warmth spread quickly to the rest of my body. "Charlie," I again spoke his name slowly, "Charlie, what is this going to turn into?"

Dresden, Germany

January 1942

"The New Year by Joseph Goebbels," Anna read aloud as her eyes scanned the latest of the letters from Dr. Goebbels to the people. "You will not fool the people much longer," Anna spoke to the photograph of the man she believed to be even more vicious than the Fuehrer himself. "If the Fuehrer is the devil, then you are his betrothed." For as much as she tried to distance herself from the war, she realized the war followed her, had changed her, and everyone she loved. It had become a part of her.

"The war will now come to us, Frieda," she had heard her father speak to her mother last night, on the rare occasion that he had shared an evening meal with his family.

"Oh, Franz, you do not know what the German soldiers, what the Fatherland, is capable of," her mother had argued with less enthusiasm than Anna had ever heard. But even that surprised her. These days her mother did not speak much of the war.

"Frieda, the Japanese have attacked the Americans! Are you really so blind? Do you not see what the Fuehrer has done? He has doomed us!" Her father had shouted as his spectacles filled with steam. To hear her father shout at all, and with such conviction, unnerved her.

Somehow he had reminded her of a raging bull. It was obvious to Anna that her father's nerves were frayed, and those of her mother had been dulled. Mama still listened to her radio incessantly, but Anna was sure it was more of a companion to her than anything else. She seemed to have little strength left for much of anything during the long winter months, when her breathing seemed most labored. Both Maria and Dieter, whom Papa had persuaded to move back to the main house with the children, had looked less than pleased with the shouting. Maria had never been one to ruffle anyone's feathers, Anna thought, yet these days Maria seemed almost a little feisty. Anna wondered whether the death of one of her twins had anything to do with this.

Anna bent down over the paper and could not resist blotting out Dr. Goebbel's face with her father's fountain pen, hoping he would not return to the study at just this moment. Whoever had rang so early this morning still occupied him at the front door. These days her father spent much of his time in Berlin. Only rarely did he come home, such as now. And when he did, he spent all of his time in his study, behind locked doors, where the smell of cigar smoke did not cease until he left for Berlin again. Anna knew her father did not feel comfortable with his "honorary" officer position, a title assigned to coerce support. Obviously these "honorary officers" did not command much respect.

Anna walked over to the windows of the study and sighed as she observed soldiers standing at attention beside two military trucks. "What do these monkeys want from us now?" she hissed between clenched teeth. It seemed a week did not pass without some type of military vehicle appearing at the estate. She questioned her father once regarding these frequent visits, but he had chosen to ignore her. When she had pressed him for information he had reprimanded her. "A young woman should concern herself with finding a husband," he had said, something she was used to hearing from her mother, but not her father.

"This war is going to kill you, Papa," she whispered, as the window fogged up with her steamy breath. Anna watched as the soldiers, most of them likely younger than even herself, stood motionless, in some type of perfect linear arrangements. Only an occasional involuntary shiver betrayed that these men were human at all.

"And why t…t…two large trucks?" Anna pondered aloud, as she recalled the large vehicle that had stolen away her father's black stallion. Anna wiped the condensation from the window and shivered, not from cold, her father's study was always kept well heated, but from fear. Whenever soldiers came a primal fear took hold of her which she barely managed to keep under control. And now, as the soldiers stood outside in the freezing cold, hardly moving, barely human, she wondered, had they come for her? She had loved a Jew. She still loved a Jew. She had given birth to a Jew.

"Are you here for me? What do you want?" she whispered, frozen with fear. Too many friends and neighbors had disappeared. "Oh dear God, when is this going to end?" she cried, praying to something she wasn't even sure she believed in anymore. "When will things be the way they used to?" Somewhere deep inside her, Anna knew things would never again be the same. They could not be the same. Deep scars remain etched in the soul after so much death and devastation. "What do you want?" she again asked in a whisper, wiping at the window with her sleeve.

As though in response to her question, she heard orders shouted from the front door. "So much shouting these days," she spoke under her breath, as the noise brought life back to her limbs. Anna rushed out of the study, nearly colliding with her mother, who was closely followed by Lena and Sigrid. Anna heard footsteps coming down the stairs and looked up to see Maria carefully coming down the stairs with a child cradled in her arms.

"Where is Dieter?" Anna whispered to her sister when she reached the bottom of the staircase.

"He left for Berlin late last night, direct orders from Adolph," Maria sneered as she said the Fuehrer's name. Surprised, no one called him anything but the Fuehrer these days, Anna looked at her sister, whose face expressed a combination of defiance and disgust.

Maria pushed past Anna and into the entrance hall where her father was in obvious disagreement with the senior-most official of this early morning visit. "These pigs take my husband at a moment's notice from me," Maria hissed between clenched teeth. It was then that Anna recognized one of the younger officers. Her father had introduced her to this officer in his study. She could not recall his name, but was frightened by the stone-faced soldier who now replaced the once nervous man she had met. Anna shuddered as she suddenly remembered his name. Officer Geist. Would he be here had she shown interest in him?

"Maria! Stay here, Maria!" her mother ordered. Maria, ignoring her mother, marched towards her father and stood by his side just as the young daughter in her arms awoke with a scream. Lena too pushed her way past Anna and cautiously approached Maria. Whispering into her ear, Lena swiftly removed the small child from Maria and retreated back to the main part of house.

There was a moment of charged silence as Maria looked from her father to the officer and back to her father, both of whom observed her, one with fear, the other with almost eager anticipation.

"What is she doing?" Anna whispered to her mother with a quivering voice, fearing the black spider on the officer's uniform would come to life at any moment to grab her sister around the throat.

"Quiet, child," her mother snapped, reminding Anna of a previous time she had stood at the corner of the hall with her mother, watching her father. For all of her authority within the home, including her influence over her father, Anna had never seen her mother interfere with matters outside of the home. The creaking staircase announced Sigrid's presence. Sigrid joined the other women at the doorway to the large entrance hall. She looked pale, with almost a green shimmer to her face, reminding Anna of the mold she had seen on the potatoes in the cellar yesterday.

Maria abruptly turned and stormed out of the hall, grabbing her daughter from Lena as she passed by her, as though some insanity had overtaken her. All the women in the home breathed a sigh a relief.

"She has gone mad," Anna hissed at her mother as Maria quickly ascended the staircase, relieved her sister had not slapped anyone. The Baroness gave Anna a warning glance as she slowly, and with great purpose, walked towards her husband. The men had resumed speaking, but at a reduced volume, making it difficult for Anna to hear what the topic of discussion was. As her mother stood by her father she could not help admire this woman who, even under these extreme circumstances, carried herself with such dignity and poise. Her mother stood in silence as the officer abruptly turned and pulled out a whistle. Anna did not know what was happening, everything happened so fast. She saw her mother gently, yet firmly, shove her father from the doorway as all of the previously frozen soldiers pushed their way into her home.

The women watched in horror as no less than ten men stormed into every corner of the house, only to emerge minutes later, carrying with them as much as their arms could hold. Anna wanted to scream out as she watched armload upon armload of clothing, linen, dishes, her mother's chocolates, and even her father's riding boots, make their way out of the house and onto one of the military vehicles. Sigrid, Lena, and Anna listened as screams of protest sounded from the upstairs living quarters. Moments later, a young soldier, completely hidden by the down comforters he carried, bounded down the stairs and rushed towards the entrance hall. A loud thump sounded as the young soldier dropped to his knees after tripping on the corner of a comforter. As he scrambled to stand up and pick up his loot, Anna noticed her mother move swiftly towards the young soldier. And in a voice Anna had never heard, her mother addressed the soldier.

"You," the Baroness pointed at the soldier, moving slowly toward the young man like a lioness stalking its prey, "You may take the clothing, the food, the serving ware, even the furniture, but you shall not take the blankets from the beds of my family, or I swear, before God, you shall kill me first!" Anna had never seen her mother filled with more rage.

"Take your hands off me," the Baroness shouted at the Baron, who now attempted to physically move his wife away from the young soldier who had raised himself from the ground. Undecided as to what he should do, the soldier stared at the very angry woman.

"Now! Set them down now!" the Baroness shouted with such intensity Anna could see one of her mother's veins menacingly poking out of her forehead. The young soldier, frightened by the insane woman before him, exercised his better judgment and dropped the comforters.

The senior officer in charge of this effort observed the scene with calculated silence. Strutting towards the young soldier, he glanced from the soldier to the comforters to the seemingly mad woman before him.

"He must realize Mama is not bluffing," Anna prayed in a whisper, as she caught Sigrid's terrified glance.

After a brief moment of silence, the officer ordered the soldier outside and blew his whistle. Within moments, the soldiers emerged from every corner of the house and filed out, one-by-one, like well-trained dogs.

The senior officer curtly nodded. "Madame, my apologies, you shall keep your blankets," he hissed, and turned to exit the house. A strange silence settled over the normally noisy house, as the family members heard the military vehicles start their engines and leave. It was not until the Baroness collapsed that noise once again filled the home, which would be forever-changed.

"Lena, find Otto...have him bring the doctor, quick," the frantic Baron said as he kneeled down beside his wife and caressed her hand.

"Frieda, Frieda," he muttered as Lena ran out in search of Otto, hoping to find him tending the cows in the barn.

Anna ran to her mother and searched for her pulse. "Sh...sh... she is alive," Anna stuttered, as she looked up at her father sitting on his knees, stiff with shock. Bending close, she felt her mother's warm breath on her cheek. "Sh...sh...she's breathing too, Papa," Anna said calmly, as she stroked her mother's clammy forehead. It felt odd to Anna to touch her so intimately, when her mother had never shown physical affection. "Is that any surprise? She isn't your real mother," the small voice inside chided as she suddenly thought of Sigrid. It was Sigrid who had always been there, feeding and comforting her as a small child. Even as a grown woman, it was Sigrid who empathized with her loss. "It was Sigrid who taught me physical affection," she whispered to herself, as she looked from the woman she had called mother all these years to her biological mother whom she had been denied her whole life. "That is not true, she has always lived on the estate," her rational voice argued. "But she disappears at will, leaving me alone," the small child in her bickered, not wanting to forgive the woman who could callously give her children away.

"Anna, Sigrid, help me bring her to her room," her father ordered, interrupting Anna's thoughts. He sounded hollow, as though only a shell of his former self remained. Anna wondered how much of her-self remained after all that had transpired over the last months.

Together they managed to move the Baroness up the spiral stair-case and into her bedroom. Anna and Sigrid stood motionless, panic stricken, as the Baron paced back and forth like a caged tiger.

"Where is he?" the Baron impatiently asked, as he continued to pace back and forth, occasionally stopping to glance at his wife who stared at him with distant eyes. She had opened her eyes shortly after they laid her on the bed, but had not yet uttered a sound.

"Maybe it is snow which delays them," Anna offered, interrupted by the sound of rapidly approaching footsteps and a soft knocking at the bedroom door.

"Come! Come quick," her father ordered the doctor in, at the same time directing Anna and Sigrid to leave the room.

"I should like to stay, please," Sigrid timidly requested, only to be swiftly ushered out by the Baron. The Baron followed shortly thereaf-ter, leaving the doctor with the Baroness.

Anna and Sigrid waited outside the room for what felt like hours. Actually no more than half an hour had passed before the young doc-tor headed out of the bedroom.

"How is she?" Both Sigrid and Anna asked in the same instant.

"The Baroness has suffered a stroke. It appears the right side of her body has been paralyzed. But, with proper rehabilitation, she may regain some motor function," the young doctor rattled on nervously.

"W…w…will she speak again?" Anna asked, terrified by visions of what kind of life this independent, strong willed woman would now lead.

"Yes, she can, but I fear she may not…she, ah, tells me life has taken her need for a voice…I am sorry, but I must be on my way. Ladies," the doctor said as he bowed, still twitching nervously, and headed towards the staircase.

"W…w…wait, p…p…please, I shall w…w…walk you out," Anna called after the doctor, leaving Sigrid to stand alone outside the Baroness' room.

"It is y…y…you," Anna said, forgetting her manners and point-ing at the young doctor with her naked finger, something her mother would look upon with great disfavor. One never pointed a naked finger at a clothed person she would have chided. Despite the dire circumstances, Anna almost giggled at the thought. "Y...y...you knocked m...m...me senseless, and then n...n...never returned to check up on me," she spoke with feigned arrogance.

"You do not remember anything else?" Dr. Wenke asked, as he nervously clasped his hands together.

"Of course, I r...r...remember everything, d...d...despite the fact that I h...h...had a lump the size of an egg on m...m...my forehead for nearly t...t...two weeks," Anna answered, insulted that he should question her mental faculties.

"No, it was I who tended you after the, ah, horse incident...I, ah, did not think you would remember me, your contusion and concussion were quite severe, you know." Anna heard his words, but somehow could not imagine that this was the doctor who had, according to her mother, "so marvelously cared for her." He just seemed too twitchy and nervous to be competent she thought, immediately feeling guilty for her unjust notions.

"Oh, I d...d...did not know, I th...th...thank you," Anna stuttered, as all traces of arrogance vanished. "A...a...and I am sorry, for...for my ill manners," she added before she lost the nerve to apologize. Why was it so much easier to commit a grave offense than it was to apologize for that same offense? Somehow she now viewed the doctor in a more favorable light.

Letter 10   *Dresden, 16. June 1942*

My Beloved Jakub,

I pray this letter finds you safe on the shore of my imaginary tropical beach. I apologize as too much time has passed since I last wrote to you, my love. I find it difficult these days to find the necessary peace of mind that came so naturally as a child. With the war now on German soil, fears run high that more bombs shall drop on unsuspecting cities. Jakub, each day I hear those cursed sirens wail I believe the end has come. One day it shall.

What news is there you may ask, beside the war? The war is the news which dominates every topic of discussion. Rumors of torture and much worse have reached even my ears, ears which have tried in vain to remain deaf to all that is happening around me. Often I pinch myself in an attempt to awaken from a dream I am sure does not reflect the reality I once knew and loved. Could this be a nightmare I have become trapped in, powerless to escape? Impotent to help others, my mother, or even myself? This cursed war has doomed future generations for years to come.

While the war dominates our foremost thoughts, life on the periphery does continue to move forward, as it must. Frau Ahrens, Mamma's old maid, passed in her sleep two months ago. While death is never a pleasant occasion, there are most certainly ways to leave this earth which are definitely more desirable than others. A peaceful, natural death while sleeping seems, given any number of alternatives, the least terrifying way to depart this world. As to Maria and Dieter, they suffered for months in an inadequately heated home, likely the reason one of their young twins passed away. Papa convinced Dieter to move his growing family to the main house, as both

Papa and Dieter spend more time away from home these days. Mama, who has suffered a stroke, spends her days in her room. It is Sigrid and I who move her each day to her chair by the window. When the weather permits, we, through great physical exertion, bring her outside where she seems to enjoy the plants in bloom. She is unable to move the right side of her body, but freely uses her left hand to still care for herself in many ways. It is her voice I fear she has lost forever, despite assurance from the doctor that she still can speak. Since the day she suffered her brain injury, I have not heard her utter a single word, Jakub. Will she ever reveal to me her true role in your disappearance now? How can life play such cruel tricks? And at a time when there is already so much suffering.

You would no longer recognize the estate, Jakub. Many of Papa's workers have disappeared as the war continues to spread. The gardens have not been tended to in many months. And it is difficult to purchase anything. I should not complain of scarcity as we continue to have more than others, yet meals consist of simple foods which do little to stimulate the pallet. Theft has become, aside from the risk of falling bombs, the main threat to the well-being of all on the estate. Less than one week ago, thieves gained access to the upstairs rooms by entering through an open window. It was Sigrid who unexpectedly discovered them. Chasing them back with a single shoe, she managed to push one out through the window and watched as the unforgiving ground did nothing to soften his fall. Papa requires all windows to remain locked at all times, which does nothing to relieve the odors that fill the house from the animals wandering freely in two of the ground floor rooms.

My work at the newspaper no longer provides the outlet to freedom it once did. It now truly depresses and horrifies me to find myself involved in this war effort in any way. Often I ride into town and find that I am unable to set foot in the office. Instead of returning home, I ride through the city. It continues to confound and amaze me that humanity, myself included, trudges forward, despite all the horrors that surround us.

My beloved Jakub, all of Germany is in turmoil. Who will it be that puts an end to our way of life? I am tired Jakub. Just now I feel I can sleep. Please know I continue to pray for you every day, to whatever greater justice or higher power there may be. Someday, Jakub, we shall be reunited. Someday.

Love Eternally,
Anna v. Marschalkt

Post Script: Last night I dreamt of you in the hayloft. But it was not I who met you at the top of the ladder, but another woman. Please forgive me, Jakub.

Anna did not wait for the ink to dry before she rolled up the letter and carefully shoved it down through the neck of the bottle. It had become more difficult to find her sacred green glass bottles. Both Sigrid and Lena had questioned why so many apple juice bottles were missing. Hastily plugging the bottle with wax, Anna wondered about the dream she had the previous night. "Why did I dream of another woman with Jakub?" she whispered, while thoughts she detested rose to the surface of her consciousness. "No, he does not have another woman," she spoke to the bottle, which felt cool to her touch. "No, no, no," Anna repeated, as though a small child.

The following day, Anna, with her bottle safely tucked in her basket, rode her bicycle into the city, depressed by the oppressive feeling that followed her even there. As she rode by the small church adjacent to the newspaper offices, she stopped and turned around. There was something about this church that seemed to draw her in. Maybe it was the fine, highly detailed architecture that fascinated her. "Maybe it was the smack on my head," she snapped, as she pulled open the heavy door. "Or maybe it is the opportunity to meet the endearing pastor and give him a piece of my mind," she whispered, remembering the words the pastor had spoken. As she walked down the aisle, with her bottle close by her side, Anna hoped to rid herself of this impending feeling of doom.

Anna sat down just as beautiful organ music began to float through the air. Setting her bottle down at her feet, Anna leaned back and allowed the music to engulf and move her soul. She was unconcerned, for the moment, with the pastor, the war, her family, or even Jakub.

It was not until she awoke that she realized the organ music had stopped and the sunlight that filtered through the stained glass windows seemed less bright. "How long did I sleep?" she whispered to the painting of a Madonna, who seemed to glare at her. Whatever feelings of peace and benevolence she had sensed in this church quickly dissipated when she realized how late it was. Quickly jumping up from the uncomfortable pew, she rushed out to her bicycle and pedaled towards home. She was almost home before she realized with horror that she had left her bottle in the church. Furiously pedaling, she reached the church in half the time it had taken her to ride home. When she did not find her bottle she pounded on the pastor's door, whose chronic, cough could be heard from behind the closed door.

The pastor eventually opened the door and denied any knowledge of a green apple juice bottle, all the while watching Anna with a most peculiar, if not antagonistic, look. Anna would never know the pastor had seen the red-haired devil sleeping in his church. She would never know that he not only found her bottle, but figured out that there was something inside. As was his most meddlesome nature, he smashed the bottle, eager to read what was written on this obviously private letter. He did not pause for a moment to consider that what he might be doing was wrong as he held the letter over his burning candle. "How can a man of God be wrong?" he spoke aloud with self-importance, dropping the burning letter onto the cold stone ground.

Travels of Letter 16
Sierra Leone Coast, West Africa
August 1993

Yenplu watched from her hidden spot on the beach as her father pushed off into the sea in his fishing canoe. Crouching behind her rock, the one she had stood behind so many times as a child, she wondered why it seemed smaller than she remembered. Did her father know she was here today? Just recently he had asked her why she stood behind that rock every morning as a child. Yenplu had been surprised by the question. Had he known all along, she wondered? "To pray for your safe return," she had answered, remembering the day she no longer came to stand behind her rock. Mother had said it was no longer safe for her. Reciting the prayer she spoke for him every day as a child, she watched as the last of the twelve men climbed into the wooden canoe. Today she did not pray for the safe return of her father alone and felt her pulse quicken as she watched Dwe jump aboard, his sheer size setting him apart from all the other men. Quite unexpectedly, she felt exposed, vulnerable, despite the solid rock that kept her well hidden. There was something about the sea that looked different today. Familiar, she thought, but definitely different. Was it watching

Dwe, the man she was to marry tomorrow, that made everything seem different?

As she watched the large canoe roll back and forth with the waves, she felt immensely grateful. Her parents had chosen her mate well. Not all matches were so fortunate. She and Dwe had been childhood friends, she had never seen him as anything different until the day she became a woman. It was her sister who told her it was no longer proper for her to play with Dwe. He was no longer a boy and Yenplu no longer a girl, she had said. There was something else about her sister she knew she should remember. Something that had happened, but, as Yenplu stared out at the magnificent blue sea, she was unable to remember. No, that was not right she thought, it was something she did not want to remember. Squinting against the glaring sun, she watched as the boat drifted farther out to sea. She was no longer able to distinguish one man from the other. How long should she wait she wondered. As a child there was no time, there were no responsibilities. An hour was a day, a day a minute. Today, there were chores to complete and a wedding ceremony to prepare for.

Yenplu knew she should leave now, it was her time, but something kept her rooted firmly to the warm sand on which she stood. Running her hands over the large grey rock, she wondered how long it had stood on this shore. She watched her own hands slowly caress the familiar rock, realizing how much of life she had experienced through her hands. She lifted her hands to examine them more closely. She had never really looked at her hands before, only her nails to make sure they were clean before food preparation. What beautiful creations these hands were, that gave one the power to create and preserve or torture and destroy. These hands which inextricably linked her to all other human beings. Yenplu did not notice the butterflies until one of them landed on her hand. Since childhood she had been fascinated with the delicate creatures. Never before had one landed in the palm of her hand. As she examined its fragile wings she wondered why the creature was so close to the beach. It wasn't until she looked up that she saw a swarm of flaming orange butterflies. It was an omen, a good one. It had to be. Extending her arms she watched as one butterfly after another landed on her warm brown skin.

She did not know what suddenly scared the butterflies away. Was it the dark cloud which appeared out of nowhere to block the sun, abruptly turning the sky dark? Was it the wind that agitated the sea that frightened them away? Within moments the swarm disappeared leaving only the dead and dying on the beach as evidence that their kind had once been there. Yenplu sat down on her knees to look at a butterfly that had chosen an old glass bottle just beside her grey rock as its final resting place. As she moved closer to better inspect the creature she realized it was still alive. She felt an overwhelming, almost unnatural, amount of sadness as she watched the ailing creature which rested on its side attempt to beat its wings. "What is wrong with this world?" she asked the butterfly as it lifted its wing one last time. "Why does something so beautiful have to die? Why does life have to end?"

It was time for her to go. Yenplu knew that now. The air had grown cold, as the dark cloud continued to increase in size like an angry demon. She felt a shiver pass over her as the wind cut through her light cotton dress. Looking out at the sea, she caught sight of the canoe, but it took her mind a moment to understand that something was not right. As she stared in horror at the capsized fishing canoe, she realized she did not see her father or Dwe in the water. They were gone, dead, all of them, she knew that much. The realization that they were all gone, that she was all alone, hit her like a freight train. Shivering uncontrollably she threw herself onto the sand, which was no longer warm.

"No! No! Not now, not yet," she screamed as she beat her hands on the icy sand.

It was a movement from the sea that caught her eye. Looking up she watched as a figure emerged from the grey churning sea. Someone had survived. If there was one, maybe there would be more. From the size of the person she immediately knew it was her beloved.

"Dwe! Dwe!" she called out to him, nearly beside herself with joy. "You did not drown," she cried, as she lifted herself up and ran towards his waiting embrace. "You did not drown," she repeated, as she felt his dry, strong warm arms wrap themselves around her chilled body.

"I did not drown, my love," he spoke warmly as he looked into her dark eyes. "It is time to go, Yenplu, the others are waiting." Yenplu did not answer. She did not need to. The memories she had suppressed surfaced the moment she felt Dwe's strength surround her like a protective shield. Nodding, she held out her hand to him. Together Yenplu and Dwe walked into the sea.

The old woman dropped her head into her hands after she watched her niece draw her last breath. She had done everything she could for Yenplu. She stared at the pools of blood on the floor. The girl had lost too much blood after the men had come and taken off her hands. The woman tried to lift herself up from the chair she had been sitting in for the last two days, but felt herself too tired to move, too tired to cry. There was no one left, they had killed the girl's father and most of the other men and boys in the village. Her own sister, the girl's mother, had been raped and beaten to death along with the oldest girl. And the three little ones, a wave of nausea passed over her as she tried to block the images in her mind of what these horrible people would do with three little girls. Why was she spared? Why did destiny place her outside the village the day the men came? Did God need a witness for these crimes? She lifted her head and leaned forward to close Yenplu's eyes. "These godforsaken men and their wars, and their cursed diamonds," she whispered to Yenplu's recently departed soul.

Sternblick Hotel, Berlin, Germany
Fall 2011

"I want to know everything about you," I said, as Charlie rubbed my left foot, something Warren had never done. "Besides the fact that you can actually touch *my* feet, corns and all." Charlie laughed as he tickled my feet and made me squirm.

"Well, I'm an attorney, I live in Los Angeles, and I can't believe I'm here in this hotel with the most beautiful foot in the world." Watching as he leaned down to kiss each one of my toes, I felt shivers, the good kind, move up and down my spine. Tousling his hair, everything felt strangely surreal. How could this be real? Everything just seemed too perfect.

"No, come on, Charlie, I'm serious, I want to know about you, where you grew up, how you grew up, you know, personal family kind of stuff," I said, looking up at the man who, if anyone had told me last week I'd fall in love with, I would have thought they were utterly insane and in more need of a shrink than me.

"Well, what do you want to know?" Charlie asked, setting down my left foot only to pick up and continue on with the right one. Somehow finding this mysterious Anna didn't seem like the most important thing right now. I had to admit, some small part of me hadn't really believed

Charlie would ever show up. First there were all the cell phone problems. I hadn't been able to reach him and then when I finally did there was a bad connection, making it difficult to understand anything. The hours passed with me sitting, waiting, in the lonely hotel room, wondering what it was I would say to him should he ever show up. Would it be awkward? So when he did walk into the hotel room, and not merely in my imagination, I almost fainted. But when he embraced me it felt like the most natural thing in the world, almost as though we had known each other for years.

"My family, hmmm, well, I've got two older sisters, a doctor and a dentist, and both married with way too many kids." Charlie scratched his head as he spoke. "And my dad, he passed away last year." I noticed a wave of melancholy wash over Charlie's face.

"I'm sorry, Charlie," I empathized, all too familiar with loss.

"Yeah, he never missed a day of work in his life. My mom used to say his work was his mistress, but you want to know what I think," Charlie looked at me with eyes as dark green as the deep sea. "I think he wanted to make sure my mom was always taken care of. I think he wanted to make sure we had a better life than he did."

As I regarded Charlie in silence, I realized, with a clarity that comes to me only rarely in life. This guy *was* for real. "What did your dad do?" I asked, pulling my foot away from Charlie to lay down on the bed beside him. I don't know if it was the foot massage or Charlie's voice, but I couldn't keep my hands off him.

"He was really a kind of jack of all trades, but he eventually opened up a small grocery store…in New York…that's where he met my mom," Charlie's smile returned to his face, an Antonio Banderas kind of smile. "I always loved the way the two of them told their *love story*," Charlie chuckled at some distant memory, as he rubbed his knuckles up and down my spine.

Listening to him speak, I wanted to know everything about this man, so wished to be a part of even his past memories.

"Mom, she's quite a bit younger than my dad. She worked for him, as a cashier…his only employee. He said he hired her for her great ass. Mom said he hired her because he was cheap, and she was desperate, and willing to work for next to nothing." There was something about the way Charlie told their love story that made me smile. This was the kind of love that one imagines, the kind of love story that I had always imagined for myself. Was sure I had. Wow, life can throw some zingers at you.

"It wasn't until much later he told her he really couldn't afford hiring her, but he just knew."

"Just knew what?" I asked, but I knew what he was going to say. Is that what I had with Charlie? I needed him to tell me this story.

"That she was the one…the one my dad wanted to spend the rest of his life with." A peculiar expression crossed over Charlie's face and I felt his heartbeat quicken beneath his chest. "You know, until this week I always thought my dad was kind of full of it…I guess I always thought, you know, maybe it was the time he grew up in, and different attitudes towards love and marriage. I never believed you could meet another person and *just know.*" I felt Charlie's grip on my shoulder tighten as we lay closely pressed against one another. "But since I met you, I know it *is real.*" Charlie lifted my face towards him and gently kissed me with his warm, soft lips, still tasting of the licorice we had recently shared.

Rolling on top of him, I felt his manhood surge beneath me, ready to go again. The two of us had not left the hotel room since he arrived two days ago, and I wouldn't mind spending the rest of my life locked up in here with him. As his strong hands squeezed my buttocks, I fleetingly thought of Warren's letters and wondered why I hadn't called the motel yet. I'd call later.

My guilt was gone. Why I no longer felt guilty was a mystery to me, but I had to say it felt good to be free of this burden. The guilt that had burdened me had magically lifted. This probably sounded insane, but I felt physically lighter.

"You know what I don't understand," I said, shifting my body closer to Charlie, "how I could so quickly transform from believing in one true love, one soul mate, to knowing that there is more than just one true love out there for me." I didn't realize exactly what I had said to Charlie until I watched his ears take on the familiar crimson color I had seen many times before, but this time the color spread over his neck and face as well.

"I love this about you...oh God, I said it didn't I?" Charlie said and laughed. I felt my own surge of heat wash over me, making my armpits begin to dampen.

"You know, when I met you I thought you were a lady's man, you know, a player. But now I'm not so sure," I teased, gently tracing his strong jaw with my finger.

"Hey, you're *not so sure?*" Charlie asked mischievously, pinching my rear.

"You're like a school boy, actually, turning all sorts of different shades of red all the time, but on the other hand, completely in control of the situation... that, is *one* of the things I love about you," I said, running my hands along the length of his solid body.

"Well, I'm ready to hear the other things you love about me... you know, any time you'd like to start. No need to keep me waiting," Charlie said smugly, obviously enjoying the direction our conversation was once again headed in.

"Don't push your luck, mister," I jokingly warned him. "But there is one thing I've been wondering about. How come someone like you isn't married? You know, how come you haven't found Mrs. Right?"

"Someone like me?" Charlie repeated with a smile. "Well, I never found the right girl...until now."

"Are you for real, I mean really, really for real? There are so many women out there," I said, "And what about your mom? What is she like?" I asked, seductively blowing into Charlie's ear.

"Well, I'm having a hard time thinking about my mom right now, if you know what I mean." Charlie said with a quickened pulse that I could see beating in his neck.

"How'd she take, you know, your dad's passing?" I didn't mean for my voice to crack when I spoke, Charlie must have noticed, as he gently touched my cheek.

"Mom...well, it's been really hard on her. I was really worried about her for a while. She takes each day at a time now. She's a survivor, Diana." Charlie took a deep breath, as though he had more to say, but decided not to.

Somehow the lighthearted mood between us had disappeared. Why'd I have to go and ask about his mom? It was obvious Charlie wasn't in the mood for anything anymore. Rolling off Charlie, I felt an awkward silence between us.

"Hey, look, I know this probably, you know, reminds you of, you know just forget it," Charlie said with a dismissive gesture, his face turning a few shades darker. Flustered and frustrated with himself, he sat up. "Hey you know what, now that I've kind of busted the mood, how 'bout you and I get out of here, grab a bite and then start our search for Anna?" He busted the mood? No, I think it was me who busted the mood. But hey, I'm not gonna argue with the man right now.

"Anna, right. I, ah, I almost forgot about her," I said with a slight laugh, trying to lighten the mood. Briefly squeezing my leg, Charlie lifted himself from the bed. "Well, obviously that was that," I whispered to myself, watching a naked Charlie walk across the room and rummage through his travel bag. Pulling a small piece of paper from his wallet, he returned to the bed and sat down beside me.

"Here," he said somewhat bashfully, handing me the paper with an address written on it. Taking the paper from him, I stared down at the last known address for Anna von Marschalkt.

"Do you think she's still alive, Charlie?" I felt my heart race as the tension in the air melted away. "What do we say to her? She'll think we're crazy." My excitement was contagious, it wasn't long before I had infected Charlie, who had been watching me closely. Leaning over, he kissed me.

"We tell her the truth, baby, the whole truth." Wrapping my arms around Charlie I kissed him and pulled him down to the bed to finish what I had set my mind on earlier. It didn't take much to convince Charlie.

Two hours later we found ourselves in the tiny Fiat rental car headed towards the von Marschalkt estate in Dresden. Unrolling Anna's letter, I stared at her name as the beautiful scenery outside whizzed by.

"Read it to me again," Charlie begged for the third time.

"Oh come on, who's getting all sentimental now? Didn't you tell me I needed to stop reading it? That I was just a tad obsessed? I see who's obsessed now," I joked, actually pleased that Charlie seemed as excited as I was. I would probably feel guilty if I thought he were just here for moral support. Taking a deep breath, I read the letter aloud to Charlie for the third time. And for the third time a calm, peaceful silence filled the car. And I had to think to myself that there are two kinds of silence, the awkward, uncomfortable kind, and the harmonious kind. This was definitely a harmonious silence, I thought, as I stared out at the harvested fields we passed by.

Dresden, Germany

Fall 1942

Sigrid and Anna carried the Baroness down to the sitting room, laying her gently on the couch with pillows propped up behind her head. The days were getting shorter and colder. In this room one could still enjoy the warmth of the afternoon sun shining through the windows.

"Her radio…we should turn her radio on," Anna said. The radio had been silent for many months now. "She must have missed it all these months," Anna assumed as she turned on the radio which had previously been her mother's constant companion.

"I am not so sure anymore," Sigrid said, as she studied the face of the Baroness. "I am not so sure."

"Here, a blanket for your legs, Mama," Anna quietly spoke, carefully placing a heavy woolen blanket across her mother's legs. How odd, she thought to herself, that such a misfortune would actually bring her closer to her mother. Anna glanced sidelong at Sigrid. What was even more odd, she realized, was that her father's former mistress now tended to her mother with such an extraordinary amount of respect and care.

"I could not even begin to imagine such a situation for myself," Anna whispered silently to herself, as she watched Sigrid pour coffee for her mother.

"Is it still two teaspoons, Baroness? And cream?" Sigrid asked, although she and Anna both realized there would be no response.

"Sigrid, can you manage without me? I was going to ride into the city today, to the newspaper," Anna lied, "I have not been there in some time." Sigrid watched Anna's ears and face turn a shade of red that matched the shade of her hair.

"I see, and when shall you return?" Sigrid asked, with obvious suspicion. Anna had little patience for Sigrid's new role of mother in recent months, with her incessant questions and concern.

"You are n...n...not my mother," Anna snapped back, not failing to notice an immediate and intense sadness sweep over Sigrid's face.

"You are right, I am not your mother...anymore," Sigrid said, with a stern voice that belied the inner turmoil she experienced. Anna wanted to apologize for her hurtful words, but somehow could not bring herself to apologize to the woman who had given her away so many years ago.

"Good bye, Mama," Anna said, briefly squeezing her mother's icy hand and turning to leave the room.

"Anna. Anna." Her mother called to her in a voice that was nothing more than a hoarse whisper.

"Mama," Anna cried, hurrying over to her mother, whose half frozen face looked up at Anna with a pained expression.

"Frieda," Sigrid called out, as she jumped to reach the Baroness. The familiarity with which she had addressed the Baroness startled Anna.

"Turn it off, turn it off! I cannot stand another moment of this," the Baroness croaked.

"Baroness!" Sigrid exclaimed, quickly turning off the radio, "I did not think you would ever speak again." A fleeting smile spread over half her mother's face, disappearing as quickly as it had come. Anna could never be sure, but somehow it was as though this look of triumph had momentarily transformed her mother. For a moment, Anna half believed her mother would jump up from the sofa and begin issuing commands as she had in the past.

"M....M...Mama, oh, Mama," Anna repeated. Overcome with emotion, she kneeled down beside her mother.

"Sigrid, leave me alone with *my* daughter," the Baroness hoarsely whispered, trying to clear her throat. What was going on, Anna wondered? What had changed these last few months that Sigrid and her mother addressed each other so informally? Anna had never heard her mother refer to Sigrid as anything other than Frau Steinmeyer. And no one would ever dare call the Baroness Frieda, aside from her father and very close friends, of which she had very few. Could this familiarity have to do with her mother's current condition, she wondered? She too, after all, felt much closer to her mother, now that she had been forced to interact with her on such intimate levels. Sigrid nodded her head slightly and left the room, turning around once more to glance at the Baroness. Anna wished she could decode the unspoken language that passed between these two very different women.

"Anna, I do not know how much time God will still have me suffer on this earth. This war may well be the end for all of us," her mother spoke with obvious difficulty, as the muscles on one side of her face did not cooperate, and never would again. The Baroness paused and stared out the window. It was obvious to Anna that her mother's half-paralyzed face caused her difficulty with speech, and it was difficult for her to look at her mother's distorted face. Anna had always thought her mother beautiful in a severe sense, unlike Sigrid, who would be considered a more natural beauty, even though she was as thick-boned as a bull. It would benefit both women to wear their hair unbound, the tight knot into which both pulled their hair did not suit either one.

Anna waited patiently as this half-paralyzed woman sat contemplatively staring out the window. Her mother was not one to be interrupted, Anna thought, even when immersed in her own thoughts. She admired how the Baroness, even in her meditative silence, could still command the attention in a room. Anna did not dare speak. Somehow the more her mother spoke, the further removed she felt from her. This bond that had formed when her mother had chosen not to speak seemed to vanish before her eyes.

"This room, it has always been my favorite. I would... like to thank you Anna...and Frau Steinmeyer, for bringing me down here so often."

"Oh, th…th…there is no need to th…th…thank us M…M… Mama…,' Anna began, but was cut short by her mother.

"Ssshhh, child, I have much to share with you…do not interrupt," her mother reprimanded her, somehow possessing the ability to transform Anna back into a scared little girl. Anna was still recovering from the shock that her mother had spoken the words "thank you." And now this, revelations from the dominant matriarch, this was unbelievable. Anna fervently waited for her mother to continue.

"I am well aware what Sigrid has told you and Maria about yourselves…and herself. There is no reason to repeat what is already known to you." It was not a question her mother asked, of this Anna was sure. Nodding silently, she looked to her mother to continue. "You may call it a cruel fate to suffer…possibly you resent Sigrid, but my child, there are far worse fates to suffer than growing up the privileged daughter of Baron von Marschalkt. Just look at the world around you."

Despite her mother's speech impediment, she could still clearly understand the Baroness. Was it this impediment that had kept her silent for so long? Anna had always known her mother to be a vain person. It had to be difficult for her to come to terms with something like this.

"What you desire to know is how I became your mother." Her mother looked at her expectantly, awaiting some kind of response. Anna nodded mutely. "Sigrid is my half-sister," the Baroness said, as evenly as though she had just told the maid to boil potatoes. Anna was dumbstruck as she waited for her mother to continue, but when the Baroness slumped back into her pillows and closed her eyes, Anna was sure she would learn no more from her mother. Anna's mind raced as she tried to piece together the puzzle that was floating around in her mind.

"If Mama is Sigrid's sister, then Mama is really my…aunt," Anna whispered to herself, staring at the Baroness, who seemed to have aged a decade in these last months.

"Sigrid could not keep you and Maria," the Baroness abruptly said, with her eyes still firmly shut.

"I d...d...do not understand M...M...Mama, how is she y...y... your sister?" Anna dared to ask, as her mother remained as though asleep on the couch.

"My father, like all men, was a philandering fool...he never could keep his hands off the maids. Eventually, as nature goes, one of the maids bore a child. This child was Sigrid. It was a disgrace, but Papa knew what needed to be done, Anna. He was a man of means." Anna watched her mothers lips tighten into a thin line as she spoke of her father. "My father had his eye on the Baron, your father, the moment he found out his own illegitimate daughter, Sigrid, had given birth to twins. Your father carried the name, my family had wealth, and now two heirs from my father's own bloodline. What more could my father want?" Anna saw the Baroness squeeze her closed eyes more tightly.

The Baroness breathed deeply. "My father had no need for additional wealth, just a title for his daughters. A propitious match had already been made for my sister, so it was arranged that I wed your father, on the condition that I raise you and Maria as my own." Her mother inhaled deeply before she continued. Anna listened with utter amazement as this woman, who normally spoke no more than a few words to her, spewed out words like an erupting volcano.

"I have been cursed from the beginning...a condition prevented me from ever having a child of my own. For my father this was all the perfect solution. I was cursed to love a man who would always love another." A tear managed to escape from the corner of Frieda von Marschalk's eye. Anna watched in disbelief as the tear slowly rolled down the side of her mother's face. As she continued to stare at her mother, she wondered what it was that influenced her mother to share these hidden ghosts with her. Never had her mother revealed anything personal to her, and, as far as she knew, not to Maria either.

"My father needed no additional wealth for his daughters, just a title. Just a title." she repeated as though to herself. The Baroness shook her head and abruptly opened her eyes. "Women have a duty, Anna. No one asked me if I wanted to marry your father. No one consulted me when Sigrid moved in as a *maid*, and I was to play the role of mother. No one could stop Sigrid from loving her children. No one could stop your father from loving Sigrid." Her mother had started to tremble all over as she struggled to catch her breath.

"M...M...Mama," Anna stammered, as she instinctively grabbed her mother's hand. "M...M...Mama, are you all r...r...right? Sh... sh...shall I fetch the d...d...doctor?"

"No...no...no," her mother gasped and then coughed, pulling her hand away from Anna. Spending so much time bedridden had done nothing to improve the health of her lungs.

After a few minutes her mother's coughing spasms eased and Anna watched her mother's face relax. She wanted to ask her mother if she needed to rest, if she wanted to be alone, but Anna couldn't. She needed her mother to continue revealing the secrets of her life, so she could understand her own life. Anna was sure her mother would never again reveal so much about her personal life. What had started this fountain of information? Anna sat impatiently by her mother's side, waiting for her to continue. She was surprised as a smile spread over half her mother's face.

"They wanted to hide the fact that you two were twins. There would have been too many questions. They made a mistake by telling all Maria was older, she was always so much smaller than you. You are just like your mother." Anna was not sure how to interpret this last comment, but again decided silence was most advantageous for both of them. "Their plan was foolproof they thought...supposedly sending me to the sea with your father to return two years later with two small children. It was Sigrid who nursed you. Sigrid."

Anna watched her mother's smile fade into something dark. The expression that passed over her mother's face frightened Anna. Why had the Baroness gone along with so much deception? Could her sense of duty have been so great as to bind her to a life where she was forced to stare daily into the face of the woman who had not only lain with her new husband, but had also given birth to two children who she was then ordered to raise? Maria shared this sense of duty, but what the Baroness had gone through, was still going through, was worse. Much worse.

Anna's pity for this woman grew. The sorrow she felt for her was great, but her mother had not let the situation she was in destroy her.

Oddly, Anna's admiration for her mother's strength grew as well. Would she have been such a commandeering, impersonal force if she had found true love without any conditions attached? If Papa had loved only her? Anna wanted desperately to ask her mother all of these questions, but she knew there were certain things she could never discuss with this woman. If it were Sigrid, she would have asked without hesitation. Was this why her mother had sent Jakub away? Did she not want me to repeat the mistakes of the woman who bore me, Anna wondered?

Anna's questions about Jakub still burned in her, but for the first time since his disappearance she no longer felt the suppressed resentment for her mother that had preoccupied her for so long.

"Somehow the past always finds a way to haunt the present," her mother whispered. Anna looked up at her mother as she tried to make sense of the words her mother had spoken. "I am tired, leave me now." Anna did not argue, she had heard enough for today. She too felt tired, drained of all emotion.

Slowly climbing the stairs to her own room, Anna realized with cold clarity that deception was the normal way of the world. One moment later the wail of the air raid sirens filled the air once again.

Letter 11   *Dresden, 25 December 1942*

My Beloved Jakub,

It is with little joy in my own heart that I wish you the very best on this Christmas morning. Snow has been falling for the last week. The world is truly a winter wonderland, yet the joy I felt as a child has been lost. As I look out my window, I cannot help but wonder how many soldiers lay freezing somewhere, waiting for death to slowly embrace them with its icy grip. How many people, even entire families, have disappeared? I cannot even begin to guess. Papa fears for our safety every day. He no longer voices his doubts about the party. It is too dangerous. And one cannot blame him with all of the rumors about what goes on in these terrible camps. They are horrible rumors, Jakub, so horrible I am unable to put them into words. I am weak, Jakub, I dare not speak out, my fear is too great. Is it better to remain mute than to be subjected to Gestapo interrogation? To see, hear, and speak no evil? They are everywhere, as though invisible eyes watch. Fear, yes, that is what rules the world these days. One trusts no one. Jakub, it is horrible, families betray one another. Fear. That is what surrounds one every moment of every day. Even the air raid sirens have become a part of life. But the fear, Jakub, the fear is something one can never become accustomed to. Oh, Jakub, is there a place in the world where I can run? Where I can be safe with you?

Never did I understand how life could become so difficult. Since mother's stroke, we have moved her downstairs. It is too difficult to transport her down the stairs when the air raid sirens sound. With Papa and Dieter gone much of the time, this is the best solution for the time being. Somehow I sense an end is coming, it is only a matter of time. I am not sure what that end will mean for my family, for me. One thing is certain, it shall not be pleasant. Even Mama seems to sense this. Seldom,

314

only when Papa is home, does one hear the radio broadcasts that continue to speak to the strength of the German position. Mama seems to have lost faith in her Fuehrer. I am not convinced she has given up on him completely, or his war, but the devastation it has brought to her own Fatherland is something I believe even she cannot come to terms with, or forgive. The war, with its evil tentacles, does not leave any unscathed, Jakub. Those who believe they can begin a war with no loss to themselves are fools.

Mama suffers great physical discomfort and pain. It is always the cold winter months that cause her the most difficulty. We fear for her health, every day wondering whether she will survive another. I am grateful that she is still amongst us. Maria and I have considered taking her to the sea. Papa has strictly forbidden it, fearing for our safety. A doctor tends to her on a regular basis, coming twice a week to observe her progress since the stroke. He too prescribes the salty sea air, but fears the journey to be too treacherous. Jakub, there is nowhere safe anymore. I must agree though, that traveling during this war is a more than foolish endeavor. Father has been home only once in the last two months. He warned us to prepare for the worst. A victory for Germany is no longer possible, he says. He urges us to use caution and trust no one. German cities are being devastated. It is only a matter of time before the fates turn against us here. Dieter has been gone for months, sending telegrams as frequently as possible. Maria fears for his safety and has suffered much without him. The only good that comes from his absence is that Maria must not carry the burden of bearing another child. It is difficult enough to face the world, especially one at war, when one has little ones to care for. Thankfully, Sigrid divides her time assisting Maria as much as possible, usually caring for Maria's children and stockpiling whatever food she can. Often I watch Sigrid and am unable to comprehend that she is the woman who bore me. How is it possible that she could live all these years under the same roof with Mama, knowing the man she loved would forever be outside her reach, yet so physically close? Worse yet, how could Mama tolerate the woman Papa loved? I now understand the circumstances surrounding the deception and have tried, without success, to no longer blame others, and to embrace forgiveness, which seems to come so naturally for Maria.

Despite the horrors that surround us, we continue to remain some of the fortunate few. We have fields and animals which, while greatly reduced in size and number, continue to ensure our survival. I cannot bear to look at the hollowed eyes and hungry faces of those who dwell in the city. It is the children who most disturb me. Only infrequently do I visit the newspaper now, rarely do I venture anywhere near the city center. There seems so little in which to find comfort and joy. We have the privilege to still have loyal farm workers, without whom the estate would crumble and we would truly have nothing, especially given Papa and Dieter's long absences. It is odd how one can live in complete oblivion when one is surrounded by plenty. Oh, but what a different world it is when one awakens one day to find that this plenty has gone. Each day is experienced with much greater awareness, with greater intensity, and possibly with much greater gratitude.

It is late, Jakub, and my hand tires. I must now go and find some rest. I no longer fear the demons that haunted my sleep. Only rarely do I dream. Mostly it is only darkness I see. Gone are the days when I dreamt of you. Is this a sign, Jakub? I continue to search for signs from you. Is this a sign that we shall never again be together? Rarely do I sense your presence. Only once in many months have I visited the hayloft. There is only a cold emptiness there. My beloved Jakub, I do not want to lose the only faith that I have. That someday you and I shall be reunited. I pray to the universe and all that it is good that it shall be amongst the living that we reunite. For now, I beg you always remember my love for you.

Love Eternally,
Anna von Marschalkt

Post Script: It is amazing how the falling snow can transform the world into one of beauty. Even the scars of war can be hidden, if only for a short while.

Anna laid down her fountain pen and blew warm air onto her frozen fingers. The small stove she had in her room did not provide sufficient heat on such cold nights. Carefully, Anna picked up the letter she had just written and silently read through it one last time. As she neared the end of the letter, she felt an odd sensation, as though eyes followed her every move. Spinning around in her chair, she scanned her room, looking for what, she asked herself. His ghost? The Gestapo? She had pressed the letter firmly to her bosom and continued to stare into the dark corners of her room. Unable to shake the sensation that she was being watched, she quickly held the letter towards the candle that burned on her desk. She watched as first the corner alighted, quickly followed by the entire letter. Tossing the flaming letter into the metal pail she had retrieved from the stable for just such a purpose she stood up and warmed her hands by the stove.

"I cannot risk my family over a letter to you, Jakub," she whispered as the flame disappeared into glowing red ash. All that remained of her letter to Jakub was black ash. Carefully she collected and poured the ashes into her green glass bottle and sealed it.

"You shall know the words I wrote to you, Jakub," she spoke into the darkness of her room. Somehow she was sure someone had heard her.

The following day Anna pulled on her warm winter boots and heavy wool coat and marched through the knee deep snow. She found her stream covered with snow and partially frozen. Raising the bottle to her lips, as she had done ten times before, she tossed the bottle into the snow-covered stream.

"In the spring you shall find your way," she spoke. Anna stood in silence a moment longer before she headed towards the stable to find her favorite cat. She would never know the bottle would be shattered by children playing by the stream ten years later.

Travels of Letter 16
South of Buenos Aires,
Argentina Coast
October 1996

The full moon reflected bright silver streaks across the rippling water. Was it a sign, he wondered? The dolphins darting in and out of the waves, were they another sign? If so, how was he to read these signs? He had told his congregation that signs are all around them, just waiting to be seen. God revealed himself in the most extraordinary ways, he had said. He now questioned what he preached to his flock. Were these all signs from God or merely natural occurrences? Occurrences to which he wanted to attach some type of meaning to justify his behavior, or rather his intentions. Father Marco Sanchez walked along the shore searching for his God.

Why had things been so easy in the past? He had been so sure about himself, about his vocation, after God revealed Himself in a dream when he was fifteen. A dream he had never spoken to anyone about, one which had been a spiritual and private moment between him and his Maker. He never had any doubt about his choice, not even for an instant during the years at the seminary. Eight years there and not once did he even secretly break a vow to his God. Of course there were sins, minor sins for which he had to atone, he was human after all. Father Marco recalled his vows of celibacy and obedience he made at the ordination. The feeling of spiritual awakening and clarity he had felt at his ordination still made him shiver. This closeness to the heavenly Father, this holy bond, had moved him to tears.

But what was this now? What was *this*? This was a sin of far greater magnitude. "I am a priest," he spoke aloud, as he watched a dark cloud slowly pass in front of the moon, all traces of silver on the ocean gone in an instant. "Well, if this is a sign, it can't be a good one," he called out to the heavens.

Father Marco had been a priest too long to know he could not ask God why He was doing this to him. But what was it that prevented him from asking God to give him the strength to resist this temptation? Why did he not want to resist? What demon had taken possession of his soul that he should not throw himself at his Maker's mercy and beg for forgiveness? "Why am I willfully shaming myself and betraying You?" he cried, watching the first shimmering silver streaks appear from behind the departing dark cloud. Father Marco inhaled deeply. The smell of the salt air and the sound of the softly rolling waves had a hypnotic effect on the young priest. He stopped walking for the first time in hours. He had no idea how many miles of seashore he had walked along, but his feet ached. Sitting down on the damp sand, he removed his sandals and enjoyed the cooling effect it had on his blistered feet. Picking up one of his sandals, he had to smile at her memory. What was it she had said to him when he was on the ladder patching the roof?

"Where do I find the Father? Father Marco Sanchez?" she had asked in perfect, but heavily accented Spanish. He chuckled a little at the memory. Why do so many believe a priest spends his day wearing vestments, he wondered. Especially in this rural environment where most of his time was spent assisting the local children. Father Marco rubbed the sole of his foot as he observed a flock of birds pass through the shimmering silver night.

"Sorry, oh I'm so sorry," she had apologized when he introduced himself. Her face had turned the color of his favorite cherries, as his own face had. What was it about her that caused this physiological response in him? "Sorry," she again apologized with outstretched hand, "I'm Virginia Washington, Ginny, the English teacher," she said, obviously flustered. "I just didn't expect a priest in jeans and Doc Martins," she added, seemingly abashed at her comment as soon as she had voiced it. "Sorry, I just can't seem to stop putting my foot in my mouth."

He had watched her from the moment they met, more intently than any other living being. This Virginia Washington, from Savannah, Georgia, here to teach the children English, she could not possibly be the Devil's temptation, could she? Father Marco felt a yearning completely unfamiliar to him, one he had never experienced before. He could not get Ginny out of his mind.

It started with harmless comments. "If you weren't a priest, all the ladies would be after your heart," he remembered her words, feeling his hands begin to sweat. Were these harmless words? Or was she responding to his obvious feelings for her? Then there was the children's festival. It was he who had offered to help her with all of the decorations, nearly falling off the ladder once as he watched her bend over to greet each child as they entered. He had thought of the female body in the past, but had managed, through strict discipline, to suppress all shameless thoughts before they led him to immoral behavior. What was it about Virginia Washington he could not get enough of? It had to be more than her beauty. There were enough beautiful women around. No, she had a charm and an inner beauty far greater than anything he had ever come across.

It was the evening after the festival that she had asked him if he wanted to stay and have a cup of coffee with her. Together they had sat on a bench and discussed the meaning of life when she gently touched his hand. "Let me see your lifeline," she said so sweetly he felt a maddening desire for her. "I can read your palm for you, I promise it isn't any kind of devil worship," she added when she saw his distraught look. His distress was not about palm reading. It was the battle that raged inside him.

"Do you believe in love at first sight?" he had asked her, terrified that he had uttered the words aloud. More terrifying was her response that she did believe.

That night, outside, under a moonless sky, Father Marco touched and made love to a woman for the first time in his twenty nine years of life on this earth. It was not the act of love-making that caused him the greatest grief. He had betrayed his vow of celibacy the moment he laid eyes on Virginia Washington. The act of love-making was merely a physical enactment of the impure thoughts he had been having since he met her nearly four months ago. An act that would repeat itself, again and again. No, it wasn't the love-making, it was the secrecy that caused him agony. How could he preach the word of God, yet live this duplicitous life? It was this deceit, before God, his congregation, and even himself that could not go on. As he sat on the damp sand, he stretched his legs out, his feet coming to rest upon a cool glass bottle. He laid back and rolled the bottle between his feet, gazing up into the heavens. Where was his sign?

"What am I to do?" he pleaded, tears trickling down the sides of his face, tickling his ears. "God grant me the knowledge to understand what has happened," he prayed with eyes wide open, searching, hoping.

Father Marco Sanchez did not know how long he had dozed off for. The moon he had stared at earlier in the evening had wandered across the night sky. He awoke, chilled, but with a warm feeling of peace and absolution only experienced one other time in his life. Was it God speaking through the angel Gabriel? The experience was more than a dream, he knew that. For the first time in months, a weight had been lifted off his soul. Leaving the priesthood was never something he had even remotely considered. Meeting a woman without whom he could not breathe was even more far-fetched. But here he was now, merely a man who had thought to know God better than he knew himself. How wrong he had been.

As he lay in the cold sand, serenely looking up at the lightening sky, he felt a sudden rush of water cover his feet as the tide came in. Quickly sitting up, he scrambled backwards to avoid the next wave rushing in. Sitting a few meters up from the high tide line, he pulled his sandals back on, watching as the bottle he had rolled between his feet was reclaimed by sea.

The man left the beach in the early morning hours. He had come searching for answers, searching for signs. His God did not disappoint him. His God did not judge him. He was right. There were signs all around. One just had to open one's eyes and ears to see and hear them. The man left the beach, and left his priesthood behind to return to his lover, with whom he would spend the rest of his mortal life.

Autobahn A13 towards
Dresden, Germany
Fall 2011

"Do you know what side the gas tank is on?" I asked Charlie as we drove into the Aral gas station. We had already been driving for a couple of hours, but then it had taken us over an hour to find our way out of Berlin. I needed to stretch my legs, not to mention empty my bladder. Thankfully our wheeled matchbox was low on gas.

"This thing's so tiny, it's a wonder there's room for a gas tank at all," Charlie mused, as he maneuvered the small vehicle close to a pump. "And no, I have no idea what side this thing's supposed to be gassed up on, but I guess we'll find out soon enough," Charlie said with a smile, obviously in a good mood. I had to laugh as I quickly exited the car.

"No gas tank on this side, sorry Charlie." Not bothering to wait around for him to turn the car around I went in search of the ladies room. As though led by an internal radar, I quickly located the WC, but was immediately frustrated to find I needed change to use the otherwise locked bathroom.

"Oh, you have got to be kidding me…you have got to be kidding me," I repeated, rummaging through my purse, desperately looking for change. "Oh come on, damn it, damn it, damn it!" I swore, pulling out two one cent pieces. "Who the hell charges fifty cents to use the restroom?"

"Here you go," a female American voice behind me in line said, handing me a fifty cent Euro coin.

"Oh, thank you so much, you're an angel." I didn't have time to thank her further, but hurriedly made my way to a vacant stall.

The woman smiled. "It was a lot worse before they used the Euro…now at least you can use the same currency in most European countries if you've gotta go," the generous stranger said. I gave her a brief smile, afraid if I said another word I'd have an accident, and deposited my coin to unlock the toilet stall.

"Thank you again," I said to the woman, feeling so much better, now that I had emptied my bladder.

"No problem," the woman with wavy light blond hair said as she washed her hands.

"I *seriously* thought I was going to burst," I tried to explain, somewhat embarrassed by what had been such a desperate situation one minute ago.

"Hey, don't worry about it. Once I couldn't find any change and the line in the gas station was out the door, so I ended up behind a bush. And from the looks of it, I wasn't the only one who'd been in that same predicament," the woman spoke loudly as the hand dryer blasted hot air onto her hands.

"Are you here on vacation?" I asked, examining my reflection in the mirror. "Scary," I whispered to myself, looking at the rings under my eyes and the crows feet that seemed to have multiplied overnight. The fluorescent lighting didn't exactly help matters. And long, late nights with Charlie didn't do much for my looks either.

"No, well, sort of I guess. I've got a conference I'm speaking at and then my best friend and I are going to travel around the continent a bit." Listening as the woman spoke, I was immediately curious as to the nature of the conference.

"What sort of conference?" I asked.

"Oh, well, I'm a professor of social anthropology. I've been invited to speak in Berlin at the annual "Society for the Improvement of Mankind Conference." Maybe it was my dopey "deer in the headlights" stare, but it must have been immediately apparent to the woman that I had no clue what she was talking about.

"Hey, I know it sounds kind of hokey, but it really tries to bring different professions together to help, you know, society...and I'm not talking about recycling. I'm talking about on an interpersonal level. How people interact with each other on a day to day basis. Just going that extra step to help someone else. You know, say a kind word, that kind of thing." She paused momentarily and looked at me with a perplexed expression. "Sorry," the woman apologized, shaking her head, "I tend to ramble on. I've never been accused of being shy."

"No, no, please, I've never heard of anything like that before, but, I think it's really great, actually, and you know, you did save me with your coin," I said with sincerity, impressed that something like that actually existed. I could use a dose of "be nice to my neighbors" thinking once in while.

"Sorry," she apologized again, "I can get carried away with this kind of stuff. I'm Sally, by the way."

"Nice to meet you, Sally. I'm Diana. You from New York?" I asked, trying to place Sally's accent.

"Philadelphia, actually. Well, that's where I'm originally from. My family's still there. I live in New Zealand now," Sally said, as she started to head to the bathroom exit.

"I'm from L.A." I said, somehow feeling an immediate connection with this woman who shared so much of what was familiar to me, so far away from home.

"Are you here on business, or for pleasure?" Sally asked.

Hesitating, I wondered if I should give her the long, convoluted, and, even to me, still incomprehensible story, or keep it simple? Keeping it simple seemed to be the right choice. "Just pleasure," I answered.

"Well, you enjoy your trip, Diana from L.A."

"You too, Sally. And good luck with the conference," I said, waving good bye to the woman I had just met.

"Hey, Hahona, over here," I heard Sally call out to her friend who was just exiting the gas station mart.

"It's nice to know there are still good people on earth," I said to myself as I turned towards Charlie and our unknown future.

"So, just how much further is it to Dresden?" I asked, turning the map upside down, trying to make heads or tails of it.

"Well, that depends on how many times we get lost between here and Dresden," Charlie replied with a smug look, obviously not bothered in the least.

"And where exactly is here?" I asked, resisting the urge to crumple up the map that had led us astray and toss the incomprehensible thing out the window. We had decided Charlie should drive and I would navigate. I had nightmares about driving on the Autobahn, especially in our matchbox car. Unfortunately, my map reading skills were worse than my driving skills. Charlie took it all in stride. At one point, when we dead-ended at a park somewhere, Charlie had suggested a stroll. I just couldn't be as calm about the whole situation. Here we were, two love-crazed Americans, who had really known each other for just over a week, who had flown across the Atlantic Ocean in search of a woman who may have written a love letter a lifetime ago, and I was supposed to be calm? No way.

"Well, we're somewhere on the A13…it should be a straight shot to Dresden," Charlie said, motioning a straight line with his finger. "Beautiful," he whispered as he stared at the road before him.

"I don't think you were talking about me," I teased, seeing a side of Charlie I hadn't expected. "Hey, buddy, don't get too excited in this wheeled coffin," I half-joked as I felt the small car accelerate.

"You know, this was great propaganda for the madman." Charlie said more to himself than to me. "Supporting a national highway system at a time when Germany was crumbling economically. What a strategic move." My mind wandered as Charlie, obviously a history buff, explained how the greatest monster of all time had done wonders for the German economy by creating jobs to improve the infrastructure. "Just think, how much more efficient troop movements were because of these improved roads." Charlie looked over at me. Was he waiting for me to say something? Maybe agree with him?

"Hmmm," I mumbled, giving him my standard non-committal response I used when I failed to listen to other people and had no idea what they had just asked. Somewhat abashed that I hadn't been listening, I looked out the window. Maybe he wouldn't notice.

"You weren't listening were you?" Charlie didn't look upset, but smiled at me and laid his hand on my leg. So much for him not noticing. I wouldn't be pulling any fast ones on this guy. "Sometimes I even bore myself," he laughed.

"I'm sorry, Charlie, I just can't get Anna and the letter, and this whole crazy trip out of my mind. What are we doing? Are we insane?" I felt my heart race as I opened my backpack to check for the hundredth time that I had indeed wrapped the letter up properly and that it was actually still in my backpack. Sifting through my backpack I caught sight of the strange green knit "nothing" and pulled it out. Why I still carried it in my backpack was a mystery to me, but I just couldn't part with it yet.

"What's that, you didn't make that thing did you?" Charlie asked, briefly wrinkling his nose in obvious disgust. I had to laugh.

"No, I did not make this *thing*. I kind of found it. Actually, someone left it and I just haven't been able to get rid of it."

"I can help you get rid of it," Charlie said, rolling down his window and making throwing motions.

"So much for a sentimental guy," I teased, as again a comfortable silence engulfed both of us as we now sped towards Dresden.

"I should drive and you should navigate," I suggested as we drove around Dresden looking for the address Charlie had received from his Interpol contact. "Or, we could just stop and ask someone for directions."

Charlie frowned at my suggestion, which was followed by an audible sigh. "We've already stopped to ask for directions three times, Diana. Most guys don't stop to ask for directions...ever. Isn't that the cliché?"

"So stop and ask again...a fourth time won't kill the man," I mused, giggling like a stupidly silly school girl. Unfortunately, Charlie wasn't amused and decided not to seek further outside assistance. Forty-five minutes later, and multiple rounds of crumpling and smoothing the map out, we finally found Kirschbaum Street, just as large raindrops began to hit our tiny windshield.

"Charlie, stop! Stop the car!" I shouted, just as Charlie turned down the street we had sought all this time. "I have to get out." I didn't know what got into me, but I couldn't breathe. The sides of the tiny Fiat closed in on me. Charlie had not even stopped the car when I threw open my door and jumped out. Bending forward, I rested my hands on my knees, counting to calm my breathing as the rain, which had turned to hail, struck my head like rabbit pellets.

"What's the matter with you, Di?" I heard a small voice echo in my mind. "It's just an old woman you're going to see." My weak inner voice was right. Anna was just an old woman, but then why did I feel another panic attack coming on? Inhaling deeply, I couldn't figure out what it was that frightened me so much. I didn't normally have these kinds of attacks during the day.

"Hey, you okay, Diana?" The feel of Charlie's warm hand on my back infused some calm into my jellied brain as cold hail rained down on me. "Let's get back in the car. We don't have to do this you know." Straightening up I looked at Charlie as the hail turned to pouring rain, blurring my vision.

"Yes, yes we do. I do. I don't know why, but I have to."

Dresden, Germany
March 1943

The air in her father's study was thick with smoke. So thick it made Anna cough as she entered. She waved a hand before her face. She stopped abruptly when her father turned around in his large chair, the chair she had despised since childhood. A wooden face, carved into the top, supposedly a Prussian prince, always stared back at her with its life-like face. Staring at her father in silence, she backed one step away from him. Anna had often seen her father wearing the party uniform, but it always startled her. Here before her sat not her father, but an imposter. Anna watched him slowly pull his pipe from his mouth and set it on his large desk.

"Anna," he said hoarsely, standing up stiffly and approaching his daughter with outstretched arms.

"P...P...Papa," Anna said as she met his embrace and looked into his haggard face. "What h...h...has happened, Papa?" Something about her father *was* different she thought, and it wasn't just the uniform. Stepping back from her father she observed him, wondering just what was amiss. Her father gazed into her eyes with a silent despair that forced her to avert her eyes, which again came to rest on the chair's wooden face. Whose face was it? The hollow terror-stricken eyes had always unnerved her.

"I must wear it at all times, Anna. It is too dangerous now..." her father sighed, as he walked to his sofa and sat down. "Please, Anna, come sit. Tell me what is on your mind." Anna hesitated. Her father looked as though he had not slept or eaten in days.

"I c...c...can come b...b...back, Papa."

"No, no, please, Anna," her father insisted, as he opened the large box of chocolates he must have traded a cow for. "Please, Anna," her father said pointing at the golden box filled with chocolates that seemed oddly out of place in this dismal world. Anna looked from the chocolate to her father and back to the chocolate.

"Well, if y...y...you insist, Papa," Anna replied with a smile as she reached for two pieces of chocolate. Dismal world or not, chocolate was chocolate, something she could never pass up.

The courage with which she had entered the room disappeared by the time she finished her fifth piece of chocolate.

"Leave some for your mother and sister," her father half-heartedly scolded, as he watched his daughter with melancholy eyes. "Now, I know you did not come here just for the chocolate Anna, please. Although, knowing you and your mother I wouldn't be surprised." Her father nodded his head, encouraging her to speak her mind.

"I n...n...need to know," Anna blurted out, "I n...n...need to know what happened to Jakub. Is he in Australia?"

"In Australia?" Her father whispered as he looked towards the window and seemed to sink into some deep place, somewhere Anna wished she could follow.

"The g...g...gardener told m...m...me Mama had h...h...him taken away. It was y...y...you who t...t...told me, years ago, th...th... that he w...w...was in Australia." Anna's voice quivered as she spoke.

"*I* told you he was in Australia?" Her father asked with feigned confusion.

"Yes, P...P...Papa, when I w...w...was ill. Wh...wh...when you all th...th...thought that I sh...sh...should die in my bed. I h...h...heard you, Papa. I heard you, p...p...please, Papa, please." Anna felt the warm tears stream down her face and made no attempt to hide them.

"I…we…had a son Papa…your grandson." Her father looked up sharply.

"A son?" he asked, as the impact of what his daughter had just said began to sink in. Did he know I had borne a child, Anna wondered? Had Sigrid shared this with him? With her lover?

Dumbfounded, he stood up and paced back and forth. It was some time before he found the voice to speak. Anna realized her father, the great Baron, had not known.

"All these years," his voice cracked as he spoke, "all these years you have…continued to search for this…this Jakub?" Her father's earlier affable tone had vanished. "How could you, Anna?" he suddenly snapped, taking a step towards her with a raised hand. Anna was sure her father might strike her, but watched him seemingly change his mind abruptly. "You are no longer a child. No….no, I can no longer make decisions for you. Nor protect you from all the evils in the world," he spoke more to himself than to Anna. She had seen this look only once before. She could almost see the gears in his mind turning as he digested what he had heard. "Where is this boy now?" Her father asked, staring past her with dark eyes; eyes filled with suppressed anger. Eyes that frightened Anna, but also incited her own demons. Was it because he did not know what happened on his own estate that his ire flared? Or did he worry there was one more family secret that needed to be hidden from the world?

Anna watched her father with increasing enmity. "You n…n…need not worry, he is dead," Anna snapped back. "Is it y…y…your reputation you w…w…worry about? What the n…n…neighbors might th… th…think? What n…n…neighbors are left worry f…f…for their own survival. N…n…no, you can rest peacefully, Baron von M…M… Marschalkt, your grandson d…d…does not live," Anna hissed at her father. Why she lashed out at her father in this manner she could not herself comprehend. Years of anger and frustration seeped from every pore on her body. "He does not l…l…live," she repeated, unable to look at her father.

"How could you, Anna?" her father repeated, "How could you… with a farm worker?"

"Like f…f…father, like daughter," she hissed, resisting the urge to throw the remaining chocolates at him. Her father turned on her like a rabid animal and slapped her across the face, hard. The shock of the slap delayed the stinging sensation that slowly moved across her face.

"I know, P…P…Papa. I know," she said caustically as her father stared at her in silence. "Th…th…they told me. M…M…Mama and Sigrid." Anna did not know what to expect when she told her father, but she did not anticipate his confused look.

"What did *they* tell you?" he asked with controlled rage, closely watching his daughter.

"E…e…everything. Everything about Sigrid and you, about M…M…Mama and you, about Maria and I. Everything." An odd expression crossed her father's face as she spoke. Anna did not know if it was relief that the truth had been finally aired, or something more sinister. Somehow the demons of his past did not seem to affect him the way she had hoped they would. His body, which moments before had appeared tense, seemed to relax as he walked back to the sofa and sat down. Abruptly his face changed as he studied Anna.

"Child, your mother has not spoken since her injury," he spoke with inflated conviction.

"N…n…not to you Papa…sh…sh…she has not spoken to you. She has nothing m…m…more to say to you." Anna knew she had entered territory that was not hers to enter, nor was it the truth, but anger pushed her to continue. "How c…c…could *you,* Papa? How c…c…could you do th…th…that to Mama? Force her t…t…to raise children n…n…not her own? And then h…h…have the woman who b….b…bore those children live in th…th…the house with you?" Anna felt she could no longer breathe. Her world had collapsed a long time ago, how was it possible that it could continue to crumble?

"It is possible to love more than one person, Anna. And would your life be better if I had sent Sigrid away?" her father stated with finality as he watched his daughter.

A heavy silence hung over the smoke-filled room. Anna heard her father sigh a number of times as he sat with his back turned to her in his chair, unmoving. He had not even picked up his cigar, Anna thought, as she sat frozen on the leather ottoman.

"I am sorry, Anna," she heard her father apologize with his back turned. "I am sorry you suffered all these years...that you continue to suffer." Anna listened to her father without much empathy.

"If th...th...there is anyone you m...m...must apologize to, th...th...then let it be Mama," Anna said flatly. All emotion had been drained from her.

Her father turned to look at her. His lips were turned up, pressed firmly together, but he was not smiling. "You are right, Anna," he admitted, surprising her with this wholly unnatural admission. "How can I judge you, when I...," he sighed, "when I am more guilty than you. And you have not forgotten."

"Forgotten wh...wh...what?" Anna asked impatiently, yet feeling the incessant itch of curiosity. Her father sighed again as he seemed to weigh what he should voice next.

"About Australia," he whispered as he removed his spectacles and wiped them clean with a sleeve of his uniform. Anna inhaled sharply and felt her pulse quicken.

"Is it true th...th...then? Is h...h...he in Australia?"

"I do not know, Anna. I do not." Her father spoke with sincerity, yet Anna was unable to accept his vague response.

"I n...n...need to know Papa. I shall n...n...never rest peacefully until I kn...kn...know for sure," she pleaded, convinced her father would reveal nothing more. She was that much more surprised when her father continued to speak. Maybe, like her mother, he needed to speak now.

"It was all so long ago, Anna...much has happened since then." As though in deep thought her father rubbed the small area on his head where the hair had thinned, revealing his pale, vulnerable scalp. "Jakub was to be arrested the following morning for...theft."

"He did n...n...not steal a thing, the g...g...gardener was lying," Anna interjected tensely. Her father lifted a hand to silence his daughter.

"Your mother had notified the authorities, but I had asked her to give me one day to figure things out. I had been expecting something like this. For some reason your mother had never seemed fond of Jakub...I forget his surname..."

"G...G...Gorski," Anna quickly said, "Jakub Gorski."

"Yes, yes, Gorski, that is right. A good, hard working man, but I know now why your mother did not find favor with him." Her father gave her a sidelong glance which she ignored. "I had arranged travel papers for him, and also provided him with a generous amount of cash for the journey."

"So h...h...he is in Australia then?" Anna asked, confused by what her father was telling her. She so desperately needed to know where Jakub was.

"I said I do not know," he said gruffly, again rubbing his thinned hair. "It was Otto and Gerold who were to escort him to the vessel, the Konstantine, to ensure that he boarded and sailed." Anna could scarcely breathe as her father spoke. "Otto and Gerold lost track of him in Bremerhaven...," her father mumbled something incomprehensible.

"Excuse m...m...me?" Anna asked, nearly burning alive with her desire to know the truth.

"I said... he never made it to the vessel, Anna. I have known the Captain, Wilhelm Beyer, for years. Your Jakub never boarded the ship." Anna tried to form her own conclusions based on what her father had said. Her thoughts were too jumbled, but one thought jumped out at her with crystal clarity.

"So he is d...d...dead." It was more a statement than a question. One she never hoped to speak aloud. The Baron hesitated before he answered his daughter.

"Anna, this too I do not know...but given the war, and he was a... Jew...I do not know, Anna." Her father was unable to state the one thing that both he and Anna were thinking.

"Do you b...b...believe he is imprisoned s...s...somewhere, Papa? Do you kn...kn...know something you are not telling me? You cannot h...h...hide the truth f...f...forever, Papa."

"Anna, some things that happen on the estate may escape me, but most do not. I have told you, and I shall continue to stand by what I say, no matter how many times you ask, I do not know the present whereabouts of Mr. Gorski." Her father seemed exhausted, as though his confession had taken much out of him.

Anna felt nothing as she sat on the ottoman. If someone had pierced her with a sword, she would still feel nothing. Every nerve ending in her body was dead. She did not care if she always remained in this state. It was a safe place to exist, after so many years of searching. As Anna sat in silence a small voice in her mind forced itself to be heard. "You have no proof that he is dead." It was not much, but it gave her something to hold on to, some small amount of hope that he could still be alive, maybe even in Australia, if he had found a different ship.

"I am sorry, Anna, I had no choice," her father's voice reached her somewhere in the depths of her spinning mind.

"N…n…no, Papa, one always h…h…has a choice," she replied without emotion, staring at the "black spider" on his uniform. Slowly lifting herself from the ottoman, she headed for the door.

"He would have been arrested," she heard her father shout after she was already well on her way down the hall. He likely was, Anna thought, as she passed into the hall.

Her head hurt as she walked outside into the cool morning air. Inhaling the fresh scents of spring, she slowly walked towards the barn, feeling her father's eyes watching her through the windows of his study. Anna stopped short of the barn and glanced up to the hayloft.

"You are not there anymore, are you Jakub?" she asked, answering her own question by turning away from the barn and heading towards the stables.

It was dark in the stables, and strangely quiet, aside from the rhythmic scraping she heard from one of the box stalls. It took her eyes a moment to adjust to the dim light. The stables, with the smells of horses and her cats, used to fill her with so much joy. Now, there were only two horses left, Estelle, her father's young mare, and Hennie, an old workhorse. No one knew how much longer they would be around. Any day they might be needed "for the cause," she thought, as she walked towards the stall from which the scraping sounded.

"Good day, Fraulein von Marschalkt," Ingo Zimmerman said without the timidity and nervousness she had witnessed in the past.

"Mr. Z…Z…Zimmerman," Anna replied with a nod of the head, suddenly remembering the last time she was alone in the stables with Ingo, interrogating him about Jakub. He had matured.

"Are you going for a ride?" The young man asked as he placed the pitchfork he held back against the stable wall. "Henni's got a sore on his leg I've been treating, and the other one, she's a bit feisty." Anna listened and considered how this previously lanky, awkward young man had grown into a handsome man with broad shoulders.

"N...n...no, I am n...n...not riding today," she said as she slowly moved closer to Ingo, whose one blind eye had saved him from being shipped to the battle fronts with the rest of the young German men.

"D...d...does it hurt?" Anna asked, startling herself as she touched his eyelid.

"My eye?" Ingo asked, suspicious of Anna's odd behavior, yet unable to move away from this beautiful woman with her fire red hair.

"Yes," she answered, "it looks d...d...different from close up. Almost as though th...th...there were a white s...s...star in it," Anna said, as she brushed her finger along his cheek. She watched as Ingo's cheeks flushed.

"My sister tells me the fever that took my sight in this eye was horrid, but I have no memory of it, I was a young child," Ingo Zimmerman answered with averted eyes, his face resembling a fresh garden tomato.

"Well, it just m...m...may have saved y...y...your life," Anna spoke aloud as she slowly reached for Ingo's hand. "Come with m...m...me, I m...m...must show you something." Anna recklessly dragged a half-petrified, half-excited Ingo out the back of the stables and towards the barn where she slipped through a side door that was invisible from the main house. She did not think about what she was about to do, but there was a passion, a burning desire in her that needed to be satisfied. One that she was sure would otherwise never be satisfied again. Her irresponsible spontaneity surprised even herself, but as she ascended the stairs to the hayloft she did not care. Ingo's silent, almost passive acceptance of what was happening further fueled her desire. Still dragging him behind her, Anna led Ingo Zimmerman to the spot she once shared with Jakub.

Ingo Zimmerman laid half naked in the hayloft, unable to comprehend what had just happened. One hour ago he had never said more to Fraulein von Marschalkt than on the day she confronted him years ago. And now he had shared the most intimate of acts with a woman he had watched and silently desired for most of his life. He had not allowed himself to believe what was happening until Anna von Marschalkt pulled up her skirt and straddled him in the hayloft. It was not how he had imagined his first time to be. The act had been fast and intense, without any of the caressing he had heard women so desired. Without a word Anna had lifted herself from him and disappeared as fast as their lovemaking, if that is what it could be called, had been. For the rest of his life Ingo Zimmerman would wonder about that one day in the hayloft.

Letter 12   *Dresden, 15. March 1943*

My Beloved Jakub,

I have pondered for two days now how I should explain this to you. More importantly even is how I should explain my behavior to myself. My whole life I have viewed as a delicate balance between good and evil, hoping it would always be the good which stacked itself in my favor, tilting the scale away from the evil that lurks behind every corner. Two days ago, my beloved, the scale tilted forever out of my favor, I fear. I should feel remorse for my actions, my betrayal of you, but I do not. I believe that I am possibly mad, and that it was my unrequited love that has driven me to this place. Jakub, I have lain with another man. I do not love this man, have never had immoral thoughts about this man, and now feel only pity for this man whom I violated. As to myself, my act did nothing but temporarily quench a physical need. I must be a wicked person, Jakub. How is it I feel nothing? Have the dark powers that be taken possession of my soul? I have judged others for so long. Held them to standards to which I do not hold myself. Jakub, my love for you still burns within me, but I cannot bring myself to understand how it is I betrayed you so horribly? What I have done to us?

As I sit alone at my desk I wonder if it is the reality of us that pushed me to act in a manner otherwise so hideous. Will there ever be an "us" again? I tell myself every day, that some-where you are alive and well, waiting for that time that we can once again be together. Somewhere, in the darkest corner of my mind, a voice whispers to me that this shall never be. I squash that voice, Jakub. Flatten it with the whole strength of my being. But this voice, it grows louder with each passing day. And with each passing day it fuels my fears in a way that nothing else can.

I have prayed for so long that I should no longer feel. Maybe these prayers have been answered. How can I continue to live in a world where I am torn between what has been and what never will be? What has been no longer exists and what I hoped so desperately for, what I still hope for with all the goodness that remains in my heart, will likely never be. How am I to continue Jakub? How am I to face this uncertain future if you are not to be a part of it? But somehow I am not prepared to let you go, Jakub, for when I do, I lose everything. The dream of us together, the dream that one day we shall have another child. Even the child I bore will no longer seem real. Just yesterday I visited our son, hoping to feel closer to you. I did not feel you. I did not feel him either. Am I truly losing both of you—have I already lost both of you? Could this be the normal progression the heart follows as time continues to tear separated souls further apart?

At times I envied Maria and wondered if I did not make a mistake so long ago. You were never the mistake, Jakub. It was the path of life I have always chosen to wander that I questioned. Unlike Maria, I was never satisfied with accepting the restraints society places on individuals. Like Maria, I too could be married now with an eternally unfulfilled love, only finding comfort in the children that I would have placed on this earth. I have never met a mother who does not agree that the love a mother has for her child is the greatest love on earth. I consider myself blessed to have witnessed this miracle, no matter how heartbreaking the circumstances. Yet, as I sit here and think of you, I know that I did not do an injustice to myself by loving you.

I do not know if, wherever you are, you can ever begin to forgive me. This was not an act to spite you or our love. It was not a premeditated act of defiance. I will not try to explain away what I have done. What is done is done.

Love Eternally,
Anna v. M.

Anna stared at the incriminating letter she had just written. The decision to burn this letter was obvious to her. While she did not feel shame, it did not mean she was ready for her letter to fall into the wrong hands. It had not occurred to her until this moment that she was not the only one whose silence mattered. She had not considered what she had done to Ingo Zimmerman. The looks he had sent her way over the years were unmistakable.

"It would only take a woman with half a mind to realize how he felt," she chided herself, suddenly feeling again. She felt a sensation of guilt wash over her, that it was not she alone who now had this burden to bear.

"What have you done now?" she heard a small voice in her mind ask as she watched the letter alight. She may not have completely understood what it was she had done or why, but she did know that she would take much care to avoid Ingo Zimmerman from now on.

It would be Ingo Zimmerman, however, who made certain he would never run into Anna von Marschalkt again. The love he felt for Anna von Marschalkt, he knew, would never be reciprocated. Whatever it was that passed between the two of them on that strange morning could not be mistaken for love. He knew he could no longer bear her presence, and decided, for his own sake, to leave the von Marschalkt estate and search for his father. Like his father before him, Ingo Zimmerman disappeared one evening without a word, without a trace.

It was four days before Anna snuck out with her bottle full of ashes and headed towards her stream by the woods. "I am mad," she said, abruptly stopping to look at her smooth green glass bottle. "I am utterly mad," she repeated, realizing the absurdity of what it was she was doing and had been doing all these years. Despite this self-aware-ness, she was unable to stop the madness, and continued on towards the stream. She did not take a moment to reflect on anything before she dropped the bottle into the water and turned to leave.

There had been enough thinking in the past to last her a lifetime. Now she was content with no longer thinking. Allowing her mind a moment of quiet would have to suffice, even if it was not the peace she desired. Thoughts of curling up on the damp ground, for the earth to reclaim her, sounded almost inviting. Closing her eyes, the smell of the earth stimulated her senses as no man-made perfume could. The olfactory sensation acted almost as a soul-nourishing experience, transporting her to a place and time where the acts of man were irrelevant. Inhaling deeply once more, Anna already regretted this moment would not last. Again dark thoughts edged their way into her mind, fueling a desire to depart this world. "Maybe this war shall take care of that for me," she said forebodingly, staring up at an ominous black cloud.

The bottle, as though having a mind of its own, would not follow the stream's current to the river, but remained forever on the von Marschalkt estate.

Travels of Letter 16
Off the Coast of Puerto Padre, Cuba
March 1999

Santiago worried about many things, including the fact that he did not speak a word of English, as he gripped the sides of the makeshift boat he traveled on. He tried to keep his fears in check as he looked at the oil drums strapped to one another with wood rafters secured on top. He thought of his mother. He had to survive for his mother. He could send her medicine once he made a better life for himself in the United States. Pulling the rope tight around his waist, he wondered whether his life vest would really keep him afloat. He was grateful for the vest his father had given him. Santiago was surprised his father did not discourage him when he told him of his plans to leave for the United States. He had heard his parents discuss the option behind closed doors when he was a young boy. His mother had never wanted to risk such a perilous journey with three young children. Santiago wondered whether he would ever see his parents or sisters again, or even his young nieces and nephews. His mother had given him the U.S. dollars her cousin had sent her, hidden in the cookies and other baked goods occasionally sent from Florida. There were never

345

any letters that encouraged leaving Cuba, but they all knew what the money was for. Bribe money for passage across.

A large swell rocked the craft not fit for a bathtub, Santiago thought, gripping the sides even tighter. He had grown up by the sea, knew its wonders, but also the deadly dangers always lurking within reach, waiting for just one small mistake. The "captain," that is what the man steering the boat and also fleeing Cuba called himself, had told them they would sail when the winds were favorable. Santiago had a bad feeling when the craft stole away from Puerto Padre in the middle of the night. The swells on the open ocean heightened those fears. They were large and coming in too close behind one another. Santiago knew a storm was coming. Not the favorable winds the captain spoke of. Watching the captain and two other questionable seamen hoist and maneuver the makeshift sails did nothing to improve his sense of foreboding.

"Get a hold of yourself," he told himself, "you knew what you were getting into. You're lucky to have made it out of the bay."

"Hey, you," the now pale-faced captain called out, pointing at Santiago, "over here, help with this sail." Santiago watched the man for a moment. He did not want to leave his seat. He did not feel safe in it, but a lot safer seated and holding on, than standing to secure sails on a rolling boat.

"Move it before I toss your ass overboard," the captain yelled, tossing him a line. He didn't seem much older than Santiago.

Santiago mistook the first drops of rain to hit his face as sea spray. Looking up, he saw the sky had pulled itself together into a huge ominous dark mass. Within moments he realized what he had mistaken as drops of sea water was a the first drops of rain from a storm about to release its full fury on anything in its path. Releasing tension on the rope he had been holding he watched as the sail collapsed and folded in on itself. Retreating to his previous seat, he barely heard the captain bellowing at him. Holding a hand to his ear he could just make out the captain cursing him. Did this captain not know it was safer to pull in the sails? With this kind of weather, they risked capsizing the whole craft. Santiago reached for the ropes that held his life vest securely tied to his body, holding on to them for emotional support. Thanking his father and saying a little prayer, Santiago watched as the captain himself leaned over the side of the wildly shifting craft to empty the contents of his stomach, followed by one of his seamen, solidifying his suspicions that these men had little seafaring experience.

Looking around at the other lost souls aboard this death trap, Santiago found some consolation in the fact that there were no children amongst the sixteen passengers, himself included. As Santiago wiped the rain and salt water from his eyes he felt the craft move over swells at continuously steeper angles. He tried in vain to block out the shrieks and screams of the others on board, but watched in horror as one of the seamen was swept off the boat. Looking around frantically for anything to throw to the man, he realized there was nothing he or anyone else could do for him. The blinding rain prevented him from seeing anything on the open ocean. Santiago watched as the captain staggered towards him with outstretched hands. The driving rain and howling winds blocked out everything. Santiago could not hear what the captain shouted.

Santiago did not require ears to figure out what the captain wanted as he began tugging at Santiago's life vest. Santiago shoved him away, yelling that the captain had his own vest, although Santiago's was definitely superior. His father must have saved for quite some time to acquire this vest for him. Even though the captain outweighed him by at least 40 pounds, no one was going to separate Santiago from this one link to the old life he still desperately clung to and the new one he longed for. With one last fierce push he freed himself from the captain's grip, just as a gigantic swell lifted the boat to an angle of no return.

For a few moments everything seemed silent to Santiago, almost as though time stood still, as he felt himself suspended in mid-air. An instant later he was launched forward, flying at top speed towards deep blue roiling water. The force of the impact shook him back to reality. Almost without thinking, he rolled his head back to assist with floatation, just the way his father had told him. Despite the gigantic swells and frequent mouthfuls of salty water, Santiago felt himself roll up and down with the swells, occasionally looking up and around to see if he could catch a glimpse of the boat or anyone nearby. Nothing, he was alone, in the middle of an ocean, in the middle of a storm. Suddenly his life back in Cuba did not seem so bad. He could have worked with his father, helped his mother, been closer to his sisters. Everything was lost now.

He felt it before he saw it. A glass bottle bumped into his head. Santiago had no idea where it came from, but he grabbed hold of the bottle and told himself it was a bottle from the boat. If he had a bottle from the boat, then that could only mean the boat was nearby, he reasoned. He refused to acknowledge his faulty reasoning. Right now, the only thing keeping him alive was this defective reasoning, and his vest. Rolling his head back, attempting to float, he wondered, would he float to the United States if he wished hard enough? Somehow he managed to repress the frantic inner voice that wanted to shout that he would suffer a horrible death by sharks, dehydration, hypothermia or drowning somewhere in the middle of the Atlantic Ocean, never to see the shore of any country again.

The sound of whirring roused him from whatever state of stupor his mind had retreated to. Was it a boat? The large rotor in the sky told him otherwise. The gigantic orange and white helicopter with the black block letters read U.S. Coast Guard. A very dehydrated Santiago felt dazed as the rescue swimmer shouted for him to raise his hands. Raising his hands, hands now without sensation, he dropped the green bottle back into the water. He hadn't realized he was still clutching the bottle, he had forgotten about the boat, had forgotten about the others aboard the boat.

The rescue swimmer, attaching a rope around Santiago's midsection, hoisted him up towards the safety of the loud whirring helicopter. It took Santiago many ounces of fluids, warm blankets, and two days of sleep to recuperate sufficiently to remember what had happened. The Coast Guard officer informed him it was lucky they had spotted the capsized wreck. After 48 hours of searching, he was the only survivor they found, miles away from the wrecked boat. The rest of the souls on board the boat had vanished, likely swallowed into the bowels of the sea.

Santiago did make it to Florida where he found his mother's cousin. Three years later he made his way to New York, where, after many years of hard work, he eventually ended up working as a reporter for the *New York Times*. But at what cost he wondered? Not a day went by that he did not think about that fateful day with varying degrees of guilt. Was there anything he could have done that would have changed anything? What if he had given the man who called himself *captain* his life vest? Why did he survive and no one else?

Dresden, Germany

Fall 2011

The cobblestone drive Charlie had turned down made my breasts jiggle uncomfortably. Crossing my arms beneath my chest, I looked ahead expectantly, wondering just how long this "driveway" could be. A strange sensation passed over me suddenly, almost as though I had been here before.

"You okay?" Charlie glanced over at me with a concerned expression, placing his hand on my neck and gently squeezing. It's no wonder he's worried, after the stunt I just pulled. He's gotta think I'm insane. Unexplained nervous breakdowns would be good cause for concern I thought, smiling over at Charlie.

"Just a little bit of déjà vu, you know, combined with a big case of the jitters," I reluctantly admitted.

"Don't worry, I'm here with you," Charlie said. I had to laugh, did he really think I couldn't handle this on my own or something? Well, if I was honest with myself, I wouldn't be here if it wasn't for him.

And he was right, I worried less with him around. "He's the one who found Diana for you," I heard the little voice in my head remind me. Strangely enough, with Charlie around, I felt more secure about the love I had shared with Warren. Even Warren's forgotten letters, which I still hadn't called about, didn't seem as important anymore.

I knew what Warren and I had was real love, and that love would always be there. I didn't need letters to prove it. I think I knew I'd never see the letters again.

Gently, I laid my hand on Charlie's leg and watched as a brief smile curled up the sides of his mouth.

"Wow," we both breathed simultaneously, as our little Fiat finally broke through the dense woods. A gigantic oval-shaped lawn spread like a majestic carpet toward a palatial-sized home situated at the far end of the lawn. The forest on both sides of the lawn looked as though it was swallowing the home from both sides. I had never seen anything so spectacular, yet in the same instant, so unsettling.

"Something doesn't feel right about this place, Charlie." I felt the butterflies in my stomach furiously beating their wings.

"Yeah, I'm getting that too," Charlie agreed, following the driveway that wrapped around the lawn toward the large house. "Oh wow, now *that* is really weird," Charlie said as he stopped the car in front of the house. "The front wall of the house is all that's left of the place. Do you see that, Diana? Kind of reminds me of a Hollywood set, don't you think?"

What was Charlie so excited about? I had hoped to find an intact home with Anna and her family inside. Not sharing Charlie's excitement, I stepped out of the car and walked slowly towards, what looked from a distance like a home, but was in fact only the front of the home, the last remaining wall. Strange, the front of the house looked untouched. Charlie was right, it was like a Hollywood set. I couldn't resist touching the wall and wasn't surprised by the goose bumps that subsequently covered my body. Was this really the place Anna had lived? What had happened?

"The war, silly girl," I heard my rational voice tease me. Of course the destruction occurred during World War II, but what had happened to the people who lived here? Why had nothing been renovated? Lost in thought, I slowly walked along the wall, touching it occasionally, convincing myself of its solid existence.

"Well I'll be…, take a look at this, Diana." Charlie led me around the side of the front wall and together we stared at the large heaps of rubble, which was all that remained of most of the house.

"How bizarre, from a distance it looks like the house is intact…
only the front façade left standing…well half, but the destroyed half is
hidden by these trees. This really must have been some house, huh?"
I heard Charlie speaking, as though to himself, but I didn't care. *That*
is what was wrong with the place. It was abandoned. Dead. Only the
ghosts of those who died here likely wandered its overgrown paths. I
felt like I had been hit with a bag of bricks. The place we had traveled
to, come so far to find, was nothing more than a large heap of rubble.
And the woman, Anna, the woman who had come to mean so much to
me could not possibly be here anymore. My heart sank. I was certain
I'd find my mysterious Anna. There had been just too many coincidences, hadn't there? Too many things had to fall in place for both
Charlie and I to be here together. Maybe that is what all of this was
really about. Maybe fate had brought me closer to Charlie this way. To
help me overcome my loss and find love again?

"Okay, that's enough of the crazy talk," I whispered aloud, looking down at a pile of bricks, one of which had 1757 engraved in it.

"This place must have been gigantic at one time. No one could
afford to live like this anymore, could they?" Charlie half shouted
with delight, making his way through the heaps of rubble behind the
one standing wall. I watched him, but had no intention of joining him
on the mounds of rock. Leaning against the solid front wall which
seemed to defy gravity, I placed my cheek against the cool moss-cov-
ered surface.

"Is this where you lived, Anna?" I asked the ancient rock, half
expecting someone from the great beyond to answer. Medication. That
was what I needed, and quite a bit of it. Just as I was about to close my
eyes, I detected movement near the edge of a dense pine forest.

"Just like a Hollywood set. There must've been some more buildings over there," I heard Charlie calling out again, but my eyes were
fixed on the person who had appeared at the edge of the wood, no
more than two-hundred yards away. Forgetting about Charlie for the
moment, I quickly headed towards the person I was sure I had seen.

"Is that you, Anna?" I whispered, picking up my pace.

Breathless, I reached the spot where I was sure the person had
been standing. And of course, just as in all of the Hollywood movies,

the mysterious stranger disappeared before the heroine arrived at the scene. The exertion of jogging left my heart pounding in my ears. Maybe this was another one of my hallucinations. The experts, whoever they were, say stress induces a lot of strange things. Looking around, I noticed I had stopped next to an untended, overgrown graveyard. Ancient, from the look of the gravestones, but then again, what did I know about European graveyards.

A rusted gate hung half open, almost inviting me to enter. I don't know what it was about this graveyard, but the gravestones fascinated me. Pushing open the creaking gate, I entered the graveyard. It seemed eerily quiet now, as though I had stepped through a sound barrier. Not a single bird call could be heard. I was sure I had heard plenty of bird calls just a moment before. Even the light breeze was gone.

Slowly I made my way between the haphazardly placed gravestones, stepping over nettles and other prickly weeds I couldn't identify. Trying to make out the names inscribed on most of the headstones was close to impossible. Most had been worn away beyond recognition, a combination of time and the elements, others were almost completely covered with moss. Whether from exertion or exhaustion, maybe both, I felt my head suddenly spin. Leaning against a headstone for support, I quickly sat down before my legs turned to complete jell-o. With my face pressed almost up against the headstone, I could smell the earthy scents of moss and lichens that covered the large rock.

"You came, I knew you would," A voice behind me exclaimed, startling me enough to seriously spike my adrenaline. Jumping up with exaggerated energy, I spun around.

Why was I not surprised to see who it was? I should be scared, she's gotta be a ghost or something, right? Then why wasn't I frightened?

"You...it's you," I muttered. It was the woman from the airport, the one whose needlework sat in my backpack in the Fiat. And her brooch. Why did she expect me to come here?

"Are you...are you Anna?" I asked with a voice that was no more than a whisper. It was then I noticed she still wore the knitting needles in her hair. The woman smiled. "You have come far, Diana, you will find her now. Return the brooch."

The woman hadn't answered my question, but I was beginning to think she wasn't Anna after all.

"Why?" I muttered, "Why couldn't you just give her the brooch yourself? Why go through all the trouble of using me?"

"Find Anna. Give her the brooch." The woman's voice echoed through my head, almost pleadingly. The woman vanished, as though she had never existed. Leaning back against the gravestone, I still heard her voice urging me to find Anna. Why me? Why not just drop off the damn brooch herself. She's the one pulling off the vanishing and reappearing act after all. I had to pay fifteen hundred dollars to get here, not to mention the hotel and the car. Somewhat frustrated with the whole situation I called out, "Who are you?" Not surprisingly I was met with silence.

The woman was gone. Real or imagined, she was gone. It wasn't until then that I noticed my damp rear end. Jeez, had I fallen asleep again? Or did I have some kind of waking epileptic seizure? Standing up, I rubbed the damp grass from my bottom and happened to glance down at the gravestone I had been leaning against before. Unlike most of the other gravestones, the name on this one was still legible, even with the moss that covered half of it. Picking up a small stick, I scraped at the moss to reveal the name.

"Sigrid Steinmeyer…is this the Sigrid of your letter, Anna?" I whispered, gently tracing the cool letters inscribed on the rough, gray stone. There was no response to my question, but, for reasons I could never explain, I knew the woman haunting me was Sigrid Steinmeyer. The only question that remained was why? And there was only one way to find out, find Anna von Marschalkt or at least figure out what happened to her.

"Diana! Diana! For God's sake, I've been looking all over for you," Charlie snapped, quickly changing his tone when he saw I was alright. The poor guy probably thought I had passed out somewhere. Relief replaced his irritated but concerned expression.

"What have you been doing here? Why are you loitering in a graveyard of all places? The place seems creepy enough not to wander off on your own without ending up in some overgrown graveyard," he reprimanded me, but I didn't mind. It felt wonderful having someone care about where I loitered.

"Good God, you're pale, what on earth have you been doing, Diana? Chasing ghosts?" Feeling about as energetic as a wet noodle, I didn't have the strength to answer him, or argue with him. He'd think I was crazier than I already thought I was.

As Charlie dragged me back to our miniature Fiat chariot, I wondered if I had indeed imagined this strange woman, possibly conjured her up in some delirious dream. It was quite possible, since I think I did drift off into dreamland at one point. And besides, if she wanted me to find Anna, wouldn't she give me an address or something? Why all the mystery and intrigue? No, this had to be my imagination playing tricks on me. Where was I supposed to find Anna now? There was nothing here besides rubble and an old graveyard I thought, as Charlie led me along by the elbow. I guess I'd just have to file this under "unexplained."

We had almost reached the ruins of the old house when a small Dachshund appeared out of nowhere, barking wildly.

"Hey, boy, where'd you come from, little guy?" Charlie asked the small creature that reminded me of an oversized rat. "Come here, boy," Charlie called to the dog with an outstretched hand, just as an elderly man with a cane emerged from the woods and limped towards us. He had a short grizzled beard and reminded me of an oversized gnome.

"Heiner, nein! Heiner, nein!" he shouted.

It didn't take the man long to figure out that we did not speak a word of German.

"Can I help you?" he asked, in heavily accented English, looking us up and down the way a butler might inspect uninvited guests. Well, I wasn't going to let him get away with the once-over he was giving us. I took my time looking over the giant gnome, wondering who he was and how he might fit into this whole puzzle.

"Maybe," Charlie the kind-hearted answered for both of us, "We are looking for a woman named Anna...Anna von Marschalkt," Charlie and I both watched the old man's expression suddenly change. How to read this expression was another thing. He definitely had heard of her, but would he know details? The old man regarded us in silence.

With raised eyebrows he finally asked, "Who wants to know, may I ask?" It was clear this little old hunched man with bright eyes and a crooked cane was not one to be fooled easily.

356

"I am Diana, and this is Charlie…we…I… have something I need to return to Anna." Pausing before I continued, I wondered how much I should tell him. He had not taken his eyes off of us, but now he regarded us with more curiosity and much less suspicion. "Is she…uh, is she still alive," I asked, holding my breath for an answer.

The old man belted out a laugh that sounded like an unhealthy smoker's cough.

"Anna? Of course she is still alive…she will tell you herself, weeds do not die." I felt my heart suddenly beating in my ears again as I stared at this funny old gnome with his green hunting cap, matching vest, and decorated cane.

"Is she here?" My voice trembled.

"No, she has not lived here for many years. Never came back here after France. She lived in Frankfurt for a while." The old man must have noticed my disappointed look and slowly continued. "She moved back after the, how do you call it in English…the reunification of West and East Germany. Many of us did, to reclaim what was ours."

"So she is here?" Charlie asked, looking as confused as I was.

"She does not live on the estate…what is left of it. She lives, oh, not more than 15 kilometers from here." He pointed in a direction which meant nothing to me. The old man spent the next five minutes trying to explain to Charlie how we would find Anna's home. After much frustration he finally agreed to accompany us if we would be kind enough to return him and his large rat back to the estate at the "conclusion of our business with Anna."

"I am sorry, sir, I know it is none of my business, but did Anna get the estate back?" I finally asked once we were all packed in the car, myself in the back seat.

"No, but I did," the old man said flatly without turning around as he pulled an embroidered cloth towel from his pocket and blew his nose.

Why did he get the estate? Was he related to Anna somehow? I realized we hadn't asked him his name or relationship to the von Marschalkt family.

"She has no more use for this place. There is nothing here but the old gardener's shed. I have fixed it up some, for now." The old man pointed at a house almost completely hidden behind vines and bushes, situated along the oval driveway.

"We completely missed that one…nice camouflage job," Charlie snorted, peering at the hidden home that could have been straight out of a children's fairy tale. "This place must've really been abandoned for some time," Charlie noted as he slowly followed the driveway back into the dense wood.

"No one has lived here since the American and British bombings," the old man spoke without hostility as he stroked the oversized rat in his lap.

"I'm sorry, sir, but do you mind telling us, uh, your name, and how you know Anna?"

"I am Thomas von Marschalkt, my father, the Baron von Marschalkt, owned the estate before the war…and my grandfather lived on the grounds. He was the gardener….the house I live in now was his." He paused to blow his nose again before he continued. "Anna is my, how does one say in your language? Half-sister?"

Leaning back in my seat I found myself staring at the back of the old man's head. This man, this little gnome like character was Anna's brother? Where on earth was this adventure going to lead us to next? This couldn't all be coincidence, could it?

Dresden, Germany

August 1943

The screams reached all the way up to Anna's second story window. Quickly she dropped the needlework she had been working on and ran down the stairs, nearly colliding with Maria on the way.

"What is it?" Maria asked with a panic stricken expression.

"I do not know," Anna answered, as the two sisters rushed down the stairs, leaving a horrified Sigrid behind to tend Maria's young girls. It could not be Mama. Anna and Sigrid had moved her to the sitting room not more than an hour ago. She could not possibly have moved herself.

"Lena," Anna half shouted as she breathed heavily. Running to the front door with her sister on her heels she heard the screams intensify. A moment later the two sisters were outside the house running towards Lena, who carried her unconscious son in her arms.

"Thomas, no, no, no!" Lena screamed between sobs. "No, Thomas, wake up, Thomas," she pleaded.

"What happened, Lena?" Maria asked, trying hard to stay calm.

Lena seemed unaware of the two women who stared from her to her young son with terrified expressions.

"What happened, Lena?" Maria spoke more firmly, grabbing Lena by the arm and digging her nails into Lena's pale skin. Lena looked at Maria, as though seeing her for the first time. Her mouth moved without sound, resembling a fish out of water.

"Lena," Maria snapped again, digging her nails deeper into Lena's thin skin.

"He,…I,…I only looked away for a moment…he wanted to see the new kittens up in the hayloft," Lena sobbed hysterically as she buried her face in the body of her young son. "I saw him fall…," she wept, as she wiped her tears with her sleeve.

"Is he d…d…dead?" Anna asked flatly, void of any external emotion, while terror threatened to take hold of her inside.

"He is not dead," Maria hissed, glaring at her sister and feeling the pulse on Thomas' small wrist. Anna noticed a look of immediate relief pass over her sister's face as she silently counted the beats of this young heart.

"His heartbeat is strong and stable," Maria announced, as though a doctor herself. She had seen enough of doctors, and had enough children, Anna thought. If anyone was to judge a strong, steady heart it would be Maria.

"Mama," the small voice, buried beneath Lena's face, quietly cried. "Mama, my leg hurts."

"Oh, Thomas, my Thomas…," Lena continued to cry. "You are awake my boy. Hush now. Hush."

"You," Maria ordered, pointing at Anna, "fetch the doctor. And you, bring the boy inside," she directed Lena who still suffered from shock. "Inside, Lena. Now!" Maria ordered again, pushing the young mother along.

As Anna ran towards the shed to retrieve her bicycle, she could not help thinking how much her sister's tone reminded her of the mother she used to know before the brain injury.

Drenched with perspiration, Anna returned a short while later with the doctor. Maria looked up in surprise when she saw her sweat stained sister return so quickly.

"I did not expect you for some time," Maria said with a relieved tone, as she quickly led the doctor up the staircase, closely followed by Anna.

"I was on my way to see Baroness von Marschalkt when I ran into your sister," the doctor began to explain, quickly stopping when he realized it mattered nothing to these women what explanation he offered. The child was the primary concern. Anna followed her sister and the doctor to Lena's bedroom where young Thomas was laying on his mother's bed with a slab of cold meat pressed to the back of his head, and his left leg twisted in a most unnatural position. The boy, obviously in agonizing pain, whimpered continuously like a small dog, but not once did Anna hear him scream out.

"His mother could learn something from him," she whispered to herself, immediately overcome with guilt for her unkind thoughts. "Why must children suffer so horridly and I have such wicked thoughts about others?" she silently wondered, as her heart bled for this young boy who had become such an important member of the family. The fact that he was an illegitimate, fatherless son of a maid had been overlooked years ago when he had come to live in the main house with his mother. In some ways, Anna felt a closer kinship to young, illegitimate Thomas than to her sister's legitimate daughters.

Anna watched as Dr. Werner Wenke skillfully touched and tapped various parts of little Thomas' body. Only when he laid a hand on Thomas' leg did the young boy grimace and emit a small moan. Anna could not take her eyes of these hands that were so different from the hands of her father and the other farm workers on the estate. The doctor had long thin hands which seemed almost delicate as they moved swiftly and skillfully over the small child sprawled out on the bed. Even Jakub, she recalled, had large, rough hands, calloused from years of hard work outside. She felt her face flush as she imagined the doctor's hands gently caressing her body. It was at that moment that Dr. Wenke looked up at her. Anna felt a heat rise up in her which she knew was more than the stifling summer heat.

"Some fresh air would do us good," she mumbled, heading to open the window, which did little to relieve the internal heat coursing through her veins.

"It is broken. Yes, the leg is definitely broken." Dr. Wenke spoke calmly to himself. Anna wondered how his voice remained so calm and confident when he interacted with a patient, yet he appeared so frazzled, and at times aloof, when she encountered him alone. "I am going to need your assistance," he ordered. Anna did not know with whom the doctor spoke, but she turned away from the window and rejoined Lena and Maria at the bed. "You and you," he pointed at Lena and Maria as though directing his own staff, "You hold his arms... and, ah, you, Fraulein," the doctor pointed at Anna, "You hold on to his right leg."

Dr. Wenke noticed the look of terror on young Thomas' face. The doctor bent down close to the boy. "Now young man, it appears you are the man of the house," the doctor looked around as though to emphasize the point that Thomas was surrounded only by women. Even Sigrid had come to the door with a gaggle of young girls in tow. "Now, we want to show these ladies what a brave young man you are, do we not? I must be honest with you, this will be painful, but I know how brave you are." Anna watched in amazement as the terror faded from little Thomas' face. The boy looked straight into Dr. Wenke's eyes and nodded, even managing a fleeting smile.

"Now then, ladies, if I may, hold on and do not let go. I will make this as quick and painless as possible." Anna stared as the young doctor placed a leather strap between Thomas' teeth and took hold of his left leg.

"Bite down on this young man," he said. With two swift movements he jerked the twisted leg back into place. It was the first time she heard young Thomas scream since the accident, quickly followed by silence as the child drifted back to an unconscious state where pain could not follow.

The doctor looked upon his work with dissatisfaction as he gently felt along the length of the boy's leg. A look of fear had been plastered on Lena's face since the doctor entered the room, and she too had momentarily blacked out when she heard the doctor straighten out her son's leg with a snapping sound. Now Lena looked at the doctor with horrified anticipation, her face almost resembling that of a gargoyle, Anna thought. She herself wondered what it was the doctor seemed discontented with.

"I believe the boy's leg shall heal, he shall walk again...the bone did not break the skin, this is good." The doctor felt the leg once more and then remained silent for a moment as he held his chin in seemingly deep thought. "He must remain absolutely still for quite some time." It was obvious he doubted Thomas' ability to remain motionless in his bed for the requisite amount of time the leg needed to heal. The odd look of consternation had not left the doctor's face as he once again prodded his way carefully along Thomas' left leg.

"What is it, please, Doctor?" Lena begged, further distorting her face as she squeezed her eyes closed to maintain a hold on her emotions.

"The leg…it is where the leg was broken. The boy may limp for some time. Possibly, always."

Anna watched as the muscles in Lena's face and neck relaxed. She had never found the young maid beautiful, with her bland combination of pale skin, hazel eyes and fair hair, but there was something about the manner in which she carried herself that she did not go unnoticed by the men that crossed paths with her.

"Not to mention the colossal size of her bust," Anna whispered to herself with some resentment, as she noted the odd way even the doctor seemed to glance at Lena's bust when speaking to her. Anna felt her face flush. She was not sure whether from embarrassment or from, could it be jealousy? Stealing a glance down at her own apricot-sized breasts, she wondered whether she should be insulted or honored that men did not stare at her bust when speaking to her. For a brief moment Anna had a vision of herself, naked in the hayloft. But the man who lay beside her with his hand on her breast was not her handsome Jakub with his large hands, but this thin, awkward doctor with his long, fine-boned fingers who had never experienced a day of farm work in his life.

"Anna!" Maria snapped at her sister with an odd expression. Anna's shifting countenance had not gone unnoticed by her sister.

"The doctor has asked you to hold that side of the splint." Anna looked from her sister to the doctor and back to her sister, noticing a faint smile pass over Maria's lips. She recognized that knowing smile, she had after all, spent most of her life in the same room with Maria.

"I am sorry," Anna apologized with averted eyes, grabbing the makeshift splint Dr. Wenke had fashioned out of wood from the stables and strips of clean table cloth. Anna stood close to the doctor as he worked. She felt his arm brush against hers a number of times, leaving her feeling week-kneed with a warm feeling spreading through her body. She had never had feelings for any man besides Jakub.

"But with Jakub it was different…it was love at first sight, an over-powering, blinding, all-consuming love," she silently whispered to herself. "With this strange doctor it is different. It is something that is percolating." Anna could not explain how, she knew there had been no initial attraction for this odd, lanky man, but over time he had grown on her. His passion and competence as a doctor moved her beyond words. Somehow his awkward nervousness around her, and she had noticed it was only around her that he behaved in such a manner, had also moved her spirit. As she watched perspiration trickle from his fair, thinning hair, a sharp contrast to Jakub's thick, dark curls, she wondered how she could be attracted to two such distinct opposites.

"You do not choose love, love chooses you," Jakub had once said to her. Their love had been mutual from the beginning. Could it be this strange doctor had similar feelings for her, she wondered, as she inhaled his warm, pleasant scent.

"There," Doctor Wenke sighed with exertion as he firmly tied the last of the strips around the splint. "The leg must remain immobilized and elevated until I return tomorrow. Under no circumstance," he said as he sat down on the bed beside Thomas and procured a piece of black licorice, "are you to get out of this bed, young man. Do we have a deal?" he asked, handing Thomas the licorice and lightly stroking his cheek. Little Thomas, eager for the sweet licorice nodded in agreement.

"There is more where this came from," Dr. Wenke smiled as he stood up from the bed and packed his things together.

Anna watched with disdain as Lena rushed to the young doctor's side and grabbed him by the hand.

"Oh, Doctor Wenke…I am eternally grateful to you," Lena blurted out, as tears streamed down her face yet again, "Please let me walk you out," Lena insisted.

Anna let out an audible sigh as she attempted to manage her own emotions. She too was grateful for the services the doctor rendered, but she had no inclination to throw herself at the man.

"I am sorry," the doctor spoke to Lena, "I have, some, ah, how shall I say, uh, unfinished business with Fraulein von Marschalkt... ah, regarding her mother."

It did not go unnoticed by Anna that this man, who, just moments before, demonstrated calm efficiency in his capacity as a doctor, had now reverted back to the nervous man who had once knocked her senseless with a church door. Nor did Anna miss Maria's curious glance as she looked from the young doctor to Anna.

"W...w...well, I shall w...w...walk you out then, Doctor. W...w...we can discuss the Baroness along the way," Anna suggested as a warmth in her abdomen radiated through her body like a glowing furnace. Anna knew there was no unfinished business to discuss, but freely accepted the invitation. Maria watched her sister leave the room with the doctor, amused by the cherry-colored faces both of them shared.

Letter 13   *Dresden, 13. September 1943*

My Beloved Jakub,

*I hope this letter finds you well. I had to write to you imme-
diately, as once again much has transpired since I last wrote
to you. It has been a dark time for everyone in my life, but
recently a ray of sunshine found its way back into my soul.
It was a difficult decision to admit to myself that what I was
feeling was true, but now that I have come to accept it, I feel
that it is only fair that I share this with you. I have met a man;
he is a doctor and a most curious creature, I might say. We
have developed an unusual friendship, which, I believe, arises
from the fact that in this dreary and horrid place, two kindred
souls have found each other. He was separated from his love
through death, while I was separated from you for reasons
that still do not make sense to me. This relationship I share
with him is nothing as ours was, Jakub. He has become a dear
friend as he spends more time tending to Mama than most doctors would, as well as to poor little Thomas, who injured his
leg not long ago.*

*With this friendship, my beloved, I hope I do not betray your
trust. I will not be dishonest, there are often times where I wish
this friendship with the doctor might progress beyond just that,
but I fear such intimacy would destroy the laughter I now frequently enjoy in conversation. Also, I fear such a relationship
would forever push you from my life, wherever you may be.
Maybe it is just that which my subconscious desires. There is
so much suffering in the world, and, my dear Jakub, I sometimes wish I could push you from my mind so that both you
and I may move forward with our lives. But then am I naïve to
believe that you have not moved forward with your life? Are
you waiting for me on the beach of some tropical paradise? It
is when I lay alone in my bed at night that I hunger for you,*

Jakub. I cannot even put into words that power of the emotion that overcomes me. What we shared is something I believe can never be replaced. Oh, Jakub, I am so confused. I wish there was someone or something who could prescribe to me what path to follow, to know what is right and what is wrong. To tell me if I shall ever see you again. To tell me if you shall ever love me again.

Yesterday, Papa and Dieter returned from Berlin together. They both appear to age much after each trip. Unlike what is broadcast over the airwaves, the future for this once beloved Fatherland does indeed look bleak. I have asked Papa if we cannot flee and begin life someplace else. It is too late for that, he says. Mama's condition makes travel anywhere, even to another town, difficult. It, however, surprises all of us that Mama continues to thrive, despite the depressing circumstances that surround her. She even manages to knit again, with assistance from myself or Sigrid. The voice of the Fuehrer is thankfully never heard booming from the sitting room anymore. However, on occasion I have heard Mama's voice booming again, for which I believe Papa is grateful. Just last week, I overheard an argument between Mama and Sigrid. I arrived too late to hear the grounds for this disagreement, but it appears Mama intends to remove Sigrid from the estate. This ongoing feud between the two is quite understandable, but the care with which Sigrid handles Mama is remarkable since the two women always seem at odds with each other. I recently confronted Sigrid regarding her relationship with Papa. I believed she would never answer such questions as I posed, therefore her response surprised me. She confided that, I quote, "I fear his heart lies with another....and it is not your mother." I do not understand her cryptic message, but attribute it to latent jealousy, as Papa has spent more time with Mama since her injury. Oh, Jakub, the human psyche can be so disturbed.

I have come to believe this war shall never end, or not until all have either starved or been blown to pieces. These are horrible thoughts, I realize, but how much longer can this suffering go on? The plight of those in the city is overwhelming. I thank the stars every day that Papa had the foresight to bury food and valuables, many of which have been unearthed to provide for our existence, as much of what was not underground has been stolen. Thievery is so commonplace now— I often hear horrible stories from the remaining farm workers. Destitute mothers with children are often chased from the estate, caught in the act of stealing anything they can carry. Despite their crimes, Sigrid always manages to find some spare milk or eggs for the mothers of young children. Oh, Jakub, what would life have been like for our young son? If he had survived, would I have had to live through the horror of watching him be taken from me?

I move through life in a state of confusion, Jakub. Now, it is only when I converse with this young doctor I spoke of earlier, that I feel I have anything worth living for. There is a life-giving energy he radiates that warms my soul, which has been frozen for so long. It only fades after his departure. What shall still come to pass cannot in any manner be affected by me. Possibly this is a passive approach to life, but I am tired, Jakub, my soul is tired. Sometimes an end seems a welcome reprieve from the hatred that surrounds this world. Oh, my love, I have burdened you sufficiently. I hope you shall someday understand me.

Love Eternally,
Anna v. Marschalkt

Post Script: Last night Death walked our floors. For whom does he reach? Both Maria and I heard his footsteps and yelled for him to leave us be. The footsteps did fade away, but tomorrow is another night. And Death never stays away forever.

Anna nervously wrung her hands. She had finished yet another letter to Jakub, a lover who, if he was still alive, had quite possibly long since forgotten her.

"When is this insanity going to stop?" she asked herself, as she stared over her carefully written letter. She no longer sensed Jakub's presence, but oddly, she sensed her son with greater frequency. It was not, however, her helpless infant she sensed, but an independent spirit that, at times when even the doctor could not help her, was the only thing that could lift her mood from the depths into which it had fallen. Picking up her letter, she carefully rolled it up and slid it through the neck of the empty green glass apple juice bottle.

"How many times have I done this?" she asked herself aloud as she prepared the wax plug for her bottle. Anna watched as a small hummingbird quickly darted in and out of her line of vision, just outside the window. It was not dark yet, but the evening sky had already turned a deep shade of grey. Anna peered out of her window, hoping to catch another glimpse of this creature that, she realized, was likely a figment of her imagination. "Why do you come to me, bird?" Anna asked. The hummingbird did not return.

It was the following day that Anna rode her bicycle to the Elbe River. As she stood on the bridge that crossed the swiftly flowing river, she was overcome by an overwhelming sense of loss, as though a dark blanket had been draped over her body. Without ceremony she quickly tossed her bottle into the river, and watched it submerge, only to surface a moment later. She watched the bottle bob away for a moment and quickly turned to leave. Anna would never know her bottle would travel over forty kilometers down stream where it would eventually come to rest on a sandy bank. Heavy rains would later deposit sediment on top of the bottle. Fifty-five years later, the Dresden City Works project would remove sediment to build a new bridge over the river. The excess sediment, along with the bottle, would be deposited, as requested, on the Thomas von Marschalkt estate to fill holes left from heavy bombing during World War II.

Travels of Letter 16
Hudson Bay, New York
September 2001

Joshua Mueller wasn't watching the skyline as the Hoboken ferry sped across the Hudson towards Manhattan. It was Sara he watched. He watched her in class, at lunch, and even on weekends at the tennis courts.

"Man, you gonna stare at her all year again? You got it bad for her, don't ya," his friend Jimmy teased, socking him in the arm.

"Not as bad as the ass whoopin' you're gonna get," he answered, smacking Jimmy on the forehead.

"Look at ole Mickey Mouse over there, got his lady killer pants on again today," Jimmy said, pointing at his teacher's bright green pants.

"Stop it, man," Joshua hissed, as he slapped at Jimmy's hand. "You're gonna get me a 'D' in class, man. I don't wanna go to summer school."

"Aw, look at the little wuss, will ya. Scared of old sissy pants over there. Waa, waa, waa," Jimmy sang, loud enough for Sara and her friends to hear. Joshua felt his face flush as he watched Sara and her two friends giggle. Why was it always Jimmy? How come he made

371

everyone laugh? All Joshua wanted was to make the others laugh, make Sara laugh, instead of being the butt of every joke.

"Yeah, yeah, smart ass, real scared," Joshua said stiffly, glancing over at Sara to make sure she was listening. "I am gonna tell him his ass looks good in those pants," he added awkwardly, waiting for Sara's approving giggles, that didn't come. Joshua watched as one of Sara's friends tugged her by the arm to the other side of the boat.

"What a freak," he heard a voice from the other side of the boat say, followed by giggles.

"What's wrong with you, dude? You sound like a friggin' freak, man, jeez. You just don't get it, do you, retard? Stay the hell away from me, you hear?" Jimmy said, shaking his head as he walked away from his friend.

Joshua stood alone at the railing of the boat unable to figure out what had just gone so wrong. What had he said? Did anyone think he was funny? What about Jimmy? How come Jimmy could say whatever he wanted to about anyone and no one looked at him like he was a jerk? Why did Jimmy always pick on him anyway? They were friends, at least Joshua had always thought he had a friend in Jimmy. Now he wasn't so sure anymore.

Joshua looked over at Jimmy, who was working his magic again. Jimmy was surrounded by a group of guys and had them all laughing. Each of the boys stole glances his way, Jimmy included, and laughed uncontrollably, causing an uneasy feeling to creep up Joshua's spine. Was Jimmy talking about him? Was he making fun of him? Jimmy had been his friend since they were both four years old and lived next door to him.

Joshua didn't know what had awakened in him, but suddenly he saw the world through different eyes. Staring down at the dirty Hudson, he briefly spied a bottle poking its neck through the surface, only to disappear again a moment later in the churning water. Whatever change occurred inside his being, he knew he would never again be the same person. People wouldn't laugh at him again, ever. From now on, they would laugh with him. Strangely, within the boundaries of this empowered self, he did not harbor any resentment towards Jimmy or any of the others who had laughed at him. With crystal clarity he knew what he had to do. Climbing on the ship's railing he heard the calls and shouts of encouragement, of fear, of approval. Balancing on the narrow railing he searched for Sara's eyes. She had to see him. Just as Joshua lost his balance, he found them. Sara's eyes, filled with horror.

"Dude, what are you doing?" Jimmy called to Joshua too late.

Joshua hit the water hard, hearing screams from the departing ferry. Suddenly, the screams were drowned out, as he submerged in the cold water. Feeling the weight of his shoes pulling him down, he kicked them off, followed by his backpack and green parka. All the clarity with which he had seen the world just moments ago was gone again. He felt a fool, was a fool, and always would be a fool. Now they would really laugh at him. He was the idiot who jumped into the Hudson.

"What were you thinking, idiot?" Joshua yelled at himself, close to tears, as he watched the ferry pull away, but at a seemingly slower pace. "Why'd you jump on that stupid railing, moron?" an inner voice of reason chided him. "I wasn't supposed to fall," he answered, as warm tears began to flow into the cold water. What would Mr. Thomas say? Would he flunk him? "Of course he will, retard. Say hello to summer school. Now they're all going to hate you," his inner voice blamed him. There was nothing he could do now but wait for the ferry to turn around and pick him up. The class would miss their tour, and he would be the reason everyone was sent back to school. "God, they are all gonna hate me!" Joshua yelled, flailing about in the water to stay afloat.

Robert Thomas hadn't seen Joshua fall. The screams of the other students alerted him that something was amiss. It took a moment to notify the Captain that a student was overboard.

"Why me? Why always me?" the eighth grade school teacher asked aloud. "Why do I always have a moron who does something stupid?" It seemed to take a long time to turn the damn boat around, the teacher thought impatiently. Jesus, they were going to miss their nine a.m. roof-top deck tour, he thought, staring out at the Hudson. Robert Thomas felt a wave of guilt pass over him. He didn't even know if his student was alright and here he was worrying about a tour.

He caught sight of Joshua as the ferry slowly approached the floating boy, and felt immense relief that the boy had not drowned.

"He's going to be alright," he whispered, trying hard to reassure himself that his student was indeed alright. "Thank the stars," he again whispered under his breath. It wasn't something he would have expected from Joshua. According to the other students, Joshua had climbed on top of the railing and lost his balance. What was the kid thinking? Robert Thomas watched as crew members tossed Joshua a flotation device attached to a rope.

"We've notified the fire department," the Captain informed the teacher, "they'll meet us once we dock." Yeah, the fire department, the police department, the coast guard, and every other emergency responder, not to mention the local news, will be there in about two minutes, he thought to himself, feeling increasingly irritated as he watched the ferry crew hoist the half frozen boy onto the deck.

It was 8:43 a.m. when Mr. Thomas and Joshua completed their statements to the New York Police Department and the paramedics had made sure Joshua suffered no lasting harm.

"We called your mother, Joshua. She's on her way to pick you up," Mr. Thomas said flatly as Joshua sat shivering with an emergency blanket wrapped tightly around his narrow shoulders. Repressing the urge to kick the kid in the ass, Robert Thomas tried not to think of how much planning had gone into this day. "And class, for your information, we'll *obviously* have to skip the 9 a.m. Twin Towers observation deck tour, thanks to the stunt your classmate pulled," he said, feeling satisfied with the humiliation this student would suffer from his peers, likely for the rest of the school year. "But, on a happier note, we can resume our tour at the Empire State Building at 11:30 am. That is, if no one else decides to jump into the Hudson."

At 8:46 a.m. Mr. Thomas heard a student yell, "Oh my God!"

Robert Thomas and his eighth grade class watched as a plane crashed into the North Tower of the Twin Towers skyscraper. They all stood, petrified with horror, as a second plane crashed into the South Tower less than twenty minutes later. Robert Thomas and his class did not make any part of their tour that day. The ferry that had shuttled them across the Hudson to Manhattan returned them safely to

Hoboken from where they watched the collapse of first one tower and then the next. Robert Thomas was not the only person to wonder about Joshua and the stunt he had pulled.

"What if he hadn't fallen in?" The question seemed to reverberate amongst the eighth grade students. "Instead of the fool, his stunt had made him the hero," Mr. Thomas said to himself, as he observed a shaken, but proud Joshua sitting next to Sara. Joshua was her hero. Joshua was everyone's hero today.

Dresden, Germany

Fall 2011

"No, my father was Polish," I overheard Charlie tell Thomas von Marschalkt as I slowly awoke from whatever state of unconsciousness I had drifted into. My body felt so tired I just wanted to sleep. Rubbing my eyes didn't help, they felt as though someone had lined them with sandpaper. I wondered how long I had been asleep.

"Ah, and your girlfriend, does she have relatives here?" I heard the old man ask Charlie. It sounded strange to be referred to as some-one's girlfriend. It had been a long time since anyone referred to me as their girlfriend. Charlie didn't miss a beat, at least not on the outside. Maybe he did consider me his girlfriend.

"No, I don't think so, not immediate family at least," Charlie answered as I pressed my head back, closing my eyes again. The sur-real events of the day had not yet settled in my mind; they fluttered about like agitated butterflies.

"When did you come back to Dresden?" Charlie asked Mr. von Marschalkt, whose dog suddenly jumped into the tiny back seat with me and darted up to the rear window, barking furiously.

"Do not mind him, he is a little, ah, soft in the head," the old man said, pointing at his temple, as he turned to smile briefly in my general direction. "It is as though he sees something I do not…always barking at the ghosts," Thomas von Marschalkt chuckled, causing the hairs on the back of my neck to stand up. Watching the agitated Dachshund dart back and forth along the backseat did nothing to ease my already jumpy nerves.

"Stop that now, Heiner," the old man said as he called his small creature to him. The dog quickly jumped back onto the old man's lap, laying down as though nothing had happened. Watching the dog, I turned to stare out the back window.

"What did you see?" I whispered, turning back to look at the dog. "What did you see?"

"And when did your father emigrate…to America?" The old man asked, seemingly to pass the time, as he was forced to share a small space with random strangers.

"I'm not quite sure, actually," Charlie answered, somewhat abashed I could tell, as he nervously ran his fingers through his hair. Now why hadn't I thought to ask where Charlie's parents were from? I guess it just hadn't seemed relevant. It wasn't something that seemed important, but maybe it would have come up later. "I know it was sometime before the war, though…he, uh, he never really spoke about his life in Europe, and for some reason I never thought to ask. None of us did actually, come to think of it. I never heard my mom talk about his past." I could see Charlie's bright red ears from the back seat, they appeared even larger than normal.

"Ah, I see…I did not know my father lived until I was…oh, about five or six. My mother was, how would you say in English, hired help…a maid on the estate." Why the strange little old man turned around to wink at me, I don't know, but he managed to make me feel less than comfortable. Somewhere I had the urge to slap his face. His wink said a lot more than his crooked mouth.

"You know, it is the same story one hears around the world… in America too, no? Rich man, poor girl…and then a baby." He laughed. At least the old man could find humor in his past, which was more than I could say for my own. God, how I wished myself out of our cramped little car, a wheeled coffin that smelled like a damp dog. Eyeing the little beast with its upturned legs, occasionally twitching on its master's leg, I caught Charlie's brief glance through the rear view mirror, and managed to give him a half-hearted smile. At least he was here with me. Charlie was right all along, I did need him here. Not just here though. I needed him. And it wasn't just the great sex.

The oversized dwarf was quiet for a while. I was sure he had finished discussing the infidelity of his father when he again began to speak.

"He, my father, recognized me as an official heir….I was still a child. My mother was killed by a bomb and I was lucky to survive." Thomas von Marschalkt wiggled himself free of his jacket and held up his right arm, showing us a one inch thick scar that ran along the length of his arm.

"I was dug out of the bunker, the only one to survive." Listening to this heavily accented speech, I wondered how much he would know about Anna and Jakub. Would he have been old enough to know? Maybe Anna or someone else had told this half-brother, as he called himself, about Jakub? I could feel my armpits begin to perspire from the excitement. Clearing my throat, I tried to find an opportune time to interrupt mister motor-mouth, who rambled on like an open faucet. His topic had now jumped to the local hunting society he belonged to.

"Uh, excuse me, Mr. von Marschalkt," I sheepishly said. The old man turned to look at me as though he had forgotten I was crammed in behind his seat. "Did you, happen to know anything about a man named Jakub? A man Anna may have been involved with?" I felt a large lump in my dry throat that made it difficult to swallow. What business of mine was any of this anyway? Hearing myself ask about Anna, a woman I didn't know, and her love life, seemed absurd and even a tad voyeuristic. It had fueled my sexual desire for Charlie, hadn't it? But I'd come a long way, too far, not to know. I hardly believed the woman existed, let alone that she could possibly still be alive. Were we really going to figure out the mystery of Anna and Jakub? Maybe Jakub came back for Anna? Was she possibly married to him right now?

Holding my breath, I watched the old man look up and try to retrieve ancient memories.

"Jakub," he said, stroking his dog. "No," he said flatly without turning around. "I have never heard of him." I exhaled audibly, sinking back into the seat of the car. My heart sank at the thought that Anna did not live with Jakub.

"So she never found him," I whispered to myself, looking down at my backpack, remembering the words from the woman at the graveyard. Why was I supposed to find Anna? Rummaging through my backpack, I reassured myself that I still had the letter. This was the second time I checked. Somehow I just knew I was missing something obvious—some missing piece of the puzzle was staring me right in the face. But then again, I sometimes walk into closed glass doors. Annoyed with myself, I leaned my head back and thought of Abe. He was always good at times like this. He knew me, didn't judge me too harshly. He was my brother after all, he shouldn't. Abe would definitely think this was an insane adventure, but he would still support me. I had to laugh, envisioning the dinner conversation between Sheila, my father, and Abe as they discussed me. Likely they'd have a shrink waiting at the airport and have me committed to an institution on the spot. My laugh caught in my throat, remembering what my father had told me once about Sheila. She had actually spent some time in an institution as a young woman. Some traumatic experience in Australia she'd never talked about. So, there I had it, insanity runs in the family. A rapid thudding sound, followed by cursing from the driver's seat, tore me from my fantasy world, as Charlie maneuvered the Fiat to the side of the road.

"Damn it….it'd be just my luck…damn it…," Charlie swore, kicking the left rear tire that was as flat as a pancake. "What the heck did I drive over?"

"Probably nails or glass…back at the estate," the old man offered with a chuckle, peering down at the flattened tire. His dog relieved itself on the tire before heading off into the forest at high speed. "He'll be back," the old man said, reminding me of a line from one of my favorite Arnold Schwarzenegger movies.

"God damn it, we're in the middle of nowhere," Charlie cursed again, kicking the tire again. "And damn it, my cell phone's dead… you have yours, Diana?"

"Yeah, I have mine. I mean, no I left it at the hotel, damn it," I swore myself. We both turned to stare at Mr. von Marschalkt.

"Don't look at me, I don't have one of those things," he said, walking off in the direction his dog had run. Charlie and I both heard the humming sound of a motorcycle engine approaching before we saw it coming around the bend in the road.

"He can help us," I said, frantically waving at the rider with both arms. We were so close to Anna I could hardly stand it.

"Hi, uh, we need help…you don't speak English do you?" I asked the man clad from head to toe in black leather, matching his black Harley.

"Sure do, Ma'am," the man answered in perfect American English, pulling off his helmet to smile at me.

"Oh, thank God," I said, feeling a cool wave of relief wash over me. Really, what were the odds? Here we were stranded in the middle of who knows where with one of Snow White's oversized-dwarves and an American comes riding along on his motorcycle. Almost like a movie. But this was real. I'd met more Americans here than Germans. There's something about meeting a fellow American in a foreign country that brought me just a little bit closer to home.

"Looks like you got yourselves a flat," the man chuckled with a voice similar to Morgan Freeman's. Bending down, he touched the flattened tire. "There's a gas station, just a couple of kilometers from here, I'll go on down there and see what I can do for you all." He was already strapping his helmet back on before I could thank him. We both watched as our helmeted hero rode off to save us.

We didn't have to wait long for our hero to return, closely followed by a tow truck. The motorcycle man pulled up alongside me and smiled from behind his helmet.

"This guy's gonna take real good care of you," he said pointing at the tow truck driver. I liked the sound of his smooth voice. It had a calming effect on my frayed nerves.

"Hey, thanks…thank you so much for all of your help." I offered him a hand which he shook without hesitation.

"No problem…I'm Jerry, by the way," he said, handing me a card.

"Diana," I said, taking his card. "Are you doing Europe on a Harley?" I hazarded a guess, looking over to his machine.

"I'm preaching through Europe…thought I'd give it a shot over here again, relive some of my youth." Jerry smiled at me with straight white teeth, a sharp contrast to the beautiful mocha color of his skin.

"Wow, that's…that's…really great," I said, impressed with the concept. I'd never have the guts to do something like that.

"Look, I've gotta get going. I've got a group of kids waiting for me at the lake. You all be safe now, and God bless," the preacher man said to us just as Mr. von Marschalkt reappeared from the woods with his dog. Raising his hand briefly, the mobile preacher started his engine and drove off.

"Hey, thanks again," Charlie called out after our two-wheeled knight. Part of me envied motorcycle man's free spirit as he drove off with so much purpose, as though he knew exactly what life expected from him. I had never had that. Looking at Charlie, I wondered if I did now. With a sigh I turned and walked back to the little Fiat whose tire had already been replaced.

Dresden, Germany

June 1944

"It has always bothered me," the Baroness spoke in no more than a whisper, dabbing at her chin with her one functional hand. Anna looked up at her mother, hesitant to ask her what it was that had always bothered her. She had learned from experience if one wanted the Baroness to divulge anything, it was best to feign a certain amount of indifference. Anna gently laid her spoon down beside her soup bowl filled with a strange concoction of left over vegetables, potatoes and unidentified meat. These days she did not question where it was the meat came from. She was grateful there was any to be had at all. "For years I resented him, more than her," her mother continued, as though she were alone in the sitting room. Anna inhaled sharply as a chill ran down her spine. She had sat across from her mother during supper for weeks, often in complete silence. She did not recall when exactly it was that she had begun sharing the evening meal with her mother in the sitting room. The formal dining room had proved less comfortable for her mother, and there was something rather impersonal and stiff about it. With her father and Dieter gone much of the time these days, and Sigrid, Lena, and Maria taking their supper with the children in the kitchen, it seemed impractical to serve a meal in the large dining room, located a farther distance from the kitchen.

Anna listened to her mother clear her throat. She could still not get used to her mother's distorted features, which reminded her of a mask she wore to Fasching one year, where half of the face turned down in perpetual sadness and the other half raised up in cheery playfulness.

"Not that Mama has a cheerful side," Anna said silently to herself, chewing on a dry lump of bread, more closely resembling wood shavings than anything edible.

"I should not have agreed to this foolish bargain...but I was young...naïve...and really I had no say in the matter," her mother said, staring into her soup as though seeing the past reflected therein.

"I have lived with Sigrid, in the same house for all these years, but the sins of her past have come to haunt her. Sigrid too must watch as your father beds another." Anna stole a glance at her mother. Who was this woman her mother spoke of? It could not possibly be Lena. A sudden realization struck her as she saw what burden this haggard woman had carried all these years.

"I would be a different woman today if it were not for Sigrid...for their foolish behavior." Anna sensed her mother's eyes on her as she spoke. Looking up at the gaunt face with deep set eyes, Anna wondered why this latest revelation, if that is what it was, did not cause her more distress.

"I was there the night he left...it was I who persuaded him to leave," her mother continued as she stared across at her daughter. It took a moment for Anna to realize it was Jakub her mother now spoke of. Choking on the last of her bread, she coughed as her mother observed her with an unnerving silence. So much had happened since her beloved Jakub disappeared all those years ago. Somewhere she still clung to a deep rooted hope that one day they would be united, but these were her private thoughts, ones she never shared with anyone. Never had she believed her mother would reveal any more information about Jakub.

"It was you he expected in the hayloft that evening, Anna. Do not think for a moment I was not aware of your...relations...with this young man. He was a thief, of that I am certain...but worse, a Jew who would have destroyed your life." Anna was dumbstruck as she listened to her mother speak of Jakub in such a manner. Her throat felt dry, and a pain shot suddenly through her chest. "I could not allow you to be so foolish Anna...you could not repeat Sigrid's mistakes!" Her mother said with finality, as though divinity had been bestowed upon her. "I gave him one evening to leave...for this you can thank your father. I would have had him arrested immediately had your father not intervened." Anna felt a wave of rage rise up in her, but somehow she managed to stem the flood of accusations and insults she desired to scream at her mother. She needed to hear her mother speak the truth. She needed to know the events that led up to Jakub's abrupt departure.

"If he were ever to return, or attempt to make contact with you, I assured him the authorities would be notified immediately. I had contacted the authorities and alerted them of a pressing matter which required their attention the following morning. Your father informed me that this common thief made the wise decision to go that evening," her mother said, dropping her spoon into her dish with a loud clang, spraying soup onto her black dress. Anna did not move to assist her mother. She sat motionless, caught between conflicting emotions to tear her mother's head off, and to remain silent until her mother had finished confessing her horrible sins.

"I did not think...you would mourn his departure...for so long, Anna." The Baroness spoke haltingly, as though weighing her own words. "I believed you would eventually let reason guide your actions. That you too could be persuaded to agree to an appropriate... marriage." Again her mother cleared her throat and swallowed hard. "Maria has thrived in her marriage to Dieter, the children are proof of the successful match." Anna had remained silent for too long. She could no longer dam the rage that spilled over.

"S...s...successful match?" Anna yelled out, barely resisting the urge to slap her mother across her half frozen face. Her mother looked up with one raised eyebrow, resembling an eagle coolly studying its prey.

"H...h...how could you do that, M...M...Mama? After all th... th...that you have b...b...been through with Papa?"

The Baroness tilted her head and glared at her daughter with narrowed eyes.

"It is *because* of what I have suffered that I do not want my daughter to suffer."

Anna heard her heart pounding in her crimson colored ears. "Y…y…you have n…n…never concerned yourself with w…w…what is best for m…m…me! It was always appearances y…y…you concerned y…y…yourself with!" Anna shouted, almost as furious about her stuttering as she was with her mother. "Y…y…you should be ashamed of y…y…yourself, Mama. You disrespect y…y…yourself…staying with Papa!" Anna expected to incite her mother's ire, but instead she watched as her mother's shoulders sagged and her face seemed to droop further.

"No, Anna, you do not understand," her mother spoke, shaking her head. "How could you understand? You have been allowed freedoms I did not have. This is a different time. A very different than when I was young." Anna had never heard or seen her mother so vulnerable. "Some day, Anna…some day you *will* understand…not now."

"W…W…Why are you t…t…telling me this now?" Anna asked the woman with a thousand secrets. She could not figure out what had prompted her mother to reveal this information she had obviously safeguarded for so long.

Loud footsteps rushing down the hall interrupted Anna's thoughts.

"P…P…Papa…you are home," Anna called out when her father opened the door, closely followed by Otto, his most experienced farm hand. Papa trusted Otto with his life, as Otto trusted Papa.

"Anna, leave the room…I need a moment with your mother… alone." Anna stared at her father. Something in his expression revealed a fear he was trying hard to suppress. "Now," her father ordered when Anna hesitated.

"Yes, P…P…Papa." Anna left the room and closed the door behind her. Listening from behind closed doors was something Anna was used to. She saw no reason to change that now.

"They are coming, Baroness. Gerold was in the city. They have been going from house to house," Anna heard Otto say. Otto had been with the von Marschalkt family for as long as Anna could remember.

"So let them come, they will not find her…if you hurry. We have made it this far. Franz, you shall keep the girls out of this." Anna heard her mother speak. What was all this about she wondered? Who were they talking about? When her father opened the door to exit the sitting room Anna had already slipped behind the door and hidden herself in a small storage space beneath the staircase, as she had done so often as a child.

"There are too many lies, too much deception," Anna whispered to herself as she crouched among the brooms in the musty space that seemed so much larger when she was a child. She heard footsteps running up the staircase. Anna waited for a few minutes and was about to leave her hiding place when she heard hushed voices and footsteps coming back down the stairs. She was unable to make out the hushed voices, but was sure one was a woman's voice.

"It will only be for a little while," Anna heard Otto speak reassuringly to someone. Whose was the woman's voice? Anna was sure she had never heard the voice before. Carefully, she pushed the door back a centimeter and peered down the hall. She caught a brief glimpse of a woman with long, curly, dark hair, just as she disappeared into the kitchen with the Baron and Otto. Anna could not recall ever having seen this woman before. Could this be the woman Mama spoke of she wondered? The one who shared Papa's bed? But then why was Otto involved? Could this be Otto's wife? Anna had never heard him speak of a wife. Anna crept out of hiding and followed the strange party at a safe distance. She watched as the woman ran to keep up with Otto and her father's long stride.

Anna watched the strange threesome enter the barn. What in heaven's name were they up too? Naturally, Anna felt she needed to get to the bottom of this mystery. Quickly, she ran around to the back of the barn, and entered through the backdoor, which could not be seen from the main house. It took her eyes a moment to adjust, but she could find her way around in the barn in the darkest of nights. She heard movement above her and knew the three had climbed into the hayloft.

"What are you doing, Papa?" Anna whispered to herself as she climbed up the back ladder, hoping her father would not detect her. She could feel the pulse in her neck as she slowly climbed the ladder, stepping over the rung she knew creaked with the slightest pressure. Anna had not been up to the hayloft for quite some time. In the past she had visited the hayloft often to sense Jakub's presence, but had stopped visiting when she no longer felt him there. Oddly though, today she sensed his presence, as though he waited for her in the soft hay. From her vantage point Anna could watch, undetected, as Papa and Otto helped the strange woman climb onto the perfectly stacked hay. Anna's hair stood on end when she noticed the infant the woman cradled at her breast. An instant later the woman disappeared, as though consumed by the haystack.

"They have hidden her inside the hay," Anna whispered to herself in the same moment as she watched Papa and Otto stack bales of hay over the spot the woman had disappeared. The men worked in silence. Anna could sense the urgency in their actions. Anna watched as Otto bent down towards the hay, whispered something inaudible, and abruptly left the hayloft with Papa. Anna felt a shiver run down her spine and the hairs on the back of her neck still stood on end. The thought of a woman with an infant, entombed in hay, did not fit in her own already illogical, absurd life. Quickly climbing down the back ladder, she inadvertently stepped on the squeaky rung. She hoped her father and Otto had already exited the barn, but she couldn't be sure. Anna stopped, held her breath, and listened. She could hear her heartbeat in her ears. Aside from the normal whispers of the old barn, all was silent. Even the woman in the hay was silent, as was her infant.

Anna poked her head out of the back of the barn. Stepping out into the daylight, she nearly collided with Otto as her eyes adjusted to the light.

"What are you doing, Anna, ah, Fraulein von Marschalkt?" Otto looked as though he had seen a ghost. Anna returned his stare with equal horror, unable to answer. What would Papa say if he knew she had followed him to the barn? He would be furious, this much she knew. Mama had explicitly told her father to keep Anna and Maria out of whatever was going on here, although Anna had her suspicions.

Anna's mind raced to find an appropriate explanation for Otto, whose facial expression changed from one of surprise to one of suspicion.

"How much did you see?" he asked, as Anna watched his face transform yet again to one resembling an enraged reptile. "Answer me, girl." Anna studied this man who had been a part of her life for so long, yet whom she knew so little about. Frustrated with the lies and deception she had lived with for the last years, Anna studied Otto for a moment. The terror she had felt dissolved like honey in warm milk. She realized what her father might think did not concern her anymore. It was he and Mama, and even Sigrid, who should be ashamed and filled with horror.

"I have seen enough," Anna replied, equally venomous, "It is time you explain yourself, Mr. Wichtelmann."

Letter 14   *Dresden, 14. June 1944*

My Beloved Jakub,

I sensed your presence yesterday, more intensely than ever before. I had not felt you in a long time, Jakub. The war moves closer every day. It will not be long, Papa says, before it is here in Dresden. I have awaited its arrival with constant trepidation. The soldiers around us and the frequent sirens are constant reminders that the war, which seemed so far away, is closing in. Oddly, the fear that surrounded me all these years has vanished, leaving in its place a void which, in itself, frightens me more than the war ever did. Jakub, with each day that passes a small part of my spirit dies. I am not even sure that I have much spirit left. How can one view life with such ingratitude, when there are those who suffer through so much to survive.

Just yesterday, Jakub, in the hayloft, I witnessed Papa and Otto hiding a woman with an infant between stacks of hay. It was a woman I had never seen before, and, as you can imagine, my curiosity was piqued. I had my suspicions as to why she was being hidden, but not who she was. As fate should have it, I suppose, I ran into Otto behind the barn and he confronted me. I was torn between revealing the truth or hiding behind a shroud of deceit once again. His aggressive behavior pressed my conscience in the direction of truth. Once I revealed what I had witnessed, Otto was more than willing to comply with my demand, which, as you would understand, was not much— merely the truth. Jakub, I can no longer tolerate deception and lies. Reluctantly, Otto explained the woman hiding in the hay, her name is Louisa, is the wife of his late brother Hartmut. Hartmut passed away a number of months ago from an infected bullet wound. Otto warned me, or rather threatened me, not to reveal their whereabouts to the soldiers who would likely arrive that same day. When I pressed him on the nature of Louisa's crime—why otherwise should she be hidden away—Otto's anger faded and fear took hold of his being. It was then that my suspicions were confirmed. "She is a Jew," I said to him. He did not answer, but only nodded. It was her mother who was a Jew. Somehow she managed to remain in hiding, while all others in her family had disappeared. It is horrible, Jakub. This woman lives in fear every moment, not just for her life, but for the life of this infant she gave birth to in a small space behind Otto's mother's closet. Otto could not, for the sake of humanity, and love for his brother, betray this woman, or his niece. I have promised Otto my silence if he should not betray me to Papa. I believe he shall honor his promise, as I will mine.

As it turns out, Otto was correct about the soldiers. They did arrive again, possibly ten of them. The soldiers searched the estate, but unlike the first time they ravaged our home, their efforts seemed less enthusiastic, almost indifferent. It is as though they knew their role in life would soon change, despite the broadcasts heard over the airwaves. The woman, Louisa, and her child were not found, as it was such a clever hiding spot. I have no idea as to her current whereabouts, but I am certain she no longer hides in the hayloft. Papa seems to exhibit a talent in helping people disappear. That Papa could be persuaded to assist a desperate woman does not surprise me—he seems to have a pathological weakness for women. What surprises me though, and I would not have believed it had I not heard it myself, is that somehow Mama was involved in this whole scheme. Did Papa mislead her in some way? Did she feel a debt towards Otto, who, I was told, risked his own life to save mine? Or has she come to understand the true nature of this war? Has the inhumanity of it all finally pierced her normally impenetrable exterior? Is it possible a soul survives in this hard woman? Over the years my feelings toward Mama have fluctuated. I am never quite certain of the woman she truly is or could have been.

Jakub, my rational mind has given up on us, on you. For years I managed to convince this part of my mind of a certain future together. One where the horrors of this war were but a distant memory— I realize now this war shall never become a distant memory, but will burn in the minds of men for countless generations to come. It is only my irrational psyche which continues to hold on to a future with you. How you could ever find your way back to me seems unfathomable, but somewhere this foolish heart of mine cannot bear to let you go. As I sit here alone I wonder if it is my destiny, my fate, to walk this earth in solitude. All these years I have waited for you, Jakub. How many more shall there be?

\It is late and my head aches. Tonight I will rest and tomorrow I will rise again to face yet another day. May you be safe, wherever you are.

Love Eternally,
Anna v. Marschalkt

Post Script: I am unable to push the image of this woman hidden in the haystack with an infant from my mind. I feel my heart beat with fear as I think of all she has lost. What more shall be lost?

Anna looked out into the dark night sky and, for one brief moment, she was sure that Jakub too looked up at this same sky. Carefully, she held the candle to her letter and watched it quickly alight, then dropped the ashes into the bucket by her side. Anna smiled without joy as she stared down at the ashes.

"A promise is a promise," she whispered. The letter could not leave her room, this much she knew. It would be foolish not to burn it. What if it were to fall into the wrong hands? Gathering the ashes, she carefully placed them into her empty green glass bottle. "If I am mad enough to believe you actually read these letters, Jakub, then I am mad enough to believe you can make sense of these ashes." Anna felt tears well up in her eyes as she briefly wondered what her son would have looked like now. Why she always thought of him when she placed her letters in the bottle was unclear to her, but somehow it had become a ritual for her. "So I do not forget either of you," she whispered to the cool bottle. Anna carried the bottle to her bed with her and placed it safely beneath her pillow.

The following morning Anna walked slowly to her stream by the woods with the bottle tucked beneath her coat. She had sense enough not to ride into the city, it was too dangerous now. She did not need Papa to remind her of that these days. Pulling the letter from beneath her coat, she kissed the bottle and tossed it into the stream. She watched as it traveled no more than five meters only to become entangled in roots along the bank. Watching as the current gently tried to free the bottle, she resisted the urge to free the bottle and toss it again. Eventually Anna left the bottle to its fate. She would return every day for seven days to watch as her bottle continued the struggle to free itself. On the seventh day the bottle was gone. Anna would never know a farm hand had found the bottle, and, realizing it was empty, deposited it in the woods where it remained. Eventually the forest floor would reclaim it.

Travels of Letter 16
Savannah, Georgia
July 2008

"I take you, Herbert Thomas Johnston, as my beloved husband," the aging woman spoke solemnly as she looked out at the sea. She had sensed his presence again today. "So close, you are so close," she whispered, "so close, yet worlds separate us." She usually felt his spirit connect with hers at some point during the day. She knew Walter thought she was mad. Possibly she was, she thought as she inhaled deeply, trying to remember Herbert's smell. It was easier when she was out here at the shore, especially on a day like this she thought.

"A day like this, Herbie, do you remember?" she asked the waves.

"Mary, are you out here talking to ghosts again? If I were the jealous type I'd think you're cheatin' on me with yer spirit folk," the woman's husband interrupted her, tearing her from the past. Walter smiled at her as he reached for her old hands.

"Old fool, there's just one of them," she replied, as she gently patted her husband's hand. "It was a day just like this, you know," she spoke slowly as though he had never heard her story before.

Walter stood patiently, and silently, as he listened to her story. In his mind he repeated the story, pauses and all, alongside his wife. How many years had he listened to her repeat this story? Could it be fifty-eight? It had become a sacred chant, to revive an ancient spirit, even he felt that much. Walter felt no jealousy, he never had. But then again it wasn't as though a dead man had ever been any sort of threat to his marriage. He had, at moments, felt as though he could never measure up to this enigmatic Herbert he knew so little about, yet had, in a most strange way, shared his wife with for the last fifty eight years. If he had felt a moment of something, possibly inadequacy, Walter had never found the courage to tell his wife about it. Did he even have a right to complain about a ghost? It was Herbert's death after all that brought him to Mary. What would his life have been without Mary, he wondered, as he watched her stare out at the sea.

Mary told Walter her story, almost unaware of his presence. As though in a trance, she relived the day 60 years ago that Herbert was unexpectedly taken from her an ocean away. It was on this beach she had first learned of the news that the military jeep Herbert was riding in had overturned, killing her young husband.

"He survived the war," she spoke, her voice barely louder than a breath, "he survived the war," she repeated in a whisper. Walter watched and waited for the tears to flow down her face, but unlike every other year Mary had come out to this beach to mark the anniversary of her first husband's death, the tears did not come. He waited, almost curious of what should come next. Should he comfort her? Ask her if she was all right, he wondered, as he tried hard to see what it was she saw so many years ago. Who was this faceless man she clung to all these years? As though reading his thoughts, Mary turned to him and looked at him curiously.

"Could you give me a moment, dear?" she asked squeezing his hand briefly as she turned to look back out at the sea.

Mary did not turn around again, she knew Walter had left, but he would be back, he always came back. Mary let her thoughts wander through the hidden paths of her memories.

"It has been a long time, my dear," she spoke to the sea. "Walter has been waiting a long time," her voice sounded foreign. There it was, the smell, it was so distinct she knew he was close, so close she could almost see him. Mary closed her eyes to see him, the way she had done for the last sixty years. At first Herbert's spirit had only revealed itself in her dreams, but for years thereafter he visited her during her waking hours. From behind closed eyes she watched as her Herbert, clean shaven with short trimmed hair, dressed in his uniform, approached her.

"What bothers you, Mary?" Herbert asked as he stood before her in all of his youthful glory, so close she could touch him. She had never tried. Somewhere she knew the moment she tried to reclaim him to her earthly world he would disappear forever.

"You do not come to see me as frequently," she spoke, trying hard to disguise any accusatory tone.

"You do not need me anymore, Mary," he said holding his hand out to her. Mary did not reach for his hand, taking a step back instead.

"I have always needed you. I always will need you," she said, almost pleadingly.

"Mary, my beloved Mary," Herbert smiled, "You have not needed me for a long time."

Mary felt a defensive emotional response swell up inside her. "How can you say these things to me? How can you? I have come here, every year, to be with you," she cried, angry with herself at her emotional outburst.

"Is it not for yourself, Mary? That you come every year? That you search the past for your present?" he asked without malevolence. "Mary, my beloved Mary, it is time for you to let me go. It is time for you to live in the present," he spoke as she sensed his presence begin to weaken.

"No, wait, please, wait, Herbert," she cried, almost reaching for his still outstretched hand. "Wait, we still have so much to talk about," she begged.

"Do not waste your time with death when you have someone waiting for you in life. Death will come, it always comes," he spoke softly.

Mary stood motionless as she looked at Herbert for what she knew would be the last time. She did not understand what overcame her, but she felt as though a blindfold had been removed. One that had blinded her for the better part of her life. He was right. Herbert was right. She had been living, no, that wasn't the right word, she hadn't been living. She had been waiting, every moment of the day, for something that was no more, while life, Walter, and everything else around her, lived each day without her. She was about to speak, say something else to Herbert, but realized with sudden clarity that there was nothing left to say. There hadn't been anything left to say for a long time. It was she who had trapped Herbert from continuing his own journey. It was she who had denied Walter her full attention all these years. Slowly Mary lifted her hand and reached for Herbert's hand. Herbert gently grasped her hand and lightly stroked her weathered cheek and disappeared.

The sky was growing dark when Mary opened her eyes. She knew Herbert was gone. For the first time since his death she did not feel his presence. Mary had feared this moment her whole life. Instead of panic and despair, she felt a sense of closure and peace she never imagined possible. Sitting down in the sand, she watched the sun set on the horizon. Down the beach she noticed Walter, slowly walking towards her with his head bent forward in concentration, repeatedly bending down to pick up something.

"Good old Walter, always cleaning the beach," she said as she watched him approach. She had seen him do this many times, not just at the beach. He couldn't pass by a rogue piece of trash without picking it up. She raised her arm to wave at him. Encouraged by her wave, Walter picked up his pace to join his wife under the quickly darkening sky. For the first time in her marriage to Walter, she realized she never gave of herself the way he did. Walter had given her his heart and soul. She had given him only a small part of her heart. There was still time though, she hoped. Still time to discover what this love could develop into.

Walter stiffly sat down beside his wife, depositing an old green bottle and various other beach litter beside him. Rubbing his aching knee, he placed an arm around his wife who leaned in to his embrace. Walter noticed something different about Mary, something lighter and happier. He wasn't prepared to ask though.

"Oh, Walter, you are a good man," she said as she looked up into his beautiful hazel eyes, "I've never deserved you."

What had happened today during her *visit* with Herbert, he wondered. His wife placed a hand on his knee and massaged his aching joint.

"He is gone," she said, still facing him. Walter did not need to ask what this meant. The difference he sensed in his wife was real. She was his alone, finally, after all these years. He did not regret the wait, but was more than happy to have this ghost, imagined or real, go to whatever great beyond it was bound for. Walter looked up at the beautiful clear evening sky and watched a shooting star race across the heavens. Had he looked up any earlier or any later he would have missed it. He did not have to make a wish, his was already granted.

"Rest in peace, Herbert," he whispered under his breath.

Mary and Walter walked away from the beach together, hand and hand, Walter's heart racing with excitement, Mary's beating full of peace. In his excitement, Walter forgot to dispose of the litter he had found along the beach. A few hours later the tide would reclaim this litter, along with a green glass bottle.

Dresden, Germany
Fall 2011

"You take a right at the next stop light," the old man directed Charlie, who slowed to turn right. "There, just ahead on the right… you see the drive? It is hidden behind the trees." Charlie slowed the car even further as he looked for the hidden driveway Mr. von Marschalkt was pointing to. I felt like a pressure cooker that was about to pop. Scarcely breathing, I reached into my backpack and fingered the letter I had carried across the Atlantic Ocean for just this moment. Feeling the letter, protected by a plastic bag, made me feel better, more secure, but my doubts still found a way to worm themselves into my mind.

"What if this was a hoax? How foolish would I look? Especially after I dragged Charlie into all of it," I whispered to myself, as the feelings of doubt threatened to unleash one of my famous panic attacks. "There is nothing you can do about it now, but breathe," I tried to tell myself. My nervous stomach wasn't calmed by breathing in and out the stale air of a small confined space that smelled like a wet dog, but I did manage to avert my imminent panic attack.

"There. That is it," the old man said, pointing an arthritic finger towards a group of large concrete block buildings. Ah, the eastern European architecture I had only seen on television. The only thing that distinguished one concrete monster block from another was a different colored stripe painted along the top of each one.

"What is this place?" Charlie asked incredulously, leaning forward in the driver's seat to stare up at the blocks of concrete, one of which housed the mysterious Anna von Marschalkt.

"It is a Wohngemeinshaft. It is a, how do you say, living quarters for the old."

Well, jeez, they didn't exactly afford their elderly the most picturesque living quarters, but at least these monstrous concrete blocks were partially hidden by a lush forest. There had to be twenty of these, at least.

"This is her tower," Mr. von Marschalkt said, interrupting my thoughts on former eastern German architecture. He pointed at the building with the orange stripe across the top of it. "This one. Stop the car," he said flatly as Charlie slowed the car to a stop. Before the old man had a chance to roll up his window, his dog once again used the opportunity to escape through the window and disappear in the woods. "He knows this place well," he chuckled, opening the passenger door and heading towards the unappealing concrete block. Charlie and I rushed to follow him.

It was quiet as we waited for the gray door on the third floor to open. We had climbed up three sets of stairs before we reached the apartment in which Anna von Marschalkt resided. Who the heck puts elderly in high rises without elevators? What are they supposed to do if they're in a wheelchair? Maybe the first floor is designated for those in wheelchairs, I thought, holding my breath as I waited for Anna to open the door. I had to use the bathroom. Nerves, damn it. Hearing the turning of a lock from behind the door only intensified my desire for a bathroom.

When the door opened I was half-disappointed and half-relieved to see an old man on the other side. He stared inquisitively from me to Charlie, but his expression changed and turned to a smile of recognition as his eyes came to rest on Thomas von Marschalkt. Charlie squeezed my hand as the two men shook hands and exchanged, what I thought, were likely pleasantries and an explanation as to why these two strangers stood at his doorstep. The old man at the door looked at us more curiously as Thomas von Marschalkt continued to speak.

"I wish I spoke German," I whispered to Charlie, regretting that I had never studied any foreign language properly. The French classes I completed in high school would barely help me find a bathroom. But then this was Germany, and not France. I couldn't find a bathroom here either. "But then again, everyone speaks English here, right?" I whispered, remembering Anna's letter was written in English.

Thomas von Marschalkt turned to us. "He says Anna will return shortly...he would like to invite you in," he translated for us, as the old man at the door nervously invited us in with an exaggerated, sweeping arm gesture.

"Does he, uh, speak English?" I asked. It was pretty amazing, to come to a foreign country where most everyone spoke English, but then again, many of the people I had met *were* Americans.

"I am not sure how good his English is. There is not much opportunity for him to speak it here. Mostly old Germans live here...who do not leave much." Thomas von Marschalkt explained, following the lanky old man into a formal sitting room.

"Please, please, sit," the old man offered with a heavy accent, nervously pulling out a carton of cigarettes. So he does speak English, I thought, sitting down on a stuffy sofa that looked as though it had been covered with my grandmother's floral drapes. I didn't want to appear rude, but I couldn't keep myself from looking around the apartment. There were photos everywhere. My eyes came to rest on an old wedding photograph, but from where I sat I couldn't figure out if it was this same old man who sat across from me, shakily holding a cigarette to his lips.

"I am Dr. Wenke, ah, Werner Wenke," he explained, awkwardly extending his hand first to Charlie and then to me.

"Charlie, Charlie Gordon, and this is my girlfriend, Diana," Charlie didn't hesitate to call me his girlfriend. I watched as again the crimson color I had become so used to crept into his face and ears. I nodded at the old man, as I squirmed on the sofa, trying to will away the urge to urinate. I was surprised by how warm and strong his handshake had been. Somehow I had expected a frail, cold hand.

"I understand you have something for my wife. Or is it you desire something from her?" My heart sank as I stared at the fidgety old man who seemed to twitch all over his body. His English was excellent for one who did not know much of it. He was obviously not the Jakub from Anna's letter. What happened to him? What happened to Jakub? Would I be able to ask Anna? Would she even be willing to speak of this Jakub I wondered, as Dr. Wenke offered first me, and then the men, a cigarette which I graciously declined,

"Actually, ah," I tried to clear away the lump that had formed in my dry throat, "actually both, but may I use your bathroom first, please?" This was an emergency.

Alone in the bathroom, I realized I had no idea how to explain to this man, Anna's husband, what it was I had found an ocean away. And then there was the matter with the woman in the graveyard, how to explain her?

"Anna will return soon. She is at, how do you say, where books are," I heard Dr. Wenke say as I returned from the bathroom."

"A library?" Charlie asked with hunched shoulders, not quite sure if that was what Dr. Wenke meant. I wondered what type of a doctor this old man was. He was a smoker, so likely he was professor of something. What medical doctor would smoke?

"Yes, yes, but of course, a library. The van should be back in the next hour…that woman goes every week. She can never get enough of her books," Dr. Wenke said with the look of a man who is completely smitten with a woman. I noticed it wasn't just his face, but his whole body language changed when he spoke of Anna. Much of the twitchy nervousness just wasn't there, and his voice sounded more smooth, his accent less harsh. What love can do, I thought to myself looking over at my Charlie. That is what he was now, my Charlie, with his beautiful dark curls and warm hands.

A few minutes of awkward silence passed. Thomas von Marschalkt had gone outside in search of his dog and Charlie, sitting straight up on the sofa, looked as though he would fall asleep at any moment. How was that possible? How could men do that? Just fall asleep when there was so much to think about. And me, with my incessant hand wringing, I looked as nervous as the chain-smoking Dr. Wenke. I couldn't think of what to say to this man without sounding completely crazy. I didn't even know if he knew about Jakub. Maybe it was a secret love affair between Anna and Jakub? I couldn't help myself, I had to ask.

"So, uh, Dr. Wenke, do you happen to know of a man by the name of Jakub?" The old doctor looked at me with a blank stare. Nothing in his expression revealed anything either way. "From your past, say from 1946," I clarified as Dr. Wenke slowly shook his head.

"No, I do not think so...but then my memory is not what it used to be." This was the first time I saw the old man smile. "So, if you don't mind me asking, how did you and your wife meet?"

It was more than curiosity that drove me to ask. Something inside forced me to plow ahead like an old steam engine. I needed to get to the bottom of this insane puzzle. The old man chuckled and then laughed heartily as he blew smoke from his cigarette.

"I nearly broke her face the first time I met her." He spoke as though he saw some faraway place. "How we came together I do not understand myself. I tended to an injury she had once, and looked after her mother...but why she would have me I will never know. Lucky, yes?" So he was a physician I thought, somewhat amazed. The old man nervously lit up yet another cigarette. The air in the room looked blue from all of the trapped smoke that had no place to escape.

"Just what is it...exactly...that you need from my wife?" For a split second I did not see the nervous, twitchy old man before me, but a competent, caring doctor. As quickly as the vision flickered before my eyes, it disappeared again. Shaking my head to clear my mind, I didn't know if it was the smoke or nerves, I reached into my backpack. I would have to explain myself sometime, why not now I thought, still digging around in my backpack to retrieve Anna's letter.

Removing the precious letter from the plastic bag, I smoothed it out and handed it to Dr. Wenke. He did not look at the letter, but looked straight at me, pulling a pair of reading spectacles from his shirt pocket. The old man stood up and moved himself to a chair beside a small oak dining table, his back turned to me. For a few minutes I sat in silence wondering if he, like Charlie who snored lightly beside me, had fallen asleep too. Maybe it hadn't been such a good idea to show him the letter. Quietly I stood up and approached him. He was definitely not asleep, but staring down at the letter on the table. He did not look up when I sat down beside him.

"She never told me of this Jakub. It was not my business to know, but now I understand." Dr. Wenke looked up at me, all twitches momentarily in check. "Where did you get this?" he asked, his German accent intensifying, as he picked up the letter and waved it slowly in front of his face.

"I don't think you'd believe me if I told you," I answered truthfully. Who would believe a crazy story like this?

Dr. Wenke stood and walked slowly towards the window, pulling out yet another cigarette. The doctor did not speak while he smoked his cigarette. He stared vacantly out of the third story window onto the parking lot below. The uncomfortable silence I experienced made my heart race. What if I had just opened some old wounds this guy didn't even know he had? What if I had now done some irreparable damage to his marriage? Nervously clearing my constricted throat, I wiped my sweaty palms on my pants.

"Now I understand," Dr. Wenke repeated to himself, his mind in a place and time I could not follow. He lit another cigarette. "All these years I wondered. Wondered what it was that made her, how do you say in English, ah, very suddenly change her mind?" I watched him exhale a large cloud of blue smoke. "It was so long ago, but I always wondered. One day she can only be my friend," he chuckled to himself, startling me. "A very distant friend, but I always knew there could be more. I followed her you know. Followed her to France. I would have followed her anywhere. But there was always something…something that kept her from taking that next step. I never knew what it was, who it was." I listened in silence, even Charlie sat up from the armchair he had melted into and appeared mesmerized.

"She could not be with me until she let go, I understand that now. For years I did not understand her resistance, and then I gave up wondering. All that mattered was to be near her. I never knew of another man who stood in my way, in the way of her feelings," Dr. Wenke continued to speak as he looked out the window, occasionally turning to tap the ashes of his cigarette into a tacky star-shaped crystal ashtray. He looked down again at the letter and smiled slowly, as though some age old mystery had been unlocked. "Even the date makes sense. It was shortly thereafter that she unlocked herself, that she became mine."

As I listened to this old doctor speak of his past I wondered why this whole situation didn't seem strange in the least. On the contrary, listening to him speak of Anna only fueled my fascination with her, my passion for her relationship with this mysterious Jakub. Where did this connection come from that I felt for a woman I didn't even know?

"I have never spoken of this," he spoke in a whisper, barely audible to me. The old doctor let out an audible sigh when he turned suddenly, as though realizing he was not alone. For a moment he studied me in silence.

"I am sorry, I speak of matters that occurred long ago. They are of no interest to you." I did not know what to say, how to tell him that this was of the greatest interest to me. I wanted to shout at him, tell him this woman, this Anna, interested me more than anything right now. But how could I tell this old man about this strange, possibly unhealthy, infatuation? That I had traveled across the Atlantic Ocean to satisfy a *curiosity?* No, it was more than curiosity. A thought struck me as I watched this old man, Dr. Wenke. He did not seem to doubt for an instant that some other Anna may have written this letter.

"I...thank you for sharing this information." The old man seemed strangely at peace. As he read the letter I had wondered what sort of impact it might have on him. Was it was even my place to involve him? The last thing I expected was any sort of gratitude.

"Well, what did you expect, Di?" my little inner voice rationalized, "did you think the old guy was gonna fly into a fit of jealousy?" No, it wasn't jealousy I thought about. I had worried Dr. Wenke, a man I had just met, might be disappointed in the woman he lived with, the woman he loved. The last thing I wanted to do was to paint Anna, the woman I had unilaterally formed some bizarre bond with, in a negative light.

"I will fetch some tea and cookies," the old man said, nervously extinguishing his cigarette and removing his reading glasses, tucking them back into his shirt pocket. "You two will be alright in here?" I think the poor guy needed a moment to himself. Charlie, awake, yet having resumed a catatonic-type stare, nodded at Dr. Wenke. My head was spinning. I needed a breath of fresh air to clear my mind, which was impossible in this smoke-filled room. Maybe I could open the window a bit I thought. Moving across the room to search for a window that could be opened in these purely utilitarian cement blocks, I tried a latch only to find it rusted in place.

"Damn," I swore aloud, taking in a deep, smoky breath. From the third story window of this atrocious Soviet-era concrete tower, I watched as a large white van approached.

Dresden, Germany

January 1945

"Is she asleep?" Sigrid whispered, fearful she might wake the Baroness.

"Yes, finally. I gave her some more chamomile tea for the chest congestion. I think it may have helped," Anna whispered, gently closing the door to her mother's bedroom.

"Are the ch...ch...children asleep? It is s...s...so quiet," Anna said as she turned to face Sigrid, who nodded silently. Anna had not felt the house settle into such a state of silence in as long as she could remember. With the makeshift barn downstairs and many small children typically running through the house, it was unusual that there should be no sound at all.

"Like the quiet before the storm," Sigrid said darkly as she reached for Anna's hand. Anna did not know why, but Sigrid's words sent shivers down her spine.

"Do n...n...not say such th...th...things, Siggi. It is n...n...not good to...to summon evil w...w...when it is already s...s...so close," Anna said as she removed herself from Sigrid's grasp and headed towards the stairs.

Sigrid followed Anna down the stairs and into the sitting room where she anxiously paced back and forth.

"W…W…What is it, Siggi?" Anna asked impatiently. "You are m…m…making me nervous with your c…c…constant movement. P…P…Please stop." Sigrid abruptly stopped moving and reached into her apron pocket.

"I have something for you, Anna. I have meant to give it to you for a…for a very long time. Since your birth." Sigrid handed Anna a red gold brooch in the shape of a rose. "I had left it in your room, but I feel you deserve to know who it is from." Anna stared at the brooch she had once seen in her room, but had forgotten about after it disappeared again. "It belonged to my grandmother. I gave your sister her wedding band, and you, Anna, my dear Anna, for you the rose." Sigrid looked distraught as she spoke. "I only wish I had more to give you, both of you." Anna did not know what to say. Her relationship with Sigrid had changed ever since she found out Sigrid was her birth mother. Finding out later that she and Maria were twins further damaged their already tenuous relationship. It was not the revelations, but the deceit that damaged their bond. There had been many times over the last years that Anna wished she could restore the closeness she once felt to Sigrid. So much had transpired; Anna doubted their relationship could ever be the same.

"Siggi, it is b…b…beautiful." Anna's voice cracked as she spoke, betraying the emotions she had tried so hard to hide. Had she been wrong to judge Sigrid so severely? She had, after all, judged her more harshly than her mother who had betrayed Jakub. Possibly it was time for her to learn to forgive.

"There is one more thing, Anna, one more thing I cannot take to my grave." Sigrid had resumed her anxious pacing, clenching her hands before her as she walked. "It has to do with…with the man you believed to love." Anna stared at Sigrid. A dark feeling crept up her spine. What could Sigrid possibly tell her of Jakub she wondered, as this darkness crept into her mind, even her soul.

"T…t…tell me Sigrid, tell me w…w…what you know of Jakub," Anna quietly demanded, as she nervously turned the rose brooch between her damp fingers.

"You blame the Baroness, your mother, for the disappearance of the young man, Jakub." Sigrid spoke with a quivering voice as she turned towards the window, away from Anna, as though unable to face her. Anna watched Sigrid's shoulders rise and fall with each deep breath she inhaled and exhaled.

"Anna, it was I who…who…paid the gardener to watch you with this Jakub…" Sigrid did not hear Anna drop the rose brooch onto the thick rug. "It was I who…who whispered in old Mr. Zimmerman's ear…who gave him the idea that Jakub was a thief." Sigrid did not see Anna's face change to the color of freshly fallen snow. "Oh, Anna," Sigrid cried as she covered her face with both hands, muffling her words. "It was I who convinced your mother to send him away, who told her he was a common thief. I did not want you to make the same mistakes I did. I wanted you to have a better life than I did." Anna listened to Sigrid as the words she had spoken slowly began to make sense.

"I did not expect your mother would want to have him arrested for stealing. I expected her to send him away, back to where he came from, back to Poland. Oh, Anna, thank the gracious Lord your father reasoned with her. Your father gave him a chance, Anna. The Baron made arrangements to have him sent away from you, from here, forever," Sigrid sobbed as she repeatedly pushed a stray hair back from her forehead. With cold rationality Anna glared at Sigrid.

"W…W…Why did mother n…n…not betray your secret to me? W…W…Why did she have me b…b…believe it was her w…w… who sent him away?" Anna looked at Sigrid with eyes that could pierce steel. Sigrid shook her head.

"She did not need to. All she desired, and continues to desire, is that you and Maria accept her as your true mother….as you do," Sigrid spoke softly as she turned towards Anna. "She has won," Sigrid said without resentment. Anna continued to glower at Sigrid as she formed a clear understanding of what had happened so long ago. It was always a competition for Sigrid, Anna thought as she looked at the woman who had changed her life forever.

"You have seared your soul, Sigrid," Anna said without her usual nervous stuttering. It had quickly become apparent to her that she had

411

nothing more to say to this deceptive woman. Anna bent down to pick up the rose brooch and gently placed it on the table before she left the room. Sigrid did not try to stop her.

Anna quietly opened the door to her mother's bedroom. She had already heard her heavy breathing from behind the closed door. Anna could not remember the last time her parents had shared a room. Grateful that her mother was able to find some rest, she wondered if her mother would survive the winter. Every winter the chest congestion seemed to worsen, leaving her weaker, with longer periods to recover. Quietly, Anna set down the heavy pot of steaming water she had carried up from the kitchen, hoping the moist heat might further ease her mother's discomfort. Somehow Anna always believed matters could not get any worse, always finding herself surprised when they did.

"The war rages on, slowly tightening its grip on us, until we all suffocate...and Mama, unable to care for herself, suffers now more than ever," Anna whispered to herself as she watched over her mother with a peculiar protective instinct. Watching her mother sleep, she suddenly wondered what her own son would have looked like as he slept.

"If there are angels, my son, I pray you are one of them," she whispered, gently reaching down to grasp her mother's clammy hand. Her mother emitted a whistling sound as she exhaled, followed by a moan.

Anna sighed deeply and wished her father were here more often to share in the burden of caring for her mother. There were days Anna did not think she could go on. Without Sigrid and Lena helping with the children and her mother she would have gone mad by now, she realized, looking over at Lena who peacefully slept in the rocking chair at the foot of her mother's bed. Anna feared Death's footsteps might claim her mother if she slept unattended for even one night. Together, she and Sigrid had figured out a schedule where she, Sigrid, and Lena would, on alternating nights, hold watch over her mother. On more than one occasion, each of the women swore they had heard the footsteps, which quickly retreated when a metal pot was beat upon with a wooden spoon.

"Tonight," Anna whispered to her mother, "I shall watch over you, Mama." Anna turned and quietly walked over to a gently snoring Lena and lightly tapped her on the shoulder. Lena let out a shriek as she reached for her spoon before realizing it was Anna who stood before her.

"It is only I, Lena," Anna whispered as she squeezed Lena's arm. "Go to your boy, go to Thomas," Anna ordered as she tugged at the maid's arm.

"Yes, alright, yes," Lena answered, still groggy with sleep, as she lifted herself from the chair and quietly exited the room. Anna watched as the shadow of Lena passed through the door and wondered if what her mother had said about Lena was true. Papa could not be the father of Thomas, could he? Fears of war, concern for her mother's health, and just the daily challenge to survive had occupied her mind, leaving little time for Anna to further ponder her father's infidelities.

"Then Thomas would be my brother," Anna said aloud as the realization struck her like a bolt of lightning. Unclear even to herself why she had not thought of what that could mean for the family, Anna breathed deeply, her chest heaving as though it carried a heavy weight.

"Oh, M…M…Mama, what shall b…b…become of us?" she asked the wheezing body of her mother as she leaned back in the rocker and gently rocked.

"I do not know, my daughter," Anna barely heard her mother murmur.

Letter 15   *Dresden 13. February 1945*

My Beloved Jakub,

There is darkness, an indescribable evil, which lurks in the shadows. I can not see it, my love, but I sense it, all around me, waiting. I hear them, again and again. Footsteps...slow and steady. For whom do they come, Jakub? This cannot be the evil I sense–the malevolent beings that tear me from my sleep and hold me prisoner throughout the night. Death itself cannot be evil, it is merely the last step of our journey on Earth. A step each of us must take. But why tonight, Jakub? What is it that beckons both Death and the Devil simultaneously? Is the noose of war finally so tight that the end is near for all of us?

It has been many months since I experienced any such dread. It soothes my soul to share my thoughts with you. It is early yet, not quite 2200 hours, yet an eerie silence weighs down on the house tonight. Mama sleeps peacefully this night, yet I know Death constantly lurks, waiting for its chance to overwhelm her. This is a night where I know sleep shall elude me. It is not often that I sense such unease, yet I know the world around me is filled with indescribable horror and suffering. Sometimes I hear the voices of those tortured souls whose atrocious departure from this world cannot be forgotten. Does this Fuehrer not know what price he makes his Fatherland pay for his insanity? You might call me mad, and others would not disagree with you, but I know those responsible for war, any war, in some place and time, shall have to atone for their crimes. Oh, Jakub, I often wonder where the woman you left behind has vanished to. What hideous woman am I who remains here in this ghastly world? Would you recognize any part of me in her? Would I still recognize you, Jakub? Who is the man I should find if ever you were to return to me? Could we still share the same love, or was this passion reserved for the innocence of youth?

414

It is a cold night, Jakub. The number of animals that reside inside the house seems to have increased. Those that remain in the surrounding buildings are protected by farm hands who, I believe, guard them with their lives. Otto, in particular, has made it his duty to protect Papa's last remaining mare—I have no doubt he would give his life to spare hers. Papa and Dieter returned home late last night. I have not yet spoken to him about the latest developments in Berlin, but if his face is an indicator of how things stand, then we have already lost the war. I can only hope for surrender before all is lost. Just yesterday the

Something outside distracted Anna. Abruptly she stopped writing and looked out her window. Red lights lit up the sky over Dresden just as the sound of air raid sirens wailed through the night sky. For the first time since this war began she knew this was not a drill. The bombs were coming. They were here. Grabbing the small bag she had prepared for just this scenario, she called out to Maria who, together with Sigrid, already hurried the children down the long staircase, followed closely by Lena with a sleepy Thomas in her arms. Anna turned as she descended the staircase to see Dieter, followed by her father who carried her mother.

"Mama, Papa, Maria…," Anna spoke the names of her family members aloud, thereby calming her nerves and ensuring all were accounted for. Thanking some higher power that Papa and Dieter had returned last night, she counted aloud again. In the confusion she felt a hand grasp her own.

"Anna…listen to me, just know that I am…," Sigrid began to speak to Anna, but was interrupted by Maria.

"Siggi, please take the little one." Maria tried to suppress panic as she urgently handed over her youngest daughter, forcing Sigrid to release Anna's hand. Sigrid received the small child and quickly followed Maria out towards the bunker.

Anna looked around the bunker as her father held up his dim light. Her father had two bunkers built across from one another, equidistant from the main house, to ensure that wherever one was on the estate, there would be a bunker to quickly reach. One bunker sat closer to the gardener's vacant house and the other across the large front garden, closer to the stables. Looking around, Anna noticed that Lena and Thomas had been separated from the rest of the family. They must have gone to the other bunker along with Papa's remaining farm hands, Anna thought. Papa, Mama, Maria and the children, Dieter, and Otto, those were the faces she could make out in the dim light.

"Did you tell Sigrid what bunker we are in?" Maria whispered to Anna, who felt a sense of dread spread over her being. Anna shook her head. Sigrid had stopped almost immediately and thrust Maria's youngest daughter into Anna's arms. Sigrid had felt compelled to save the animals still locked on the ground floor of the main house. Not only her father, but surprisingly her mother too, had urged Sigrid to leave the animals and come to the bunker.

Sigrid could not, however, be persuaded to "let the animals perish," as she had said. Anna had watched with a sense of horror as Sigrid, with knitting needles still in her hair, similar to how her mother often forgot them, disappeared into the darkness with her green knit work slung over one shoulder.

"No," Anna answered with a sense of dread. She hoped Sigrid would find her way into this bunker. Despite what Sigrid had done to Jakub, to her, and for as little as Anna had spoken to Sigrid over the last few years, there had never been a crisis in her own life when Sigrid had not been there for her. Suddenly feeling like the small girl who needed comforting, Anna felt tears well up in her eyes that spilled over and could not be stopped.

An eternity, which was in reality no more than a few minutes, passed before a loud, high-pitched whizzing noise filled Anna's ears. This was quickly followed by a violent explosion that shook the bunker and everyone inside it. The high pitched whizzing noise came again and again, always followed by the sound of loud explosions. Anna listened as glass food jars, carefully prepared and stored in the bunker for just such an attack, rattled against one another, threatening to shatter.

The whizzing noises became more frequent, as were the subsequent explosions that followed the impact of the bombs. The smell of smoke that seeped into the bunkers stung Anna's nostrils. Strangely, she did not fear for herself, but mourned all those perishing in this senseless war. It was the young innocents she mourned the most. Closing her stinging eyes she prayed for the first time in a very long time, almost certain whatever higher power existed had long since abandoned her Fatherland. With her eyes firmly squeezed shut, she prayed, still holding Maria's infant in her arms. Her life did flash before her eyes, as it had once before, but this time it wasn't only Jakub's vision she cherished, but that of her whole family. It was in this moment she remembered the half- finished letter to Jakub she would never again see, destroyed by one of the many bombs that fell on Dresden that night.

Two days and nights of bombing left everyone in the bunker rattled and near deaf. Anna did not think she would ever regain her hearing. When she, along with her small party of survivors, emerged from their underground sanctum, they were horrified by the devastation that surrounded them. Anna followed her father as he hurried to the other bunker from which no survivors had emerged. His shouts and calls for help made Anna fear the worst once she caught up to him at the bunker.

"Oh, please no," she whispered aloud as she rushed to aid her father. It was clear a wall of the bunker had collapsed in on itself, due to the proximity of an exploded bomb.

After hours of intensive work, with assistance from surviving neighbors, young Thomas was the first to be pulled from the rubble. He was to be the only survivor from this bunker. For the rest of her life Anna would not forget the horror she felt as one by one, the remaining, lifeless victims, Sigrid and Lena included, were pulled from the destroyed bunker. Anna watched as her father cradled an injured Thomas in his arms. "He *is* Thomas' father," Anna whispered, finally understanding.

Travels of Letter 16
Belfast, Maine
September 2007

He had been riding all night. It was a relief to smell the salty air. He inhaled deeply. The smell of salt mixed with forest evoked a feeling in him that was almost indescribable. Was it happiness? He never really felt happy anymore, everything seemed so trivial, so pointless. But for these few moments, out here, under this unbelievable sky, he did feel God's presence and maybe, just maybe, happiness. Maybe it wasn't all pointless after all. The feeling passed as quickly as it had come, leaving him feeling depressed and worthless again. He could hear the waves now. He knew he was almost home. Wherever home may be for the rest of this night he thought. Jerry rode into a deserted campground at the sea.

"Who would camp on a night like this anyway?" he asked himself. Maybe he should have found a motel, like most other nights. There was something about the ocean, especially the North Atlantic Ocean, that always attracted him. He had spent many a night on beaches throughout the world, but nothing compared to this coastline. These days he spent most of his time within the boundaries of the United

419

States. Preaching overseas wasn't without its dangers, he thought, as he parked his Harley under a large tree.

"Heck, preaching here isn't without its dangers either," he said aloud, remembering the time a group of teenagers in Alabama chased him with baseball bats. Maybe it wasn't my preaching, but the color of my skin they wanted to beat off me. He half-chuckled at the absurdity of life, removing his gloves and helmet and placing them on his seat. Preaching wasn't what it used to be anymore. People didn't want to hear the word of God anymore. Maybe they were just too busy with life, he told himself. Maybe it was time for him to pack it in, it was all pointless anyway. As he drew in another breath, he wished it was light out so he could see the fall leaves. "You will, soon enough," he said to himself as he removed his sleeping bag, hoping it would be warm enough for a fall night in Maine. Unbuckling his saddle bag, he searched for his flashlight, his bologna sandwich, and the Mickey's Big Mouth he kept hidden at the bottom of the bag for just such a night. Jerry touched his coat pocket to make sure he had his cigarettes and lighter. Switching on his flashlight, he ate his sandwich and moved closer to the water to set up a temporary camp.

Standing close to the waters edge he drank deeply, washing away the dry, limp sandwich and the thirst of the day. He always remembered his own father when he drank a beer and smoked his cigarettes. It didn't take him long to realize he was not alone on this beach. He was never sure whether he actually heard the young woman or if it was her presence, her desperation, he sensed. Swinging his flashlight around, he searched for something, he didn't know what. Moving down the shore he found her sitting, drenched and shivering, with a revolver in her hand. She didn't seem to notice his presence, or maybe she just didn't care, he thought.

The girl couldn't be more than seventeen years old, but given the weak flashlight and surrounding darkness, he couldn't really be sure. Without thinking, he unrolled his sleeping bag and placed it around her shaking body. He didn't think it was a good idea to suggest removing her clothing.

"Whadya do that for?" she asked flatly, surprising him when she spoke.

"You're freezin' and gonna catch pneumonia out here, all wet like that," he answered, trying to sound casual.

"Whaddaya care what I catch?" she asked staring straight into his flashlight. Jerry switched off the flashlight and sat down beside her.

"Whaddaya gonna do now, rape me?" she asked in a monotone voice.

"No," he answered, taken aback by the question.

"Do your parents know where you are?" he asked with sincere concern.

"I ain't got any, they're dead" she hissed, obviously annoyed by the question. "What's a black man doin out here late at night anyway?" she asked the darkness.

"How do you know I'm a black man? Everyone's black on a night like this." he answered, concerned about the revolver he had seen in her lap. Was she going to kill herself or someone else?

"You sound black," she said in her monotone voice again. That made Jerry laugh out loud, despite the possible grave situation she, maybe even he, found themselves in.

"What's so funny? You laughin' at me?" she asked, sounding angry.

"No, no, you just surprise me. You're pretty observant," he answered, still laughing. "What's a smart kid like you doin' out here, and soakin' wet to boot?" he asked, hoping his question wouldn't trigger some type of irrational response from the young woman.

"Killin myself. I couldn't shoot myself, so I thought I'd freeze myself, ain't workin though," she said between chattering teeth. Was she crying? Turning the flashlight back on he shone it up at the sky where the light disappeared into the darkness. Resting a hand on her gun, he looked up into the sky.

"You know, I wanted to kill myself once. Actually, sometimes I still want to. We ain't gonna freeze ourselves to death out here just yet, just get ourselves a nasty ole bladder infection," he said still watching the heavens. "Lemme tell you, get one of those and you'd wish yerself dead," he said, slowly lifting the gun from her lap. The young woman did not try to stop him. "Mind if I shoot myself first? I wouldn't wanna clean up yer mess if you do it first," he said, remembering the day he sat in his garage with a pistol in his own lap.

"I told ya, I couldn't shoot myself," she said, irritated with him. That was good he thought. Get angry, let it all out. He had the gun after all.

Together they sat in silence under the moonless sky, an occasional bug passing through the beam of light still pointed skyward. It was the young woman who finally broke this silence.

"Yer already killlin' yerself, smokin those things," she said with a lightness he could detect through the darkness.

"Oh yeah, well how bout you and that bottle you got? A little young to be drinking wine, don't ya think?" he asked as he shone his flashlight at a glass bottle by her feet.

"That ain't mine, it just washed up here." He detected a tone of sincerity in her voice he had not yet heard. Was now the time to ask her why she wanted to kill herself?

The young woman interrupted his thoughts. "They ain't dead ya know, my parents."

"I know," he answered as he emptied the chambers of the revolver and tucked the bullets in his jacket pocket.

"You wanna talk about it?" he asked, wondering whether he was pushing her too hard, too soon."

"No," she said flatly but continued to speak. "He don't love me. He ain't never gonna love me, he told me so." Jerry listened quietly as the young woman poured out her heart and soul, suddenly erupting into loud sobs. Jerry remembered how devastating a young, broken heart could be.

Gently he placed a hand around her body, still engulfed by his sleeping bag.

"I don't know who he is, but God loves you," he said warmly, knowing in his heart that he spoke the truth.

"You some kind a preacher man?" she asked as her sobs ebbed for the moment.

"I am," he responded. He didn't know what else to say.

"You ain't really gonna shoot yerself are ya?" she asked just as the sky began to lighten in the east.

"Na, but you aren't gonna kill yourself either are you?" he asked trying his best to sound confident. He didn't know how to read her silence, but somehow felt her internal storm had passed. Would she try to kill herself again? Hopefully not, but anything was possible. But for today, her soul had been saved.

The young woman stood up and removed the sleeping bag from her body.

"Keep it, kid," Jerry said with a smile, trying to capture this moment in his mind forever.

"Yer okay, man, ya know that," she said as she wrapped herself in the sleeping bag again and turned to leave. Jerry watched as the walking sleeping bag made her way towards the trees. Had he just saved her or himself? Reaching in his coat pocket he pulled out his cigarettes and studied them for a while before crushing the box between his hands. He noticed the girl stop and turn around.

"Dee Dee's my name," she called out and quickly turned back towards a life she would never again take for granted.

"Dee Dee," he repeated as he watched her disappear into the trees. Jerry stood up and stretched his stiff limbs, barely cognizant of a green bottle that rolled back into the churning surf. Maybe it was time to go overseas, he thought, might be a lot of young kids he could help. Jerry smiled to himself as he envisioned himself cruising through the Bavarian Alps on his Harley. "Yep, Europe, I think it's time for some preachin."

Dresden, Germany

Fall 2011

"Ah, the two must be back," the old doctor said as the rustling of keys and muffled voices could be heard outside the front door.

"Two?" I mouthed to Charlie. Who were they I wondered, chewing on my nails.

"Give me a moment, please," Dr. Wenke requested as he opened the front door and slipped into the long hallway. I couldn't see a thing, but was dying to see her. I could barely keep myself from bouncing up and down on the sofa. Charlie looked like he was about to burst with nervous energy himself. Why did Father Time decide to slow down at times like this? I could swear the tacky, flowered wall clock hadn't moved in two minutes. Standing up to shake out my nervous energy, I heard the door open. A moment later a tall, sturdy old woman burst into the room, followed more slowly by a much shorter, frail old woman.

"W...w...where is it? W...w...where is the letter," she demanded in English that held little traces of a German accent. The woman didn't notice me, let alone Charlie, as her eyes darted back and forth searching for the letter the old doctor had obviously told her about. Slowly I walked over to the small dining room table where Dr. Wenke had left it. There was no time for me to pick it up. The sturdy old woman moved like a cougar and snatched the letter just as I reached for it. This had to be Anna. It just had to be her I thought, staring at the finely wrinkled skin in which I could find no traces of the woman I had imagined. Yet in the same instant she seemed so familiar, almost as though I had known her my whole life.

The old woman's face paled as she read the letter. "W…w…where did y..y…you find this?" She stammered, without moving her eyes from the letter that trembled in her hand. "Please, where did you find this?" she repeated more calmly, as though she had been dazed. It was in this moment that she first looked up at me that I knew. The similarity this old woman, Anna, shared with the woman I has seen at the graveyard and at the airport was undeniable. How were they related? Was that her mother? Or more likely, as mad as I might sound, the ghost of her mother? But why me? Why not just confront her daughter directly?

"Please," the old woman begged as her eyes filled with tears. I had to shake myself out of my own trance. "I…uh, I found it at the beach," I stammered, clasping my hands behind my back to keep from chewing nervously on my nails. Doctor Wenke observed his wife with interested silence, as she was clearly captivated by this letter from the past.

"Wh…wh…where?" Anna stammered, looking up at me with desperation. It was then I realized this was something that had never been resolved in her life. Looking at her I could suddenly envision a much younger, vivacious Anna, with her life still ahead of her. Just as quickly my vision blurred and before me again stood an old woman, desperate for absolution. It may have been a much younger woman who wrote this letter so long ago, but it was still this woman.

"I don't know where you tossed it in, but I found it in the United States. On the Jersey shore, ah, New Jersey, in Cape May is where it was."

Anna gasped and covered her mouth with her free hand as she stumbled backward and dropped onto the sofa. "I…I…I can not believe this…I cannot b…b…believe that after all th…th…these years…," Anna's voice drifted away as she again looked down at the letter. The tears that had filled her eyes now freely streamed down her face. "I…I…I have not thought of th…th…these letters in so long…, th…th…there were sixteen of them. Sixteen letters I wrote him. T…t…to Jakub." Dropping the letter onto her lap, Anna covered her face with her hands as the past flooded her mind.

Doctor Wenke resolutely crossed the room and picked up the letter that rested in his wife's lap. "It is best that you leave now. Thank you for coming," he said, sitting down beside his wife. I looked at Charlie who shrugged his shoulders. So that was it? I hand over the letter, the old woman cries, and her husband kicks us out? I felt my heart sink, there were so many questions I had for Anna about Jakub. I…we had come so far to deliver this letter. This was not what I had expected.

"Did you think Anna would rush into your arms and thank you for your efforts?" I heard my rational mind ask. Well, actually, yes, I did think she'd show some gratitude. Standing up, I dejectedly walked over to Charlie who tried hard to mask his own disappointment.

"I'm sorry," I muttered to the old couple whose backs were turned to us. Dr. Wenke briefly raised his hand as I followed Charlie to the door. Charlie took my hand, kissed it, and together we walked down the hall toward the staircase.

"Wait! Wait!" a woman's voice called out to Charlie and I just as we reached the end of the grey hallway. She was the small, frail woman who had watched Charlie with an odd expression from the start.

"Leave them, Maria," I heard Dr. Wenke call after her as she slowly hobbled down the hallway towards us. She was out of breath by the time she reached us. I hadn't paid her much attention, but had noticed the interest with which she observed Charlie. Looking at her more closely, it was clear how much she resembled Anna, only she was a more petite version.

"Wait, please…," the old woman gasped, reaching to Charlie's arm for support. "Please…you…I know you," she said to Charlie with a much heavier accent than Anna. "I am Maria, Anna's sister."

Charlie looked at her curiously. Did she really know him I wondered? But how?

"You do?" Charlie asked with raised eyebrows, obviously somewhat taken aback.

427

"I have seen your face. Please, please come speak to my sister… please let her see your face," the old woman said, tugging at Charlie so he would follow her. I watched the bizarre scene unfolding before me, but nothing surprised me anymore. I followed Charlie back into the smoke filled apartment, grateful for a moment of semi-fresh air.

"Please, wait…I will get my sister," the old woman said, distract-edly raising a hand as though unsure what direction to go next. Anna and the doctor no longer sat in the living room. "Just wait, please, one moment." The old woman left the room. Moments later I heard hushed female voices speaking, and a much louder male voice obvi-ously protesting whatever the women discussed. I sent Charlie a ques-tioning glance, but he merely shrugged his shoulders and gave me a nervous, lopsided smile. A moment later Maria appeared in the room, tugging a reluctant Anna behind her, closely followed by the irritated Dr. Wenke.

"Look, Anna, look! Do you not see? Anna!" Maria shoved her sis-ter towards Charlie with more force than I would have expected from so frail an old woman.

Anna, previously absorbed with the letter, had not noticed the man who had accompanied the strange American woman with red streaked hair. Somewhere she was conscious that he had been in the room, but her letter to her beloved Jakub, after so many years, had taken her breath away. How was it possible that it could have traveled so far? Her husband, Werner, was not the jealous type, but she knew how pro-tective he was of her. The letter had made her cry, not the woman who brought it, but Werner did not see it that way. It was these foreigners who caused her stress that her heart did not need, he had told her after he sent them away. But now, here they were again, in her living room. She allowed Maria to drag her into the living room, where the young woman stood once again and the young man nervously stared down at his shoes.

Anna could feel Werner's eyes on her back. She had never told him of Jakub, there had been no need to. But now, now she felt as though she had betrayed Werner all of these years. Yet Werner, God save his soul, she thought, cared nothing of this Jakub. He had just told her so, and she believed him. It was only her that Werner cared for. Werner was her soul mate, but then so was Jakub. It is possible to have more than one soul mate, Anna had realized long ago. Anna felt Maria shove her forward until she stood face to face with the young man Maria had insisted she see.

Anna looked upon his face and paled. The scream she emitted caught in her throat and came out a croak. Was it a ghost that stood before her?

"Jakub! Jakub!" Anna whispered reaching out to touch Charlie's face.

"No, ah, sorry, the name's Charles, Charlie Gordon." Charlie looked at this old woman, sounding more sure than he felt. Jakub must somehow have resembled Charlie, or why else would Anna be acting like this? Anna still clutched the letter in her hand.

"Y…y…you…are his son?" Anna cautiously asked, as though the question and its answer may explode in her face.

"I'm sorry, my dad's name was Jacob Gordon…," Even as Charlie spoke an eerie feeling crept up his spine and spread throughout his body. "Jacob Gordon," he whispered again, with an expression of disbelief crossing his face. No, it couldn't be, I thought to myself. His dad's name was Jacob, and Anna's lost love was Jakub. I felt Charlie staring at me. He looked pale, even under his olive-colored skin.

"Jakub Gorski," Anna whispered, loud enough for Charlie and me to hear. Of course, he must have changed his name when he came to the United States—Gorski to Gordon. Obviously Charlie was coming to the same conclusion from the look on his face.

Anna stared at Charlie as though dumfounded. Of course the young man who stood before her was Jakub's son. How could she have been so foolish to think, if just for a moment, that he was a ghost? The young man looked up at her.

"I remember my dad…," Charlie paused and scratched his dark curls, so like his father's, Anna thought. Even the way in which he moved his head when he spoke was like Jakub. "He, ah, he told me once he had changed his name to Gordon when he came to the United States. I was just a kid, I had forgotten all about it…until now. He never really wanted to talk about it." Charlie looked at Anna and took hold of her hands, feeling the sturdy bones beneath the warm, soft skin.

"His name...my father...his name was Gorski...before he came to the U.S...I remember that now." Anna felt her heart racing. After all these years, all this time, Jakub had become a distant memory. How had this young man and young woman found her? Anna briefly glanced at the attractive woman who had accompanied Jakub's son.

"Please sit down, young man," Anna offered with shaking hands, still holding on to Charlie. "We must speak."

This whole time I stood on the sidelines, like a spectator, watching as something miraculous unfolded before my eyes. Was all of this real? The chances of winning the lottery would be greater than all of the strange coincidences that had happened over the last two weeks.

Coincidences, ha. I've kind of lost faith in coincidence. Destiny. Now that is what this is, but whose? Mine or Charlie's? None of this really has anything to do with me, besides my relationship with Charlie. Overcome with emotions I did not understand, I observed these two strangers, who really weren't strangers to one another, slowly understand the full impact of what they had just discovered.

An hour had passed and Charlie still answered every question Anna Wenke asked about his father. It was the first time Dr. Wenke had seen his wife smile this way. It was the sort of smile that only distant memories or faraway persons could evoke in someone. A smile no other could join in. Intermittently, tears streamed down Anna's face as she sat across from Charlie and listened to him describe his father in a way not even I had heard before. When he pulled an old, wrinkled picture of his parents from his wallet and handed it to Anna she nearly fainted. Dr. Wenke brought his wife a glass of orange juice and spoke to her in German, likely urging her to reconsider further entertaining guests. Dismissing him with a wave, Anna sat in silence studying this man who resembled his father to such an extent she could have sworn it was Jakub.

"America," she whispered as she searched Charlie's face, "D...d...do you know w...w...we had a child together? M...m...my only child. He did not live. Your father never knew. All these years I h...h...had hoped he was in Australia, b...b...but my heart believed he had p…p…passed so long ago." Anna inhaled deeply. "I h…h…had a dream some time ago…it w…w…was Jakub, your father, h…h… he had come to say auf wiedersehen." Anna glanced over at me. I had been listening intently, but then my mind had wandered back to a familiar place, to Warren. What was his role in all that had happened these last couple of weeks? All of the visions, all of the signs, they had to mean something.

"I wouldn't believe any of this if someone else had told me the story," I whispered to myself, remembering the day I found the letter on the New Jersey shore.

My head began to spin again when I suddenly remembered the woman at the airport and the graveyard. As though sensing I had more to say, Anna asked me to repeat the story of how I had found the green glass bottle. Clearing my throat, the reality of all these so-called coincidences unnerving me somewhat, I took a deep breath and began again.

"It was…uh, it was on the New Jersey shore, at the same time I met Charlie, uh, again. You see, I had met him on the airplane…uh, never mind about that, anyway…," My mouth was dry and my throat felt constricted when I spoke, but then a thought struck me. "The bottle, I found it just before I ran into Charlie on the beach…this might sound crazy, but, uh, I think we were supposed to find it together." I looked from Anna to Charlie, unable to read either one. Did they both think I was nuts? Maybe, but I had begun to think it was Charlie the bottle had sought out, not me. I was just peripheral to the whole story, wasn't I? A convenient addition for the main protagonist—Charlie finds his lost history, and love, at the same time.

"Why not kill two birds with one stone?" I whispered to myself, realizing suddenly that I might be jealous that this love story really wasn't about me at all, but about Charlie finding love. What if some other woman had found the bottle with Charlie? Would he be with her now? Swallowed by my own thoughts, I noticed Anna looking at me, waiting for me to continue my fantastic tale. First, I needed to calm down. Locking eyes with Charlie I sighed, feeling some of the tension flow from my body, and reminding myself that I wasn't alone in this. Charlie, with the corners of his mouth just slightly turned up, nodded at me to continue.

"It had just washed up, right where I stood. At the time I didn't know it was meant for Charlie, at least that is what I think now, you know, given this situation. And, I don't know, but that's it, I think. We found the bottle and then it was Charlie here who found you." And that was the end of my fairytale.

Anna stared at me in silence.

Nervously picking at my fingernails, at least I wasn't chewing them, I remembered the brooch I was to give to Anna. Fumbling with the latch on my backpack, I didn't know I had muttered "brooch" aloud until Charlie asked me what it was I had said.

"The brooch," I repeated, forgetting that he had no idea what I was talking about. I hadn't told him about the brooch I had found on the knit "nothing." Dr. Wenke, who had been pacing the length of his dining room like a caged tiger stopped to stare at me. He too was curious about the brooch.

"Um, a woman, she…she told me to give you this," I said to Anna. Charlie looked as confused as Anna as he watched me hand a small rose brooch to her. "She, uh, looked a lot like you. I…I think this might be…yours," I added, realizing how crazy all of this sounded.

I don't know how much time passed before Anna reached out to take the brooch. She had closed her eyes, mumbling something under her breath I couldn't understand. Maria joined her sister to look at the brooch, casting repeated glances my way.

"Who gave this to you?" Maria demanded, somewhat red-faced, standing protectively beside her much larger sister. Geez, don't shoot the messenger, old woman, I thought. I felt like I was on trial for some crime I didn't commit. I didn't steal the damn thing for God's sake. Is that what she thought? The truth did sound somewhat incredible though, I had to admit.

"I don't know why she gave it to me." I felt the blood rushing to my head. Did all of this really happen? The sisters stared at me, hanging on every word, but the small feisty one looked at me as though I belonged behind bars.

"Uh, she told me to give it to Anna. I don't know…I don't know anything anymore. I didn't ask to get involved." The smoke filled room was too much for me, I had had enough of all of this crap to last me a lifetime. "Look, if it's yours, please take it. I don't know why I felt compelled to fly across the ocean to bring you the letter. Maybe it was so you could find closure. Maybe that's why she asked me... because I found the letter." I directed my comments at Anna, avoiding her sister's stares. What I told Anna actually made sense to me now. I was *chosen* because I found the letter. That had to be it. Waiting for some response from Anna, I felt Charlie's arm reach around my waist, gently pulling me towards him.

"Sigrid, oh, it was Siggi," Anna suddenly blurted out, abruptly standing up.

"Yes, Sigrid," was all I could answer. I remembered the grave stone. Pacing back and forth in the small living room, Anna came to a sudden halt before me.

"Thank you," Anna whispered, as the years of guilt she carried with her suddenly fell away. She had denied her birth mother so much, denied her absolution. There was no greater sin than that. But now, now she knew that she had been absolved. Now she could live and die in peace, and Sigrid might finally find peace as well.

"Thank you," she repeated, standing up to walk towards her husband. "I think I shall rest now." Anna did not turn around again and left the room with the brooch clutched firmly to her breast. Shortly thereafter Maria, with a silent nod, followed her sister.

"I shall see you out," Dr. Wenke said, leading us out. The knit nothing, how could I have forgotten it? Pulling it out from my backpack, I handed it to the old Doctor. "This...please give this to your wife."

Neither Charlie nor I said anything of what had transpired as we delivered Thomas von Marschalkt and his sleeping dog back to his estate. Nor did we speak of anything as we drove back to the hotel. What the heck was going on in Charlie's head? All this time I thought I had gotten him into all of this, but as far as I could tell, it was always about Charlie. I just happened to be there at the right time. Did he understand that now too? Is that what preoccupied him? I wasn't sure how to bring up the subject of Anna and his father. I wasn't sure I really wanted to know anymore. Ever since I handed over the brooch and the knit work, the feeling that someone was watching had disappeared.

This unsettling feeling had been replaced by an inner calm I hadn't felt for years. More than a calm, it was a satisfaction or contentment with what life offered me at the moment, and life had a lot to offer. What I did with this offer was my choice, but I knew Charlie was the best part of this choice.

Neither of us spoke when we walked into the hotel room. Charlie pulled me towards him and gently kissed me with his warm, soft lips. Running my hands through his lush hair, he removed my top and bra with experienced hands. Before I knew what was happening he swooped me off my feet and gently laid me on the bed. Somehow I felt like the heroine in a novel, saved at the end by her handsome hero. Only Charlie wasn't really the cheesy novel type. But he was stealthy. I hadn't noticed him dispose of his pants until he lay down solidly on top of me. Kissing my neck, he gently caressed my breasts, slowly pushing my legs apart with his own strong leg.

"Charlie," I whispered into his ear, gasping as the warmth of his manhood penetrated deep inside me. Placing his finger on my lips, he slowly, rhythmically, moved back and forth.

It wasn't as though this was the first time we made love, but somehow if felt like it. This was the passionate lovemaking that comes when both souls are freed, if just for the moment, of all earthly concerns. When all that matters is the person you're with right then. This is the kind of lovemaking that makes one remember the beauty of life, and what life can create. I don't know how long we lay, side by side, in comfortable silence. There had been no room for words. Only the physical expression of our love was necessary. Necessary to somehow cement the bond we had formed just a short time ago. We were both different people now. I had always thought one needed the institution of marriage to bind two souls, at least that was how I felt with Warren. Now I knew I didn't need a piece of paper telling me I was bound to Charlie, neither of us did. Somehow this whole experience…the letter, Anna, my visions, all of it, had started both of us on a path I now truly believed was our destiny.

Feeling Charlie stir, and then clear his throat, I waited for him to speak, which he did.

"I feel…almost guilty," he said, "But let me back track…this is, by far, the craziest thing I've ever, and I mean ever, had happen to me…us actually." He cleared his throat and almost absent-mindedly stroked my arm. "My dad never mentioned anything about Anna, but why should he, to me at least. I wonder if he ever mentioned anything to my mother. I mean, here's this woman who spent her whole life wondering what had happened to my dad. Did he ever think about her?"

"Hmmm," I answered. I didn't really know what to say about the whole thing any more. And honestly, I had already begun to put it all behind me. I was ready to move on, out of the past and into our shared future.

"And all this other weird stuff…I don't know how else to describe it." Charlie rolled over on his side and looked at me as I ran my hand through his thick dark curls. "You know what…I can't explain it, but I know we gave Anna closure…and she, or whatever *it* was, brought us together," Charlie said.

I nodded and laid my head on Charlie's chest. I was grateful Charlie didn't say anything more about Anna after that.

"Are you going to keep in contact with her?" I finally asked, holding my breath for the answer. The thought had weighed on me ever since we left the Wenke home. I was grateful for this whole experience, but I too needed closure.

"No," Charlie answered. And he meant it. Never again did I hear him so much as utter a word about Anna.

Brest, France,
November 1946

That she had found an unbroken green glass bottle amongst the rubble of her home still amazed her. That the bottle had survived the trip to France surprised her even more. Anna stared at the empty bottle she had transported with her from what was left of Dresden. There would be no more bottles after this she realized, cradling the bottle with affection not normally reserved for an inanimate object. The journey from Dresden to Brest had been an arduous one. It was not only the physical toll that exacted itself on her family, but the emotional toll of leaving behind not only a home, but loved ones as well. Anna felt her throat tighten at the thought of Sigrid and Lena. Her mother had said they were the lucky ones. They had not been left burned to unrecognizable lumps of charred flesh, only to be dumped into anonymous mass graves.

"They received proper burials with gravestones," her mother had said without the strong emotions Anna had felt whenever she thought of those horrible days. Did Mama mourn their passing, she wondered, looking out over the war-ravaged city of Brest. It too had suffered greatly during the war, but miraculously their summer cottage had been spared.

It had been difficult, especially for her mother, to leave Dresden behind; to leave Germany behind. She left behind not only her past life, but her past ideals. None of which had survived the war.

"Yes, Mama suffers," she whispered, as the cool breeze carried her voice over the white capped waves of the Atlantic Ocean. "She has always suffered. But she is not the only one who suffers." There seemed to be no one left who had not suffered some catastrophic loss. Anna's thoughts turned to young Thomas who had not spoken a word since the untimely death of his mother. His arm had been crushed beneath a large section of collapsed bunker wall. Miraculously, Dr. Wenke managed to save the arm, as he had saved his leg in the past. Even the doctor had doubted whether the arm could be saved, given the horrific injury it had sustained. And then there was Papa. Lena's death did not go unnoticed by the Baron either, nor Sigrid's, Anna thought with a heavy heart. Her father, who now constantly hovered around Thomas to the point of obsession, grieved not the loss of one, but two women he had loved.

"It is a large price to pay for betrayal," Anna whispered, running her finger along the smooth neck of her glass bottle, wondering whether the universe adhered to its own sense of moral obligations or justice. Did Papa feel responsible for their deaths, in the same way he felt responsible for the deaths of his farm hands and animals, Anna wondered? She too mourned their passing, but it was Sigrid, the woman who had carried her for nine months, the woman who had attempted to reclaim their relationship, whom she missed more than she would have thought possible.

"I turned my back to her, and with this guilt I must forever live. If I could only turn back the clock," she whispered as thoughts of the Sigrid filled her mind. It surprised her that it was her mother who had managed to survive the past winters, as well as the war.

"Weeds do not die...wither, yes, but we do not die," her mother had said to her upon their arrival in Brest. It was not just her iron constitution that had assured her mother's survival through all of this Anna considered, but the attentive nature of Dr. Wenke. He had cared for her as though she were his own mother, who had passed away years ago. The doctor had followed the family, to tend to her mother he had said, but Anna knew the truth.

Anna felt her face flush as she thought of Werner Wenke. In the last few months her thoughts lingered less frequently with Jakub, and more often with the odd Dr. Wenke, who made her heart skip when he was near.

"He m…m…makes me laugh. In this w…w…world we live in… he m…m…makes me laugh," she said, as a smile briefly passed over her lips. Until this moment she had not realized how important laughter was to not just life, but to hope, to survival. It was not until she enjoyed it again that she became aware of her ability to feel again. To feel something true for Werner Wenke that was more than a basic animal desire. For the first time in a very long time, she felt safe enough to let her guard down when they were alone. Even an exhausted Maria, poor Maria who had suffered through yet another child birth, had been able to see the transformation occurring in her sister. It had been Maria who had urged her, no, who had insisted she "move forward" with Werner. Again Anna felt a heat rise in her face as indecent thoughts of Werner fueled a desire in her that set her body aglow.

"I can f…f…feel again," she cried out, as a few rays of sunshine fought their way through the eternal blanket of gray that seemed to cover the fall French sky. Lying back in the damp grass, she stared up where the Sun once was.

"I can f…f…feel again," she repeated more quietly, acknowledging for the first time how desperately she wanted to feel again. For too many years she had isolated herself from any human touch. A void that she sensed would soon be filled.

"I believe it is time," she whispered to the empty green bottle which rested on her gently rising and falling chest. Anna recalled Maria's persistence, always urging Anna to move forward with Werner. With a smile she now realized she no longer needed prodding from Maria to know the time had come to say goodbye to Jakub. The war was over. Jakub was gone. It was time to live again.

Anna sighed deeply as she enjoyed this momentary respite from the confines of the small cottage which threatened to drive her mad.

"Only Werner's humor maintains my sanity," she whispered as she felt the coolness of the ground slowly penetrate her wool coat. She knew she should return to the cottage. It would grow dark soon enough, and of course Maria would worry, but somehow she could not leave this peaceful place just yet. From her bag she pulled out her uncle's fountain pen and the scraps of paper she had salvaged from the rubble in Dresden. For a moment she stared onto the blank paper. Thoughts of betrayal pushed their way to the surface, which she quickly repressed.

"No, it is not you I betray, Jakub. I have betrayed myself for too long. It is time I release you and free myself," she whispered, as a small hummingbird darted into her line of vision, hovered, and sped off again.

"A sign, Jakub?" she asked as the hummingbird, whether real or imagined, returned once again, leaving little doubt in Anna's mind that *this* must be a sign.

Anna picked up her pen and wrote her sixteenth letter. She wrote for what she knew would be the last time to the man who had carried her heart away with him. Somehow though, amongst the death and destruction, she had found her heart again, and her way. She would be eternally grateful to Jakub for carrying her through the dark years of the war. Long years, where there was no one she could physically hold onto for comfort and support. It was Jakub's memory, and that of her long since deceased son that kept her grounded, and sane. Still, she mourned her child's death, she always would, but there was no one to blame for the death of her child.

There was only a sense of gratitude to Jakub that came with knowing their love had created something wonderful—a true miracle. It did not matter how briefly the child lived inside her, for Anna would never forget the tiny lifeless body she held close to her breast, nor his strong vivacious father who had held her often in his arms. Anna did not look up as she wrote. Time had no meaning when the soul healed itself. It was nearly dark by the time she finished her letter and rolled it up one last time with nearly frozen fingers. As she gently guided the letter down into the bottle, she felt a warm breeze tickle the back of her neck on this chilly evening. Looking up, she saw the brilliant colors of the setting sun pushing through the thick blanket of grey which painted the world. The beauty of the natural world had always moved her, but tonight it took her breath away.

"It is like heaven," she whispered, looking past the ravaged city and out to the great sea beyond. She knew she had to get back to the cottage. Dinner would have been served by now and Anna did not want to miss out on Werner's company on such a miraculous evening. As she sat up, she straightened her skirt and coat, wondering for the first time if Werner too envisioned a shared future. A momentary dark fear threatened to take hold of her as she realized that Jakub would soon be gone forever. Breathing deeply, she looked towards the future. There was no telling what the future may bring, but she saw that she would no longer be alone.

"Anna," she heard the man to whom her thoughts had turned call out to her. "Anna, here you are," Werner Wenke said without the nervous energy he normally radiated.

"Y...y...yes, here I am," Anna replied, as she studied this odd man her heart had grown so fond of.

"I have been looking everywhere for you, Anna," Werner spoke as he caught his breath and dropped himself into the soft grass beside the woman he had fallen hopelessly in love with. "I ran up here to find you... actually I have run up a number of hills looking for you, Anna," he said, without the accusatory tone she was so accustomed to from the rest of her family. Anna watched with a flushed face as this man to whose sentiments she had never been immune, yet had managed to sufficiently insulate herself from, reached out to touch her chilled hand. Anna surreptitiously tucked the bottle she held beneath her coat and held on to his warm hand.

"The h...h...house is...too full," Anna said with a guilty conscience, "One d...d...does not have room to th...th...think."

Werner smiled as he moved closer to Anna. "I know," he whispered with warm breath into her ear, "That is why I have not been able to do this." The sparks Anna saw as Werner passionately kissed her for the first time with soft lips left her feeling warm and vulnerable; a vulnerability she welcomed for the first time in her life.

"I love you, Anna von Marschalkt. I have loved you since the first day I almost ruined your face," he spoke with a smile. Anna laughed. And she continued to laugh. Anna von Marschalkt laughed until the tears streamed down her face and washed away all of the hurt of the last years.

"And...I love you, Werner Wenke," Anna spoke without stuttering.

The sea was rough the morning Anna walked to the shore with her green glass bottle tucked beneath her coat. She stood for a long time, alone, watching as one angry wave after another crashed against the shore. Somehow she felt she had come full circle in her life—a life which was far from over she hoped. She was no longer a child, yet she was far from the old woman she hoped to someday become. Life still had much hope and opportunity for her, she thought, as she bade her first love farewell. As she watched her final glass bottle begin a journey she could never begin to imagine, she realized she had the most important thing in her life—true love.

Tegel International Airport,
Berlin, Germany
Fall 2011

Seat 16 C. Thank God, an aisle seat, and Charlie's in 16 B, right next to me.

"Perfect," I spoke aloud, grateful to find our seats on the packed United Airlines flight destined for Los Angeles, with a short layover in New York. Looking over at the window seat, I briefly pitied the guy who had to sit next to two tired lovers. Not to mention my upset digestive tract, which I hoped would not come to be too much of an issue during the long flight.

Exhausted, I melted back into my seat as the events of the last few days and weeks threatened to take over my mind again. Gently resting my hand on Charlie's warm arm, I closed my eyes and tried to concentrate on anything but the last few weeks. Too much had happened. Too much I didn't understand and really was through trying to figure out. All I knew was that I was on a plane, with a man I had fallen in love with, and we were going home. Breathing a deep sigh of relief, I shifted and tried to keep the miniscule airline pillow from falling between the seats. Eventually I drifted off into a welcome oblivion.

"Uh, Ma'am, you're gonna have to bring yer seat up for take-off," a young and annoying flight attendant shrieked in my ear, as she reached over me to push the button and straighten my seat.

"Hey, Dee Dee, you have any air-sick bags over there? This kid's gonna be sick," I heard another flight attendant shout from the front of the cabin.

"Jesus, we haven't even taken off," the flight attendant at my side hissed without any sign of compassion, violating my personal space once again to confiscate *my* air sickness bag. I had half a mind to protest. What if I needed my bag? What if I was going to be sick? Well, then she'd just have to get down on her skinny little knees and wipe it up. Getting a grip on the two year old with a temper caught inside me, I looked over at Charlie, already peacefully asleep.

With our stop-over in New York came a passenger who squeezed past Charlie and myself to claim his window seat. Charlie and this random stranger immediately dove into a conversation as though they had known each other for years. I envied the ease with which Charlie could hold a conversation with just about anyone. I swear, he could talk to a duck.

"Yeah, you know it's actually safer to fly than drive, at least that's what I'm trying to tell myself," I heard the man who introduced himself to Charlie as Robert Thomas say.

"Well, Charlie and Robert, have a nice chat," I whispered, grateful for the aisle seat. I reclined my uncomfortable airline seat and tried to block out the world.

Alternating between fitful sleep and uncomfortable waking periods, our long journey finally came to an end. Unattractive fluorescent lighting lit up the plane. Heaving my suitcase down from the overhead bin, Charlie said farewell to his new friend, Robert, a teacher who was visiting Los Angeles for the week. With Charlie's easy-going, good-natured personality, I wouldn't be surprised if this guy showed up at our place. What was I thinking? There was no "our place." I've got my place and he has his. What if everything suddenly changed now? What if everything that happened the last weeks suddenly disappeared now that we were both home and the drudgery of normal life took over again? He goes to his place, I go to mine. We call each other, but over time the phone calls decrease and then end altogether. What if this was it? What if I never see Charlie again? Irrational panic attacks were one of my many weaknesses, but I didn't think these thoughts were all that irrational. For lack of anything better to do, I rummaged through my backpack. Finding my beret, I placed it firmly on my head and turned on my cell phone with God-only-knows how many unheard messages.

"Abe," I said to myself. I hadn't called my brother since I left for Germany. Neither he nor my parents had any idea where I was or with whom I was traveling the streets of Germany. This thought alone calmed my rattled nerves, as I envisioned the frantic phone calls Abe likely received from Sheila at all hours of the day and night.

"You sleep as well as I did?" Charlie asked teasingly, pinching me in the rear.

"Charles Gordon," I sternly reprimanded him with a hint of a smile, "Keep your lascivious hands to yourself." Charlie raised his eyebrows with feigned shock as he pinched me again, much to the disapproval of the old woman in the seat behind me. Ensuing laughter did nothing to appease this blatant offense. My laughter, if I was honest with myself, was more to relieve my pent up anxiety than in response to Charlie's behavior. I hadn't mustered up the nerve to ask him where we were going from here, or if we were going anywhere at all. Figuring he would be the one to take the initiative, I felt my heart sink as we walked off the plane together in silence.

"You okay, Di?" Charlie asked as we awaited our baggage. He had never called me Di before, not that I minded. It just felt new, and different, but definitely more familiar. This was a good thing, I tried to tell myself, as Charlie first pulled my suitcase and then his off the conveyor belt.

"So, I thought you'd stay with me, you know, until you...ah, you know, felt comfortable enough to have me stay over...and then we could see from there." That's what Charlie said. Just like that. All of my fretting and anxiety disappeared in an instant. Not only had Charlie thought about us and our joint future, he already had everything figured out in his mind. Speechless, I stood and stared at him.

"What? Hey, Di. I didn't mean to assume you'd even...Christ... did I just royally screw this up, Di? I didn't mean to make assumptions about you…about us, I mean. If you'd rather go back to your place… alone…I'd understand." A look of defeat passed over his face, as he nervously slid his hands into his pockets. The smile that spread over my face and my passionate kiss relieved Charlie of any self-doubt.

Together we pulled our suitcases towards a waiting cab. Charlie never did let go of my hand. Not until we stood at the steps of his home. It was wonderful to once again know love.

Epilogue

Los Angeles
April 2, 2012

"Wow, he actually did it. I never thought I'd see the day my baby brother actually got married," I whispered to Charlie, who gently placed his arm around my shoulders. Nervously I tugged at the black stone, a moon stone, the jeweler had called it, that I had attached to a necklace. That Abe actually married Akila, the one I thought would be out of his life by the time I returned from my trip, was more than surprising. A sense of guilt surrounded me as I recalled my thoughts before I left on my strange adventure to Cape May and beyond. I watched my brother, with his new bride in tow, head straight for us. Well, as straight as he could manage after all those drinks.

A man passed behind Abe carrying a ratty shoe box. It was only a flicker, as though someone had changed the channel on the television and he was gone, but I knew. A feeling of calm passed over me as I imagined, or truly did feel, the first fluttering of life in my lower abdomen. Absent-mindedly, I stroked my expanding midsection. Maybe there was something poignant that needed to be said at this point, but I couldn't think of anything. Instead I felt content with the inner peace that washed over me just as my brother and his bride stumbled towards us.

"Hey, hey, hey, Charles my man! How you holdin up with the old woman here?" Abe teased, nodding in my direction while reaching for Charlie's hand to pull him close for a "man" hug. I couldn't help thinking of two gorillas pounding chests.

"Hey, hey, yourself. Congratulations to you, Abe, and my condolences to you, Akila," Charlie teased, winking at Akila.

"Wohoho, Di. Wohoho, what is this I see?" Abe asked, pointing at my swollen lower abdomen. No, I hadn't told him yet. Maybe I should have, but I didn't want to detract from his wedding. This was his time.

"Either someone's got a bun in the oven or you've really packed on the pounds," Abe said, gesticulating wildly in his penguin suit, eliciting the stares of his wedding guests. "Maybe this living together isn't the best thing after all," Abe teased as he puffed out his cheeks like the Pillsbury dough boy and offered Charlie his best macho wink.

"We were going to tell you, Abe" Charlie answered, protectively covering my bulge with his large hand. "Just after the wedding, you know. It's your time now, and Akila's, we've still got a few months to go."

"No way, man, this is great, great stuff," an intoxicated Abe shouted, as he roughly embraced both Charlie and me simultaneously. "Great, great stuff," he repeated as he looked at me with eyes that threatened to overflow. "Really, Di, this is great," he whispered to me in a brief moment of sobriety and kissed my cheek. "Guess the next wedding's yours," Abe smiled.

Charlie and I looked at each other and smiled. "Maybe," I said.

"Yes," Charlie said.

Made in the USA
Charleston, SC
05 April 2013